c
D0413104

A CORNER OF MY HEART

MARK SEAMAN

The Book Guild Ltd

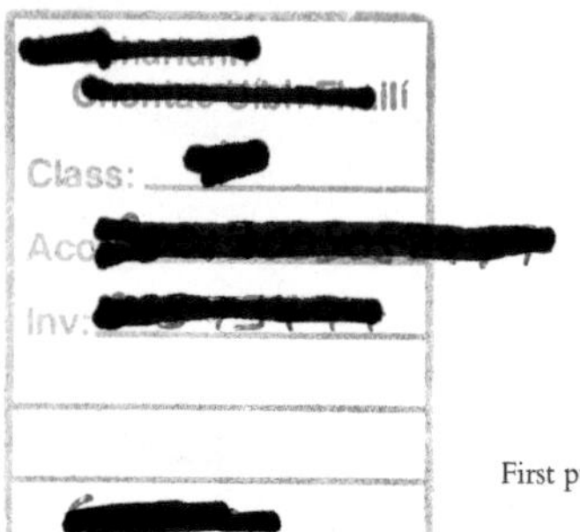

First published in Great Britain in 2017 by
The Book Guild Ltd
9 Priory Business Park
Wistow Road, Kibworth
Leicestershire, LE8 0RX
Freephone: 0800 999 2982
www.bookguild.co.uk
Email: info@bookguild.co.uk
Twitter: @bookguild

Typeset in Adobe Garamond Pro

Printed and bound in Great Britain by CPI Group (UK) Ltd, Croydon, CR0 4YY

ISBN 978 1912083 091

British Library Cataloguing in Publication Data.
A catalogue record for this book is available from the British Library.

FOR SANDRA. THANK YOU.

ONE

I wrote to my mother a few days ago. I wasn't going to. I thought I'd come to terms with being adopted and in not wanting to know anything about her or the circumstances of my birth. After all it was she who gave me away, abandoned me at seven weeks old. What could I have done at such a young age that was so awful and would cause her to want to get rid of me like that? And, if I was the result of an unplanned accident then why carry me to full term in the first place? Why hadn't she had an abortion and simply erased me from her life without bringing another unwanted child into the world? Why bother going through the whole experience of pregnancy, coupled with the physical ordeal of giving birth, if her intention was to let me go almost as soon as I arrived?

I'd never really allowed myself the time to think about these questions in the past, or seek answers to them, especially having been so thoroughly loved and cared for over the years by James and Carol. They'd told me I was adopted when I was younger and I'd never felt the need to know any more than that, or to hurt them by searching for answers to questions that none of us might want to hear.

It certainly wouldn't have changed our feelings for each other. As far as the three of us were concerned, they were my parents and

I was their daughter, so why cause any unnecessary ripples in the calm and settled waters of our happy family unit?

Yet if all of that was true what had caused this sudden change of heart within me, this sudden desire to know the truth?

It was my daughter Jenny who persuaded me to write, not directly but just in something she said one day almost as a passing remark. Jenny's ten and for most of that time it's just been the two of us, apart from James and Carol of course.

Gerry was okay and we enjoyed each other's company, certainly early on, but I knew as soon as I became pregnant that I'd made a mistake. I had no intention of spending the rest of my life with him. He made it clear he felt the same way too.

I hadn't intended to get pregnant and certainly not by Gerry, who I'd never viewed as anything more than just a boyfriend. I had always said no to him before whenever he had suggested sex, but on this particular occasion I was feeling a bit emotional after a stupid argument I'd had with Mum and Dad about arriving home late from a night out with some friends. I was just being a stroppy teenager with my emotions racing, but at the time I felt I wanted someone to make a fuss over me, to make me feel special, that I mattered and had a right to make decisions for myself, no matter the outcome.

Unfortunately, as it turned out, that *someone* happened to be Gerry who happily pretended to offer the listening ear and hand of comfort I was seeking. What he actually provided was heavy breathing in my ear and a hand up my skirt. And, more fool me, even though I knew what was happening, I let him continue. Perhaps I did it to get back at Mum as I knew she would be horrified to think I'd been having sex, not just with Gerry but with anyone, especially after I'd promised her that I'd wait for Mr Right. Of course, in retrospect I wish I had listened to that inner voice telling me this was a bad idea and wouldn't be realised as one of my proudest moments, but at the time I was filled with traditional teenage angst, raging hormones and rebellion all of which determined me to go for it and hang the consequences. Of course, after that first time it then became harder for me to say no whenever Gerry broached the subject of a repeat session, especially if Mum and Dad went out for the evening, leaving us alone in the house.

And so, rightly or wrongly, occasional sex became a part of our relationship.

It still came as a shock to discover I was pregnant though, but as soon as it was confirmed I was determined to have the baby, keep it, and not abandon it as I had been by my own mother. Gerry was relieved when I told him I didn't want him to have any part in the baby's upbringing and I knew in that instant that I'd made the right decision, not only about him but for all three of us. Mum and Dad struggled early on when I told them I was expecting, but I think that was more in disappointment really that I'd had sex against their wishes, let alone become pregnant. If truth were told, I'd let them down, failed them, as I had myself of course.

It certainly felt that way, especially when I considered my true feelings towards Gerry and in my having been stupid enough to agree to our having sex in the first place.

"Come on, Mary, it'll be fine, bring us closer and all that."

It brought us closer alright, but getting cramp on the back seat of his car, no matter how hurt or rebellious I was feeling, still wasn't the romantic setting I'd imagined or hoped for when making love for that first time, or in "going all the way" as we used to say whenever I talked to my girlfriends about that great unknown taboo in our formative teenage years. And whilst the settings for our future love making encounters became more comfortable and better planned the truth was I never really felt relaxed or happy about what we were doing.

Mind, once Jenny arrived all earlier disappointment and regret about what I'd done with Gerry was soon forgotten. Mum and Dad couldn't have been more supportive either once they held her in their arms. And of course, their natural grandparenting skills kicked in alongside an overwhelming sense of love for Jenny just as it had done when adopting me as their daughter some eighteen years earlier. I hardly got a look in in those early days of Jenny's life when it came to bathing and feeding her.

"Let me do that, Mary," Mum would say, desperate to be involved and wanting to spend time with this new and precious life that had overtaken their home.

Dad did his bit as well but was quite happy to take a back seat when it came to changing nappies.

"Not sure where to start," he'd say. "Anyway, you girls are better at that sort of thing."

Mum would wink at me as Dad would hand Jenny over to one of us as if she were a fragile parcel of hazardous material about to explode.

"Coward. Honestly, Mary, what would you do with him, eh? Men, they're all the same. They're happy enough to get their hands mucky and covered with oil doing something to their precious car but give them a baby that needs changing and they run a mile."

I felt in those early days of Jenny's existence that my relationship with Mum and Dad grew stronger as they sought to support me in raising my beautiful daughter, *their* beautiful granddaughter. Of course, I'd always considered them to be my real parents even though I knew they weren't. Now though, with the arrival of Jenny and having to think again about my own birth and life to date, all the previous security I had so readily accepted and taken for granted from James and Carol suddenly shifted. For a while I felt vulnerable and unsure about myself along with my place in the world. It didn't last long though with the ever present love and care poured out on the two of us by Dad and Mum. They encouraged me personally each day in my efforts at motherhood and couldn't have made more of a fuss of Jen as they welcomed her into their home as an immediate and much loved addition to the family. The only difference now being they were playing the role of doting grandparents; a role they accepted with the same natural gifting and ability they had done so many years earlier when adopting me as their daughter. And although I was feeling an increasing sense of confusion about my own birth mother and place in her life I was, at the same time, aware of a growing affinity and closeness between James, Carol and myself. It was as though our relationship had moved to another and far deeper level, with each of us becoming ever more committed to the other.

I may have given birth to Jenny, but without Mum and Dad's love, understanding and support I could never have coped. I quickly came to appreciate it was Jenny who provided the glue in completing this family circle and cemented all of our relationships forever as one. I think this was especially true for Mum and I with her not having been able to carry a child herself. Following Jenny's arrival I feel we both experienced a new, if undeclared, union between us.

"I'll love her like my own, Mary, you know that, don't you? Just the same as I have always done with you."

"Then she'll be every bit as lucky as I've been, won't she?"

Over the next few years it became increasingly natural for me to share the role of mother with Carol knowing I could call on her or Dad for their help and support whenever I needed it, which I often did, certainly in the early days of Jenny's young life.

TWO

I received a letter from my daughter today. It's a letter I've been praying for and yet dreading receiving in equal measure for the past twenty eight years.

They called her Mary. That's a nice name, but to me she will always be Rebecca.

The day after she was born I looked out of the window and saw a rose which had been my mother's favourite flower. It was dark red, almost velvet like in appearance and very beautiful just like my baby and so I decided to name her after my mother, Rebecca. Born of my blood and as fragile as the petals on the rose itself; yes for me, she would always be Rebecca. Even now whenever I see a red rose it reminds me of them both and of the precious link between us.

I felt my hands shaking as I tore open the envelope. What would she say and why was she making contact after all these years? There was no detail about her own life, no expression of warmth or affection in her writing, just blunt and to the point: where was she born, who was her father and why had I given her away and abandoned her at only seven weeks old?

Given her away! Abandoned her! I'd never have done that. I had fought to hold on to my beautiful baby daughter as though my life depended on it right up until the moment they took her from me and out of my life, seemingly forever, in that dark blue car.

I could hardly breathe; a sense of dread and panic overwhelming me as the car pulled away and I struggled to comprehend what had happened, my eyes filling with tears and my heart breaking. I fell to the ground, arms outstretched and pleading for the return of my baby. I screamed her name as loud as I could but that only appeared to make them drive faster in their effort to get away and take my precious baby to God knows where, but always away from me, of that much I could be sure.

The nuns offered no words of encouragement or comfort for my loss, choosing rather to focus on my perceived failings.

"It's for the best; you'll come to see that in time. The child will have a much better life than you would ever have been able to provide for her. She'll be brought up in a proper Christian home, not some back street slum with never enough to eat or real bed to sleep in."

Of course I hadn't abandoned her, how could I have done; I was given no choice.

But how could I tell her that or any of what had happened in those first few days and weeks of her life on the single page of a note pad? How could I explain in just a few short sentences all that had happened during the early years of my life that had led to the events of that day? How could I tell her of all the mistakes I'd made and of the sadness I'd carried for so many years that had so cruelly shaped my life and had now resulted in this potentially life changing moment in time for both of us?

She wants to know why I let her go, to get some closure on what happened, but doesn't want to see me, meet with me, or even speak to me. Even worse, she doesn't consider me in any way to be her mother apart from the physical act of having given birth to her. She says she is part of a family already and so doesn't need another mother in her life, certainly not one that had so little regard for her as a baby.

In a way I can understand her professed feelings of betrayal and abandonment, but without speaking to me how will she ever learn the truth. And knowing of her pain now only serves to increase the hurt I felt on the day our lives were ripped apart.

That overwhelming sense of utter loss and despair is something that still consumes me even today. Being told I would never see my child, my precious Rebecca again, along with the years spent alone in not being able to watch her grow into the young woman she is today haunts my every waking hour and often my dreams as well.

And so after all those years of hoping and praying for almost any form of contact with her my prayers are finally answered in the shape of this short and spiteful letter I hold in my hand now.

I've spent the past twenty eight years pretty much on my own. I've made a few friends here and there, mainly women, but never a soul mate, not someone I could really share my heart and feelings with. There has never been anyone I could trust enough to allow myself to be open and vulnerable with, not since Rebecca was taken from me. The world seemed to lose its colour for me after that, life and everything it had to offer becoming black and white and without purpose.

Whenever I went out I found myself watching other women with their babies and children. I'd notice young girls playing with their friends and wonder if they might be her, my Rebecca?

On April 23rd each year, her birthday, I buy a card and write in it all the things I have been unable to tell her over the past twelve months; how much I miss her, love her, and am thinking about her. I write about how she will have grown and become even more beautiful than the first day I held her, and how a corner of my heart will be forever hers.

I've kept all those cards in a box at the bottom of my wardrobe. I get them out occasionally to look at and to talk to, as though she's there in the room with me.

How do I tell her all of that in the page or two of a simple letter, the story of a life torn apart by her going and a story that she says she doesn't want to hear? She knows nothing about me, nothing about my childhood and the unhappiness I experienced growing up; a childhood that saw my own parents and brother taken away from me to die in unspeakable horror. If she would just meet with me, and let me explain what it was like growing up as a young Jewish girl during the 1930s in North London and beyond.

We had a good life there. My father worked in a local tailor's shop along with my mother who helped behind the scenes with the orders and accounts as well as bringing up my brother Joseph and I at the same time. My parents were so happy together and dreamed one day of owning their own tailoring business, with Papa making the clothes and Mama looking after the books and finances. She would laugh and say that he might know how to count the inches on a piece of cloth required to make a suit but that he couldn't add up the pennies it cost to make if his life depended on it.

"You focus on taking the customers' measurements and I'll focus on taking their money."

Our house was always full of joy and laughter and my brother and I never doubted how much we were loved.

"One day when you have children of your own you will understand how precious they are to you," Mama told me once. "You would give your own life for them in a heartbeat."

When Rebecca was born I knew in that instant what Mama had meant. I've felt that same all-consuming love for her ever since even though the greater part of our lives have been spent apart. They say after a patient has had an arm or leg amputated they can still feel the limb in place even though it is no longer there.

That's the way I feel about my Rebecca. She may not be physically with me but when I close my eyes at certain times during the day or at bedtime I can still feel her tiny body nestling in my arms the way she used to in those short weeks we had together in the home before she was taken from me.

It has been a constant sadness and regret to me that we weren't able to spend those all important early and formative years together as she grew. How different our relationship would have been had we spent that time together as mother and daughter, along with all the love and shared adventures we would have experienced between us.

I can remember when Joseph and I were children and the excitement we felt when we moved, as a family, to Guernsey, with our parents finally able to realise their long held ambition of opening a tailoring business of their own. I can still see the look of emotion of my father's face when he told us, "We're on our way children. God has decided to shine His light on us and bless our dreams, my dears."

Life was good for all of us in those early days on the Island and Papa's work flourished until the Germans arrived. They tolerated us briefly for a while but it was obvious they had other plans for any Jews left living there. Things rapidly became more difficult, not only for my parents but also for the others living and working in that tiny Jewish community. Most of Jews who had lived on the Channel Islands had already left, making the move to England in the late spring of 1940 just before the Germans arrived. My father said that he and Mama had worked hard for their business and didn't see why they should be made to give it up because of an unwelcome threat posed by a group of Nazi bullies. Mama wasn't so sure and begged him to think again, but my father was a proud man and wouldn't be turned. Things changed very quickly once the Germans established themselves on the island and over the next two years. It was clear that for the few of us left, mainly women, life was going to be made very difficult. Even the established island authorities made no move to protest, allowing the Germans to rewrite many local laws and regulations in their favour. They agreed to all Jewish business being labelled as such and eventually sold or handed over to non Jews, with many of them winding up under direct German authority. My father's business came under the same rule and he was forced to place a sign in his shop window saying, 'Owned by Jews'. Although we were small in number we were made to wear the Star of David on our clothing to mark us out as being different from the rest of those living on the island. The Germans told my father that he had to work directly for them and that they would handle all the paperwork in future instead of my mother. Mama may have feared the Germans but she wasn't one to lie down easily and so protested, quite determinedly at first, against the unfairness and injustice being exacted on her and Papa. After a while though she relented, having little choice but to obey the orders that were barked at her; orders that became increasingly threatening in nature as each day passed.

"We make the rules from now on and you would be well advised to obey them," a German officer snarled at my mother one day, placing his hand on his gun holster as he sat in front of her at the small desk where my mother managed the accounts. She realised any further protest was futile, and so along with my father simply got on with the work demanded of them, keeping their heads down and doing as they were told. After all how do you argue with the threat of a Luger pistol being pointed at you or worse, at your children?

Papa was forced to make suits, uniforms and other items of clothing for the German officers, but we never saw any money. I remember him asking one day about a certain payment that was overdue. He said with all the work he was being forced to do for the soldiers he was falling behind with his other clients and that it was becoming increasingly difficult to make ends meet financially. One of the German's started shouting at my father.

"Filthy Jewish dog. You should see it as a privilege to support the great German war effort in this way. How dare you ask for money and seek to make a profit from us."

"I'm simply saying that I need some form of income if I am to buy food and meet the needs of my family."

The officer became instantly more aggressive in his demeanour, taking hold of the roll of material Papa was holding and throwing it to the ground. He took his pistol from its holster and beat my father around the head with it, threatening to shoot him if he continued to protest.

"If you argue with me once more I will make sure you are never able to work again, and then how will you feed your stinking Jewish family." My mother and I begged for his life and the officer replied that soon we wouldn't be a problem for him to deal with as plans were in place to deport us along with the other remaining Jews on the island.

"Soon you and the others will be gone, and we will be able to walk the streets without having to hold our noses from the stench of you Jews." Whilst we were shocked at his language we weren't entirely surprised at the decision to expel us as they had already confiscated our passports and identification papers.

"You will have no need of these documents now as it will be us who decide your future movements from now on."

Over the next few weeks arrangements were put in place to have any remaining Jews on the island placed under house arrest and readied for deportation. When the time came for us to leave we were allowed only one small suitcase each for our clothing and personal belongings. Anything of any monetary value was removed, supposedly to help raise funds for the German war effort although we witnessed watches, rings and the like being put straight into some of the soldiers pockets. We presumed these items wouldn't make it to the war fund but would be held onto for more personal gain. Mama managed to hide a few pieces of jewellery in her bag and by concealing others in the hems of her dresses and coat, but everything else was taken from us.

We had no real idea of our final destination on the day we were herded onto the ship, except we were told it was bound for France and that we would be moved on from there. As we made our way gingerly up the gangplank to the ship's deck we were surrounded by soldiers shouting and pointing their rifles at us.

"Keep moving, Schnell," they bellowed as we moved slowly forward holding hands, as much for our own safety as for any comfort with the walkway swinging to and fro over the choppy waters below. We were forced towards the end of the ship and made to sit on rough wooden benches directly above the engine room which belched out foul smelling smoke and fumes that made us feel sick.

I remember looking back at the island, the distance growing between the ship and the coastline as we sailed away from our home towards an uncertain future, but one we knew would be very different to the life we had come to know and love in the couple of years we had lived on Guernsey, certainly in the early days.

I felt a sense of fear and growing unease in the pit of my stomach as I looked at my parents, noticing the expression of concern on their faces. Mama turned to Joseph and I, telling us not to worry and that everything would be alright as she hugged us close into her. This was not only to protect us from the stinking fumes and chill wind blowing across the ship's deck, but also from equally icy stare of the German soldiers standing guard alongside us.

"Don't worry, my dears, your father and I won't let anything happen to you." Joseph and I glanced at each other not doubting the sincerity of her words, but more perhaps her ability to see through those intentions as we watched the soldiers grimace and pull their long overcoats tight around themselves, seeking shelter from the spray being thrown on to the ship by the increasing wind against the waves. They were quite happy for us to get soaked of course as we turned up our own collars in an effort to gain even the limited protection from the elements they afforded. We held on tightly to each other for safekeeping whilst the soldiers grasped just as firmly to their rifles; a reminder, as if we needed one, that the real risk to our survival was not to be found in the turbulent seas tossing us from side to side but in the far darker menace standing beside us and threatening our very existence.

THREE

Everything changed about a year ago when I met Chris, he took to Jenny straight away and she really liked him as well; it felt good having him around. I also enjoyed being in a proper relationship with a man again for the first time in a few years, especially a man who appeared to be interested in me as a person and in what I thought and had to say, rather than simply getting me into bed as had been Gerry's primary objective. I'd been out on a few dates after Jenny was born but nothing serious as I hadn't been looking for anyone else to share my life with at that stage, certainly not with all of the demands that raising a young child brings, not until Chris came along anyway. We'd only been out once before but I knew I liked him, so when we met up in the pub that night for the second time I decided to tell him the truth and get everything out in the open. I didn't want any hopes I had for a deeper relationship to come crashing down once he found I came as part of a package or not at all.

"Blimey, you're a girl of surprises I'll give you that. A ready made family, eh, not sure I was looking for that."

"If you want to stop seeing me that's fine," I replied, desperately hoping he wouldn't.

"I just wanted to be honest from the start."

We spent much of the next hour talking about my time with

Gerry and how Jenny had come into the world. Chris listened to all I had to say and then slowly got to his feet. "This is it," I thought, "he's going to leave." He stood for a moment looking down at me and then smiled. "Tell you what, how about I meet her and we'll see what she makes of me. Same again, is it?"

"Yes, thanks." I looked at him quizzically. "Makes of you?"

"Yeah well, if she's anything like her mum I'll need to be on my best behaviour, wont I?" He smiled again, obviously sensing my confusion at his reaction.

"You know, so I make a good impression. I mean, I may be able to pull the wool over your eyes about certain things, but in my experience kids can see right through us grown ups, so I don't want her eyeing me up and telling you to dump me do I?"

I smiled back at him, knowing in that moment I had done the right thing in telling the truth about my beautiful little girl. As he moved towards the bar I uttered a silent prayer that she would feel the same way as her mum did about this special man. I sat with a fixed grin on my face for the next few minutes until Chris returned carrying our drinks.

"They do a nice Sunday lunch here, perhaps the three of us can come this weekend. Mind, I hope she's cheaper to buy for than her mum," he said laughing as he placed my drink on the table in front of me. "Lemonade, wasn't it?"

Spending time with Chris over the next few weeks made me feel vibrant and alive again in a way that I hadn't experienced for some time. I felt valued, both as a woman and as a person in my own right, and more significantly for me, as a mum. I sensed from their very first meeting that he liked Jenny and would care for her. Within a few weeks it became obvious that she was becoming as important to him in our relationship as he was to us.

It wasn't long before she and Chris would happily go off to the shops together or the park and Jenny would always come back asking when she could see him again. "Mummy, we had such a good time, can Chris come back tomorrow?"

I never had any concerns about the two of them spending time on their own, and quickly learnt to trust Jenny to his care. There were times they would pretend to gang up on me and, even though I knew they were only teasing, I would still feel a little jealous in how close they had become in their relationship.

"Shall we go to the park tomorrow, Jenny? Would you like that?"

"Only if it can be just the two of us. You know what a scardy cat Mum is when I go up high on the swings and she worries about me falling off. You never do that, do you, Chris? You push me as high as the sky."

"I know, she can be a bit of a fuss pot at times."

"I'm her mother; I'm allowed to worry about her."

The two of them would then fall about laughing and say they were only joking.

"Of course we want you to come with us, you daft brush we were just messing about, weren't we, Jenny?"

"I suppose so."

Chris would always be the first to stop if he sensed the two of them had overstepped the mark with their teasing and would make a special fuss of me later or buy some flowers to reassure me that I was still first in our relationship.

Although I was encouraged by Jenny's enthusiasm for him it was sometimes difficult to know how best to respond to her childish questions and reasoning about this new man in our lives.

"Chris is so funny, Mummy, why didn't you meet him before and then he could have been my real daddy?"

Mum and Dad also took to Chris pretty much straightaway as I think they could see for themselves that his concern for both Jenny and I was genuine and also, that he wanted only the best for the two of us. His relationship with them was important to me as well of course, but more especially, I felt, to Jenny with her now being old enough to know what was going on, and with her grandparents already being so caring and protective of her.

One day when Jenny and I were talking about Chris she asked me directly about our plans for the future and wasn't shy about making her own suggestions.

"Mummy, I love Chris and I know you do as well and Granny and Granddad really like him so why don't you marry him and then he can be my proper daddy and not just a pretend one?"

"Well you certainly say what you think, young lady, I'll give you that, but it's not that simple. It's not just up to you and I, Chris has to want to get married to me as well. And for now we are still getting to know each other at lots of different levels, some of which you will only really understand when you get older. Anyway, what's brought on this sudden urgency for us to get married?

"All my friends have got proper dads and I want to be able to talk about Chris and moan about him like they all do when they're in trouble or grounded and the like, and I can't really do that while he's just your boyfriend. You can dump your boyfriend but you can't just get rid of him like that when you're married, can you?"

"That's very true, and also the reason we have to think very carefully before we consider taking such a big step."

I didn't want to get into a serious discussion between the two of us that I knew we wouldn't resolve and so tried to move the conversation on by injecting some humour into it.

"It seems to me you're more interested in having a dad to moan about to your mates than you are in the happiness of your mum?"

"Oh, Mum, you know what I mean."

Actually I wasn't entirely sure I did know what she meant but on talking with some of her friends' mothers I discovered that moaning about how strict fathers could be at times was some form of perverse badge of honour that youngsters liked to wear, and one that Jenny felt unable to fully join in with. Even though I had been known to lay down the law at times when she misbehaved or got into trouble at school it still wasn't the same as being able to complain about your dad being unfair and out of touch. He was the greater threat apparently in response to any perceived acts of disobedience by a youngster when it came to demonstrating appropriate respect for the family book of rules. It was your father who was deemed to be the real ogre in the relationship when it came to handing out differing and supposedly unwarranted forms of punishment; at least as far as Jenny's circle of friends were concerned. Mum's threats it appeared just didn't carry same weight in the battle of child against parental understanding and discipline. I wasn't sure if this was an attack on mums for being more understanding than the man in the house or a compliment. Either way I decided to leave that particular line of questioning unanswered for now.

Although this started out as a bit of fun the more we talked over the days ahead the more I think Jenny felt she really would like to have a permanent father figure in her life rather than just my dad who, although wasn't particularly old, still carried the name of "granddad" as far as she was concerned.

This led on to conversations about her own father, such as, who he was and where had I met him that sort of thing?

"You never really talk about him, Mummy, what was he like?"

She'd never really asked these questions before, previously just accepting what I'd said when she was younger; that we hadn't got on and that we didn't see each other anymore. When we'd had those sorts discussions in the past I'd always concluded by adding that it didn't make any difference to the way I felt about her. I told her since the day she was born that she was the most precious thing in my life and that nothing had, or ever would happen to alter that truth. She'd seen a picture of Gerry in the past but had shown no real interest in knowing anymore about him. Even as she grew she'd never really wanted to know where he was or indicated that she might like to meet with him. I think she'd just got used to the fact that he'd never been a part of her life. He clearly didn't matter to me, so why would she want to have any involvement or contact with him herself? Yet suddenly here she was asking some very real questions about him, about the two of us, questions that began to bring back memories about times and events that I'd placed firmly at the back of my mind and had all but forgotten about.

"Was he a nice man? If you didn't like him why did you choose him to be my daddy?" The harder I tried to answer Jenny's increasingly challenging questions about Gerry the more it raised fresh doubts and uncertainties in my mind about my own birth, my parents, and why I'd been abandoned at such an early age. This went on for some time until I finally realised I did need some answers to these misgivings and unanswered questions; questions that became louder in my head with every passing day and each one now demanding a response.

"Who was my father, what was he like? Had my mother made a mistake in getting pregnant as I had?" And if that were the case, the most telling question for me still remained, "Why had she given her baby away? Why hadn't she kept me and tried to do the best for me as I had done with Jenny?" Our experiences in becoming pregnant may have been different but surely a mother's love for her child is still absolute, no matter what the circumstances, or was I being naive?

I knew from the first that I would keep Jenny, that she was my daughter and my life, and I couldn't understand why my own mother wouldn't have felt the same way about me. I decided I needed to find out what had really happened and who this woman was; a woman who, although I didn't know, was occupying more and more of my waking thoughts each day.

Mum and Dad were great about it, although I think Mum was a little concerned that if I did discover who my birth parents were and met up with them that I might not love the two of them in the same way anymore, or want to spend so much of my time with them.

"If you do find your mum, Mary, you won't move away will you? You'll still let us be a part of yours and Jenny's lives?" She paused, her voice beginning to crack. "We love you both very much, you know that, don't you?"

"Don't be daft; you'll always be my real mum. You and Dad are the best parents anyone could ask for, and certainly the best grandparents any little girl could want, you ask Jenny." I gave her a hug. "Whatever happens, Mum, this will always be our home – at least I hope so?" Mum laughed, wiping a tear from her eye as she did so.

"You silly thing, of course it will, for as long as you both want."

"Well that's settled then." I hugged her again and smiled. "Time to put the kettle on, I think."

We spent the next 20 minutes drinking our tea and chatting together as I explained in greater detail why I needed to know more about this woman who hadn't apparently loved me enough to keep me, nor wanted me as much as she and Dad had. I couldn't comprehend why any woman wouldn't hold the same affection for their child as I did for Jenny, in loving them, caring for them, and protecting them for as long as a breath of air remained in their body.

"I just can't understand why she didn't feel the same way about me as I do about Jen."

I looked at Mum and sensed her need for reassurance.

"Or in the same way that you and Dad feel about me, okay, Mum? Never doubt that I know absolutely how much the two of you love me, and Jenny, that's a given, yeah? But I need to know the reasons she made the decisions she did. I need to make some sense of how and why she let me go, and maybe in the process discover more about myself as a person?"

Mum said she understood and would talk to Dad about what they could remember from the time of my adoption. "Your dad's better at detail than me, Mary, especially about that time. I just wanted to get you home and didn't think too much about the logistics of it all or the paperwork."

True to her word they both spoke to me a day or two later and told me everything they could recall about how I had come into their lives after they had discovered they couldn't have any children of their own and so had made the decision to try and adopt.

"We weren't given much detail about your mother," Dad said, "except that she was a young girl who had got herself pregnant by an unnamed man. Apparently she had no desire to keep you or means of supporting the two of you even if she had done and so you were taken into care. As far as I can remember you were put up for adoption pretty much as soon as you were born, with your mum and I agreeing to take you just a few weeks later."

They said they didn't really know much beyond that as it wasn't deemed advisable or appropriate at that time, in the late 1940s, for the birth mother and the adoptive parents to have any form of contact between them, nor any discussion regarding the adoption itself, or in the physical handing over of the baby.

"We were told this was best for all parties as it allowed for a clean break for the mother and a fresh start at life for the baby and its adoptive parents."

I was grateful for their honesty and that they had chosen me to be their daughter, bringing me up as their own, but I still couldn't reconcile how any woman, even a young teenage girl as I had been, could give up her child, her own flesh and blood without at least some form of protest or fight to keep it. I also knew that in those days the birth mother wasn't allowed to make contact with the child's new family, but times had changed and I was determined to discover the truth, no matter how painful that truth might prove to be for the both of us, even accepting that she had obviously learnt to live her life without me. There still had to be a reason why she hadn't at least tried to keep me and I wanted to know what that reason was, as much for myself as in responding to Jenny's own curiosity. Perhaps these questions had lain dormant in my heart for years and Jenny's interest had acted as the catalyst needed to stir them back into life, but alive they were and I knew they wouldn't go away again until they had been answered.

Dad helped me with those early letters to the adoption agency in trying to trace my birth mother and getting permission for me to approach her.

The law has changed in more recent years and it is easier now to obtain that sort of information, but back in the late '40s such legal procedures were carried out very differently and so I needed to get the detail right. I was really nervous, and if I'm honest a part of me had half hoped they would say no, but they didn't and so after staring at the mountainous pile of forms and paperwork that arrived for a few days, Dad agreed again to help me fill in the required detail and send them off.

It was a few weeks later that I received a letter informing me that my mother had replied and given permission for me to contact her. The envelope was lying on the table when I arrived home one day, and Mum was looking at it nervously as I entered the room. She could see where it was from because of the post mark and official stamp on the front. "There's a letter for you, love." She nodded towards it trying to look indifferent but failing miserably. "It looks like the one you've been waiting for."

I felt a sense of trepidation as I picked up the envelope, staring at it for a moment before opening it carefully in some form of needless deference to its official status. I knew deep inside, for all my misgivings, what I wanted to see and hear the letter say, but I was also fearful that if it was the yes I had been hoping for then perhaps I would now be opening a Pandora's Box that couldn't be closed again and one that would potentially change all of our lives forever, but to what end?

The letter itself, whilst looking very official, didn't say much in truth apart from the fact that she had agreed for me to get in touch with her. It also offered me an address that I could write to if I decided I wanted to progress our contact to the next level. It wasn't her home address but one that would act as a sort of intermediary between the two of us; this in turn would allow her the space and time to decide if she wanted to continue the process further herself. I suppose it was also to ensure that I couldn't simply march round to her house demanding answers to a list of questions she may or may not wish to answer, or even feel entirely comfortable in doing. Also, progressing slowly in this way meant that if things didn't work out we could both simply return to the lives we already knew without any undue embarrassment or the potential for either of us to do or say something we might later regret. Either way I felt in agreement that this was probably the best way to proceed, certainly at this early stage, although a part of me was disappointed not to have been able to arrange a meeting there and then to get the whole thing out in the open and dealt with. But I also recognised that in maintaining some sort of distance between us, at least for now, would also allow us to have second thoughts and to act on them if the prospect of what we were contemplating became too much for either of us.

Until that letter arrived I had felt increasingly confident about the detail of what I wanted to know but now, having been given permission to pose those questions, my thoughts became more confused and I was unsure about how best to couch them or what to say.

I must have started writing my reply a hundred times but nearly always beginning with the same obvious demands to know about how I came to be in the world and why had she let me go. I would look at this page of self-centred rage and indignation for a moment before tearing it up in frustration and starting again.

Sometimes I would attempt to be polite and make small talk but would quickly find myself going off at the deep end once more, ranting on about what sort of an awful woman she must be and demanding to know how could she desert me, her own child, a baby of only seven weeks?

This went on for ages until in the end Mum suggested that I write just a very simple letter, introducing myself and asking only the essential questions such as where I was born and what could she tell me about my father?

"You've waited all this time, Mary, so another few weeks of taking things slowly won't hurt. Just go gently to begin with and see what happens. Remember this is probably as difficult for her as it is for you, maybe harder. After all she's the one who let you go; she's the one who has to explain herself, not you. You don't want to scare her off at the first hurdle."

Mum said by moving slowly this would allow for the opportunity to establish some common ground between us and not make her feel under any immediate threat or pressure to address the more difficult issues and harder to answer questions so early on in our relationship. Also, that once we had established some sort of basic rapport this might hopefully facilitate the two of us being able to move forward more easily, thus allowing her to feel more relaxed when addressing the more exacting detail of what had actually led to her letting me go at such a young age.

"You need to gain her confidence, love; you can't simply bully her into answering you. I'm not sticking up for her but I bet she's every bit as nervous as you are about all of this, and for both your sakes you need to get it right. Once you've gained her trust and she knows you're not just out to vilify her you'll both be in a better position to open up to each other and address the things you've probably both wanted to say, or ask for years. I'll bet there are a hundred things she's desperate to know about you, whatever your misgivings or feelings about her might be. She's still a human being, Mary, and your dad and I have brought you up to value and respect everyone as an individual no matter how hard that might be to do at times. Once you know more about each other and why she was happy for you to be adopted by your dad and I then you can decide for yourself whether you want anything more to do with her or whether you're simply happy to say thank you and goodbye. At least you'll have the answers you're looking for then, for both you and Jenny. And remember sweetheart, whatever you ultimately decide your dad and I will stand by you."

I accepted this as good advice. After all, as Mum had said, I didn't know this woman and all of these events that were bothering me so much had taken place some twenty-eight years ago; times had changed and perhaps she had as well? Maybe, like me, she had made a mistake in getting pregnant and had agreed to let me go in a panic, having no-one to support her as I had been so fortunate to have had in James and Carol? And now after all this time perhaps she has managed to put all that happened in the past behind her and feels it is too late for us to start over again, or maybe she has a new life and doesn't want me to be a part of it? And what if she hadn't really wanted to have a baby at all and that had been the reason for her letting me go? After all, she'd apparently never made any attempt to get in touch with me during the past twenty eight years, or more recently since the laws regarding contact between adopted children and their birth parents had changed. But if that were true, why agree to any further contact now unless it is to tell me to leave her alone once and for all?

I continued to torment myself with these thoughts for a few more days until in the end I did as Mum advised and just wrote a short and simple letter asking where I'd been born, who my father was and why she'd agreed to my adoption. I said I didn't want, or need, to know about her life as we would probably never meet and that as we'd survived this long without each other, why get into a lot of personal details that had no bearing on the people we were today, nor would go on to become in the future.

As I sealed the envelope I was suddenly filled with regret that I hadn't listened to my head which still wanted to know more, but in the same instant my heart reminded me it couldn't bear the disappointment of hearing things that might potentially break it, or call into question the sanctuary and security I already knew in my life with Jenny, Mum and Dad. I couldn't and wouldn't threaten those precious relationships at any cost.

FOUR

We were to be sent to the death camp at Birkenau, although we had no awareness of this as we journeyed by ship, road and rail over the next week towards our final destination.

I remember the German soldiers arriving at our house on the morning we left; they banged on the front door, shouting at us to come out. "SchnelI, Schnell. Come quickly."

I looked out of my bedroom window and could see them standing in their uniforms laughing with each other, their dogs barking at our door as if telling us to hurry as well.

I looked up the road and saw two women and a little girl making their way down the street carrying their bags and battered cases as they walked side by side flanked by more soldiers and their dogs. I noticed one of the women, a friend of my mother's, Mrs Goldhirsch, turn to pick up her little daughter, Hannah, who was moving too slowly for the soldiers. She handed a bag to the other woman as she swept Hannah into her arms, struggling to hold onto her case as she did so. The case dropped to the ground and as she moved to pick it up a German soldier kicked it forward and shouted at Mrs Goldhirsch. I couldn't hear what he was saying but he pushed her so hard that Hannah nearly fell from her arms. As she stumbled and picked up the case I could see she was upset but trying not to cry as she held Hannah close to her in an effort to reassure her. The soldier forced her forward with the butt of his rifle and yelled at her again. I watched as Hannah began to cry and Mrs Goldhirsch did her best to comfort her as the soldiers continued barking orders at them to keep moving. My parents called for me to hurry. "Come on, Ruth, quickly, we have to go now." I felt a shudder of fear run through me as I made my way down the stairs carrying my own small bag containing a few treasured belongings including my favourite doll. I had already determined in my own mind that she wouldn't be knocked from my grasp by the bullying soldiers outside no matter what they did to me.

Once outside we were forced on to the back of a truck and taken to the port ready to board the ship that was preparing to sail to France for the next part of our journey. The weather on the crossing was rough and did little to ameliorate the mood of the guards towards us as we sat huddled on the windswept deck with both the rain and the spray from the sea soaking into our clothing and dampening more than just our spirits.

Mama and I felt seasick for most of the journey and so were relieved to see the French coastline ahead of us as we approached the calmer waters of the harbour.

After disembarking we were taken to a large warehouse along with many other Jewish families who had been rounded up from various towns and villages, both locally and from other districts. Like us, they had the Star of David attached to their clothing and wore the now familiar look of fear on their faces as we all stood cramped together in almost total silence, exhausted and waiting for whatever it was the German's had prepared for us next.

A short while later a German officer entered the building accompanied by two other soldiers carrying rifles. They pointed the guns menacingly towards us as the officer stood on a wooden box to speak.

"Soon you will board a train and be taken to a special camp where you will be held for the duration of the war. Once you are there you will be given work to do in supporting the glorious

German war effort against our enemies, and in defending the German people from attack." He stood to attention and threw his arm forward outstretched in front of him. "Heil Hitler."

One of the men standing near the front of the crowd stepped forward.

"Please could you give us a little more detail of exactly where it is we are being sent to and what will happen to us when we arrive?" There was a murmur of approval from those standing nearby and another man stepped forward.

"Can we also have some food and water as well? Many of us haven't eaten for some time and the children especially are hungry and thirsty."

The soldiers pointed their rifles directly at the men and forced them back into line as the officer bellowed his dismissive reply.

"I do not have time to concern myself with feeding your Jewish bellies; my orders are to get everyone loaded onto the train and transported to the camp as soon as possible. There will be no more discussion about this. You will follow my orders and those given to you by my soldiers without question." He stared menacingly at us and especially towards the two men who had been brave enough to speak; "Is that clear?" The officer stood motionless for a few seconds his gaze focused on those who had been foolish enough to question him as if daring them to speak out again. They recognised from his brutal response any further attempt at discussion or protest would, not only be futile, but more than likely be met by some form of active aggression against them as a chosen means of reply.

When the soldiers had satisfied themselves there would be no further questions or complaints, at least none that we felt brave enough to verbalise, they left. There was a moment's stunned silence as we processed in our minds what the officer had said; then just as suddenly the building was filled with raised voices and the cries of children as the realisation of what we had been told took on a terrifying reality of its own. Whatever the Germans had in mind for us it clearly wasn't too make our immediate, nor presumably, longer term existence anything less than uncomfortable.

Some of the men started suggesting we should stand up to the Germans and demand to know what they were intending to do with us.

"There are not that many of them, perhaps we could overpower them." A large woman pushed herself through the crowd. "Are you mad? There may be more of us but they have guns, and listening to that officer I am sure he would be more than happy to tell his soldiers to shoot us if we made a move against them."

Another woman spoke out. "And then what will happen to us, with many of our men and perhaps even some of our children dead? They would still send the rest of us of to the prison camp. If I am going to have to live as a prisoner I want it to be with my husband and children beside me, not dead and buried in the ground hundreds of miles away."

These arguments went on for a while but eventually it was decided it would be best for us all to do as we were told for now and see what the future might bring.

"After all," one woman said, "things can't get much worse than they are now." Little did we know.

Around fifteen minutes later another group of soldiers arrived to march us to the station which was situated some half a mile away. As we arrived a train pulled in but the carriages looked like wagons used for transporting cattle rather than human beings. They had wooden planks slatted along them and no sign of windows for us to look out of during the journey. We were hurriedly marshalled into a long line outside the station, with little patience or regard shown towards the elderly and smaller children who struggled to maintain their balance at times as we jostled together in our efforts to form the orderly procession being demanded of us. My parents smiled nervously at some of the other families who were standing alongside us. It was as though they each sensed things were about to get a lot worse, perhaps in ways we couldn't yet imagine. Although we had all agreed to stay quiet for now, some of the men were still arguing amongst themselves about what was happening and why as they struggled to come to terms with this sudden and dramatic change to their lives and of those they loved.

They realised, as we all did, that whatever the outcome, none of it was intended for our good.

My mother tried to comfort Joseph and I by telling us we were going on an adventure but, young as we were, we were still aware of that same sense of dread and apprehension that our parents were experiencing as we were hurried towards the train and our journey into the unknown.

"Schnell. Get a move on, come along quickly," the soldiers demanded as we filed forward onto the platform. A real sense of fear came over me as we were bundled into the bare wooden carriages that were to transport us to our eventual destination. There was no seating and it soon became difficult to stand or sit as the soldiers kept pushing more and more people on, young and old alike. The carriage filled quickly until there was no more room and it became hard to breathe in the claustrophobic conditions as we were forced ever closer together. I felt as though I might suffocate as Joseph and I were pushed further towards the back of the carriage and the light faded with so many adults standing tall above us. Any last remaining daylight eventually disappeared as the huge wooden door screeched and slid across the rusting metal runners, slamming shut on us. Joseph and I hung onto each other tightly as shouts of protest rang out from our parents and the other families and as our eyes adjusted to the darkness.

One elderly man had apparently fallen as he tried to clamber into the carriage to be with his family and we could hear his wife scream as one of the guard dogs outside was encouraged to attack him.

"Please no," she cried out. "Somebody help him." As she was forced back into the carriage by the sheer weight of bodies fighting for space I remember glancing across to see her eyes searching for him in an effort to say a last goodbye before the door was locked shut leaving her near to hysterics and wondering if she would ever see her beloved husband again. We could still hear the man yelling for her as the dogs barked and snarled at him on the platform. I'll never forget the look on her face as she yelled out his name, the tears running down her face as she collapsed into the arms of those around her.

"Levi, I'm here, I love you, my darling."

My mother leant across in an effort to comfort her. "It will be alright, you will see him again soon I am sure." I could tell by her expression that she didn't really believe what she was saying.

The train suddenly lurched into life throwing us around and into each other which caused women to scream and the children to panic, crying out for their mothers.

We felt like animals all pressed together, having been herded into this bare wooden wagon with its cramped conditions. There was practically no fresh air which rapidly created an atmosphere that was both stifling and overbearing. This coupled with a growing sense of foreboding caused many to lose any last remnant of hope as we rattled along the track in this makeshift wooden coffin, the only difference being that for now we were still alive, but for how long? Just a few days before and we had all been living safely in our own homes; yes, concerned about what the future might bring, but not in our wildest imagination had any of us considered our lives might change so dramatically in such a short space of time.

The train quickly picked up speed, rocking from side to side with many of the men holding onto each other and struggling to keep their feet having allowed their wives and children to sit on the floor as space allowed. Some of the smaller children wet or soiled themselves which made matters worse as mothers tried to comfort and change them in the overcrowded and unsanitary conditions. Tempers quickly became frayed amongst those without young families complaining about the smell and the women's failure to deal with their children's toilet needs.

"Isn't it bad enough being forced together like this without having to inhale the smell of shit as well? Why don't you clear it up?

What could they do, there were no proper changing facilities and even for the adults no basic sanitation with only a single rusting bucket in the corner serving as a toilet. This quickly filled and overflowed onto the rough wooden flooring. One very young baby was crying out with hunger and a man shouted at its mother to keep it quiet as she struggled with her blouse in an attempt to feed it.

"For God's sake can't you keep the child quiet? Are we expected to put up with that noise for the rest of the journey?" The woman's husband leapt to her defence.

"My wife is doing her best so why don't you shut up. Your bellowing certainly isn't helping either." Eventually with the two men on the point of exchanging blows another man stepped in between them.

"Stop it; you're scaring the other children now as well as her baby. Arguing amongst ourselves doesn't help any of us. Please, both of you, we all need to keep calm."

The two men weren't really angry with each other and quickly made up their differences, recognising the sense in the other man's appeal for understanding. They were just frustrated and concerned for their own family's needs like the rest of us. But as the journey continued so individual tempers and the potential for aggression rose again, especially amongst the men. Nerves became increasingly ragged and a few minor scuffles eventually broke out as parents looked to protect their families and children. There was no escape from the growing sense of fear and trepidation amongst us all as we were jostled about in the confines of that overly crowded carriage, occasionally being thrown against each other as the train sped forward along the track towards its destination. One woman cried out in pain as a man accidentally trod on her hand as the carriage lurched from one side of the track to the other.

"Watch out, you fool," shouted the woman's husband.

"I'm sorry, but I can't even see my feet let alone your wife's hand."

"Well you'll see mine soon enough if you're not more careful."

Disagreements like these continued to break out from time to time throughout the journey, although ultimately everyone recognised it was the cramped and inhumane conditions we were being forced to exist in that was the real cause of the tension between us rather than any lack of concern for each other's welfare or individual rights as human beings.

There was a broken slat on one side of the carriage and it was agreed to let the elderly woman who had lost her husband at the station sit there for a while to gain access to the little fresh air it afforded. She was still in a state of panic about what she had witnessed and as to what might have happened to him. After a while though other people pushed forward demanding their turn to garner access to the only clean air available in the claustrophobic surroundings of that tomb-like edifice.

"She's been there long enough, my little boy has asthma and needs some air," one woman shouted.

"And my daughter is not well either, let her through," another mother added.

These sorts of exchanges as to whose turn it was to gain a few moments respite from the increasingly airless environment of the carriage continued for much of the rest of the journey. Whoever sat by the broken slat was encouraged to tell the rest of us what they could see as the train hurried along the track, not that there was much to report as we appeared to travel mainly through endless woodland and countryside. Even when we did pass a town or rail station we didn't slow long enough to identify where we were.

Early on in the journey my mother and one or two of the other women tried to encourage some of the smaller children to sing in an effort to keep their spirits up. After a while though some of the adults without families complained and shouted for them to be quiet.

"Not only are we forced together like cattle but now we have to listen to your children wailing like their offspring as well?" I could tell from my mother's expression that even though she and the other women were making a brave attempt to comfort and distract us from our grim surroundings, they were also putting on a brave face for each other. They too were as fearful as everyone else as to where we might be headed as the miles rolled by on that dreadful and seemingly endless journey.

Mama put her arms around Joseph and I and pulled us close to her, giving us both a kiss. "Don't worry, my darlings, Mama loves you. This horrid train ride will soon be over and we will be settled in our new home." I wasn't sure that I believed her, but it was good to hear her say it all the same. I leant across to my father and squeezed his arm in an effort to comfort him as well. "I love you, Papa." I tried to sound confident but was also aware of the tears filling my eyes. He smiled down at me but even in the shadowy light I could still see his eyes were also full, more from the injustice of what was happening to his family I think than with regard to his own personal discomfort.

Also, to the same outrage that every other man on the train was feeling that any of us, especially women and children, should be treated in such a shameful and degrading way. As a man it was only natural for him to want to protect those he loved, but I think he also recognised, for now at least, there was nothing he could do, either for us or about our circumstances.

The journey itself appeared to go on forever and there was little food or water, only what my mother and a few of the other women had managed to bring with them, but they shared it around unselfishly as best they could. Some of the adults on board, especially the older ones became quite dehydrated, and sadly there was very little that could be done for them. One elderly man, overcome by the stifling heat and lack of fresh air died during the journey. One of the other men, a doctor, tried to save him but in those dreadful conditions and with no medicines available there was nothing really that could he could do. The man's wife sobbed as the doctor held her hand.

"I think with the lack of clean air, coupled with the cramped conditions and heat, his heart simply couldn't cope with the stress being placed on it, I'm sorry." He squeezed her hand and smiled. "At least he's at peace now." Someone put a coat over his face as the doctor moved away and another woman knelt down to pray with the man's wife. We children were discouraged from looking, partly to stop us becoming further upset ourselves, but also to give the woman a little space and dignity as she mourned the loss of her man. She sat in silence for the rest of the journey holding his lifeless body in her lap and weeping gently to herself. Following the man's death tempers cooled a little and the impatience demonstrated towards others receded as everyone realised the same thing could happen to them if common courtesy and the well being of their fellow internees didn't override any personal frustrations.

During the remaining hours on the train the men took it in turns, as space allowed, to either sit or stand. This gave them the chance to rest their legs for a while and also afforded them the brief opportunity to gain a little sleep in that confined space.

Eventually, after more than a complete day of travelling the train began to slow before shuddering to a halt a few minutes later. A woman sitting by the gap looked out and shouted.

"It looks like some sort of station and there are many soldiers." Before she could say anymore we heard German voices shouting outside, then after a few moments the door that had shut us off from the outside world for so long creaked as it was unlocked and wrenched open along its runners. The sudden change in light made us blink as we attempted to adjust our eyes to the bright sunshine now pouring into the carriage. We gulped in the fresh air that was also suddenly available to us after having survived with only the stench of human sweat, urine and faeces for the past twenty four hours or more. The momentary elation we felt in seeing daylight and breathing normally again almost immediately turned to despair as our gaze fell upon a new and arguably even greater horror than the one we'd encountered on that awful journey and that now stood alongside the carriage waiting to greet us.

Rows of German soldiers in their steel grey green uniforms began shouting at us to get out of the carriage.

"Schnell. Schnell. Get out, move."

We saw their guns pointing in our direction and heard their dogs barking and snarling with their own particular brand of ferocious welcome.

One elderly lady who had been lying in the same restricted position for much of the journey and had lost the feeling in her legs struggled to stand as she was ordered from the train. A soldier rushed forward and, grabbing her arm, pulled her out of the carriage; she fell awkwardly and hit her head on the ground.

"Get up, Jewish bitch." I could see blood coming from the side of her head as she struggled to her feet, looking around for help, but the soldier pushed her to one side and shouted again for the rest of us to get down.

"Move, quickly. Come on get out of there."

The noise was overwhelming with the steam and shrill whistle from the train accompanying the screams of mothers and their children along with the soldiers shouting and their dogs growling and snapping at us; the apparent chaos and increasing tension only serving to further encourage their aggression.

Once we were all on the platform a German officer stepped forward and ordered us to form ourselves into separate lines of men and women, with any children of the age of twelve or older being herded into their appropriate gender groups as well. I was nearing twelve with Joseph almost a year younger but as we had always been tall for our age the soldiers wrongly assumed we were older. I tried to cling on to my father's hand but another soldier forced me away and I moved into line with my mother who was still, at this point, holding onto Joseph. A soldier with a dog moved forward and shouted at my brother to get in line with the men but my mother held him back in an effort to protect him. The soldier, in response to her act of defiance, encouraged the dog forward as if to attack my mother as she shouted at him.

"He's not twelve; he's still only a boy. Can't you see that he's scared?" The dog tore at her coat and as my father moved to help her the soldier turned the dog onto him which bit his hand drawing blood.

"Please don't hurt him," my mother begged, "he's bleeding." The soldier, ignoring my mother's pleas continued to encourage the dog's active aggression and was clearly enjoying himself in witnessing both my father's fear and pain. He made as if to let the dog attack him again and Joseph, fearing for Papa's life and recognising any further protest was futile, bravely moved over to our father in an effort to shield him from further assault. I hung on tightly to my mother's arm; she was crying and looking at my father with an expression of panic and dread that I will never forget. Papa attempted a smile of reassurance towards her as he placed his bloodied hand around Joseph's shoulder and drew him into himself for protection.

Once we were separated into our lines another officer arrived with two other men who we were told were doctors.

"While you are here at the camp you must work to support the German war effort and to pay for your food and shelter. The doctors will decide which of you is fit and healthy enough to join in this work. Those who are not will be moved to another part of the camp and held in detention until the end of the war when we have gained our glorious victory."

My father, thinking he might be making things easier for my brother, said he had a weak chest and shouldn't be made to do manual work. A number of other parents said similar things also hoping to save their children from any forced labour. What they didn't know, what none of them could have known, was that the doctors were not only deciding who was fit enough to work, but also the more immediate and terrifying fate of those who weren't; they were to be taken away and killed.

Without realising it my father had, in that instant, along with so many other parents' unwittingly signed their own childrens' death warrants. The doctors worked their way through the rows of men and boys extracting all those considered too old or unfit to undertake the duties planned for them. Once this was done they were then marched away in two separate lines: one containing those considered fit and strong enough for labour and the others deemed too elderly, frail or sick to support the "Glorious German war effort", as the officer had described it.

That was the last time I saw my father and brother alive as they were marched away, waving goodbye to my mother and I briefly as they went. Tragically, in having Joseph declared unfit for manual labour my father had placed him amongst the first to be executed in the gas chambers.

I heard later that once my father realised the fate to which he had condemned Joseph he had pleaded with the guards to let him take his place. A man told me the soldiers had said because my father was so concerned about Joseph they would be generous and allow him to die with his son at the same time, and so they were both gassed in the first wave of executions that afternoon. They would have died, along with hundreds of others within an hour of arriving in the camp. The only comfort I take in the horror of that knowledge is in the belief that at least they were together in that terrible moment; that my father would have held Joseph in his arms telling him how much he loved him as the gas was released choking their lungs with its poison and ending their earthly existence.

I cried for a long time when I heard the awful truth about their deaths.

I also tried, without success, to comfort my mother who stood gasping in utter disbelief when she was told what had happened to her men.

After my father and Joseph had been taken away with the rest of the men the process was repeated with the women, again with the very young girls and those considered unsuitable or incapable of labour joining the elderly in separate lines to the rest of us. Those of us who survived that first interrogation were taken to a long barn like building and ordered to strip, placing our clothes on a numbered peg attached to the wall. Our bags and suitcases were taken from us along with our jewellery, hair grips and slides. We felt embarrassed and ashamed standing naked before our sisters and mothers. This feeling only increased when a number of male guards entered the building alongside their female counterparts. We could see the men talking to each other and nodding towards the women with larger breasts as they stood, rifles by their side, waiting to direct us to our next station.

We were taken to a large room with a long run of showers and ordered to clean ourselves in the ice cold water that spewed from the rusting faucets. There was no soap so we had to wash ourselves down with our hands. Once the water was turned off we had a white powder thrown over us. This we were told was to rid us of lice. It smelt foul, stung our eyes and irritated our skin. We trooped back into the other room cold and confused before being given different clothes to put on, much of it unsuitable and ill fitting. Some were given striped pyjama-like tops and trousers, again with no consideration for size but at least they covered our naked bodies and to a small extent our shame and embarrassment. Others were less fortunate and were handed only a slip or shirt to wear.

There was almost no underwear available and one poor woman was given a bright green ballgown which looked all the more ridiculous being at least two sizes too big for her. It also had traces of blood on it but she had learnt, like the rest of us, even in the short time we had been at the camp, not to complain or ask for a more appropriate set of clothing.

Our heads were also shaved, with all the hair sorted into different shades and lengths and taken away. We heard it had been the same process for those who had been separated from us earlier with the frail, the very young and those who were sick forced to walk, still naked, to the gas chambers, or "the showers" as they were also described to them. "It is important for you all to be clean and with no disease," they had been told by the female guards as they were marched away. For those unfortunates however it was death that was poured out upon their heads rather than the icy waters we had endured. In that moment, no matter how appalling our circumstances appeared, we realised we were the lucky ones; we were still alive.

Word soon got out to the rest of us about these alternative shower rooms and their fatal cleansing properties. Some guards would sit on motorbikes outside these buildings revving their engines to drown out the screams of those fighting for breath as they suffocated to death in those gas-filled chambers.

Those of us who survived this first experience of organised mass murder were left to make the best of what was available to us at the camp. We were directed to barrack style buildings that were to become our homes during our internment or until we were too weak to work and it would be our turn to face death at the hands of our aggressors.

There was just very rough flooring in the barracks with wide slatted bunk-style beds down each side of the walls on which we would sleep, sometimes four or more to a bed and with perhaps only one tattered blanket shared between us. There was little or no sanitation and this, coupled with the totally inadequate diet and ongoing stomach complaints, meant the stench of urine and human faeces in certain areas of the building soon became our constant and unwelcome companion. If you had your period the best you could hope for was a bit of old rag that you would try and wash out when you could, but with fresh water rarely available this was a luxury that often went unattended.

Food was also in short supply and whilst most people shared what they had initially, such thinking quickly became forgotten as the days went by and the hunger pangs, coupled with the desire for self preservation, took precedence over any sense of self-sacrifice and other forms of basic humanitarian consideration. At times, such disregard for others could also include your own family. Life soon became a daily struggle for personal survival rather than affording any thought towards helping your neighbour. The Germans appeared to enjoy watching the most fundamental acts of human decency and moral code evaporate from our mind-set and corresponding behaviour towards each other. Also, in the growing disagreements and fights that would ensue at meal times, perhaps even over a piece of stale bread. At times these disputes could become particularly aggressive if it was suspected that the offending crust might be hidden away for later personal consumption when traditionally, under different circumstances, it would have been shared. The guards also made great play out of making sure that others knew if any of the women had been giving sexual favours to the German soldiers in return for additional food rations or other gratuities. This would cause immediate outrage amongst the other women in the camp. On one such occasion some of the older prisoners meted out their own form of justice for this unforgivable betrayal by hanging one of the younger women because she had slept with a soldier. Apparently she had done this in an effort to gain extra food for herself while the others in her hut continued to starve. It was only after the event they discovered she had agreed to sex, not for food but, to save the life of her daughter who the soldier had said he would shoot in front of her if she didn't do what he wanted. After they'd hung her, the soldier had the woman's daughter taken to the gas chambers with another group to be executed, telling the other women from her barrack that the child's death was now their responsibility.

"You killed her mother and so there is no-one to look after her. Her blood is now on your hands."

There seemed to be no end to the ways in which the guards would try and foster disagreements, conflict or even physical violence between the prisoners, men and women alike, in an effort to engender a constant lack of trust between us. Our captors' reasoning, if they could divide our loyalties towards one another as human beings we would function more like animals, with the instinct for self-preservation taking precedence over any thoughts or consideration we might traditionally afford our fellow inmates. Correspondingly, when any display of tension did spill over into an argument or a fight between us the guards would then mete out their own form of retribution in the shape of a public beating or execution. This would be carried out in full view of the other prisoners thereby causing an even greater sense of foreboding and anxiety amongst us. After a while it became a never ending cycle of fear and death, either brought about through the actions of the guards themselves or via the gas chambers. All of this was designed to destroy, not only, our physical bodies but also any form of mental resistance left within those of us still alive. Under almost any other circumstances these actions might have prompted us to fight back against such depraved and nihilistic oppression, but the overriding awareness of the Germans' brutal retaliation in response to our obvious defeat, if we were to even consider such a protest, was palpable and hung heavy in the air. We quickly came to realise that all forms of protest were pointless and would only add to our, already unbearable, suffering. This of course was exactly the outcome the Germans were seeking, and had so masterfully instilled throughout the camp.

Following our arrival in Birkenau those of us deemed fit and able enough were quickly put to work sorting through the clothes and belongings of the other prisoners who arrived at the camp. All new prisoners went through the same humiliation and degradation we had on arrival at the camp, initially being stripped of both their clothing and their corresponding dignity. They then had their heads shaved and were showered before being sprayed with the same foul white powder as us to rid them of lice. As well as burning our skin and itching terribly it also had little effect on the lice themselves which continued to thrive and infest all areas of the camp. Any money, watches and jewellery, indeed anything of any value was handed over to the Germans immediately on arrival as it had been with us. Much of the rest of our personal belongings were burnt and destroyed. Some of the prisoners were forced to take the dead from the gas chambers and transport them to a particular area where any gold teeth or fillings were removed before the bodies were moved on to the ovens for cremation.

These workers were called *Sonderkommando.* They would carry out their duties transporting the dead to and from the gas chambers and the ovens for three to four months until it was deemed they knew too much about the eradication of their fellow internees and it would be their turn to be executed and a new group of workers would be selected for this soul-destroying task.

I remember one day soon after our arrival my mother and I were working with a group of other women when one of them found a Jewish tract, a piece of scripture, in a coat and thinking no-one had seen her put it in her pocket, presumably to read and pray over later. All bibles, scripture readings and anything to do with our faith were taken from us and destroyed on arrival at the camp, along with everything else we held dear. One of the guards had seen this particular lady hide the piece of paper and marched towards her, shouting for her to stand still. As he approached her he hit her full in the face with his fist sending her sprawling to the ground as he demanded to know what she had taken. "What did you put in your pocket? I saw you take something, you filthy Jewish whore, what was it?" Struggling to her feet and with terror in her eyes she tried to speak, but the soldier continued to scream questions and abuse at her in broken English.

"Don't try to hide it from me, you bitch, I saw you take something, where is it?" She took the tract out of her pocket, trembling with fear and attempting to explain, as a piece of scripture, it was very precious to her as a Jew. He tore it from her hand and incandescent with rage hit her again. She was now visibly shaking and tears were streaming down her face. He shouted once more, this time loud enough for all of us to hear.

"It is strictly forbidden to keep any such artefacts or other religious items, you know that, don't you?" The woman nodded meekly as the guard stepped towards her, his face almost touching hers as he leant forward and spat out the next few words menacingly at her. "If this piece of paper means so much to you then keep it. If it makes you feel closer to your God then maybe you should go to be with him now."

We all stood frozen to the spot as he forced the piece of paper into her mouth, then drawing his hand gun from its holster shot her full in the face. "Now you can give it to God personally," he snarled. We watched as the woman fell to the ground, a pool of blood gathering in the mud around her shattered head. The soldier stared at her for a moment and then looked up as if daring one of us to say or do anything in response to his actions. After a few moments he walked away shouting at my mother and another woman to come and take her body to the crematorium. As I stood there, young as I was, I resolved not to be shocked by anything I saw in that camp ever again, no matter how horrific or bloody it might be, not if I wanted to survive.

FIVE

I wish I'd never written now, never filled in those papers, never asked to make contact. I could have told Jenny I didn't know how to get in touch with my mother, and as it had been so long since she'd let me go she probably wouldn't want to hear from me anyway. I could have said she would have built a new life for herself, along with whatever family she might have today and so wouldn't want to be reminded of the past. Also, that any family she had probably wouldn't be aware of me, so what effect would such news have on them, especially any children, in discovering they had a sister and their mother having a secret past they knew nothing about? What impact would such a revelation have on them as a family and on their relationship with her?

Much as I resented what she'd done to me, I still didn't feel comfortable in the thought of tearing her world apart again after so many years, and yet here I was potentially about to carry out that very act.

I should have said I would find it too painful and that Granny and Granddad were now my parents, and had been since the day they brought me into their home. Also, that I didn't want to hurt them by seeking answers to such awkward questions, questions perhaps they had hoped would never see the light of day, and none of which would make any difference to the way we felt about each other now, nor to the love that had grown between us so deeply over the years.

Why would I want to tell this woman about Jenny and how I'd brought her up, as if appearing in some way to seek her approval, or as though I were trying to prove that I'd been a better mother than her by not deserting my child as soon as she had been born.

Jenny would have understood that surely? So why put any of us through even greater pain by raising issues and questions about a life I'd never known, or in looking for answers that might not be forthcoming anyway and certainly wouldn't make any difference to the people we were today. It wouldn't heal any wounds, certainly not for me. What if I'd discovered she was dead; where would that have left us, having stirred up those long forgotten memories only to find out she was no longer around to provide the answers to my questions anyway? All I would have achieved was to remind myself, yet again, of the sorrow and heartbreak I had experienced in those earlier years but had, over time, come to acknowledge and accept.

I had the love of Jenny and Chris to sustain me now, along with the ever present care and affection they had showered on me throughout my life. The two of them had only ever given of their best to me, so why was I even attempting to make contact with someone I didn't know to ask for answers to questions that I didn't really want to hear, or did I? It was too late now. I'd thrown the pebble into the pond and the waters of my seemingly calm and peaceful life had been disturbed, perhaps never to settle again.

SIX

I remember lying on the bare wooden slats of our bunks at night, and even though it was cramped and uncomfortable and I could hear other children crying I still prayed for those nights to go on forever. It was the only time I knew I could lie safely in my mother's arms and think back to the lives we'd known before the war, remembering when Joseph and I would sit on our father's knee as he bounced us up and down playing with us. I would lie quite still listening to my mother's steady heartbeat as she slept and rest in the warm and protective embrace of her body enfolding me. Sometimes she would cry out in her sleep, perhaps struggling once again with the memory of losing my father and brother to the gas chamber. I would stroke her brow and whisper words of comfort until she would settle again.

"It's alright, Mama, I'm here, we've still got each other. I love you." Safe for these few hours at least from the horrors of the day I could pretend all the terrible things we had witnessed were just a bad dream, and that in the morning I would wake again in my old bedroom back on Guernsey with the sun shining through my window warming me as I looked across the inviting waters of the sea.

The seagulls would call out as they circled in the clear blue sky above and the waves broke on the rocks below.

At other times the true horror of the nightmare we were living through would overtake me and, with my heart heavy with emotion, I would recall the shocking events that had taken place during our time in the camp, and of the day we heard that Papa and Joseph were dead. My mother and I had been appalled to discover that instead being held in another part of the camp they had been taken straight to the gas chamber. One of the guards confirmed what others had told us that both Joseph and Papa had been "disposed of" as they had nothing to offer to the German war effort and its great leader, The Fuehrer.

"There is no room or time to waste in keeping alive those who cannot make a contribution to our glorious Fatherland. They are a drain on the limited resources of the camp." The guard smiled at my mother and nodded towards the buildings that we knew by now housed the gas chambers, suggesting that if she wanted she could be reunited with her men folk. "You can join them if you want?" his offer tormenting her as she battled to counter between the prospect of an eternity spent with her men folk or in continuing the horrifying existence of daily life in the camp with me. Facing death no longer held any fear for her personally but the thought of leaving me behind to survive in this living hell on my own was one she could not even bear to consider. I knew that her life counted for nothing in her own eyes anymore, save being there for me. I looked on in tears as my mother shook visibly at the frightening prospect of what the soldier had proffered and as she struggled again with the cruel reality of losing my father and brother. She tried, as best she could, to stand firm, taking my hand and squeezing it for reassurance, not wanting to give the guard the satisfaction of seeing her own tears flow until after he had left.

She wept a lot in the days that followed, especially at night when she thought I was asleep as we lay together on those sparse wooden planks and she recalled the last time she had seen Papa and Joseph alive as they walked to the gas chambers. They had glanced over their shoulders, smiling briefly as they caught one last glimpse of the family they loved but, as we now knew, were leaving behind forever.

I felt so hurt and angry for her and could hardly conceive of the pain she was experiencing as wife and mother to them both and in knowing their lives had ended in such a terrifying and unspeakable way. I tried to imagine the fear that would have gripped Joseph as the doors of the gas chamber slammed shut behind them. How, in the ensuing darkness and panic he would have clung tight to my father for reassurance and comfort before the deadly gas took full effect and filled their lungs as they fought for air and the very life that was being sucked from them.

I endeavoured to be brave for Mama, trying to detach my own thoughts from what had happened and focusing my mind only on her and her grief. It was never easy though as the gruesome reality of daily life in that crucible of death was never more than another child's or mother's scream away. As those cries of hopelessness and desperation tore into my brain I was reminded once more of my own sense of heartbreak and loss, and the whole cycle of fear and dread would reinstate itself, with my efforts to be strong for my mother failing yet again. Even so, I would try not to cry openly as Mama re-lived the shocking end to Joseph and Papa's lives in the nightmares of her restless sleep and as we lay there together on those bare and unforgiving strips of wood.

I did cry of course, many times in the weeks and months ahead but rarely in front her. Somehow my external emotions became the only thing left I could attempt to have any control over and I was determined that the Germans, especially, wouldn't see me broken no matter how vile or horrific the portrait of inhumanity they paraded before us each day.

During my time in the camp I made a few friends although always attempting not to become too close. We were all acutely aware that each day might be our last and therefore the prospect of any deeper relationship was a luxury that none of us could, or felt able to, afford ourselves. So whilst we formed these loose associations we also made the conscious decision not to say or do anything for each other beyond the immediate, recognising that all of our lives were under daily threat and therefore any favour or promise made to another might never be fulfilled. It could also result in our own death should such a momentary act of benevolence be discovered by our captors. That said, the human spirit at times overrides common sense and sound judgement, making its own decisions based on feelings from the heart rather than the logic of the mind.

Sarah arrived at the camp a short while after me but we developed an immediate affinity with each other and soon struck up a dangerously close association. Of course we knew this was a mistake, understanding only too well we could each lose the other at any time. But in a way because life in the moment was so precious some relationships did become intense very quickly no matter how hard we tried not to let them, apart from those within our own family of course. That said, even here we learnt over time not to hold even those dearest to our hearts too close for fear they might also be taken from us in an instant. You can't break a heart that is already detached from emotion, or at least that was the theory. The guards also sought to maintain this division between us. They appeared to view it as some form of sport, relishing their ability to break trust and relationships, even between close family units. They would continually spread rumours through their chosen informants about those supposedly hoarding food or extra bedding in the differing barracks, even when the stories were fabricated and untrue as they most often were. This, as with the young woman who had been hung by the other prisoners for supposedly having sex with a guard in return for extra food rations, would in turn set off arguments or fights between us so that eventually there was little or no trust between any of those held captive in the camp. All of this, in achieving its desired result, meant that the prison population remained always distrusting of each other's motives and actions. It also affirmed the total authority of the German soldiers and guards over us, in spite of the fact we outnumbered them by many thousand. Consequently, this meant if you did form a close friendship or deeper connection with someone outside of your immediate family it could quickly become irrational in nature and obsessive in its make up with you then seeking out this individual for practically any form of contact, be it a brief conversation or some form of physical relationship. Such reliance on even the most fleeting of smiles or touches from another human being rapidly became as precious as a crust of bread or drink of water to those of us who were, quite literally, being starved of all external forms of nourishment, sustenance and human interaction. Sometimes you would hear of individuals having sex behind the barracks or in the squalid conditions of the latrines. More often than not these couples wouldn't be married as families were separated on arrival at the camp.

Chance encounters as well as dangerously prearranged liaisons took their part in these brief and sordid associations with both men and women risking their lives once they found a way through the barbed wire and electrified fences that kept us apart. Such wretched acts of lust and desperate animal desire would also take place between couples of the same sex on occasion. It wasn't simply the physical act itself that emboldened individuals to go to such desperate extremes, but more the need to feel vital in some way, to feel the touch of another human body against their own skin. This despite the ever present reality of contacting a venereal disease which became rife inside the camp as increasingly more prisoners risked their lives to attain even the briefest moment of human intimacy. When you are continually forbidden almost any form of bodily contact the instinct to revert to animal basics appears not only acceptable, but even pleasurable as the appalling surroundings in which you exist fade momentarily from your mind, along with the very real threat to your life should you be discovered.

I remember one couple found having sex by the guards

being marched out before us in the courtyard and made to stand naked as a German officer screamed abuse in their faces.

"You filthy Jewish pigs, have you no shame in fucking together in full view of others? You know the penalty for such actions." He waved his luger pistol in their faces before ordering his soldiers to release a number of dogs on to the terrified couple. We were made to stand and watch as they were torn to pieces, their screams eventually fading as they were drowned out in death by the snarling and barking of their highly trained attackers. We knew only too well that the horrific scene being played out in front of us was not only an act of punishment for the poor couple who had been caught but also as a warning to the rest of us as to what would happen if we chose to do the same thing. Once the dogs had finished ripping the bodies apart they were called to heel by their handlers as the officer turned to face us again.

"The rules you must obey here are very straightforward. And the punishment for breaking them is equally straightforward and direct as you can see."

Even with such appalling evidence lying on the ground before us, there would still be those, in the days and weeks ahead, who would take the same risk for a moment's intimate release from the horrors of the camp just as this tragic couple had done. They would do so in the full knowledge of their meeting an equally horrific end to their lives if caught. When you have nothing to start with there is little your enemy can threaten you with but death, and for many that eventuality became seen as a form of blessed release rather than a punishment. In a perverse way this became the only victory left available to us in our daily battle with our oppressors, and if this victory was to be achieved in our dying then so be it. After a while it was only the method of execution we feared, not the end itself.

And so, even with the potential of our young lives being ended in an instant Sarah and I chose to risk all by becoming friends. Almost from the start ours developed quickly into a relationship of great depth, trust and growing dependence. The ability to share stories and experiences, at times beyond traditional comprehension was such a relief. Often they would be the very things I might want to speak with my mother about but knew I couldn't for fear of bringing her own dark thoughts and demons back to the forefront of her mind once more. The two of us loved talking about the things we had done with our parents as youngsters; things again that I feared might upset Mama if I raised them with her.

"I loved sitting by the fire when I was small, and having Mama brush through my hair as it dried." Sarah smiled in recognition of the simple pleasure this had brought me.

"My mother would do the same, and I would look into the fire as she embraced me. I would imagine I could see angels dancing with their bright orange wings reflected in the flames."

We shared many childhood tales and secrets in the time we spent together in the camp, memories that would help us escape briefly from the awful realities of our lives, even if only in our minds and imagination.

I first became aware of Sarah when she appeared one night asking if she could squeeze in beside my mother and I. Another train load of prisoners had been sent to her hut on their arrival and consequently she had been forced out of her sleeping space and more especially the barrack itself. A German soldier had taken an inventory of the new residents ready for the next day's early morning roll call and with Sarah now apparently removed from that register she had been put outside.

"I have my list for this barrack and you are no longer on it, so you will be outside tonight. It is cold and so you will be dead in the morning. Then the only list you will be on will be the one for the ovens." Sarah knew he was right and so with nowhere else to go had found herself at our door, or rather the broken slat of wood by the door that she had crawled through in an effort to find shelter. She walked the length of the hut until noticing a small gap between my mother and I the end of our bunk in which she begged to find rest.

"Please can I stay here, at least for tonight?" she pleaded, her thin body shivering in the cold. My mother nodded wearily as Sarah clambered in beside me. The two of us lay together talking in whispers for much of that first night, quickly establishing a common bond with our shared love and loss of family and Jewish faith. She told me she had been in the camp for about three weeks, but that her mother had become sick just a few days after they had arrived and so, as with my father and brother, had been sent to the gas chamber.

She said she had been forced to hold her mother's clothes while she and others were ordered at gunpoint to strip and ready themselves for the showers.

"We knew what was happening of course, but what could we do? I felt my heart break as I held her clothes against me and mouthed that I loved her. I could see she was crying as they led her away to her death."

She said the horror of what was unfolding in front of her, watching this pitiful procession of naked women and children walking towards their end was a scene that would stay with her forever.

"I saw a man running towards his wife as she shuffled forward in line with the others. He was calling out her name as the door of the gas chamber swung open like a hungry monster waiting to devour its next obscene meal of human frailty and flesh. One of the guards shouted for him to get back in line, releasing his dog which tore into the man and savaged him badly as it dragged him to the ground screaming. Once the gas chamber was full and the doors had closed the guard took his pistol from its holster and shot the man in the head while the other guards looked on, ignoring his pleas for mercy."

Sarah told me that she and a few of the others had then been ordered to take the rest of the clothes away for sorting, but that she had managed to tear a little piece from her mother's dress to remember her by. She took it from her pocket and showed it to me, holding it up as though it were a precious gem. Although it had been the dress she had been given on entering the camp and was not really her mother's it still meant the world to her.

"It's all I have left, but when I look at it I can still see her wearing it and the smile on her face when she would speak to me." Even in the darkness of the hut I could still see the tears in Sarah's eyes as she struggled with her memories and so sought to change the subject in an effort to lighten her mood. I asked where she was from and commented at how good her English was, albeit a little broken.

She told me she was from Poland and that her father had been a teacher there. The whole family had learnt to speak English as the intention had been for them to move there eventually.

"Once the war began though, it became impossible to move anywhere." She told me they had been amongst the last to be deported from the ghetto they had been forced to live in as Polish Jews. The German Jews were the first to leave in an effort to cleanse the "Master race" from any further Jewish contact. She said there had been little food and practically no work in the ghetto and that when the Germans came back it was decided to level the area and send all those still living there to the death camps. She told me her father had been amongst those who, because of his good education and being a teacher, had helped with the writing and distribution of leaflets which encouraged others in the ghetto to form underground groups and fight the Germans.

"He knew what would happen if he was caught, but he felt he had to do something to help. When the Germans arrived they arrested some of the men and tortured them to get the names of those who had organised the leaflets and acted in the recruitment of resistance fighters, including my father. My mother and I, along with the other families, were taken to the town square to watch as my father and the other men were lined up against a wall and shot. They were made to face the wall but my father refused and, despite being beaten for his defiance, stared straight ahead at the soldiers as they took aim and shot him along with the others. We all screamed out and wept as our men folk fell to the ground, but I also felt proud of my father for defying the Germans in that way. My mother said, they may have shot him but they hadn't been able to kill his spirit, which would live on in us forever. I didn't really understand what she meant at the time but I do now and I take strength and encouragement from my father's brave actions. I hold onto his memory and try to demonstrate that same spirit of defiance towards the Germans every day."

As we continued to whisper stories to each other in the darkness of that overcrowded hut I told Sarah about my time in the camp and how my father and Joseph had been gassed on our arrival. I said that I was worried about my mother and feared she was giving up on life a little more each day. "I know she loves me, but it's as if the life blood has been drained from her since Joseph and Papa where killed."

I knew if she continued to show weakness then she would be gassed as well, but how could I cajole her into fighting her growing depression, understanding as I did how seemingly pointless life had become for her after losing the men she loved in such an unspeakable way.

"Of course she still has me but we have both witnessed other families being ripped apart since we have been here, so what hope is there for her that we'll be able to survive together? Or worse, she might have to watch me being taken to the gas chamber if my health fails and then she'd be left on her own?" I felt my body shiver as I looked at Sarah. "How can I reassure Mama against the possibility that her final days might be spent in the knowledge that all her family had met their end in those awful gas chambers, and that our lifeless bodies had been thrown onto hand carts and taken away to the ovens. What crumb of comfort can I offer her in that?"

My mother's heart had been broken, as had mine, but I was determined not to demonstrate, at least outwardly, any sense of acceptance towards our seemingly inevitable fate, nor to the apparent hopelessness of our situation. I wouldn't give in to our German captors or to their arrogantly assumed supremacy over us, whereas my poor mother had now all but given up on any hope of a possible route to survival or future outside of the camp. She could no longer see a way out for either of us other than our own deaths met at the hands of the guards or in the gas chamber. Dreadful though that prospect was, in a way, for her at least, it did offer a final release from the daily fight for existence that we had become accustomed to but also for the longed prayed for reunion with my brother and father. "I miss them so much," she would say, her sadness only furthering my determination not to demonstrate any personal weakness to the Nazis. I had decided the only thing I would reveal to these monsters was my total contempt for both them and their Fuhrer, even if it cost me my life, which eventually it almost certainly would. I knew my mother was worried about me but also recognised she didn't have the strength or ability to protect me any more, and so felt it my duty to be strong for the both of us. I told Sarah how much I loved Mama and how concerned I was for her.

"I pray for her every day, but what can I do to make things better for her? I just love her so much and hate to see her like this."

We both acknowledged our joint revulsion as to the sorry acceptance of daily life in Birkenau by the camp population and were drawn ever closer through the shared similarities of our family's journey and circumstances.

We often talked about the work we did in the camp, and how we had both been forced to sort through the belongings of those who were to be executed or who had already died. We wept together as we shared our joint sorrow in recalling how we had spent time emptying the suitcases of toys and other personal effects from the small children who had arrived at the camp and whose innocent young lives were almost immediately wiped from the face of the earth in the gas chambers. Sarah spoke movingly of the effect those times had on her.

"When I hold their dolls or other toys it makes me think of my own childhood and how happy I had been when I was smaller. I sometimes watch the guards as they march the little ones to the gas chambers and wonder, if they are parents themselves, how can they do such an evil thing? Do they really have no feelings for such young lives?"

Of course, the Germans would tell us that everybody must work and that, young or old alike, if they cannot carry out the duties allotted to them they become a drain on the limited food supplies and other vital resources of the camp. Also, the demands of these small children on their mothers, who could be better employed working and serving the German war effort, necessitated their extermination. After all, in the eyes of the Nazi guards these precious young bundles of life were nothing more than Jewish scum, human garbage to be destroyed and erased not only from existence but from the world's memory itself as part of the Fuehrer's great "final solution". Such twisted logic might appease their own perverse view of life but it would never assuage or lessen the reward awaiting them when standing before God and the "final solution" he has prepared for them on the day of judgement.

We knew without doubt how we were viewed by our oppressors and such emotionless rationale left Sarah and I cold and in a state of utter disbelief. This feeling of incredulity only increased as we continued each day to sort through an ever growing mound of children's belongings including, much loved playthings, comfort blankets and other treasured possessions they had carried with them to the camp only to have them snatched away moments before they were killed. We talked at length about these dolls and other toys that we were ordered to put into differing piles according to size and style. They would then be ripped open by other prisoners searching for hidden family valuables that might have been secreted inside them for safekeeping. We comforted each other as we tearfully recalled the many coloured ribbons and hair grips that had been removed from the young girls' shoulder bags and cases or directly from their heads. These would be stacked high next to the mountain of hair which was then sorted for its colouring, having been collected from the children's newly shaven heads. The Jewish human body may have been viewed of as waste but everything that had gone in it or on it was picked through in minute detail to garner anything that might be of worth to the German authorities. What sort of value system was this to live by?

Sometimes, the true horror of what we had witnessed grew too much and we would simply hold each other in silence, both recognising words alone were futile in attempting to further describe the deeper feelings of repulsion, sadness and loathing we held towards those responsible for carrying out such brutal acts.

One night Sarah began to cry as she told me how a German soldier had seemingly befriended her after her mother had died, giving her extra food rations and allowing her to have a proper shower before turning predator and forcing her to have sex with him.

"I suspected his motives from the start, but the offer of additional food and a chance to be clean, coupled with the overwhelming grief at the loss of my mother all served to confuse my already fragile state of mind even further."

When you no longer have anything to live for and all around you is dark, the offer of a little comfort or sustenance becomes a light you reach out for no matter the source of its provision, nor the cost of its acceptance. I understood what she meant only too well; recognising, as I did, the circumstances of our lives now demanded they be lived in the moment and often, in Birkenau, the moment was all we had.

"I told him I was only thirteen and a virgin; I begged him not to do anything to me. But he just laughed and ripped my clothes off, saying that my being a virgin meant I would be clean and not diseased already by having been fucked by some filthy Jewish boy. He said he enjoyed sex with young girls, the younger and tighter the better."

I sat holding Sarah's hand as she re-lived the horror of that experience. "He raped me nearly every day after that, sometimes more than once. At first I would cry out, pleading for him to stop, but after a while I realised that my protests and fear were part of the excitement for him, and simply encouraged even greater acts of sexual violence towards me. Eventually, I just closed my eyes and lay still, praying it would soon be over, but that only served to increase his anger and aggression towards me. He would beat me whilst raping me and force his gun into my mouth threatening to shoot me just to make me cry or beg for mercy. He would make me do all sorts of things to him, filthy, disgusting things to excite him and degrade me even further as a human being."

"What did you do?"

Sarah took a deep breath to steady herself before answering. "In the end I decided I would rather he pulled the trigger when his gun was in my mouth, so the next time he threatened to shoot me I told him to go ahead and do it. Of course I was scared, but the fear of death had become less terrifying than the threat of him continuing to violate me every day." Sarah's whole body was shaking as I squeezed her hand in a vain attempt to comfort her. "What happened; why didn't he shoot you?"

"I think he realised he could only kill me once, but by continuing to rape and mentally torture me each day I would remain his victim for as long as he wanted. Ultimately, I think his dominance over me as a human being was the bigger thrill for him, far beyond any form of perverse satisfaction he gained from his brutality towards me or the act of sex itself."

"Is he still raping you?"

I noticed Sarah's expression change from one of defeat to determination, as if recalling a particular memory or event.

"No, it finished a couple of weeks ago. One day I began my period, the first in months."

I had also been irregular with my periods, as had many of the other women, which was hardly surprising considering the inadequate food rations and resulting malnutrition amongst those of us held in the camp.

Sarah took another deep breath as if preparing herself for what she would say next. "This particular day when he took me to the room I told him I was having my period. He looked at me for a moment and then slapped me hard across the face calling me a filthy Jewish slut, and saying I was no use to him if I was bleeding." I could see the pain etched on her face as she lifted the ragged top covering her upper body to reveal a deep blue and yellow bruise along the lower part of her rib cage. I felt my eyes sting with tears of outrage at the thought of her being beaten in such a way.

"Did he do that?" I asked, already sensing and fearing her reply.

"Yes, he knocked me to the ground and kicked me a few times." She stopped talking for a moment, her expression changing again as she re-lived the moment. "I thought this time he *was* going to kill me, especially after saying I was of no use to him anymore."

I squeezed her hand again as she continued.

"I lay on the floor holding my side, anticipating the weight of his boot crashing into my body again or perhaps a permanent end to my ordeal with a bullet to my head."

"But he didn't?"

"No. He knelt down beside me and spat in my face, telling me to get out and keep out of his way in future or I would be sorry." Sarah looked at me. "I don't know why he didn't kill me, and much as I had wanted to die at times over those past few weeks I was suddenly grateful to be alive, even in the filth and the squalor surrounding me."

I smiled at her again, acknowledging the truth of what she was saying, a truth that so many outside of the existence we endured in Birkenau would fail to understand. Sometimes even when all hope is gone and death appears as a welcome visitor there remains something deep within us all that fights to hold on to life, no matter how fleeting or irrational that desire may be.

"Have you seen him since?"

"Only once, he's been moved to another part of the camp. Apparently he's found himself another couple of girls, even younger than me." She looked at me again struggling with her emotions. "Yes I feel sorry for them, but at least he's not coming near me anymore."

I smiled in recognition of her sadness for what the other girls were experiencing, but also of her appreciation that, for now at least, her nightmare experience of that particular physical and mental torment was at an end.

"I just hope he forgets about me all together because if he doesn't, and much as I want to live, I will find a way of killing myself before I let him touch me again."

She looked at me with tears of pain and determination in her eyes.

"I'm serious, Ruth, I can't go through that again." She wiped her eyes, smearing dirt across her face as it merged with her tears. "I can still smell his foul breath and the stench of his sweat as he lay on top of me. There were times when he was raping me that I actually envied those who had been gassed or shot. At least they were at peace, their own tortuous existence at an end, while mine continued with each day proving more sadistic and brutal than the one before."

We wrapped our arms around each other as we struggled once more with the unspeakable truth, that for so many in the camp, there were indeed occasions when death proved the more desirable option to life. Although I had no real words of comfort to offer Sarah, I knew exactly what she meant as we lay there holding onto each other for warmth and reassurance on those bare and unforgiving boards. I felt the tears of sadness and frustration sting against my cheeks; tears not only of sorrow for my friend but also of indignation towards God. How could he allow such pain? Yet even as I struggled for an answer I knew deep down that it wasn't God who was responsible for the horrifying conditions we were being forced to endure, but rather the depraved and twisted logic of man. I reasoned that God, if he truly existed, would be crying himself at watching so many of his children suffer and die under the fist of such naked aggression.

The two of us talked a lot over the next few days becoming really close and even allowing ourselves the occasional smile when we were sure no-one else was looking, especially the Germans.

One night as we struggled to sleep Sarah asked if I could remember what my life had been like before the camp, before the war, when we had been a family living happily together in London and Guernsey. I smiled. "Yes. I love to think back to those days. Sometimes when things are too bad here I recall a day or event from the past to replace the horror in front of me."

"Do you have a favourite?"

I thought for a moment. "Not really, although I do remember one particular birthday party from when I was younger. My parents gave me a beautiful doll dressed in traditional Jewish costume. Mama had made the dress out of some off cuts from a piece of material my father had been using for one of his customers. The dress itself was bright blue and she had made a long frock-style coat to go with it fashioned from some deep red velvet material. It had been a wonderful birthday party, with Mama also baking me a large cake with pink icing and candles on it. My friends and I had spent the afternoon playing games in the garden with the sun shining down on us. I remember how warm it felt and the sky was as clear and bright as our childish laughter as we ran around together."

I lay still for a moment on the rough wooden boards of my bunk, my eyes shut tight as I fought to recall the sound of my friends and I laughing and enjoying ourselves as we played contentedly on that summer's day just a few short years ago. But my brief escape into the past and those happier times quickly returned to the frightening reality of today when I opened my eyes and focused once more on the bleak surroundings of the camp. I closed my eyes again in a desperate attempt to re-visit the memory of that birthday party. It had been such a fun day, but one that might have ended very differently if it hadn't been for the forward thinking of my parents.

After my friends had gone home Mama and Papa said as it was such a special day I would be allowed to stay up later than usual and continue to play with my doll and other presents for a while. What I didn't know and was too young to understand was the real reason behind their surprising but welcome offer. It was because they were concerned if I had gone straight to bed following the earlier excitement of the party along with all the cake and other treats I had consumed still swirling around inside me, the day might have ended very differently, so they had wanted to give my tummy a chance to settle down.

I turned and smiled briefly at Sarah before closing my eyes once more in an effort to see my beautiful doll again, dressed in all her finery. I loved that doll and called her Dinah after my best friend who had left Guernsey with her parents when the war had started. We used to have long conversations together Dinah and I about all manner of things although, being a doll, it was always me who did the talking. Even so I felt a comfort in her just being with me.

She became my constant companion, staying with me wherever I went and reminding me of my special friend and a wonderful time in my life.

When the Germans had ordered us from our home and sent us to Birkenau I had taken Dinah with me. I managed to smuggle her into our barrack under my dress and kept her from being found by the guards by hiding her under the wooden base of our bunk. Although I was older now and didn't actually play with her anymore I still spent a lot of time each night whispering to her about my fears and how much I missed Joseph and my father and also as to how worried I was about my mother. I would hold my precious doll close to my chest, confiding my innermost thoughts and secrets to her before placing her back under the bed the next morning in the hope that no-one would discover her or steal her from me. Although she quickly became dirty and ragged and had her left leg chewed off by one of the rats that roamed freely about the camp I was still happy to find her there at the end of each day.

"Presumably the guards did find her eventually," Sarah asked, "as you don't have her anymore?"

I explained how one day when I had been feeling particularly sad I had made the terrible mistake of taking Dinah outside the barrack with me.

"I was waiting by the latrine for my mother and became so engrossed in talking to Dinah that I forgot about the guards for a moment. A soldier saw me and demanded to know where I had got a doll from, thinking I had taken it from one of the piles of toys and children's belongings that we had been sorting through following their arrival in the camp; mistakenly I told him it was mine. He started yelling at me, shouting that it was strictly forbidden to have dolls or any sort of toys in the camp.

I stood rigid, rooted to the spot as a warm wet sensation ran down my leg and I held my breath in fear of what he might say or do next. He marched towards me, removing his rifle from his shoulder and screaming abuse at me. He tore Dinah from my hand and threw her to the ground, stamping on her with his boot and grinding her body into the mud."

Sarah, recognising my distress stroked my arm. "It's alright, Ruth you don't have to say anymore."

"No I want to, I want to tell you." I paused briefly, allowing the memory to overtake me once more.

"The soldier looked down at me as I stood before him trembling, my emotions veering between total hatred and absolute fear. My mother came out of the toilet and saw immediately what had happened and how upset I was. I was worried she might say something and make matters worse. As she came to my side the soldier glared at her as if willing her to defend me, but she just put her arm around me and we walked away, both too terrified to turn around and praying desperately that he wouldn't call us back to inflict further abuse or punishment onto us."

Sarah and I shared many such stories during the time we spent together in Birkenau until one day she became sick. She developed pneumonia, and because there was no proper medication or any way to care for her properly she died very quickly. We spoke intimately of our deep and genuine feelings for each other in those few short days before her death and also of our family circumstances, and more especially of our determination not to be beaten down by the ever present fist of inhumanity so eagerly administered towards us each day by the Germans.

I had wanted to send Sarah to the medical area where some of the very sick were taken, but she was too frightened. She thought the doctors would say there was nothing they could do for her and so end her life there and then.

"I will have more chance of surviving if I fight the infection myself." We both knew without the proper drugs and an immediate change to her surroundings and diet this couldn't happen.

I think, although she knew she wouldn't recover she was more fearful of our being separated than of the prospect of actually dying. Death, after all, was something we had all come to accept as our eventual fate in Birkenau.

I woke one morning to find Sarah lying next to me; her eyes wide open in a stare and her thin, fragile body unresponsive and cold. I cried and held her in my arms, pulling her close into me even though I knew she was gone. I just hoped in some supernatural way she might know that somebody still cared about her, that I cared. I prayed that she was now reunited with her family and, stroking the hair gently from her face, gave her a brief kiss on the forehead as she lay in my arms limp and unresponsive. Mama said we would have to tell the Sonderkommando because if we left Sarah there the rats would soon arrive to gorge themselves on her emaciated remains. We told the transporters about my friend and a short while later two men came to the hut, picking up Sarah's lifeless body and throwing it, without ceremony, onto a cart with some of the other corpses that were being taken to the ovens. It seemed so sad that this young and vibrant life should meet its end in such a way. I cried again that night as I lay on those unforgiving strips of wood, struggling with my emotions over the loss of both Sarah and Dinah and seeking comfort in the loving and supportive haven of my mother's gentle embrace. At least we still had each other, but for how long?

SEVEN

I knew it was a mistake to contact her, but it's too late to rewind the clock now. I should have simply told Jenny only what she needed to know at the time about her father, the detail of my adoption and what I knew, or didn't know, about my own parents could have come out later, presuming she ever bothered to ask again. It would have been easier to explain my reasoning once she was older, having gained some life experience of her own and when she could better understand things from an adult's point of view. But I have made the mistake of writing and now this woman, my birth mother, wants to see me. She says there is too much to discuss, too much to explain about all that has happened over the years to be swept away or dealt with in one short letter. She wants to arrange a meeting and present her side of the story face to face.

It's not that I'm not interested in hearing what she has to say because, in a way, I am. It might even be good for me to hear the facts directly from her as she suggests, and perhaps try to understand her motives and purpose in letting me go. The truth though, certainly for me at least, is that I've grown up without her, learnt to live my life without her. So what's the point in revisiting a past that contains no shared memories or experiences between us and then seeking to start all over again? It certainly won't change what happened or the people we've grown to become in the years since.

I've always thought of James and Carol as being my real parents, even after I discovered I was adopted; they were still the ones I went to in times of trouble, the ones I learnt to love and trust over the years. And now I discover that my real mother is a woman called Ruth who, within a few short sentences of a letter, has thrown my life into complete turmoil by saying that she wants to meet with me and hopefully build a relationship between us again, a relationship that, for me at least, died the day she gave me away as a baby. What makes it worse is that I'm the one who started all of this by writing to her in the first place and so have nobody to blame but myself.

How am I supposed to sit down with her and share a cup of tea as she pours out her side of a story, true or false, that still sees me rejected and given up for adoption after seven weeks because she couldn't, or wouldn't, keep me. I suppose it might help to salve her conscience, if she has one, help her to feel better in being able to talk about what actually happened, what she did, and about how hard it had been, or not, for her to give me up. But why now, and only after I've been the one to physically make contact, does she say she wants to meet up with me and talk about the events of almost thirty years ago? Presumably she hasn't worried about me enough over the intervening twenty-eight years to make any attempt at contact herself, no matter what the law may have said in the past. Surely, if you love somebody then those laws become merely an obstacle to overcome in your quest to reunite yourself with the true desire of your heart and ultimate focus of your attentions? Even respecting the fact she may have felt unable to take on the authorities herself in an effort to find me; presumably she still hadn't been concerned enough about me following my birth or she would have fought harder to keep me in the first place. But if all of that is true, then why is she so interested in opening up these old wounds again now after all this time?

On occasion over the years, if I have been feeling low or unsure of myself, I've tried to reason in my own mind as to what might have happened and to understand what could have made her want to abandon her own baby?

I realise she would have been young herself at the time, but I was young too when I had Jenny and never once thought of giving her up or letting anyone take her from me. And yet here she is asking to meet with me and wanting to hear about the person I've become, and of what I've achieved in my life. What can I say about the past twenty-eight years or of my feelings towards her compared to Jenny? Where do I begin to tell to her about the people and events that have shaped my life, a life she's never known or been a part of since the day she let me go?

What if we don't get on, or she thinks I've been wrong in the choices and decisions I've made in my life so far? What if she questions how I've bought Jenny up as her mother? Would I have to listen to her criticisms or suggestions as to what I might have done differently as a parent? Then what? Do I tell her politely she is entitled to her opinions, that I'm grateful for them and then perhaps feel duty bound to act upon them? Does she even have the right to comment? And if she does, am I expected to respond as a scolded child, ashamed of some of the decisions I've made simply because she gave birth to me. Or what if she thinks I've done well and says she is proud of me how do I respond to that. Do I smile, shake her hand and thank her for her approval? Do I tell her it means a lot to me when in truth it doesn't?

She wasn't the one I went to at eight years old broken-hearted because a boy at school had told me Father Christmas didn't exist or at nine when I broke my arm falling off my bike. It wasn't she who held me gently in her arms and wiped away my tears as we sat in the back of the car while Dad drove us to the hospital to have it treated and put in plaster. She wasn't the one I ran to in despair when my pet rabbit died and asked if I would see him again in heaven, or if God would know that he liked a bit of carrot at bedtime. She wasn't the one I confided in about my first kiss or who sat on the end of my bed when I was twelve and explained how to use a tampon when my periods started or why boys wanted to put their hands up your jumper once you started to develop breasts. Where was she at school parents' evenings or at the end of summer and winter terms encouraging my performances in plays and pantomimes despite constant nerves and my inability to remember lines?

I don't remember her being there to applaud me the year I gained my sports certificate for captaining the girls hockey' team to victory in the inter schools cup when I was fifteen. And it certainly wasn't her that I went to that day, shamed and with my head bowed, to tell I'd become pregnant.

Mum and Dad couldn't have been more loving, understanding and forgiving as I sat in that chair confessing to what I'd done. Dad especially was hurt, although he tried not to show it at the time. After all I was his daughter, his precious little girl, who in his mind, had been violated by another man.

"We all make mistakes in life, Mary, and I can't pretend I'm not disappointed, but I want you to know this won't affect the way your mum and I feel about you, or that we'll love you any less. We're a family and you're the most precious part of it to us, I hope you know that?"

In that instant, as he and Mum held me close and reassured me of their unconditional love, I knew I had done the right thing in being open and honest with them. I also knew they would look after me, and that whatever happened in the future both my baby and I would be cared for and safe.

Increasingly over the next few days these and other memories along with my doubts and questions about Ruth herself raged through my head, battling with each other to achieve the resolution and answers I was seeking, but the more I struggled with them the more confused I became. The one thing I could be sure of however was that she hadn't been the one to advise, comfort or encourage me in any of the choices I had made over the years, good or bad. Also, in how I'd lived my life day to day, with both its successes and failures.

And if that were true, aligned with the fact she had never been there to offer that same degree of love and support as James and Carol, then why should I be interested in hearing what she had to say now, no matter how well intentioned her words might be?

That's when Mum and Dad spoke to me in greater detail about my adoption. Up until that point I don't think any of us had wanted, or felt the need, to go into any real depth about the circumstances that had brought us together, outside of the basic facts we already knew and accepted. I think we all held a fear that if we talked about a truth different to the one we had come to believe over the years then something might change in our relationship and, unspoken though it was, we all knew that was something none of us wanted to happen.

I knew early on, from around seven or eight, that I had been adopted. We had been talking about our families at school and Dad and Mum decided that this might be a good time to tell me the truth, or as much as I needed to know at that early age. I did ask about what had happened but they said there would be plenty of time to have those sorts of conversations when I was older.

"All you need to know for now, sweetheart, is that in our eyes and hearts you are our daughter and we love you more than anything in the world; always have and always will."

Of course, being told I was adopted came as a bit of a shock. I didn't fully understand all they were saying, but I knew I felt secure in our relationship and that I didn't want to be anywhere else, or for anyone else to be my mum and dad.

I think when you're younger you're more relaxed and less questioning about situations or the things adults tell you, especially if you're settled and content. And so although I didn't really grasp the detail of what they were saying I was still happy to accept I was their little girl; that they loved me and would always be there for me.

But now ten years on as a young woman, pregnant, with my maternal instincts and hormones racing around my body the true reality of being adopted suddenly unnerved me, as did the prospect of discovering more about my birth mother and the circumstances of why she had let me go. Here I was carrying a baby of my own, one that I knew, even at this early stage, would be a part of my life forever. Yet in the same instant I was being told, in far greater detail than had been the case as a child, that I had been given up for adoption by my own mother at only a few weeks old. Mum and Dad did their best, when explaining the circumstances of my adoption, to be as gentle as they had been in understanding about my telling them I was pregnant, even though I knew I had hurt and disappointed them. I think they were saddened I had got pregnant so early in my life, and of course that it had happened with someone they felt wasn't going to be the man they would have chosen to be my long term partner or the father of my child, their grandchild.

On that point I had to agree. Mum in particular hadn't been keen on Gerry and I certainly wasn't going to defend him now.

"Gerry was nice enough, but I'm sure deep down you knew he wasn't the man for you. It's just a pity you both let it go as far as you did, although I'm sure he more than played his part in that decision, knowing how persuasive men can be when it comes to sex."

I remember the day I told them I was expecting. I was scared of how they might react but, as I say, they couldn't have been more generous in their love and support for me. It might sound strange but I think in a way that's why they decided to tell me more about the circumstances of my adoption, or at least the detail they were aware of and could remember. I knew it wasn't going to be an easy conversation for any of us and felt for Dad as he rubbed his hands together, staring at the floor and glancing at Mum for support as he took the lead.

"Perhaps this is the time for that bigger conversation, Mary? The one we avoided when you were younger and first told you that you were adopted."

Mum became quite emotional as she remembered their disappointment in not being able to have a baby of their own.

"We always knew we wanted children, even after discovering I couldn't carry a baby long term myself so we decided to adopt. That wasn't an easy decision to make, not because we were against adoption but more because by agreeing to adopt we were also admitting to ourselves, finally, that we would never be able to produce a little one of our own." Dad smiled and squeezed Mum's hand as she struggled to continue. "All that changed once we saw you of course. We knew straightaway you were the one for us. It was like God had made this precious little bundle just for your Dad and I, and not in any way as a substitute because we hadn't been able to produce a baby of our own. It was more like a special gift for the two of us and one we could pour all our love into as he knew how much we had to give. And that's never changed Mary, we love you just as much today as we did the first time we saw you and held you in our arms."

I had known from early on that Mum couldn't have children herself and that's why they'd chosen to adopt. As I got older she explained that she'd lost a baby girl when she and Dad had been married for less than two years and that she'd nearly died from complications resulting from the miscarriage. This was the first time though that they'd shared the full detail of the events and circumstances that had led to their decision to adopt.

"We were advised against trying again, and eventually after further tests and examinations the doctors told your dad and I that we would never be able to have children of our own."

"Do you still think about her, the little girl you lost?"

"Sometimes, but only about how old she might be, simple things like that."

Dad smiled. "Once you came along there was more than enough to think about in keeping you fed and watered. You certainly made your presence felt in those early days I can tell you." He looked at Mum and rubbed her shoulder. "But yes, sometimes we think about her. Your Mum called her Holly because she would have been born at Christmas."

"I was about four months pregnant when I had the miscarriage. I developed an infection that carried through to her and affected the supply of blood and oxygen to her little body which meant she was unable to survive.

Whatever caused the infection was associated with the change to my body during pregnancy and the doctors advised I shouldn't try for any more children as it could carry a threat to my own life next time if we did. I was poorly for a while afterwards and had to stay in hospital for a few weeks, but we were still hopeful, at least early on, that we might be able to try again."

I could see this wasn't an easy conversation for either of them.

"You don't need to tell me about this if you don't want to; this is something personal between the two of you."

Mum smiled, appreciating my sensitivity. "No, we want to." She squeezed Dad's hand as if confirming their decision to speak out. "It was after your dad and I had spoken to another doctor and asked again about the possibility of my getting pregnant that he confirmed I would never be able to carry a baby full term. There was something in my system that would reject the foetus after a few weeks or months as had been the case with Holly, and because of this any future attempt to carry a baby could also pose a serious threat to my own health. We were heartbroken to think we would never have a baby of our own, but we knew we still wanted a family, and so after coming to terms with the loss of Holly and what the doctors had told us we began to think about adoption."

"Why didn't you choose a boy? Surely another girl would only bring back painful memories after losing Holly?

"We always wanted a girl, even before I got pregnant with Holly." She paused and caught her breath. "It was devastating when we lost her, but it also made us all the more determined to have a girl once we decided to adopt.

And, as we said earlier once we saw you we both fell instantly in love with you." Mum leant forward, taking my face in her hands. "Your dad and I love you, Mary, not because we adopted you but because you're our daughter, maybe not by birth but in every other way possible. I can't tell you how precious you are to us." She paused, stroking the hair from my forehead in affection as she had done so many times before when I was younger. "Unconditional love is not easy to explain, but it is something your dad and I have for you." She took her hands from my face and placed them on my tummy. "And I do know it is something you will also feel for this baby of yours when it arrives, as will your dad and I all over again, never doubt that."

We sat holding hands, allowing this shared moment of intimacy and understanding to wash over us. Eventually I broke the silence.

"I love the two of you as well. Thank you for your support, and for not suggesting I might have an abortion."

Mum squeezed my hand tightly. "Don't ever think that, Mary, not even for a second. We would never ask you to do such a thing; your dad and I know only too well how precious a new life is." She smiled. "Especially our grandchild."

Their support throughout my pregnancy meant so much, especially with Gerry proving less than useless when I first told him I was expecting. He was a nice enough bloke, at least early on; he even respected my decision not to sleep with him until we'd been going out for a while, or so he said. But after that first time in his car it became the usual story of him assuring me that regular sex would only add to our relationship and help us become even more committed to each other.

"It'll help make us more of a couple, bring us closer." It certainly brought us closer alright, every Tuesday night when Mum and Dad went to the social club to meet their friends.

"Now behave yourself, you two, okay? Mum and I are trusting you, especially you, Gerry. No funny business with our daughter, alright?"

Gerry would leer at me, checking that Dad couldn't see his hand from the doorway as he placed it on my knee and ran it up my leg before answering.

"She'll be safe with me, Mr Rowland, she's in good hands."

Then as soon as we heard the car start Gerry would be all over me. "Come on, girl, we've got the place to ourselves now, no point in wasting the opportunity for a bit of you know what."

If I'm honest I'd always felt guilty about sleeping with Gerry, especially after promising Mum and Dad we wouldn't.

There was one night we were doing it on the bedroom floor and as Gerry put himself inside me it felt different. He said he hadn't got any protection with him, but that it would be okay because he would come out before anything happened.

"It'll be fine; soon as I get worked up I'll whip it out."

"No, Gerry, I'm serious, get off me."

"Relax; just enjoy the ride, you know you like it."

I could feel him getting more excited and tried to push him off but he kept saying it would be okay. I felt it go warm inside me and I panicked, shouting at him again to get off but it was too late.

"That's the last time we're doing it, Gerry, what if I'm pregnant?"

"Sorry, Mary, I've never done it without anything before. It just felt different and got me worked up quicker than usual." He knew I was upset and tried to reassure me. "You'll be fine, it was only a bit and you can't get pregnant from just that little amount. I promise I'll never do it again, not without a Johnny okay?"

I stared at him, furious for what he had done but equally angry with myself for allowing him do it.

"There won't be a next time, Gerry, rubber Johnny or not. I'm serious."

He grinned and put his arm around me. "Come on Mary, you know you don't mean that, you like bonking as much as I do."

"Actually, Gerry I don't, and yes I do mean it. A kiss and a cuddle's one thing but that's the last time we're having sex."

Gerry smiled again, weakly this time, realising, at least for the moment, he shouldn't push his luck, not that it mattered as once had been enough.

EIGHT

I've been trying to write to my Rebecca again, or Mary as she signs her name now. I want to tell her more about my own life and why she was taken from me, but I can't seem to find the right words to say, certainly not on a few pages of a cheap notepad.

For some time after Sarah died I just did whatever I was told by the Germans, giving up almost totally on my earlier resolve to be strong and in allowing myself to dare to believe there might be something better for my life in the future.

I became like a robot, cutting myself off from any feelings or emotion. It was easier that way, and I certainly didn't feel able to function as a normal person in any traditional sphere either. How could I with the stench of death drifting through the air both day and night as the smoke rose from the ovens, reducing to ash the cart loads of rotting human flesh that were endlessly ferried to them for cremation. Or as the enthusiastic chatter and laughter of children turned to petrified screams every time the doors closed behind them in the gas chambers. It was like living in the very bowels of hell itself, and the struggle for life we were forced to endure appeared ever more senseless and meaningless. Yes, the natural human instinct to survive still remained, but the reasons for it became increasingly blurred and all but disappeared after a while.

My mother became sick shortly after Sarah died; I think on top of everything else her heart had been broken as well. She missed my father and Joseph so much. I know she also felt guilty she couldn't do more to protect me, although I never said anything or gave her reason to think that. The constant look of despair that reflected in her eyes whenever we were together said more than words could ever do.

"I love you, Ruth, but I don't know what to do anymore. I don't have Papa here to tell me or to help me."

I would try and encourage her but knew in my heart she had lost all hope and my words of support provided little comfort to someone whose mind was now lost to a sea of misery and desolation.

"It's alright, Mama, I love you too. Don't worry; we'll come through this together."

One day when we were in the courtyard sorting through another pile of belongings from the new arrivals she collapsed from exhaustion.

I moved to help her but a German soldier standing nearby shouted at me to leave her alone.

"Get away." It was raining hard and she was lying face down in a mud-filled puddle.

"Please let me take her face from the water," I begged, but the soldier hit me with his rifle and I fell to the ground with the power of the blow.

He kicked my mother. "Get up, Jewish bitch."

The other prisoners glanced briefly towards my mother but quickly resumed their work terrified the soldier might focus his palpable aggression towards them at any moment. The rain beat down hard against my face causing me to blink as it merged with the tears now stinging the backs of my eyes. I struggled to my feet wiping my face with the back of my sleeve as I waited to see what the soldier would do next. My mother tried to stand as he kicked her again, but the strength and fight had gone from her and she fell back to her knees in the mud. Just then a cart passed by carrying bodies to the crematorium. The guard ordered two men to throw Mama on to it.

I screamed in protest, "No please, let me help her."

He pushed me to one side. "Get back to your work unless you want to join her?"

My mother was too weak to struggle. I screamed at the soldier, "She's still alive, the bodies on the cart are going to the crematorium, you can't take her there she's not dead."

The soldier looked at me for a moment before taking aim with his rifle and shooting my mother in the head. "She's dead now."

I stared straight ahead in shock and horror, the rain and tears cascading down my face in disbelief as I watched the mud stain a dark red around my mother's head.

The men threw her limp body onto the cart without any show of emotion and, anaesthetised as we had all become to such brutality, continued their sorrowful journey to the ovens.

Time stood still as I felt my body shake, not from the effects of the cold and the rain but more from the fact that, in that never to be forgotten moment, I had lost my mother forever in such an appalling way. Even the other prisoners stood motionless as they struggled to absorb this latest display of inhumanity playing out before them. The soldier shouted at us menacingly, his rifle still raised in our direction.

"Schnell, get on with your work unless you want to die as well." Almost without pause everyone turned their attention back to sorting through the piles of soaking clothes and baggage laid before them, fearful that even the slightest glance towards me offered as some form of consolation for my loss might result in a final journey of their own to the ovens. For myself, if only for that brief second in time, I truly didn't care what happened to me as I watched the cart, along with my mother, disappear from view. I turned to look at the soldier as if daring him to do the same to me. He recognised the passion and anger in my expression, something he had no doubt witnessed from other prisoners many times before and happily responded to with the same exhibition of brutality that he had demonstrated towards my mother. However, on this occasion he chose to ignore my glare of hatred, secure in the knowledge there was little, if anything, I could do in response to his actions and that enough time had already been wasted in completing the work before us. His tolerance of my obvious loathing towards him only served to emphasise once again the absolute control he and his fellow guards had over me and every other prisoner in the camp.

After all it was they who made the final decision as to whether we lived or died. It was a decision they were free to make at will and without fear of punishment or reprisal. I knew that on a different day and with such impunity extended towards him he would have been just as happy to add my body to that already overcrowded cart of death which had carried my mother away.

After Mama died I simply existed from day to day as though in a fog. My life becoming a downward spiral of increasing hate and despair lived out in equally gruesome and shocking proportions, and one from which there appeared no escape.

The only occasion I can remember as providing any light from the time I spent in that Godforsaken camp, apart from my brief friendship with Sarah, is the day we were set free.

We were all locked in our sleeping areas as usual the night before the liberation, but were aware that something different was happening beyond the traditional end of day routine outside of our barrack walls. I had developed a temperature over the previous few days and had been placed in one of the sick bays to recover.

This was an almost pointless exercise as there was little if any form of medication available within the camp and certainly not for us prisoners. I was scared because so often those who became ill and referred to the infirmary would then be further selected and sent for the ultimate cure, to the gas chamber.

There had been growing rumours for some time within

the camp that the Germans were suffering heavy defeats on the battlefront and that our liberation might not be far away. This came as welcome news but many of us also feared that if these stories were true then our masters were more likely to kill us all; so making sure that no-one was left alive to tell the truth about what had taken place in the camp. Our suspicions were further heightened by a growing number of changes in our routine during the days prior to the liberation. The Germans suddenly became even more meticulous and exacting in their schedule as to how their orders were carried out in the running of the camp. There seemed to be an increased sense of urgency to all that went on as things moved at a new and increasingly frenzied pace.

On this particular night as we lay on our rough wooden bunks, fearful of what was happening outside we listened intently to the constant barrage of noise: the soldiers shouting at each other accompanied by loud explosions and the roar of vehicles moving to and fro within the confines of the camp and beyond. We could see fires burning as we looked through the gaps in the planks of our make shift prison and watched as the Germans ran around like an army of demented rats in a state of self induced panic. We also noticed lines of prisoners being marched out of the camp led by the guards along with their dogs who snapped and snarled at anyone who failed to keep up. We fell into excited conversation as we gazed on the events unfolding outside.

"Where are they taking the prisoners?"

"Maybe they are letting them go if the allied troops are really on their way?"

"Don't be stupid, why would they let them go, to tell what has been happening here? More likely they are taking them to the woods to shoot them."

"Then why don't they come for us?"

"Maybe they'll just set fire to the building and burn us all to death. After all there are many here who are too sick to make it to the forest."

"Nobody slept that night, frightened by the increasing clamour of noise and apparent confusion outside; also in wondering what the Germans might have in store for us. Suddenly, as if a prearranged time had been agreed amongst the guards and soldiers there was silence. We lay there in the cold as the first light of dawn crept through the slats of wood not knowing what to do or think. We were scared the Germans would come back for us at any moment and mete out some new and even more sadistic form of punishment.

After what seemed like an age and as the light improved we looked at each other wondering what, if anything, we should do. Still nobody came for us, which only added to our bewilderment. After a while one of the women peered out of a small knot hole in a plank by her bunk.

"I can't see anybody, maybe they really have gone?" We knew the Germans and their cruel ways only too well to trust her early optimism, even though we prayed it might be true. If they had left, then where and why had they gone, and more importantly when would they be back, as they surely would?

As we talked, exchanging various theories as to what might have happened, we heard shouting again, but this time the voices were in the distance, not loud and outside our barrack as they had been for so much of the night. At first we didn't recognise the language, but knew it wasn't German. As the sound of voices got nearer and louder a woman cried out. "It's Russian, they're speaking in Russian." We had heard rumours that the Russians were gaining ground near to the camp but had been too afraid to believe it might be true. A few minutes later we watched in almost disbelief as the doors of our barrack were flung open, and there indeed standing in front of us were Red Army soldiers in their camouflaged uniforms.

We discovered later that the Germans, being aware of the impending arrival of the Russian troops, had fled but had also attempted to conceal the evidence of what had been happening in the camp by blowing up the ovens and the surrounding buildings along with any incriminating evidence contained within them. They had also built huge fires to burn the paperwork and corresponding detail of all those who had been murdered in the previous months and years. Apparently some of this work had been going on for a while, hence the changes in routine we had noticed in the days previously. We didn't know what had happened to the thousands of other prisoners who had been marched away from the camp during the night but, as life in Birkenau had taught us so well, were just happy, for this moment at least, to think only of ourselves and to know we had survived to see another sunrise in this stinking arena of death.

Initial shock and trepidation at the arrival of our saviours turned quickly to relief and joy as we began hugging each other along with the smiling Russian soldiers. We cried, tears of elation running down our hollow cheeks as the freedom we had prayed for for so long and an end to the unspeakable existence we had endured in the camp became a wonderful reality.

I remember one Russian soldier coming towards me and handing me a piece of chocolate.

"Take, it's good, you will like."

I couldn't remember when I had last tasted chocolate or that anyone had given me something simply to enjoy for myself.

"Thank you." Tears of disbelief and stunned appreciation filled my eyes.

I took the precious piece of confectionary nervously from his hand, unsure at first as to whether he might snatch it back. Then, cramming, into my mouth, I let the sweet taste of the chocolate thrill my senses in a way I had all but forgotten during my time in Birkenau.

"Good, yes?" The soldier smiled again as he witnessed an expression of absolute bliss spread across my face. If I close my eyes, even today, I can still feel the smooth shape of the chocolate as I bit into it and let it melt in my mouth.

The soldier told me in broken English that our captors had

fled, presumably fearing for their own lives now they had become the hunted.

"No more Germans. We here now, you safe." As the reality of what he was saying seeped into my brain and took root I shuddered for a moment as feelings of guilt and joy surged through me in equal measure. I had survived whilst so many others had died and yet how could I not be excited at being alive and able to witness this incredible day? A moment later and with my body shaking almost uncontrollably I allowed myself to break down and weep. It was the first time in as long as I could remember that I had permitted such an open display of emotion, and for the next few minutes the tears flowed as if they would never stop. I cried for my mother, for Joseph, and of course for my father. I cried for Sarah, and all the others who had died in that filthy camp. No more would I be hostage to the threat of torture and extinction each day from the Nazis, nor the ever present infestation of the lice and rats that occupied every corner of this Godforsaken place. It was a shared moment of overwhelming grief and release I'll never forget. The soldier took my hand to comfort me and I felt myself fall into his arms as he hugged me close, aware of both my sadness and new-found joy, but unsure of what to say.

"You safe now. Don't cry, you safe, no more Germans."

I lifted my head, the tears of elation still cascading down my cheeks. "Thank you." It was all I could say, but those two words, whilst expressing my feelings at that moment, felt so inadequate a response to this man who had literally in an instant changed my life and my world, so obviously for the better, and prayerfully forever. I fought to smile at him as he put a blanket round my shoulders and handed me the rest of the bar of chocolate.

"For you." I looked up at his smiling face, his deep blue eyes demonstrating an expression of kindness and affection I hadn't witnessed for so long. I stood, not knowing what else to say, my gaze alternating between him and the chocolate that was beginning to melt in my hand.

"Thank you." Once more I became overwhelmed by the moment and my tears fell again in grateful appreciation at such a simple act of humanity. After what seemed like an age I pulled the blanket tight around me and, taking another bite of my chocolate, stepped forward into a new and uncertain future, but at least one that now appeared to offer hope, something I and so many others had all but lost during those dark days in Birkenau. The cold morning breeze stung my nostrils as I breathed in deeply but, today, instead of the stench of fear and death filling my senses, there was a new and heady fragrance in the air, freedom.

NINE

Perhaps I should meet with her and hear what she has to say. After all the one truth I can't deny, no matter how much I might like to, is that this woman, Ruth, is actually my mother. I will always think of James and Carol as my parents of course but I did come from her body and now that we have this loose form of contact I am beginning to feel unless I seek, and gain, answers to certain questions I'll never really know, nor fully understand, the truth of what happened. And I do want to know the circumstances as to how I came to be in this world and why she let me go, if only for Jenny's sake if and when she begins to ask those deeper questions herself, questions that I can't begin to really answer without having spoken to Ruth first. So it appears I am left with little choice but to meet with her, but when I think about the two of us spending time together my mind races and becomes confused. What about Jenny? What will she think and how will she react? What if she wants to meet Ruth herself at some point, get to know her real grandmother? I can hold off on that for now but not when she's older and making decisions for herself? And what if I don't meet with her? What effect might that have on our relationship when she discovers she has a grandmother who she was never told about even though I knew existed but had chosen not to talk to or to meet with because I had decided to act like a truculent teenager and not consider the feelings of others? Would that be fair to Jenny or Ruth, or in the longer term to any of us? And what if they did meet at some point in the future and got on well together? Do I have the right to deny Jenny, or Ruth for that matter, a relationship of their own simply because I made the selfish choice to shut her out of my life as an act of revenge for apparently shutting me out of hers so many years before? Where is my sense of charity and forgiveness in all of this, what sort of example am I setting for myself and for my own daughter? What if the roles were reversed and it was me asking Jenny to agree to meet up and allow me the opportunity to explain what had happened, even if it wasn't something she thought she wanted to hear or accept. Wouldn't I hope she would allow me to tell my side of the story, no matter how unacceptable it might appear to her? Don't we all deserve a second chance, or at least the right to seek forgiveness, perhaps even to be reconciled?

So, maybe I should meet her; then at least if we don't get on I've tried. I won't have lost anything, and I'll know I've done the honourable thing and made the effort to learn the truth if only for Jenny's sake. Who knows, maybe by meeting with her it will confirm my long held suspicions that she got pregnant by mistake as I did but, that unlike myself with Jenny, just didn't care enough to keep me. At least I'll have given her the opportunity to explain what really happened, even if I'm not entirely sure I actually want to hear it.

Then again, if by some miracle she hadn't wanted to let me go or had been forced to give me up then perhaps we're being given this second chance to build a proper relationship and to sort our differences before it's too late.

Mum and Dad said the nuns didn't really talk about Ruth when they adopted me. They told them she had been like a lot of other young girls who came into their care with no real family of her own and a liking for the boys and not particular about the company she kept.

"To be honest, Mary, we were just grateful for the chance to have you in our lives and that she didn't fight to keep you."

Dad smiled in agreement.

"That's right, we were told only the basics about her. That she was a young girl who, like so many others, had got herself into trouble and didn't have the resources or the wherewithal to care for her baby. That's why she turned to the nuns for help, and to find a proper home for her child."

Mum looked at me. "If we're honest we didn't really think about her, we just wanted you to be our daughter. Her apparent mistake, however it had come about, was our blessing and that's all we really cared about. I'm sorry if that sounds selfish, but it's true."

Dad put his arm around Mum's shoulder to comfort her as he could see she was becoming upset.

"And we reasoned that if she'd really wanted to keep you she would have found a way and not gone to the nuns in the first place, or allowed us to adopt you."

He was right of course, and none of what they said painted the picture of a caring young woman who having made a mistake then fought to keep her baby as I had done with Jenny.

I suppose in those days it might have been harder to care for a baby if you didn't have the support of a loving family to help you. There had been no history offered to Dad and Mum about Ruth's upbringing or her parents, nor in how they might have reacted to their daughter's pregnancy. Perhaps my father was only a young lad himself and didn't fancy the responsibilities of bringing up a child, or threatened to abandon Ruth if she had decided to keep me.

After all Gerry made it very clear that he didn't want me to have Jenny, or for him to have any part in her upbringing if I did choose to go ahead with the pregnancy.

It won't be easy though, telling Mum and Dad if I do decide to go ahead and meet with Ruth. I think Mum was secretly hoping I might get a simple letter explaining the basics, and find she lived in Australia or somewhere so far away that I would never actually get the opportunity to spend time with her. With my first letter I had been told to send it via the adoption agencies and that they would pass it on to her in case she didn't want any further contact and could say a simple no to my request in her reply. But her response was the complete opposite, saying that she had been really pleased to hear from me and would be more than happy for me to contact her directly the next time if I wanted to. I looked at her address and noticed it was less than a ninety miles away which shocked me for a moment and left me unsure again as to what to do next. I hadn't expected her to be so close and for a while my desire for information turned to fear realising that the woman whose existence I had tried to ignore for so many years lived less than half a day away by car or train.

I wrestled with this fact for a few days, but eventually realised I did need to say yes and to meet with her if only to learn the truth of what had happened all those years ago, no matter how difficult or unpalatable that truth might be for me to hear. Much as I resented what she had done, how could I totally condemn her actions without hearing her side of the story? If I was to have my say then she deserved the same courtesy, or at least that was what I told myself for now.

What if she had experienced the same lack of support from my father, as I had with Gerry? Could I allow the anger and resentment I had held towards her for so long to continue if that was the case? And what if she'd been left alone to fend for herself after falling pregnant? How could I continue to condemn her, especially knowing how blessed and grateful I had been for the love and support poured out on me by James and Carol over the years?

I remember Gerry's reaction the night I told him I was pregnant.

"You're bloody what? Well it can't be mine 'cause I always use a rubber you know that."

"And what about that night you didn't use anything?"

"I told you at the time it was hardly anything and I wasn't even right inside you by then either. You can't have got pregnant from that little bit."

"It might not have been much but I felt it alright. It was warm and it seemed like it was deep inside me."

"It can't be mine. Bloody hell it was only the once."

"You can deny it as much as you like Gerry but the truth is I'm pregnant, and you're the only boy I've ever had sex with so it is yours and that's that."

"You must have shagged someone else, 'cause I still don't reckon you can have got a bun in the oven from that small amount; that's if any did get in there in the first place whatever you say."

"I've told you, I've never done it with anyone else you know that. I only agreed to have sex with *you* because you said it would bring us closer, and I thought you might go off with someone else if I didn't. You know I never really wanted to do it in the first place."

"That's bollocks, you like your rumpy pumpy as much as I do and don't tell me any different, otherwise why would you have been up for it every time your mum and dad went out eh?"

"It was you that wanted to do it not me."

"Oh so it was all my fault was it? What are you saying, that you never enjoyed it ever?"

"No I'm not saying that, of course there were times when it was nice. I just wish we'd never started to do it in the first place and that *was* down to you. I don't like lying to Mum and Dad either."

We stared at each other in silence for a moment.

"I'm sorry if you think I'm being unreasonable Gerry or that I led you along. I liked you and wanted to please you. Like I said I didn't want you going off with someone else and doing it with them if I didn't."

Gerry looked at me, frustration and anger showing in his eyes. "Bloody wish I had gone off with someone else now, at least I wouldn't have had all this crap to deal with."

After that our conversation just descended into an all out argument that neither of us was going to win, not until I made the announcement I wanted to keep the baby.

"I'm not having an abortion and that's final, we may have made a mistake but it's not the baby's fault and I intend to have it and to keep it."

Gerry's mood changed immediately as the potential of prospective fatherhood took its terrifying hold on him.

"Now listen, girl, we may not agree about me being the father and all, but if you have it and name me as its Dad that'll be both of our lives buggered, and I'm not ready to exchange my fags and my dancing shoes for a pair of slippers and a pipe, know what I mean?"

I smiled at him, but it was a smile of pity not empathy as I recognised, perhaps for the first time, what a weak and pathetic individual he truly was.

"Don't worry, Gerry, I can't think of anyone I would like less to be involved in the birth and upbringing of my baby than you."

He thought for a moment about protesting, but then realised I had given him a way out of accepting any responsibility for our baby.

"Yeah well that's just as well, 'cause like I say I'm not ready to take on some sprog that I'm still not sure is mine anyway. What about your parents, what are you going to tell them when they start asking questions?"

"I'll tell them the truth. I'll say we made a mistake and I got pregnant, but that I don't want you to be any part of the baby's life, either now or in the future."

"Can't see your dad accepting that."

"Don't you worry about my dad, he'll be more concerned about me than he will you. Although he may just consider killing you of course." I smiled to myself enjoying Gerry's obvious discomfort as he considered the prospect of trying to appease my father and explaining as to what exactly we had been doing on those nights when he and Mum were out. After all they had trusted him to honour his promise not to do anything with, or to, their precious daughter that he might later regret. Gerry looked at me and shook his head. "I don't…"

I interrupted, not really interested in what he had to say at that moment.

"Well he's hardly likely to congratulate you, is he? Of course he's going to be angry with you, Gerry, probably even more than I am, but like I say I know that both he and Mum will be more concerned about me and my decision to keep the baby than they will be about you and your pathetic excuses."

"So what are you saying, that he'll give me a smack and tell me to piss off, is that it?"

"No I don't think he'll do that, but I am pretty sure he will accept my view that this baby will have a better chance in life without you around, although I'm equally sure he'll want you to help with the costs until it's older." I knew Dad would insist on Gerry meeting his legal obligations and pay something towards Jenny's upkeep as she grew, certainly until she was twenty one. Although I'd told Gerry he wouldn't hit him I also reasoned it would be difficult in keeping Dad away from him, certainly once he discovered it was him who'd got me pregnant. However, I was also sure I couldn't present this weak and self-seeking individual to my parents as the father of what was to become their first grandchild and tell them that he was the only man for me. I realised now what a terrible mistake I had made in even going out with Gerry, let alone sleeping with him. I knew my parents, especially Dad, would feel the same and ask what I could have been thinking about in allowing myself to become pregnant by such a pathetic excuse for a man.

As suspected, Dad *was* furious and did insist on Gerry meeting his full financial responsibilities with regards to Jenny's upbringing, even if he couldn't manage to get him to meet his moral obligations as well.

"I trusted you with the well-being of our daughter, and even though she is equally accountable for what has happened it is you I hold ultimately responsible. Yes I know it takes two to tango, but I'll tell you this, even though I was a young man myself once I don't remember any of my early girlfriends asking me to do what you did with our Mary. It's always been the man who tries his luck first and it always will be, and that's why I believe her when she says it was you who promoted the idea of having sex and not the other way round. Luckily for you Mary has told us she doesn't want anymore to do with you, and that's about the only thing that's stopping me from knocking your block off right now." Gerry moved to speak but Dad interrupted. "And before you make matters worse for yourself by trying to tell me any different I should think again and keep your lips firmly closed, that's if you don't want them split, okay?"

I'd never seen Dad so angry and knew I should also remain silent, thankfully Gerry decided to do the same. Dad went on to tell him he would arrange for a solicitor to contact him informing him as to how the money for maintenance was to be paid. I was grateful for that and knew Dad would continue to help and oversee that side of things in the months to come. Gerry's pitiable reaction later when were alone only confirmed my thoughts about him as a man and potential father for our baby.

"He better not speak to me like that again or he'll be sorry, yeah, I don't let anybody get away with slagging me off like that."

I smiled sarcastically. "I'm sure Dad will be relieved to know that. So are you going to tell him you won't be paying anything towards the baby's keep as well then?"

Gerry shrugged his shoulders not really knowing how to answer as he struggled to maintain his mask of false bravado.

"I'll do what I have to, but it's a lot of aggravation for a couple of minute's pleasure." He shrugged his shoulders and shook his head. "I still don't reckon it's mine."

We stood for a moment in silence, any sense of lingering affection between us finally gone.

"Goodbye Gerry."

Turning to leave he sneered. "You know what I'm pleased it's over between us 'cause you weren't much of a shag anyway. Not as good as some of the other birds I've been with."

In those two short sentences Gerry had epitomised all my worst suspicions about him, making me wish I had seen through the paper thin veneer of his character earlier, even before going out with him, and certainly before agreeing to sleep with him.

I explained to Mum and Dad again about my feelings towards Gerry and not wanting him to be involved in any part of my pregnancy or in the upbringing of my child, their grandchild.

"I know I shouldn't have slept with him, but having made one mistake with Gerry already I don't want to make another one by having him be a part of this baby's life."

Although I knew they agreed with my decision about Gerry I still recognised this was painful for them to hear.

"I'm so sorry I've hurt you both like this, but I know Gerry isn't the one for me and I certainly know I don't want him to be a father to this child."

Dad, especially at first, had been upset to think that his little girl could let them both down in such a way, but in the end agreed that we would make the best of things as a family without Gerry's involvement. That was, apart from his monthly payments towards Jenny's expenses and future, Dad was adamant about that and wasn't going to back down on Gerry's financial responsibilities towards her. I couldn't argue differently. Bringing up a baby is an expensive business and I certainly couldn't expect my parents to foot the bill, nor would I have wanted them to, but even here Gerry failed us. The first couple of agreed payments arrived, albeit late, and then on the third month nothing. Our solicitor informed us that, following enquiries, he had discovered Gerry had apparently left home without any forwarding address and that without one it would prove difficult to gain any further payments, at least in the immediate future.

Gerry had made the first couple of payments in cash as he didn't have a bank account which meant the solicitor couldn't readily trace him to access any future monies.

Dad went to speak to Gerry's parents, but they were equally unhelpful saying that if I hadn't been so promiscuous in leading their son astray he might still have been living at home and not felt the need to leave after being hounded to make payments towards a child who's birth he had reasonably suggested might be terminated earlier to save everyone a lot of pain, trouble and expense. They even suggested Gerry had only agreed to help initially because of his feelings towards me and his generous nature. "Our Gerry's a good lad and wanted to help, but paying out for all those years towards a kid he wasn't sure was really his just didn't seem fair and so he's decided to make a fresh start somewhere else. He was so upset and desperate to get away from all this he hasn't even told us where he's gone."

I'm not sure Dad believed that particular story and got really angry with Gerry's father, almost coming to blows, with Mum having to call the police who advised them both to calm down and leave the matter in their hands.

"We will continue in our investigations to locate him Mr Rowland and once we do we will remind him of his legal obligations as far as the support of your daughter's child is concerned. In the meantime, you and Mr Porter threatening each other is not going to help the situation. We can understand your frustration but you really need to leave the investigation as to his son's whereabouts to us."

I'm not sure whether the police had some sympathy for what Mr Porter had said or they weren't really interested in finding Gerry but we never heard from him again. And after a few months the updates from the police in how their efforts to find him were proceeding also became less frequent until in the end we gave up on ever hearing from Gerry again and just got on with ours, and Jenny's life.

TEN

After the war I went back to Guernsey, but the tailoring business had gone. The Germans had changed the papers about ownership and had sold it on. The shop itself had become a food store, and the flat above that we used to rent out had been turned into storage and office space. There was nothing left for me. The new owners were very nice, but said they had bought the business in good faith, including the lease on the flat. They obviously felt sorry for me and gave me a little money to keep me going but, in truth, I think this was more to salve their own conscious than as to any form of real recompense.

"We're really sorry to hear about what happened to you and your family and that we can't do anymore for you but this is our business and future now. As we told you we paid a lot of money for the lease and all that goes with it."

Painful though it was, I understood and was grateful for the small gift of money they offered as I had no financial reserves of my own.

The Germans had stolen everything from us in the years previously, and in taking the lives of my parents and brother in such horrific circumstances along with our home and business I was left with nothing but memories, and even here they only served to remind me of all that I had lost.

I stayed on Guernsey for a while working in a hotel but, as I'd been quite young when I first left the Island along with the rest of the Jewish community living there, there was nobody I really knew anymore and so felt no real sense of loyalty to remain, nor in seeking to build a new life for myself there. After a while just being on the island made me think more and more of my parents and brother and what had happened to them and so I decided to move back to England. I arrived in the spring of 1946 returning initially to North London. There were some former friends of my parents, Mr and Mrs Goldblum, still living there, who were pleased to see me and made me welcome in their home.

"We were so sorry to hear of what happened to your mama and papa, and Joseph of course. You are welcome to stay with us for as long as you want, it is the least we can do."

A neighbour, Mrs Stein, was a teacher in a local primary school and helped me to get a part time job there looking after the children in the breaks between lessons, helping to serve the lunches and watching over them at play time, that sort of thing.

"It's not a lot, but it will get you started and who knows what might come from it. From little acorns mighty oak trees will grow. You will see, Ruth, my dear, one day God will put a smile back on your face."

I still didn't really have a plan for my life but it was good to be surrounded by the sound of children laughing and playing together once more. I found great pleasure in watching the little ones run around the playground shrieking with glee and gaining such obvious delight from each other's company in the secure surroundings of the school and with a freedom they would never have been afforded in Birkenau. Even as I watched this new generation of youngsters sharing food and playing happily together my mind was drawn back to the years of despair in the death camp when the only sounds to be heard from the children were their sobs and cries of misery. Even worse, when they made no sound at all, moving around like the living dead as they battled to survive, along with the rest of us, against the brutal and unforgiving regime of our Nazi oppressors. Most of the small children were exterminated on arrival at Birkenau and so to witness the simple pleasure of them playing and laughing together once more proved a joy in itself.

It felt like such a long time ago since Joseph and I had shared the same freedom and happiness as these youngsters. It was as if we had lived another life altogether and in so many ways we had.

I was talking to Mrs Goldblum one day expressing how happy I was living with them and working with the children but also how at some point I would need to move on.

"You have both been so kind and I really do appreciate everything you have done for me but I think I need to look for more full-time work, especially if I am to afford somewhere of my own to live one day."

"Please, you don't need to worry about leaving, my dear. As I told you when you first arrived, you are welcome to stay for as long as you like. I hope you know that?" She smiled at me. "But I also understand why you would like to make a life of your own. Now you have been working at the school for a little while, perhaps with the experience you have gained you could think about finding work at one of the big houses locally and helping to look after the children who live there. It would offer you more of the full time work you would like, and with the right employer there might also be accommodation for you as well. Many of these houses employ a live-in nanny and you could gain further experience in learning from her"

It was a good idea and certainly one I would think about. Mrs Goldblum smiled again.

"And as I say, my dear, if you did manage to find such employment nearby but it didn't work out for any reason, then you would always be welcome to come back here." I was touched by her offer.

"Thank you, that's very kind. You and Mr Goldblum have been very good to me."

I was also grateful for the fact that, happy as the Goldblum's might be for me to stay on as part of their family, they had also recognised I would need to stand on my own two feet at some point and make my way in the world. I also didn't want to outstay my welcome even though they had assured me otherwise. I think the other thing that concerned me was that if I didn't move on soon my daily routine and existence would be more associated with my past than with whatever new adventures and challenges lay ahead, no matter how uncertain they might be.

There were a number of families locally who were doing well again now the war was over and were often seeking help in the shape of reliable housekeepers and other staff to look after their children while they were out at work, or while the lady of the house entertained guests. With the prospect of a truly fresh start I followed Mrs Goldblum's advice and applied for a number of vacancies in some of the larger houses locally. I was fortunate to gain one or two temporary positions over the next few months, working successfully for a few families and really enjoying my time with them. I learnt many new skills, both in general service and as a nanny's assistant caring for the children of the house. I also regained much of my personal confidence after years of having all thoughts of self-worth and individual choice stripped away from me. Initially, with this new work being part time I continued to live at the Goldblum's, saving as much as I could from my wages in the hope of eventually affording my own lodgings. After a few months I had saved enough to make the deposit for a tiny bedsit locally. I was so excited and even though it was only a small room it was still somewhere I could call my own. I was now free to enjoy the luxury of choosing whom I invited in to share my personal space. This was another indulgence I had all but forgotten after living for so long in the overcrowded and claustrophobic conditions of Birkenau where all personal choice was denied and any form of social interaction was forbidden. Being able to close my own door on the rest of the world at the end of the day was an experience

I never tired of. Such a simple act of freedom, for so long denied and one that most people accepted as part of their everyday life, always felt fresh and exhilarating to me. Just being able to come and go as and when I pleased after being locked up for so many years was something I knew I would never take for granted again. How could I ever forget those endless days in the death camp when our every move was monitored and dictated by the Nazis?

It was the late winter of 1947 that I started work for Mr and Mrs Taylor and really thought I'd landed on my feet when entering their employ. Mr Taylor was the Manager of quite a large bank in central London and very well respected by everyone in the area, both professionally and in their social circle. Mrs Taylor was a lovely lady and we got on well from our very first meeting. They invited me round for an interview after a recommendation from some friends of theirs, Mr and Mrs Blyth, who I had been working for but were now heading off to a new life in America. Mr Blyth worked in engineering and following the war he and a number of industrial managers and engineers were offered work in America as the country continued to grow in its perceived role as the "land of opportunity" for so many young families seeking to make a new life for themselves after the war years. They asked if I would like to go with them and take on the full-time roll of nanny for their two young children as they had been more than happy with my work in the time I had been with them. They also thought I deserved the promotion and might enjoy the opportunity to travel to this new and vibrant country and make a truly fresh start for myself after so many years of sadness and uncertainty. Their regular nanny who I had been assisting had decided not to go with them as she had elderly parents living nearby and didn't want to leave them behind. It was an exciting offer and one I was truly grateful for but in the end I thanked them and said no as I had had enough of moving around myself since the war had ended and I had gained my release from Birkenau. The prospect of making a fresh start in America was of course an attractive one but I also felt, for now at least, that I wanted to be settled and remain in one place for a while. I explained this to Mrs Blyth and she said she would keep an eye out for me as to the potential for a similar role amongst her friends should one present itself.

"You've proved a real treasure to us, Ruth dear, and I would be more than happy to recommend your services to any of our friends." And so when Mrs Blyth heard that the Taylor's were looking for a new nanny for their four year old daughter, Elizabeth, true to her word she suggested me for the position. Apparently their current nanny was seeking a return to the north of England to care for her mother who had become sick and the Taylor's were now desperate to find the right replacement as soon as possible with the other nanny hoping to leave within a fortnight. Mrs Blyth explained this would be my first position as a full time nanny but that she had no hesitation in suggesting me for the post when considering the diligence and dedication I had demonstrated during my time with them.

"You obviously have a gift for this style of work, Ruth, and as far as your care for our children is concerned, well, I think Edward and Violet would happily supply you with a glowing reference of their own if they weren't so sad about your leaving." She smiled at me. "You have been a real blessing to me, Ruth, both personally and in your care for my family, and I thank you for that."

I felt both humbled and grateful for her kind words and recommendation. Mrs Taylor was more than happy to consider me in her desire to find an alternative nanny quickly as she had recently discovered herself to be pregnant again and so her need for assistance was soon to be doubled. Mrs Blyth assured me if I presented myself well at interview the position could be mine.

"As I said, Ruth, we are more than happy to recommend you to Helen and Robert, and I have no doubt if you demonstrate the same genuine ardour and enthusiasm for your work with them as you have done with us you will continue to do very well."

"Thank you, Mrs Blyth, that's very kind of you. I will try my best to fulfil the faith you've shown in me, although I can't say I am particularly looking forward to facing another interview. I still suffer with a lack of confidence in those sorts of situations. I never find it easy to talk about myself after everything that has happened over the past few years."

"Now don't you worry, dear, I will speak to Helen again before you meet with her to smooth the path a little for you. She is a lovely lady and a very dear friend of mine. You just be your usual polite and delightful self and I'm sure everything will go swimmingly."

I tried to remember Mrs Blyth's words of encouragement about how nice the Taylor's were as I approached their large, black and very shiny front door, but I could still feel the butterflies of uncertainty fluttering in my stomach as I rang the bell. I stood back a little and looked up at the tall elegant building in front of me wondering how just one family could live in such a large house. After a few moments a maid opened the door. She was a young girl like myself and dressed in a black skirt and pristine white blouse. I remember thinking the collar looked so starched and stiff I could have probably cut my finger on it, none of which helped to settle my nerves. I offered her my hand as I entered which caused her to smile.

"Household staff don't greet each other with a handshake, and certainly not in front of Mr and Mrs Taylor. You'd be advised to remember that if you're lucky enough to get the job." She took my coat and showed me through to a large room that I presumed to be a library as there were shelves of books almost floor to ceiling on the walls around me.

Mr Taylor was the first to enter and I stood fixed to the spot not daring to move in case I knocked something over. He moved towards me and as we shook hands I wished that I'd remembered to wipe mine on my jacket first as I knew it was moist with nervous perspiration. Sensing my unease he smiled and informed me that Mrs Taylor would join us shortly.

I was immediately impressed by his air of confident authority and his smart blue pin striped suit, the jacket of which was buttoned neatly at the front. I couldn't help but notice he was a very attractive man with dark brown eyes and a head full of jet black hair cut short and groomed immaculately. As he moved to close the door and as a way of making conversation I remarked that I had rarely seen so many books in a library before.

Mr Taylor smiled again and informed me the room was actually his study.

"I spend the majority of the day at the bank where the demands on my time appear never ending and fraught with activity and so I enjoy the calm this room affords me along with the peace I get in being able to work uninterrupted amongst my many reference books." I smiled, embarrassed that I had already made a wrong assumption and not knowing what to say to in response to redeem myself. He nodded towards two comfortable looking armchairs. "Please do sit down." I was grateful for the opportunity to rest my legs which were now beginning to shake. There followed a brief awkward silence as we sat opposite each other and with neither of us quite knowing what to say next. After what seemed like an age Mr Taylor leant forward and smiled at me again.

"Have you had to come far?"

"No sir, only from Mr. and Mrs Blyth's house. They recommended I should apply for the position I believe?"

He nodded and looked down scratching the side of his head.

"Yes of course, how remiss of me, Helen did mention something." He looked up at me again. "I apologise. As I said my day is taken up with so many differing responsibilities at the bank that it slipped my mind for a moment." He paused briefly and then smiled. "That's not to say our meeting with you is not important, it's just that usually I leave staffing matters to my wife. She tends to run things more proficiently than I in that department."

I smiled back at him as best I could sensing my growing

nervousness had now frozen my face into an expression of what I could only imagine must have looked like that of a grinning chimpanzee.

"I fully understand, sir, you must be very busy. Please don't apologise."

We looked at each other in silence once more, unsure again how best to continue our increasingly stilted conversation. A few moments later a palpable sense of relief swept over the two of us as the door opened and Mrs Taylor entered the room. Mr Taylor rose to his feet, clearly relieved at the arrival of his wife.

"Ah, Helen darling, there you are. Miss Cahn and I were beginning to think you had got lost."

She smiled at me and rolled her eyes.

"No you weren't, Robert, you just don't like having to make polite conversation or indeed any conversation if it hasn't got something to do with the bank." She smiled at me again. "Please forgive my husband. Like most men he feels anything to do with domestic arrangements are not of any great importance and should be dealt with by the lady of the house. That is until something goes wrong. Then he will make his views and presence felt in no uncertain terms, similar to that of a bull in a china shop I think is the phrase?" They clearly had a relaxed and happy relationship with her being able to tease him in such an open way and him readily accepting her remarks in the humorous light they were intended. She looked at him lovingly. "That's fair, isn't it, darling?"

He smiled at her knowingly and reaching into his jacket pocket took out a silver cigarette case.

I warmed to her straight away; her broad smile putting me at ease even before we had been formally introduced. She was dressed in a highly patterned and colourful sleeveless dress with a pale blue cardigan covering her shoulders. Her long blond hair was set up high and swept back to make the most of her natural beauty, and she wore just the right amount of make up to highlight her obvious good looks. She shook my hand warmly and encouraged me to sit again as I had felt myself stand automatically on her entering the room.

"Please my dear," she said, motioning towards the chair, "we don't stand on ceremony around here, do we, darling?" Mrs Taylor smiled at her husband who was clearly relieved at having his wife present despite her light hearted aside regarding his ability to make small talk with their proposed new employee.

"So darling, have you been keeping Ruth here entertained?" She laughed as he told her about my mistake in thinking his study was the library.

"It might as well be a library, Ruth, what with so many books and the insistence on quiet whenever any of us enter his special room, especially when he is working, which I might add is something he still appears to take delight in even after a long day at the bank. Isn't that right, darling?" Mr Taylor looked slightly less amused at her criticism of his work.

"That's not entirely true, my dear, I do try to spend as much time as possible with you and Elizabeth when I am at home. It's just that we are particularly busy at the bank at this time which necessitates my having to work a little longer than we both might like. My study here provides all the necessary detail I require, along with a little *peace and quiet*, as you so eloquently put it."

Mrs Taylor laughed.

"Don't be such a stuffed shirt, Robert, I was teasing you. You'll make poor Ruth here even more nervous than she probably is already if you carry on like that." She smiled again and winked at me.

"We are all aware as to how busy you are in saving the nation's finances dear and so of course appreciate the small amount of time you are able to afford us as your lowly family." She walked over to her husband and kissed him lightly on the cheek as if to reassure him that her remarks were intended to be light hearted and not taken seriously. He smiled, first at his wife and then at me as he took a cigarette and placed it between his lips.

"I'm sorry if I have unnerved you in any way, Miss Cahn. My wife is right of course, I do rather become preoccupied with my work at times." I smiled back at him but didn't really know what to say in reply and so was more than grateful when the maid, who had answered the front door, knocked and entered with a tray of tea and cake. She smiled at me as she placed the tray on a side table; her naturally bubbly character visibly lightening the atmosphere in the room.

"Would you like me to pour the tea, Mam?" She began to take the cups and saucers from the tray and place them on the table.

Mrs Taylor moved towards her. "No, thank you, Nelly, I'll do that. We'll ring if we require anything else." Nelly turned to leave, smiling briefly at me again as she closed the door behind her.

Mrs Taylor began to pour the tea. "Milk and sugar, Ruth?"

"Just milk thank you."

"Nelly is an absolute treasure, isn't she, Robert? I don't know where we'd be without her. She has such a wonderfully infectious smile doesn't she dear?"

Mr Taylor looked slightly embarrassed again, evidently unsure as to how much of a treasure Nelly actually was to the household, and clearly not aware of her smile, infectious or otherwise.

"Yes dear, as you say an absolute treasure, I'm sure." He lit his cigarette. "As always I am more than happy to defer to you in all matters appertaining to the day to day staffing requirements." He nodded towards me. "I've already informed Miss Cahn of our differing strengths as to the domestic arrangements within the house, haven't I, Miss Cahn?" I nodded as Mrs Taylor continued to pour the tea, glancing briefly at her husband and rolling her eyes again in mock disapproval.

I'd never had tea in a china cup before. As I sat there allowing the hot liquid to soothe my dry and nervous throat my thoughts drifted back to the horrors of Birkenau when we would happily drink what was purported to be our tea from a rusty tin plate or battered tin mug. There were certainly never any cups, china or otherwise to be found, and even the few mugs that did exist were a sought after and much treasured rarity. I remembered one lady though who, envied by many, did manage to smuggle a real cup into the camp. She took it everywhere with her, fearing it would be stolen if she left it in her barracks. Eventually though, even this small luxury was exchanged for a crust of bread with another prisoner following her not having eaten for almost three days.

As I watched Mrs Taylor, with her long elegant fingers and beautifully painted nails, pour the tea into the other cups from a matching china pot I thought how far I'd come in such a short period of time from those dark days spent scavenging for food and drink in the death camp. On the one hand that terrible existence seemed a dark and distant memory, and yet the reality of my time spent there was never truly far from my mind, especially when I thought about my brother and parents, along with the thousands of others who had lost their lives in that awful place.

"Would you care for a piece of cake, Ruth? Our household cook Mrs Devlin makes wonderful cakes doesn't she dear?"

Mr Taylor smiled and nodded, clearly struggling with such mundane conversation.

I looked at the freshly made Victoria sponge, which did indeed look delicious and thought once again what I would have given for such a treat just a few short years before. Even so the thought of my attempting to steady a plate of cake along with a cup and saucer whilst trying to maintain any air of self-confidence at such an important moment outweighed my genuine desire to take a piece.

"No thank you, I've not long eaten," I said, hoping they couldn't hear the rumble from my stomach in protest to my denying it the opportunity of such a delicious looking treat. In truth I had been far too nervous to eat anything before leaving for my interview. Mr Taylor took a draw on his cigarette.

"Tells us more about your time with the Blyth's Miss Cahn and of your duties?"

Before I could answer Mrs Taylor spoke up as if to reassure her husband and steer him away from this line of questioning; one that, as earlier, she had obviously already made him aware of.

"They gave, Ruth a glowing reference dear if you remember? Dorothy especially enjoyed having her in the house. She said she was only sorry that Ruth had turned down the opportunity of discovering a new life in America with them and of making the full time position of nanny to Edward and Violet her own. Mrs Temple had already decided not to travel with them for family reasons. We spoke about that as well, dear." Mrs Taylor smiled broadly at me. "Dorothy also said that their loss would be our gain should Ruth agree to join us here and care for Elizabeth along with the new addition to our family on its arrival."

I felt a little embarrassed by such a glowing reference, but equally encouraged that I had been so highly thought of by my previous employer. I hoped it would stand me in good stead should I be offered this new position with the Taylor's, although I felt from her demeanour towards me that I could already count on Mrs Taylor's approval. Mr Taylor looked at me for a moment as he took a long draw on his cigarette. Then exhaling a cloud of smoke he addressed his wife with a nod of his head and a smile.

"Well that all sounds in order to me. And as you will be making the final decision as to the best for Elizabeth, my dear, I will leave you both to have a more detailed discussion about the terms of employment etc. should you decide to offer Miss Cahn the position?" He placed his cup on the table and put his cigarette out in the ashtray next to it. "And of course, presuming she decides to accept?"

Mr Taylor got to his feet and walked towards me. I put my cup down and rose to meet him.

"If you'll excuse me, I have an important phone call to make. It was a pleasure meeting you, Miss Cahn, and I look forward to seeing you again soon should you and my wife come to an appropriate agreement with regards to your joining our household." He smiled and shook my hand warmly. I felt encouraged to have come through what I had feared might be the most difficult part of my interview relatively unscathed and trusted I might experience an easier time with Mrs Taylor once her husband had left the room. He moved to his wife once more, kissing her briefly on the cheek before turning to leave. "I'll see you later my dear and you can let me know the outcome of your conversation. Goodbye, Miss Cahn, I wish you well."

Mrs Taylor watched him leave before offering me another cup of tea.

"And this time I insist on you having a piece of cake, it really is delicious." I think she had sensed my earlier fear of embarrassment at the potential of dropping crumbs on the carpet coupled with my overriding desire to actually take her up on her offer. We exchanged pleasantries for a while as we relaxed in each others company and I became so confident in our conversation that I ended up enjoying a second slice of cake, thankfully without a crumb leaving my plate.

After a while she moved our discussion onto the role of what might be expected of me should I be appointed as Elizabeth's nanny, along with the formal duties both she and her husband envisaged me undertaking.

"I understand you might feel a little nervous at the prospect of taking on the role of full time nanny with us, especially as this would be the first time you will have acted as such? But I should hasten to reassure you that Mr and Mrs Blyth have both emphasised to me that they consider you more than competent in your abilities and entirely ready to take up such a responsible position." She paused, taking a deep breath as if deciding how best to continue. "If I'm honest with you, Ruth, I also took the opportunity of speaking with Mrs Temple their current nanny whose expertise and counsel I have sought on a number of occasions in the past with matters regarding Elizabeth. She told me that she would have no hesitation in recommending you for the post. She emphasised that, not only were you highly proficient in carrying out your official duties as far as the care of Violet and Edward were concerned but that you also displayed a natural affinity towards them as children, an attribute I also regard highly.

"That's very generous of them and of Mrs Temple. I've been very fortunate to have worked under her and to have learnt so much in the time we were together. I'll be sorry to leave."

"Now as part of your employment here, should you agree to join us, and to assist in you're ability to provide the appropriate daily care for Elizabeth we would be offering you your own room. It's situated at the top of the house and has its own wash basin and associated facilities nearby. This will allow you, not only too fulfil your full time role as nanny to Elizabeth but also provide you with your own space in which to relax when you are not employed with any additional household duties associated with our daughter's care."

"That's very kind of you, but I do have my own accommodation elsewhere. It is local though and so wouldn't present a problem in my performing all of the duties you've outlined."

Mrs Taylor looked at me, her face displaying a degree of concern. "I'm sorry, Ruth, but Robert and I are very clear in what we are looking for as far as the care and well being of our daughter is concerned, and that most definitely includes her nanny living in. This is not only to meet Elizabeth's immediate daily needs but also to provide the consistency and continuity of attention such a role demands." There was a brief but awkward silence between us. "To be honest with you, Ruth, I am not sure how you could hope to undertake the full list of responsibilities associated with the role if you did not live in. What if Elizabeth or I were unwell, what would happen then?" She paused to allow the detail of what she had said to settle fully in my mind.

"You must remember, Ruth, this is very much a full time position. As household nanny your new duties and hours spent here will far exceed those you have been fulfilling under Mrs Temple's tutelage."

We looked at each other, both recognising perhaps that we had reached some form of impasse. After a few moments Mrs Taylor smiled. "Ruth, I do know a little of your past from conversations I have had privately with Dorothy, she told me about your difficult time during the war." I could feel myself stiffen, not wanting to open old wounds again, especially with somebody I had only just met.

"I really do understand your desire to have a space to call your own, along with the associated authority that such an arrangement provides, especially when considering your past." She took my hand. "I promise Robert and I would respect your room here as very much just that, *your space,* and I would ask that you might feel able to trust us to honour that agreement. And, in so doing feel able to agree to meeting *our* request that you live here within our household, not only as part of our staff, but as time progresses we would hope, more as part of the family."

I hadn't thought of myself as truly belonging anywhere since my life on Guernsey and certainly not as part of a family; yet here was someone offering me just that, a chance to belong again and encounter a depth of relationship I had all but forgotten over the past few years. I could feel tears beginning to fill my eyes as Mrs Taylor leant forward and squeezed my hand.

"The truth is, Ruth, I need someone to help me, not only with Elizabeth but also in many other areas as the time approaches for me to deliver this new baby that I am expecting. If I am to believe Dorothy, as I do, then I can't think of a better person to have by my side than you, so please say yes?" I swallowed hard, fighting my desire to break down and cry in the presence of such genuine affection being demonstrated towards me. I sat for a moment recalling how many times I had prayed for an opportunity to be a part of a family again, and wondered if this was indeed an answer to those prayers, it certainly appeared as such.

"Alright, Mrs Taylor, I'll accept your proposal and move in if that's what you want and truly believe is for the best." I prayed again that I was making the right decision.

Mrs Taylor sat back in her chair, a look of relief spread across her face as she smiled at me. "Thank you so much for that, Ruth. And yes, I truly do believe you have made the right decision, not only for Robert, Elizabeth and I, but also for yourself." She laughed, and patted her tummy. "And of course for this little one as well once he or she decides to arrive and join the rest of us in the family."

We continued to talk for some time about how vital she felt it was for Elizabeth to have someone she could trust to turn to when the new baby was born. How it would be my job to reassure the little girl of her mother's continuing love despite appearing, at times, in her daughter's eyes at least, to care more about this latest addition to the family than to her own particular needs and demands. Mrs Taylor emphasised to me again that she didn't want me to be seen by Elizabeth simply as someone who looked after her when her mummy and daddy were either too tired or seemingly occupied with other things.

"It's that natural ability and affinity you possess in engaging with children that I want to encourage, Ruth. I want you to become a friend to Elizabeth, and hopefully to our next child as well every bit as much as I want you to care for them in your official role as nanny. Trust is such an important attribute in life, Ruth, and I want the children to be able to trust you every bit as much as Robert and I will be trusting you in return with their care".

Although I still held a few reservations about giving up my own room I also felt that, in Mrs Taylor, I had found more than just an employer, rather perhaps someone with whom I could establish genuine bonds of friendship and personal understanding. These were feelings that had been missing for so long in my life and I hoped were ones she might also envisage developing between us as well.

Of course, no matter how well Mrs Taylor and I got on, I knew the real test would be in how I related to Elizabeth and so after finishing our tea Mrs Taylor sent Nelly to fetch the little girl and bring her to the study to meet me. Suddenly all of my new found poise and self-confidence drained rapidly away again. What if she didn't like me or we struggled to get on? Admitting to myself I was nervous about meeting with Elizabeth was also an acknowledgement that, after spending time with Mrs Taylor, I recognised how much I now desperately wanted this job. Here I was being given not only the opportunity of promotion and regular work, work that I enjoyed, but also the chance to be a part of a loving family again. That was something I hadn't really felt or known for almost longer than I could remember. Whilst I recognised that neither Mr nor Mrs Taylor could ever take the place of my own parents, nor Elizabeth my brother Joseph, I still felt this was a home where I might find love again and that was something I had truly missed and very much wanted back in my life once more.

As we sat waiting for Elizabeth to arrive we talked about many different things, our conversation warm and relaxed with no hint of the awkward silences I had experienced with her husband.

She was genuinely moved to hear about my time in Birkenau, although I didn't go into any great detail so early on in our relationship. Her understanding and genuine sensitivity convinced me just how much I wanted to spend time with both her and her family.

Suddenly the calm atmosphere of the study was shattered as the door opened and Elizabeth bounced into the room and ran towards her mother with all the confidence of a child clearly loved and cherished by her parents. She was a pretty little girl with long dark curls held in place by a bright red ribbon. She wore a highly patterned dress and red shoes that matched the ribbon in her hair; hair I felt I could happily spend hours brushing through as we grew to know and trust each other in the weeks and months ahead.

Mrs Taylor introduced Elizabeth to me and, as I had done with Nelly, I held out my hand to greet her. She walked towards me, but instead of taking my hand looked me up and down, then standing right in front of me asked quizzically, "Do you like playing with dolls' houses?" I was rendered speechless for a moment, having been caught out by the nature of both her question and her greeting. I smiled down at her. "Yes I do, I like playing with dolls houses very much, although it is quite a while since I have done it."

Mrs. Taylor burst out laughing. "Elizabeth, really, that's no way to greet somebody, especially when meeting them for the first time. Now shake hands with Ruth and say hello properly."

Elizabeth turned confidently towards her mother. "If she is going to be my new nanny then I only want her to be here if she likes playing with my dollies and my doll's house like my other nanny did."

I smiled at Mrs Taylor and then again at Elizabeth who was staring at me once more as if still unsure whether I should be treated as friend or foe?

"I really do like playing with dolls Elizabeth, in fact when I was about your age my Daddy made me a doll's house of my own."

"Really," she said, suddenly becoming very excited. "Tell me about it, was it very big? Mine is a big one and has a red roof; did yours have a red roof?"

I struggled for a moment trying to recall the exact detail after so many years. "Yes, I think it did have a red roof and a green front door I seem to remember as well."

"Mine has a black door just like Mummy's and Daddy's."

Following this slightly protracted conversation about our dolls' houses, Elizabeth eventually asked if I would like to accompany her upstairs to see her room and her dolls house, along with her other toys.

"I've got lots of dolls and I could tell you all their names if you'd like to meet them?"

"If your mummy says it is alright," I asked, glancing at Mrs Taylor, not quite knowing how best to answer. Elizabeth turned to her mother. "Is it alright if Ruth comes up to my room, Mummy? Please say it is." Mrs Taylor looked at me and smiled.

"It appears you have the royal seal of approval Ruth. Not everyone is allowed to enter Elizabeth's room and meet with her dolls so early on in their relationship. I am presuming you would be happy to accept her invitation?"

"Yes please, I'd love to see Elizabeth's room." I glanced down at the little girl before me now hopping excitedly on the spot in anticipation. "And her toys, of course. That is providing you're happy for me to go up with her?"

"Of course. Off you go the two of you, and play nicely, Elizabeth, we want Ruth to come again remember." We smiled at each other as Elizabeth took my hand and tugged on it. "Come on, Ruth, let's go."

With that we were released to enjoy the first of many shared adventures together as we began what was to become a very special relationship between the two of us. We quickly developed a genuine bond as I learnt to love this little girl who had been placed in my care and as she grew to trust me, not only with her well being but her innermost thoughts and secrets as well. I knew in those first few minutes we spent playing together I had found someone I could pour my heart and love into again.

We spent more than half an hour together that first afternoon just talking and playing with her dolls house and toys. Mrs Taylor joined us for part of that time but was happy to simply watch the two of us and in how we related to each other. I didn't feel under any pressure though, far from it, indeed Elizabeth and I became so lost in each others company we were hardly aware of her presence at times. For me especially the opportunity to play little girl games again after the recent years of darkness was something I relished and happily threw myself into. Mrs Blyth's children were a little younger than Elizabeth and so the opportunity to engage with them in the same way and on the same level was different. Elizabeth and I got on really well and the time seemed to run away until eventually I said I ought to be leaving as I still had my duties with Mrs. Blyth to attend to. Mrs Taylor apologised.

"Of course, I'm sorry we have kept you for so long."

Elizabeth wasn't quite so understanding. "But we haven't finished playing yet," she said, looking decidedly unhappy at the prospect of her new play mate having to leave half way through a game. Mrs. Taylor smiled at her daughter, chiding her gently.

"Now that's not very nice is it, Elizabeth, remember what I said? Dear Ruth has to go back to see Mrs Blyth and finish her work there. She still has to care for Violet and Edward, at least for a while."

"But you said she could be my nanny?"

"Well she can be if that's what you would like, and providing of course that Ruth would still like to be a part of our home?" Mrs Taylor turned to me, a look of pleading in her eyes. "It appears the job is yours, Ruth, that is if you'd still like to join us?"

"I'd love to; yes please, if that's alright with you?" I looked down at Elizabeth who was jumping up and down in front of me. "And of course if it's alright with you, Miss Elizabeth?"

The little girl beamed. "Yes please." She turned to her mother. "Can Ruth start tomorrow, Mummy, can she?"

"Well maybe not tomorrow, but hopefully very soon." She took Elizabeth's hand and turned to me. "I will speak to Dorothy and arrange a date for you to start once they have agreed the final arrangements for their move to America, if that's alright with you?" I nodded in agreement.

"Can I suggest a month's trial just to be fair to all parties?" She smiled again nodding towards her daughter. "Although I think there is little doubt how successful you will prove to be if this little lady is any sort of barometer to go by." Elizabeth pulled away from her mother and grabbed my hand again, jumping from one foot to the other as she did so.

"I'll think of some new games to play when you come back, Ruth, so don't be long."

Mrs Taylor and I looked at each other and laughed, encouraged not only by how well the two of us had got on, but more especially because we had gained the most important affirmation to our proposed relationship, that of young Elizabeth.

"I apologise again for having kept you so long."

"Please don't apologise I've had a wonderful time." I looked down at Elizabeth. "And I hope I've made a new friend as well?"

The three of us made our way downstairs and after assuring Elizabeth I would see her again soon she waved me off excitedly as we said our goodbyes.

"Don't forget to come back and play with me as soon as you can, Ruth."

Mrs Taylor and I shook hands and smiled at each other.

"Thank you again, Ruth, I'm really looking forward to your joining us. I'm sure you'll be very happy here."

As the large front door closed behind me I grinned to myself reflecting that I had gained not only a wonderful opportunity to care for a delightful little girl and her family but more especially I had found somewhere I might truly be able to settle and find myself once more after so many years of loss and insecurity. For the first time in a long while I felt a real sense of joy rise in my heart as I made my way confidently back to the Blyth's to tell them of my good news and to prepare myself for this new and exciting chapter in my life.

ELEVEN

And so my life as a single mother began. Naturally I had the support of my parents, James and Carol, and would always be grateful for that but at the same time I knew I had to make a go of things for myself, and for Jenny. Once she arrived my life altered dramatically, even more than I had imagined, although Mum had tried to warn me of some of the changes I could expect. Dad converted the dining room into a bedroom come nursery for the two of us as my old bedroom was too small what with my bed, Jenny's cot and everything else that was required for those first few months of her young life. We also turned my former bedroom into a small sitting room where Jenny and I could spend time together if we wanted to be alone, which we rarely did. In those early days I was grateful for all the support and advice I could get in how to bring up a new baby. Carol may not have been my birth mother but there wasn't much she didn't know or wasn't able to advise me about in those first few weeks of my becoming a mum.

She came in to our room one day when I was struggling with Jenny's nappy.

"Certain things may have changed, Mary, what with modern technology and ideas for bringing up babies, but one thing that never changes is the shape of their bottom, along with the need to clean them and change them. It's not so much the folding of the nappy that's the problem, but more in trying to keep baby from wriggling free when you're attempting to put it on." With that she took hold of Jenny's legs and, raising them in the air, positioned her bottom onto the nappy and proceeded to wrap it around my daughter in one self-assured move, pinning it seamlessly into place. Whilst still wriggling around in protest Jenny allowed Mum to complete the process without the anger and tears she had displayed during my own inexperienced attempts. Clearly she recognised Mum's confident authority or perhaps it was my own inadequacy that had provoked her earlier remonstrations.

"The thing you need to remember, Mary, is what I said to you on the day we brought Jenny home from the hospital, that precious though babies are they don't break when you handle them." She laughed. "And sometimes you need to handle them quite firmly, as I'm having to do just now." I smiled as I watched my little girl do her best to wrestle herself free from Carol's determined grip as she fought a losing battle to keep Mum from completing the job of securing her clean nappy. Much as changing Jenny wasn't my favourite job I did love to watch a washing line of her clean nappies blowing in the wind to dry. Mum said the same scene had given her a feeling of pride and a job well done when she had watched my nappies flap in the breeze on a sunny day during my baby years.

The greatest lesson I learnt from Mum and Dad during those early days was the gift of unconditional love. It was something they had demonstrated towards me for as long as I could remember and were continuing to display with their unquestionable care and concern for Jenny. As time went on so that same unconditional love took root in me for my own beautiful baby as well. A child conceived perhaps in a moment of irrational thinking and juvenile fumblings on a bedroom floor, but now a living breathing human being in her own right, and one that consumed more and more of my heart and life with each passing day.

In those early weeks of Jenny's life Mum and I spoke at length about how she and Dad had come to adopt me and of the actual circumstances of the adoption process itself. This wasn't so much the detail of why they had decided to adopt as they had already explained that earlier when I first got pregnant, but more the physical procedures and legal requirements necessary for adoption. I hadn't realised before now that they had come to see me, or "view the baby" as the nun's and the agencies had termed it, a few weeks before they had physically taken me from the home. Mum told me they had waited a few months before deciding to adopt once they discovered they couldn't have any children of their own. Also, that in the late 1940s and early '50s the process for adoption had been very different than today.

"It took your dad and I some while to get over the fact we wouldn't be able to have a baby of our own; before that we'd never really thought about adoption." Mum also told me about the lengthy process she and Dad had had to go through and of their being vetted by the various agencies they had approached before finally finding me. I'd never heard of the Catholic Crusade for Orphans and Destitute Children before or the National Adoption Agency as it was called then, but Mum explained in those earlier days these were the traditional routes for prospective adoptee parents to pursue in the hope of gaining a baby or child for themselves.

"We visited a number of homes and institutions before deciding on the one run by the nuns. They appeared to be the most caring, certainly as far as the welfare of the child was concerned, and that was the most important thing to us. We often felt awkward, even guilty at times when looking at pictures of babies or in going into a room full of cots and trying to choose a child for ourselves when we knew they all deserved a loving home." She paused, becoming emotional as the memory overtook her.

"I said to your dad after a while that I couldn't look at any more babies, viewing them as puppies or kittens in a pet shop and trying to decide which one we liked the best. That said, we knew from the moment we saw you that our search was over, it was as if you had been born just for us to love."

We smiled at each other for a moment with tears filling our eyes as we shared an embrace that said so much more than words could ever do.

"It might sound silly, but I said to your dad when I held you in my arms that first time it felt as though God had healed the heartache I had been holding onto for so long after learning we couldn't have children of our own. Far from being a substitute for the little girl we had lost we knew he had given you to us as a special gift, a precious new life to love and cherish in every way."

As she was talking I was reminded of the first time I had held Jenny in my arms and even though the circumstances of our becoming mothers had been very different the maternal bond we shared in that moment as we held each other close felt no less real. As we regained our composure Mum explained that following their decision to adopt me and after filling in all the various paperwork and gaining the necessary permissions and clearances from the differing agencies and authorities they were finally allowed to take me home.

"Did you ever see her or meet her, my birth mother?"

"No we never did. In fact we were told it wasn't a good idea for her or for us. The nuns said she was just a poor girl who had got herself into trouble and couldn't keep her baby.

They said she didn't want to keep you either and was grateful that we would take you on and that you would be going to a home where you could be cared for properly. So no, we never knew who she was, never wanted to if I'm honest, but I still thank her every day for bringing you into our lives. Apparently, many of the babies put up for adoption at that time were born to young girls who had got pregnant by mistake and had no husband or family to care for them. Even if they did, what with rationing still in place there was little money left to feed an extra mouth. And sadly a number of these young girls would have been rejected by their own parents and told to leave home and make their own way in life after bringing such shame on the family. Others might have been girls who had turned to prostitution to bring some money in and of course they didn't have access to the pill in those days so any idea of contraception would probably have been left to the man." Mum smiled at me. "And as you know yourself with Gerry, most of them keep their brains in their trousers and so are more interested in having their five minutes of fun than they are in giving any thought to the girl or the consequences of getting her pregnant."

I'd never really thought about how different things had been for girls back then. I tried to imagine for a moment how I might have coped if I had found myself in those circumstances. I looked at Mum and felt ashamed as I recalled those "five minutes of fun" Gerry and I had had which led to my own pregnancy. Mum took my hand, aware of my embarrassment.

"I wasn't trying to make you feel guilty, Mary. I'm sure it was the same with you and Gerry, with him assuring you that everything would be okay right up to the moment you told him you were pregnant. Then no doubt he decided it was all your fault?

His father certainly looked to blame you if you remember when we spoke to him about Gerry helping out with the costs of bringing up his baby."

I nodded sheepishly, acknowledging my part in letting Gerry go so far but also aware that if I hadn't I wouldn't have my beautiful daughter now.

"The fortunate thing for you, Mary, is that you had your Dad and I to stand by you, but in those earlier days when babies were born outside of marriage attitudes and circumstances were often very different. You have to remember this was just a few years after the war and a lot of men had to find work wherever they could which often meant them travelling a long way from home. Then while they were away, and with men being men, they would get themselves involved with a young girl locally, not thinking about her again once they went home to their families, not until she declared herself pregnant that is. Then of course they would run a mile, not wanting the emotional or financial responsibility of a baby, especially if they already had a girlfriend, or perhaps even a wife back at home."

I looked at Mum, knowing she was trying to ease my concerns and say something positive in defence of my own mother even though she had no reason to. I counted my blessings in having such caring and understanding parents and knew they couldn't love me more if they had actually been my birth parents. "Thanks Mum."

It was good to spend time talking together as we exchanged experiences about motherhood and in bringing up our respective daughters. We spoke again about my adoption and how the nuns had said they would expect to see my own mother back at the home within a couple of years with yet another unwanted mouth to feed. I was shocked to think this might be true and began to wonder perhaps if I had a brother or sister somewhere that I didn't know about. Mum said in the late 1940s and early '50's about twenty-five thousand babies a year were born to young girls like my mother, and that the vast majority of those children would find themselves put up for adoption. Some girls apparently even tried to sell their babies just to make a bit of money on which to survive after living rough on the streets or in the appalling slum conditions that many of them had to endure in those days. Mum said she was grateful that she and Dad hadn't met my birth mother because if she had proved to be as the nun's portrayed her, careless and heartless, they might have looked at me through different eyes and have been put off the idea of adopting me altogether, viewing it as more of a business transaction rather than the act of love they had intended.

"I know that might sound silly and that we shouldn't determine our attitude towards others simply by what we're told or presume to know about them, but sadly as human beings that's something we do all too readily in every walk of life and often to our regret and shame."

As I sat there listening to her, my mind racing with the many thoughts and questions I had never truly considered or asked before, I realised I did want to know the truth about the circumstances of my birth, and not just for Jenny's sake but also for my own. And who knows perhaps even for her, this woman I had never known nor met but who had brought me into the world, a world that was becoming increasingly fractured and distorted for me. This despite all the love and assurances I had been given, and continued to receive, from both Mum and Dad. I realised no matter what was said by others to comfort and reassure me, I did still need to hear for myself the true circumstances of how this young girl had become pregnant and brought me into the world. Also whether, as the nuns had intimated, she had been pleased to see me go or had cried out in protest as I was taken from her as I certainly would have done if my beautiful Jenny and I had been parted in such a dramatic way.

Much as I knew I was loved by James and Carol a part of me suddenly felt bereft, as though I had lost my true identity. I needed to know who I was, along with how and why I'd come to be in this world. I also knew that if Jenny ever asked me similar questions in the future about her own birth I would want to be able to answer her, not only with honesty, but also with facts. I realised without actually meeting this woman and talking to her I would never really hold those truths, either for myself, or for Jenny should she ever want to hear them. I felt a sudden, almost, irrational panic to discover the truth. I knew if I didn't grasp this opportunity I might lose it forever, along with the answers to so many unspoken and vital questions that where now demanding their answers.

Carol struggled initially with my decision to seek out my mother but softened after a while, becoming more relaxed in her attitude as she accepted my need for information. I think she also understood this wasn't about my wanting to build a separate relationship with this other woman or, worse perhaps, that I might consider moving away altogether to be nearer to her, it was more in being able to understand the truth about my own birth, and as to why I had been given away at such a young age. If I could gain the answers to these and other unresolved questions I might be able to find a renewed sense of inner peace and belonging, not only in my relationship with her and Dad but within myself. This wasn't about my wanting to leave but more about my truly coming home and finally being settled, both as their daughter and as mother to Jenny myself.

"I'll never stop loving you and Dad or want to stop being your daughter, but for all our sakes I need to know the truth."

"I know, sweetheart. It's just tough for your dad and I. Old as you are, you're still our little girl, and…" Her voice cracked. "We just don't want to lose you, that's all."

I tried to lighten her mood. "As if? You're stuck with me now whether you like it or not. After all where else am I going to find a couple of live-in babysitters when I want to go out with my friends?"

She laughed. "That's the Mary we've come to know and love."

We smiled and held hands in silent recognition that, whilst the fabric of our relationship might be about to change, the love and commitment we had for each other would stand for all time.

"Please trust me, Mum," I said, pulling back a little. "I never want to leave what Jenny and I have here; you and Dad mean everything to both of us." My body shivered involuntarily as I shrugged my shoulders. "I just…" It was my turn to be at a loss for words.

She looked at me with tears filling her eyes. "I know love, it's alright. You do what you need to; the two of us will always be here for you; for the both of you."

As I walked back to my room I became acutely aware this had been a truth I had secretly wanted to know from the first day I had discovered, even as a young girl, that I had been adopted. I hadn't been able to express it then of course, nor in the years that followed; not until today. I wasn't sure whether it had been from fear of hurting Mum or Dad or in my potentially hearing something that might upset me, but none of that bothered me now. Mum had given me her and Dad's approval and permission to seek answers to those very real questions that had burnt within me for so long and I knew I couldn't let the opportunity pass me by. I also knew that, whilst I was no longer afraid of asking those difficult questions, I still had to be prepared for the answers. Was I truly ready for what she might have to say or what I might discover? I felt my body like my courage quake a little as I made my way upstairs. But even with these slight misgivings running through my head I was still determined to grasp this chance and finally face those dark recurring thoughts and ghosts that had troubled me for so many years; prayerfully laying them to rest once and for all. I took a deep breath as I recognised that in having taken this first tentative step, there was no turning back now.

TWELVE

Mr. Taylor sent a car for me on the first day I began working for his family. I was grateful for this as I had envisaged having to carry my case and other belongings half way across town on the bus. Mrs Taylor was at the door to greet me. She wore a bright yellow dress with a pristine white cardigan buttoned up at the front. I noticed her hair fell free beyond her shoulders and down her back, very different from our first meeting when she had worn it swept up high. She looked equally as beautiful as before and I envied her her natural good looks and confident manner.

"Leave your case here in the hall for a moment, Ruth, and come through to the sitting room where I have a pot of tea waiting."

The sitting room itself was warm and welcoming with two large arm chairs set either side of a polished marble fireplace which had a clock placed in the centre along with a few family photographs on either side. The sun shone through a long window opposite and threw a bright and cheery glow across the deep blue carpet which felt soft and giving beneath my feet. Mrs Taylor gestured for me to sit as she poured the tea.

"We hope you will be very happy living here with us, Ruth, dear, as I am sure we will be with you. I have taken the liberty of placing a small posy of flowers in your room to welcome you, I hope you like them?"

"Thank you, that's very kind."

Although Mrs Taylor couldn't have been friendlier in her welcome I still felt my back stiffen with nerves as I sought to present myself in the best possible light to my new employer.

"I have arranged for Elizabeth to play with a friend who lives nearby after finishing school today so as to allow you time to unpack and meet the rest of the staff. Hopefully you will be able to settle in a little before she arrives home and assumes full control of your time as she surely will. She is very excited about you joining us; indeed she hasn't stopped talking about you since your first visit. She has already made a list of games she wants to play with you along with all of the names of her dolls so you can learn them." Mrs Taylor placed a cup of tea on the small side table next to my chair.

"Elizabeth is a lovely little girl, Ruth, as you will discover for yourself. However, she can also be rather dominant at times, often demanding her own way, especially when faced with the prospect of an alternative idea to a suggestion or proposition of her own. She is quite happy to stand her ground no matter how reasonable that suggestion or request may have been expressed to her."

I smiled, feeling slightly embarrassed and not really knowing how to respond as I lifted the cup to my lips. Mrs Taylor sensed my nerves and affirmed me with a smile of her own.

"I tell you this because I want you to know from the start that you have our full blessing to exercise your own wisdom and authority with regards to such matters or indeed to any differences of opinion that may arise between the two of you. This is particularly true regarding issues such as an appropriate time for bed, or as to how much jam she is allowed to spread on her toast. Elizabeth always takes too much and then ends up spreading it on herself or her clothing rather than on the bread itself. Her dresses tend to spend more time in the wash than they do on her."

I smiled again, sipping at my tea, still a little unsure as how best to react.

"Thank you and I'll remember what you've said. Hopefully we will get along well."

"I'm sure you will but she also needs to know from the outset that you are the adult in the relationship. With that in mind, please do feel free to approach either Robert or myself for a final decision about any particular issue or concern you may have with Elizabeth should you find yourself at loggerheads with her on some occasion or if she becomes overtly difficult or demanding in some way. To be honest, and between you and I, you would be better to speak to me whenever possible as Robert can be rather autocratic when dealing with concerns over Elizabeth. He tends to forget she is a little girl and not one of his bank employees willing to respond with due deference to his every whim and instruction." She laughed as if to reassure me.

"But I'm sure none of that will be necessary with you, Ruth, as I have no doubt you and Elizabeth will soon set about building your own bond of trust and respect for each other. It will probably be Robert and I who will feel left out with the two of you plotting against us."

"We would never do that, I am sure. I wouldn't dream of doing anything to displease you or go behind your back in any way, Mrs Taylor, I promise you."

"I am sure you wouldn't, Ruth, I was only joking with you. Indeed I am hopeful you will prove to be the sobering influence on our daughter that I feel she has required for some time now."

"I'll certainly do my best for you both, and for young Elizabeth."

"Of that I'm sure, my dear, but I am equally convinced there will be days when Elizabeth, no matter how sweet she may appear to be, may also become rather too possessive or demanding of your time. And so I am simply saying that on such occasions you have the right to say no to her. Mrs Bradley, our previous nanny had exuded the same confidence as you when she first joined us, but soon became grateful for the authority afforded her with regards to having the final say over some of our daughter's, occasionally, unreasonable demands. Although, as I say I am hopeful that won't prove to be the case with you, but one can never quite dismiss the possibility where our dear Elizabeth is concerned." She smiled at me again. "That said, she is an absolute joy to be around for much of the time as you will discover for yourself. It is just that she also needs reminding of certain boundaries within a relationship from time to time. This is part of the reason Robert and I decided on trying for another baby so that she will come to realise the world does not simply revolve around her." She laughed again. "Mind you, to see Robert with her at times you might be forgiven in wondering as to which one of them is actually the grown up? She appears able to wrap him around her finger whenever she chooses despite his protestations. I wonder at times if it's because he feels guilty for not spending more time with her through the demands of his work, or as I said earlier it is more the fact that she doesn't respond to him in the manner that one of his employees at the bank might? Whichever it is I do feel Elizabeth has a much better grasp on the rules of engagement within their relationship at times than he does, only please don't tell him I said that."

The two of us laughed together sharing the humour of the moment.

"I really do think we are going to get on very well you and I." She smiled at me again, placing her cup and saucer on the tray and getting to her feet. "

"Now, don't let me keep you any longer, or Elizabeth will be home and you won't even have had time to unpack your case." She moved to a chord hanging by the mantle above the fireplace and pulled on it. A few moments later there was a knock on the door and Nelly entered, bright and bubbly as ever. "You rang, Mrs Taylor?"

"Yes, thank you, Nelly. This is Ruth our new nanny; I think the two of you met when she came for her interview?"

"Yes, Mam."

"That's good. Please would you show her to her room and then take her downstairs to meet the rest of the staff once she's unpacked her belongings?"

Mrs Taylor offered me her hand and I remember thinking how soft her skin was.

"I'll speak to you soon Ruth and certainly once Elizabeth gets home."

Nelly winked at me as we left the room and nodded towards the front door.

"Don't forget your case."

"Thanks."

I smiled to myself as I picked up my case and walked towards Nelly who was waiting for me at the foot of the stairs. "What would Mama and Papa say if they could see me now," I thought, "a nanny to a rich family in a big London house?" I heard Nelly's voice waken me from my daydream.

"You coming or what?"

"Sorry, I was just thinking about something."

We started our climb together up the winding stairs; they were so wide that we were able to walk side by side. The plush stair carpet was a deep red with different coloured swirls in it and very different from the almost threadbare covering on the narrow creaky stairs at my bedsit.

"She's alright is Mrs T. You do right by her and she'll do right by you."

Nelly appeared to refer to everyone by their surname initials alone.

"What about Mr Taylor?"

"Bit of a stuffed shirt, if you ask me. Still I suppose that's what bank managers are like, you know, full of their own importance and not caring much about the likes of you and me." She stopped for a moment. "To be honest I don't have a lot to do with him. The only person he seems to bother with is Mr D, his driver, and he can be a bit of a bugger at times. Mind, Mrs D is lovely and a smashing cook an' all." She smiled as we continued our climb. "Get on the right side of her and you'll never go hungry, nor want to either, what she can't cook ain't worth eating believe me."

"I've already tasted one of her cakes when I was here for my interview so I know what you mean, it was delicious."

We reached my door which was set to the side of the landing at the very top of the stairs. "Here you go. Ruth, wasn't it? This is your room." She laughed. "Nice little room it is and all, but I'm glad it ain't mine what with all them stairs to go up and down all the time, you'll be knackered before you start with her ladyship I can tell you."

"Her ladyship?"

"Yeah, you know, young Elizabeth. She's a lovely kid alright, but she ain't half got a mouth on her, especially if she doesn't get her own way." Nelly blew out her cheeks. "You've got your work cut out there once she gets to know you I can tell you. She'll get the measure of you in five minutes flat and then you'll know all about it."

I smiled, feeling slightly less confident than I had five minutes ago in the sitting room. "Mrs Taylor did say she can be a bit boisterous at times."

"Boisterous! Well that's one way of putting it. More like a ruddy little whirlwind if you ask me. Mind, she does love her mum and tries to keep *her* happy at least. It's the rest of us she winds up. It's like she knows we can't say anything to her, not unless we fancy her dad telling us off. Honest, if you upset her and he gets wind of it he'll give you a right ear-bashing I can tell you."

"She seemed lovely when I met her the first time I was here, we played quite happily together."

"I bet Mrs T was there?"

"Yes, for some of the time, but she left us alone for a while as well."

Nelly smiled again as she opened the door. "Well maybe you've got something the rest of us ain't then if she was good for you. Anyway, I'll leave you to get sorted, see you later."

"Thanks, Nelly. Yes, I'll see you later."

I watched her for a moment as she disappeared down the first flight of stairs and out of sight before entering my room and closing the dark brown door behind me. It certainly was an attic room as Mrs Taylor had described it to me earlier, having a slope at one side of the ceiling and a beam of wood stretching between the joists at the other. This ran the full length of that particular side of the room. A single bed was situated along the wall directly under the beam with a small brown wooden bedside table placed next to it. The bed had a pink candlewick bedspread covering it and there was a lamp on the table with a colourful flowery shade which had little cream tassels hanging from it all the way round. The wall behind the bed was decorated with similarly patterned wallpaper to the lamp shade; something I felt added a feminine touch to the room along with the pink bedspread. The rest of the walls were painted white with the brown door standing out rather starkly against them. There was a single, equally dark brown wardrobe standing near to the door, also making its mark against the white background. On the floor was a green patterned rug surrounded by highly polished floor boards. I placed my small case and bag containing my worldly goods on the bed and stood for a moment taking in my new surroundings. Once again my thoughts returned to Birkenau and how, not so very long ago, there would have been a dozen or more of us forced to sleep in a space this size and with none of the basic luxuries such as the bedding and floor covering that were set before me now. I felt tears in my eyes as I rejoiced in the fact that this room, small though it was, was all mine and, even better, had a door that I alone had the power to decide whether it was open or closed. I had lived away from Birkenau for some time now, and had enjoyed the luxury of sleeping in clean sheets and a proper bed both at Mrs Goldblum's and on occasion at the Blyth's but nothing could detract from the joy of having the freedom to choose who came into my room or not. This never failed to delight me in a way that is almost impossible to describe. I had felt the same way to a certain extent about my small bedsit prior to joining the Taylor's, but now I had somewhere I had been given permission to genuinely call my own and without the threat of a landlord coming in whenever he chose to check that everything was alright. Mrs Taylor had told me it was up to *me* who came into this room and that I could spend time there on my own as I wished and yet I wasn't living in isolation, I could also enjoy the benefits of being under the same roof as others who actually wanted me there, not for my rent or to threaten my life at every turn as the Germans had done but because I mattered to them. It was such a simple pleasure and one taken for granted by so many, but it was a privilege that would never be lost on me again.

As I unpacked my case I said a little prayer of thanks for how far I had come in so short a time, and how distant the nightmare of Birkenau appeared to be from where I found myself today. I was struck a stark reminder of how much life had changed for me as I placed a picture of my parents, Joseph and myself on the small table beside my bed. A neighbour had found the picture, taken some years earlier before our move to Guernsey, in her home and had given it to me on my return to London after the war as a memory of happier times. That picture took pride of place on my little table and I looked at it every night as it sat by my bed reminding me, as it did, of the family I had loved and lost in the horror of that awful concentration camp. Whilst I understood that I no longer had my brother and parents physically present in my life, I also knew they would remain forever in my heart. I kissed their faces as I placed the photograph by my bed, determining to make them proud of me as I proved myself in this new position and settled into my new surroundings. As I hung my clothes in the small wardrobe and sorted out the rest of my things I spoke to my parents and told them about my new job, and how I would do my best to uphold the family ethic of hard work and maintaining a caring attitude when addressing the needs of others. This was something they had instilled into Joseph and me from an early age. I remembered how Mama had cared for our friends and neighbours when I was younger; how she would make a cake for them or share what we had if she knew they were struggling. She and Papa set an example for Joseph and I to follow and I was determined to honour their name and that family tradition as best I could in the days and weeks ahead.

I finished unpacking and, looking around my room once more, smiled to myself as a sense of anticipation and excitement swept over me. It felt similar to the day I had walked away from Birkenau when fresh opportunities and a new road to travel had lain before me. As was the case then I had no idea where this particular journey might end but it was one I was eager to make. As I stood there my eyes were drawn once more to the photograph of my family.

"I won't let you down."

I was placing my empty suitcase on top of the wardrobe when Nelly knocked at the door.

"Mrs T said you might like another cuppa. Serves me right for laughing about you having to go up and down these stairs all the time, she must have heard me and sent me back up here as a punishment. Mind it'll probably be cold by now." She laughed as she handed me the tea. It was good to see her again and I hoped we might become friends both at work and in our own time as well. I hadn't had a real friend since losing Sarah and although Nelly was very different in character I still felt she was someone I could become close to and trust. We talked for a few moments and she told me of some of the unspoken house rules shared amongst the staff with regards to our employers.

"Always try and keep out of Mr. T's way if he appears distant or grumpy and make sure you keep Elizabeth out of his way an' all if he's in a huff 'cause Mrs T doesn't like her to see her daddy upset or in a bad mood. Although to be fair when Elizabeth is around he does his best to be sweetness and light, at least in front of her, but it's best to be aware all the same."

"Does he often lose his temper?"

"He's alright most of the time, it's just the odd occasion he seems to go off on one and we can't seem to do right for doing wrong. I've heard Mrs T having a go at him over his moods a couple of times, but like I say you just keep your head down and do your job."

"They don't seem like a couple who argue though; they were really nice to each other when I talked to them earlier. She even teased him a bit."

"Don't get me wrong, most of the time everything's hunky dory it's just sometimes you can tell Mr T's not happy and so we try and ignore it. She knows we know but never says anything apart from sticking up for him. Just says he's under pressure at work or whatever, she'll never admit to their falling out. Defends him to the hilt she does. I do remember saying to her once how Mr T seemed to be unhappy about something and asked if there was anything I could do to help? She tore me off a right strip. More embarrassed I think that I'd overheard them arguing but also letting me know in no uncertain terms that my job was to be their maid and not to get involved in family discussions or in how they should be as a couple. That wasn't like her at all. I could see she was upset and so I said sorry if I'd caused any offence. I think she knew I hadn't meant any harm and said sorry herself for being short with me. Mind, I did overhear her later telling Mr T that I'd heard them and that he should keep his voice down in future if they were having a disagreement, especially if any of us were around. She really loves him though you can see that. I think in the main they're happy enough, same as the rest of us I guess."

"Thanks Nelly, I'm grateful for the advice. I'll certainly keep an eye on Elizabeth if I sense any misgivings between the two of them, especially over the next few months with the new baby due and Mrs Taylor likely to have the odd day when she might not be feeling herself."

"Good for you, she'll appreciate that. She always likes to protect Elizabeth from any sort of upset. She says she's a gentle soul at heart even if she does rule the roost at times with the odd tantrum, so you keeping her away from any signs of trouble or argie bargies between Mr and Mrs T is a good idea. Although like I say she's normally as sweet as they come, it's just him you need to watch out for, especially if he's had a long day at the bank." Nelly laughed. "We just keep smiling and saying "yes sir, no sir" until he cheers up, and then it's all back to normal. Bit like any family I reckon."

Although I was saddened to hear the Taylor's had their differences I also knew, as Nelly had said, that such occasional disagreements were indeed a part of normal family life. I could well remember my own parents arguing on occasion, especially if my father had promised to be at the table with the rest of us for a family meal only to be late because he had been busy at work and had lost track of time.

My mother would tell him off and complain that mealtimes were an important occasion for the family to share food and spend time together. And whilst my father would, in the main, agree and apologise for his tardiness, he could also become irritated if he felt my mother was berating him unfairly, or if he was having a particularly challenging time with one of his customers. Then he might bite back and defend himself, saying that if he didn't work so hard there wouldn't be any money to put food on the table in the first place. He knew he was in the wrong of course but, as with most husbands, he didn't enjoy being put in his place by his wife, especially in front of his children. Joseph and I would retreat to our rooms on these rare occasions knowing that almost as soon as an argument had begun it would blow over again with both my parents apologising to each other, and assuring Joseph and I that all was well. "Just because your father and I disagree at times doesn't mean that we don't love each other, and more especially the two of you." Then when she and I were on our own she would say to me with a smile on her face, "Men like to think they hold the answer to everything, Ruth, but they learn eventually that it is us women who really know what is best, although they would never admit to that of course. Remember that if you ever get married, my dear."

Joseph and I knew with absolute certainty that we were loved and never doubted our parents' feelings towards us even during those rare times of unrest or family disagreements. I had always presumed that to be true for most families and so was not unduly concerned by Nelly's remarks about my new employers. However, I also acknowledged the obvious sense in my being aware of how best to react if I were to experience a family dispute, certainly as far as my duty of care towards Elizabeth was concerned.

I followed Nelly downstairs, cup and saucer in hand as we made our way to the kitchen.

"Come on I'll introduce you to Mrs D."

Mrs Devlin struck me immediately as good-natured and welcoming, her thick Irish accent oozing warmth as she spoke.

"Welcome to the mad house, Ruth, I'm sure you'll fit in just lovely so you will." She was everything I imagined a household cook to be from books I had read in the past: wise, friendly and passionate about her kitchen and also, not overly tolerant of unwelcome visitors when she was preparing a meal, as I discovered to my cost on a couple of occasions in the weeks ahead. That said, I quickly learnt this lesson and we soon formed an easy relationship between the two of us. She had a kind, almost maternal nature and so it wasn't long before I sought out, and readily accepted, both her wisdom and advice as to how I might best contribute personally to the continued smooth running of the house, along with its demands and daily routine.

As we were talking Mr Devlin entered the kitchen carrying a pair of shoes. "Have you seen the polish," he demanded, ignoring Nelly and I as he held the shoes up in front of his wife.

"Not since you last had it no. And would you please not wave those mucky things around in my kitchen while I'm preparing food."

Mr. Devlin turned to leave.

Mrs Devlin shook her head, wiping her hands on her flour covered apron. "And before you go you can say hello to young Ruth here, she's to be the new nanny to little Elizabeth."

He turned, glancing in my direction as he left the room. "We've already met."

"Of course you have." She shook her head again. "You see, Ruth, I told you this was a mad house. I couldn't even manage to remember that you'd already experienced the delights of meeting himself earlier when he picked you up. I hope he was polite?"

"He was very polite." This was not entirely true as I remembered he hadn't exactly gone out of his way to make me feel welcome when he'd arrived at my lodgings to collect me.

"That's just as well for him then, or he'd have had me to answer to so he would." She waved her rolling pin in mock protest towards the door that Mr Devlin had just exited. The three of us talked together for a few minutes and I asked Mrs Devlin if there was anything in particular I should know about Elizabeth's diet when planning her meals.

"You leave all of that to me, my dear," she said with a knowing smile across her face. "Mrs Taylor and I have a very clear understanding about that young lady's eating arrangements."

"That sounds like there might be a problem?" I was immediately concerned that Elizabeth may have some special dietary needs that I should be aware of.

"The only problem young Elizabeth has as far as her eating habits are concerned is that she would rather consume sweets and puddings all day than vegetables and savoury dishes. Her mother worries that she has too sweet a tooth, but I tell her she's no different to any other child." She smiled, patting her own fuller figure. "And perhaps some of us grown ups as well. I mean who wants a plate of greens and carrots staring up at them when they know there's a nice big cherry pie and custard waiting in the wings?" We all laughed.

"I'll keep an eye on her."

"The only other thing I would ask is that you keep young Elizabeth away from my kitchen when I am preparing the meals themselves. I would hate for there to be an accident with hot food around."

"Of course."

"That said, she does like to come down and help me bake on occasion and, little madam though she can be at times, I do still enjoy spending time with her. That is when I'm not too busy and I have advance warning that she's coming."

"That sounds fun. What sort of things do you cook together?"

"Simple things like fairy cakes or scones for Mr Taylor for when he comes home from work. She likes to please her father, as we all do." She smiled knowingly at Nelly.

"I'll look forward to that. I love cooking myself; maybe you'll let me help as well?"

Mrs Devlin looked at me, her face taking on a more serious expression. "You've heard the term too many cooks?"

I nodded nervously.

"Well I'm sure that won't apply to you, Ruth," she said, her broad smile quickly returning. "You'll always find a welcome in my kitchen so you will. Just remember the same rule applies to everyone in the house when I'm preparing hot food: don't get in my way."

"I certainly will remember that, Mrs Devlin, I promise. And with young Elizabeth as well."

As Nelly and I walked back upstairs we talked about how different Mr and Mrs Devlin were in their personalities and general demeanour.

"Maybe he's got a lot on his mind just now," I said, attempting to defend Mr Devlin's less than sunny disposition.

"No he's always like that. Mind, I do feel a bit sorry for him at times. He used to have his own garage but it got into trouble so he had to sell up and he had no work for a while."

"That can't have been easy?" I remembered how my own father had felt when the Germans took control of his tailoring business.

"It wasn't. Mrs D used to come to work and say how worried she was about him, or that they'd had a disagreement because he felt he wasn't doing his bit to help with bills while she was working here every day to support the both of them."

"How did he get his job here?"

"Mr Taylor's previous driver left and he needed a replacement fairly quickly as he was always going to different meetings for the bank and the like. So Mrs D suggested Mr D and Mr T said he would give him a month's trial to see how they got on." Nelly paused for a moment. "He found that hard at first. You know, after having had his own business and being the one giving out the orders and so on. And now here he was just a driver and on a month's trial an' all for good measure."

"He must have done okay though, he's still here?"

"Yes, Mr T liked him and they got on right from the start what with him having some idea about business and finance having worked for himself in the past. It meant he understood straight away how important it was to be on time for meetings and in making a good impression and the like. In a way though that made it worse for him, at least early on, 'cause it only emphasised again he was now just a driver and Mr T was the one calling all the shots and telling him what to do."

"At least he was working again."

"Yeah, and it's alright now, but like I say it weren't to start with. Him and Mrs D had more than a few words about it I can tell you."

I felt for Mr Devlin and understood how difficult it would have been for him, certainly early on, in losing both his business and his status in the community. I could hear my mother's voice trying to comfort Papa after the Germans had forced him to work for them, often for nothing, and then eventually when they took the business away from him completely. They offered no acknowledgement of the effort he had put into establishing it nor did they give any thought as to some form of recompense in payment towards the customer loyalty and goodwill he had built up over the years. I recalled how low his feeling of self worth had become as he struggled to provide for his family and maintain some degree of dignity as he battled against the unrelenting grip and dictate of the German authorities. I hoped Mr Devlin would eventually be able to fully appreciate his new position rather than deride it as he had appeared to do at the beginning. After all his life wasn't under physical threat as had been the case with my father. Perhaps one day I would have the chance to share these thoughts with Mr and Mrs Devlin? For now though I resolved to remember them in my prayers, along with my heart felt thanks for this new challenge and fresh start in my own life; one that I was truly looking forward to fulfilling in the days ahead.

I really enjoyed those first few weeks with the Taylor's and my time spent with Elizabeth. Mrs Taylor especially appeared pleased with my work and always smiled with approval whenever Elizabeth told her of some great adventure we had been on together, even if it was only the result of a simple game we had been playing.

"Elizabeth has certainly taken a shine to you, Ruth. In fact I think she enjoys your company at times almost more than she does mine."

I knew she was joking, but it was still a nice thing to say and I took it as a compliment. I certainly felt as though Elizabeth and I were developing a strong bond between us.

She would often entrust me with her childish secrets and confidences, although I was equally aware she shared many of these seemingly important stories with her mother as well. I was also encouraged by the fact she didn't appear threatened by the growing depth of our relationship, nor of my growing affection for her daughter. Indeed, she would often comment how good it was that Elizabeth felt able to trust me enough to confide in me so readily. This would prove especially true at the end of the day during

Elizabeth's bath or at bed time when Mrs Taylor would become tired, and perhaps not best able to demonstrate the necessary focus and attention demanded by Elizabeth when recounting the detail of her busy day for the umpteenth time. She knew I would happily pass on these ostensibly vital facts from her daughter's bath time ramblings at a time when she was less exhausted. This would often prove the case during the latter stages of her pregnancy and as the day predicted for the birth itself became ever closer.

There were occasions during those early weeks in working for the Taylor's, and as I became more deeply involved with my new responsibilities in caring for Elizabeth, that I could allow the horrors of the past to fade from my mind almost completely. This was partly due to the demands of my work occupying so much of my thinking, but also as I began to feel a sense of personal well-being and confidence returning. I could never forget the past entirely of course, with night time often proving the hardest. I would lie in bed staring at the picture of my parents and Joseph, remembering all we had experienced and suffered together. But even here I felt I was beginning to make a start in releasing myself from some of the worst memories and pain associated with our time in Birkenau. Just a few months ago it had been something that had so readily occupied my every waking thought but was now slipping further away from my mind as the daily demands and delights of my new job began to take greater prominence in my life. I still held that picture close to my chest each night though as I prayed for my family, thanking God for them and for the blessing he had bestowed on me in bringing me to this new place of safety, and one I felt was fast becoming home.

My life had changed so much, and seemingly all for the better. What could possibly threaten my future now? I was soon to find out.

THIRTEEN

Jenny spoke to me about Ruth again today, asking if I had discovered any more about her. I told her I hadn't but that Granny and Granddad had said they were happy for me to meet with her if that's what I wanted to do.

"It isn't just about the two of us, Jenny, this is really difficult for them as well. Granny and Granddad have treated me as their own practically all of my life even though they have been aware all along that I wasn't. As for you though, they've known you from the moment you were born. You have and always will be their granddaughter. But now that I've traced my real mother poor Granny and Granddad have to face the truth all over again that I'm not actually their daughter. Our true family bloodline is connected to this other woman and that's what makes it so difficult for the two of them. Also, that she is just as keen to meet with me now as I am in hearing the truth from her about what happened all those years ago when she let me go. None of this is going to be easy for them Jen, we mustn't forget that."

I explained that although James and Carol knew we loved them, things would change now. Also that Granny, especially, was feeling a little scared to think she could perhaps lose a part of her family to another woman, a woman she had no legal right to keep us from meeting and building a relationship with now that I'd decided that's what I wanted to do.

"Having said that, Jen, I want you to know it will only be me that meets with Ruth and talks to her, certainly to begin with. I'm not saying you can't see her at some point, but there are things I need to know for myself as her daughter before we even think about you meeting with her."

"I understand that, Mum, but I am interested to know why she didn't keep you as a baby and put you up for adoption."

"I know that, sweetheart, and that's the very reason I need to talk to her first, so I can decide whether her story is one that I am happy for you to hear."

No matter how much I tried to assure Mum that I would never think of her and Dad as anything other than my parents, there was still an understandable fear in their minds that I might choose to spend more time with Ruth, and by so doing they could lose touch with Jenny in the process. What if we decided to move away and live nearer to her? No amount of reassurance could alter the fact this would change the dynamic of our relationship entirely, potentially destroying the happy family idyll we had come to know and appreciate over the years.

In a way I knew how Mum felt, especially when I looked at Jenny and contemplated anything like that happening between the two of us. What if Gerry suddenly reappeared and decided he did want to be a father to Jenny, demanding access to her, or even worse applying for custody of her? How would I feel or respond to that? My blood ran cold even thinking about it. So yes I understood what Mum was going through, but it still didn't dampen my desire to meet with Ruth, even though I knew from the moment I did it would change my life, indeed all of our lives, forever.

Jenny and I talked together about many things over the next few weeks as I explained in more detail my reasons for wanting to meet with Ruth. Also, how important Mum and Dad were to me, to the both of us, and that they would always be our family.

"I think if anything this has brought us all closer to each

other, more dependent on each other, if that makes sense? Never doubt Granny and Granddad's love for either of us, Jen. You mean everything to them, as you do me. You know that don't you sweetheart?

She gave me a hug. "Yeah of course I do, Mum, I think you're pretty great as well."

Young as she was Jenny always did her best to understand and respond in a way that would encourage me. I felt so proud of my little girl watching her grow, both in her understanding of life and, physically into the pretty young lady she was fast becoming. I well remember her first day at school; she looked so vulnerable, and yet it was me who cried as we parted at the gate, Jenny just smiled and ran in with the other children, laughing as she went. "Goodbye Mummy," she shouted, disappearing into the school building for the first time and demonstrating none of the nervous apprehension I was feeling, my stomach churning with anxiety for her. I was back in the afternoon a full fifteen minutes before the children were due out of their classes and stood waiting nervously in case she hadn't enjoyed herself. I needn't have worried as she ran towards me waving a drawing she'd done and shouting that she couldn't wait to come back the next day and go on the planned nature trail to search for caterpillars and snails.

"It was great, Mum, I really enjoyed it. I'll find a really pretty caterpillar for you tomorrow, I promise."

She settled very quickly at school and soon made many new friends who always seemed to be in and out of our house, so much so that I found myself apologising to Mum and Dad for the endless stream of muddy shoes and little people careering through their home.

"We love having them here, it's what your dad and I always hoped for, a real family home with lots of children playing and having fun together. I promise you, Mary, we enjoy it just as much as they do, don't we, love?"

Dad looked over the top of his newspaper and smiled. "Most of the time."

"Oh shut up, you know we do."

I loved them all the more for that and reminded myself how fortunate I was to be a part of their family, brought up in a home with so much care, love and affection. I resolved once again whatever happened following my meeting with Ruth that James and Carol would always be Mum and Dad to me, and more especially Granny and Granddad to my beautiful daughter.

As Jenny grew Dad became more protective of her, just as he had of me when I was younger.

Once when Jenny brought a young boy, Toby, home for tea Dad began questioning the poor lad about his career choices.

"So what would you like to do when you leave school?"

He was very disappointed to hear young Toby didn't have any concrete plans for life beyond his own birthday party the following week, that and a trip to the cinema to see the latest animated adventure film.

Mum intervened, dragging Dad into the kitchen while Toby and Jenny shared their romantic meal of fish fingers, chips and lemonade.

"He's a young boy, give the lad a chance; he isn't even in long trousers yet."

In the end Dad conceded he might have been a little unreasonable in expecting so much from Jenny's suitor, especially when I pointed out that he was still only six, or at least for the next seven days.

Over the next few years at primary school Jenny excelled on so many levels, but by far her favourite subject was English where her individual creativity was encouraged and flourished as she wrote endless stories, making the best of her vivid imagination and producing a variety of colourful characters and storylines. She always seemed to have her head stuck in one book or another and was forever asking what a particular word meant, words that sometimes I would struggle to explain as I looked on in wonder at this little person growing in so many different ways before me. She had a real appetite for life and was genuinely excited by all it had to offer, always grasping at any opportunity to learn something new that came her way.

Watching Jenny grow along with her passion for learning reminded me of my own time as a youngster and the support I had received from Mum and Dad during my years at school and in my early teens. They had encouraged my interest in so many areas of learning including the arts, literature and even pop music, although they did struggle with my passion for Jimi Hendrix who Dad viewed as no more than a noisy long-haired rebel.

"Is he actually playing that guitar or just tuning it up? It all sounds like a bit of a row to me."

I thanked them again in my mind as I observed and encouraged this same passion for learning and life express itself in Jenny.

It made me realise just how much they had helped and supported me over the years and served to confirm yet again my earlier commitment to honour their efforts on my behalf no matter what sort of relationship I eventually formed with Ruth.

Mum and Dad had readily accepted their roles as grandparents with the same dedication and commitment they had shown as adoptive parents to me, and I was determined they would always have access to Jenny for as long as life allowed. I felt a love for her now that possibly I hadn't fully been aware of in the years previously. In part this might have been because of the previously undeclared insecurities about what had taken place in my own early life, but more so as I came to understand just how precious the people we truly care about are to us. Like Jenny I was continuing to grow and learn new truths about life and people, truths that would hold the both of us in good stead in the years to come. I couldn't bear to think about not having her with me or my not being involved in every aspect of her young life. And now, as a mother myself, I could also understand why Carol was initially so fearful of my meeting with Ruth and of the effect it might have on our own relationship.

"Don't worry, Mum, we'll be fine." I did my best to reassure her that everything would remain the same between us but in reality I couldn't honestly say for sure what the final outcome would be until I actually spent time with Ruth, none of us could.

If truth be told, much as I wanted to talk with her and hear what she had to say, the unspoken fear as to what might actually transpire from the result of our meeting was beginning to unsettle me as much as it was Carol.

FOURTEEN

As the time for Mrs Taylor to give birth grew nearer she became increasingly tired and I was asked to do more and more in helping with Elizabeth's day to day care.

"Thank you, Ruth. You're such a blessing, I don't know what we would do without you."

I didn't mind helping of course, and as my relationship with Elizabeth grew closer each day so did the bond of friendship and trust between us. She would often tell me she loved me, although this display of affection could alter rapidly if I appeared to take her parents side when it came to having an early night or to end a game because a visitor had arrived and her presence was required elsewhere.

"Why do I have to get changed and say hello to Daddy's friend? I'm happy here with you and my dolls."

"Your daddy is very proud of you, Elizabeth, and he wants his friends to see what a clever and pretty girl you are."

"Well you go down and tell them to come up here. I will be just as pretty and clever in my playroom." She would look at me, her big blue eyes pleading for me to take her side. "Please, Ruth, if you're really my friend you won't make me go."

Eventually I would manage to cajole her into going downstairs to say hello or into agreeing to participate in whatever it was her parents wanted her to do. Most of the time we remained the best of friends and despite the occasional difference of opinion usually found some common ground on which to rebuild our relationship. This would often include my sneaking her an extra biscuit or treat for her supper or in agreeing to read her an additional bed time story. Deep down I think Elizabeth knew she could trust me and that at least I would attempt to see her side of things or argue her corner when appropriate, even if I didn't always agree with her motive. Once when she and Mrs Taylor had experienced a falling out over her refusal to do something her mother had requested she came running over to me declaring that she didn't love her Mummy any more.

"She's being horrid to me, Ruth. I want you to be my new Mummy, you tell her."

I explained this would not be possible, and how upset her real Mummy would be if she thought for a moment her little girl didn't really love her.

"Your Mummy loves you so much, Elizabeth. Sometimes mummies and daddies say things or ask us to do something we don't really understand or want to do but it doesn't mean they don't love us or that we should stop loving them. When I was a little girl I got angry with my mummy at times if she wanted me to do something I didn't really want to, but in the end when I did it I always felt better because I had made my mummy happy. And I know that really you want your mummy to be happy as well don't you? She would never ask you to do anything she didn't think was right for you. So why don't you go and say sorry to her? I bet if you do she will say thank you and give you a great big hug."

My young charge stood in front of me, her gaze fixed to the floor considering what I had said and torn between doing the right thing or giving in to her childish petulance. After a few moments she looked up at me. "Alright, Ruth,but I would still like you to be my other mummy as well."

"That's very sweet of you, Elizabeth, and one day if I have

a little girl of my own I hope she will be a lovely as you, but for now I think the mummy you have is the only one you need. I will always be here for you though as a friend, alright?"

"Do you promise?"

"I promise."

Thankfully, Mrs Taylor had been standing outside the room during our conversation and was impressed with my handling of the situation, especially as I had persuaded Elizabeth to apologise, something the previous nanny hadn't been able to achieve despite a number of valiant attempts during her time in service. I suggested that Elizabeth was a little older now and therefore more open to reason, but Mrs Taylor wouldn't hear of it.

"You have made a difference not only in Elizabeth's behaviour and general demeanour, Ruth, but also in her attitude and appreciation of others and their concerns. And that, to us, is every bit as important as her education and learning at school. I assure you that none of what you have achieved with Elizabeth to date has gone unnoticed or unappreciated by Robert and I. We are very grateful to you."

I was touched by her comments and generosity towards me which only served to further confirm my regard for them as a couple, as well of course as my growing affection towards Elizabeth.

Nelly would often tease me about my relationship with the Taylor's, along with my growing list of duties and responsibilities within the house.

"How is Miss Goody Goody today? Has Mrs T asked you to help his lordship at the bank now as well as running the house for her?"

I knew her comments were meant in fun and accepted them as such, often teasing her in return by saying that Mrs Taylor had asked me to have a word with her and tell her she hadn't made the beds properly or cleaned a room in a certain way.

"I'm afraid if you don't make more of an effort to get things right Mr and Mrs Taylor will have to review your employment, or at the very least put me in charge of you to oversee your duties and to make sure your work improves." We would laugh together knowing that neither was serious and that if ever the situation demanded we would both be there to support each other.

Nelly and I became good friends during those first few months and with the added appreciation of my efforts in caring for Elizabeth from my employers to encourage me I quickly settled into life at the Taylor household. Even the horrors of Birkenau continued to fade from my mind and I found myself able to smile at the picture of my parents and Joseph as I got out of bed each morning rather than viewing it merely as a sad reminder of their loss. I would talk to them, telling them about the tasks that lay before and how much I was looking forward to all I had to do in the day ahead. But this new sense of joy and contentment I was experiencing was soon to come crashing down around me.

A few weeks before the baby was due Mr Taylor called me into his study. I was a little unnerved by this request as he didn't usually ask to see me on my own. I knew that Mrs Taylor had gone out with Elizabeth and was concerned perhaps I had done something wrong or upset them in some way and that Mr. Taylor, as head of the house, was going to tell me off or worse, let me go.

I entered his study with a sense of trepidation, immediately apologising for anything I might have done wrong, even though I had no idea as to what it might be. He smiled and reassured me that all was well, adding that both he and Mrs Taylor were so pleased with my work and care for Elizabeth that they had decided to give me a small rise in my pay.

"I know Helen has spoken to you already about how indebted we are to you for all you have achieved with Elizabeth to date. Also for the help and support you have demonstrated towards Helen herself during this difficult time with her pregnancy. That is something for which I am personally very grateful to you for as well. And so after discussing this together we have agreed that as a token of our appreciation and ongoing commitment towards you as your employers we feel it is right to reward you in this way."

I took a deep breath, mainly of relief.

"Thank you, sir, that is very kind. I do feel my work is appreciated and I will continue to do my best for the family and especially Elizabeth."

As we were talking Nelly knocked and entered the room with a tray containing a pot of tea along with two cups and saucers. She winked at me as she placed the tray on a small table by the side of Mr Taylor's chair.

"Would like me to pour the tea sir?"

"No thank you, Nelly, I think we can manage that for ourselves can't we, Ruth?"

I smiled, nodding my agreement but also wishing he had let Nelly do it, assuming it would fall to me to fill the cups and fearing that nerves might get the better of me and I would spill some in the saucer or on the tray.

Nelly curtsied and turned to leave, smiling at me briefly before making her way to the door and closing it behind her.

Mr Taylor leant forward and nodded towards the tea tray. "I wonder if you would mind doing the honours, my dear, tea pots and I don't enjoy the happiest of relationships. I tend to get as much in the saucer as I do the cup, or at least that's what Helen accuses me of."

"Of course." With my suspicions confirmed I nervously placed the cups in the saucers and taking great care slowly poured the tea, thankfully without spilling a drop. I set a cup in front of him before taking my own from the tray.

"Please, my dear," he said, indicating for me to sit opposite him again so we could continue our discussion.

"I trust you are beginning to feel settled here with us, Ruth, and that Elizabeth is not proving too demanding?

"I am very happy thank you, sir and Elizabeth is a delightful little girl. I also appreciate all that you and Mrs Taylor have done for me by taking me into your home. If you feel there is anything more I can do to be of assistance please let me know, especially with the new baby due soon."

Mr Taylor took a sip of his tea before placing the cup back in the saucer and rising. He walked towards the big window that overlooked the garden and stood silently for a few moments before turning to face me again. He smiled.

I wasn't sure how to react so I smiled back in the hope this was the right response to whatever he was about to say.

He walked slowly and deliberately back to his chair before sitting and taking another drink from his cup. Looking directly at me he took a cigarette case from his jacket, then removing one placed it between his lips as he reached into his waistcoat pocket for his lighter with the other hand.

"I trust you don't mind my smoking, Ruth? Helen doesn't really like the habit; she says it leaves an unpleasant odour around the house and especially on Elizabeth's clothing, although I can't really say I have noticed it myself."

I nodded my approval, having neither the right nor an overriding desire to object.

"Of course, sir, although I have never tried it myself, never wanted to really. Neither of my parents smoked and so I think I never really saw the need or the attraction."

This seemed a silly thing to say as his employee as I had no right to comment on whether he chose to smoke in his own house or not, and was only sitting in his study drinking tea at his invitation. Also, the fact that I had never smoked or felt the desire to was clearly of little or no interest to him.

"Wise girl." He smiled. "My wife is probably right but it is a habit I enjoy, at least here in the safety my study where I am safe from her critical eye." He lit the cigarette, drawing on it deeply before slowly exhaling, a large cloud of smoke rising into the air above our heads.

I sat nervously waiting for whatever it was he was about to

say, remembering what Nelly had told me about the times when Mr Taylor's mood could change in an instant. I had never spent time alone with him before and was concerned not to prove a disappointment in whatever it was he was about to discuss with me. Equally, I wanted to remain faithful in my duties to Mrs Taylor and Elizabeth both of whom I had developed a genuine fondness for, and to whom I felt that ultimately my greater loyalty lay.

Mr Taylor took another draw on his cigarette. "So, you are enjoying your duties with us?"

"Yes sir. As I said earlier I am very happy and find Elizabeth to be quite charming. You must be very proud of her?"

He smiled again. "We are." Pausing he looked down at his cigarette before flicking some ash from it into the ashtray next to his cup. "Perhaps I should phrase my question differently."

I felt confused, not sure how to respond but desperate to appear willing if he thought I should be doing more or was falling short of their expectations in some way.

"Is there something else you would like me to do, sir, with Elizabeth perhaps? I truly do want to please you and Mrs Taylor and would hate to think I am failing you in some way."

He sat looking at me for a moment, almost quizzically, which only increased my sense of unease; then finishing his tea he took another long draw on his cigarette. I noticed his hand was shaking slightly as he leant forward to stub out the cigarette in the ash tray.

"Actually there is something else. Although I should add that it doesn't concern Elizabeth. Both my wife and I are in full agreement nobody could do more for her than you are and, for which, as I have already said, we are both entirely grateful."

I smiled by way of thanks for his compliment. "I'm sure I'd be prepared to help in any way I can. I know how busy you both are at the moment and how tired Mrs Taylor gets, especially at the end of the day."

"Thank you, Ruth, that's exactly the response I was hoping for." He stood up and moved to his desk. I smiled again, thankful

I had said the right thing. He sat on the edge of his desk, the light from the window reflecting behind him and throwing a shadow over me. He sat for a few moments without speaking and with the sun behind him I couldn't see his face which unsettled me slightly. After what seemed like an age he leant forward towards me.

"As you quite rightly say my wife does get very tired of late, fully understandable in her present condition of course." He paused. "Perhaps you have noticed a little tension between us recently? Helen and I are both feeling a degree of anxiety about the forthcoming birth and this has led to the occasional difference of opinion between us."

"I have noticed Mrs Taylor has been resting more of late which is quite understandable in her condition but as to any tension between you I am not sure it is my place to comment. Actually I think you have both proved a real example to us all in recent weeks, demonstrating so much patience towards Elizabeth and all of the staff considering everything you are both having to deal with at this time, if I am allowed to say that sir?"

He smiled at me. "That's very kind of you Ruth, but the truth remains that Helen and I have struggled a little in our relationship of late."

I placed my cup and saucer on the tray. "I'm not sure you should be telling me this, sir, if you don't mind my saying. What goes on between you and Mrs Taylor is none of my business. Perhaps I should leave?"

I wasn't sure as to which direction our conversation was headed but was beginning to feel uncomfortable and didn't want to appear to be betraying my relationship with Mrs Taylor by continuing to speak in this way.

"I apologise if I have embarrassed you, Ruth, that was never my intention. Indeed I was hoping to ask for your assistance in helping me to alleviate some of that tension. That is if you are truly of a mind to help?"

Although I couldn't see his expression because of the light

shielding his face his voice and manner appeared calm and reasoned which encouraged my response to be equally relaxed.

"I'm sorry if I spoke out of turn, sir, but the last thing I want to do is to come between you and Mrs Taylor." I sat upright in my chair. "I would be only too willing to help in any way I can, providing of course you feel I have the appropriate skills required?"

He leant forward allowing the shadow to move from his face. He was smiling at me. "Thank you." He rose from the desk and moving back to his chair sat opposite me again.

"Would you like some more tea?"

"Thank you but no. Would you like me to pour you another cup?"

He smiled again and settled back into his chair. "I think like you, Ruth, I have had enough for now."

I was beginning to feel awkward again as I still wasn't sure in which direction our conversation was headed, but tried to rationalise my thinking by telling myself I was worrying unnecessarily. After all, I had never spent any real time on my own with Mr. Taylor before so of course it was only natural that I would feel a little ill at ease. I attempted to look composed but became aware of my right leg beginning to tremble involuntarily as if developing a mind of its own. Mr. Taylor lit another cigarette.

"What I would like you to help me with, Ruth, is something of a personal nature, and one that I don't want either of us to trouble my wife with. As we have agreed already she has more than enough to concern her at this time, especially with the arrival of our new child so imminent."

"Of course, I fully understand." I was trying my best to sound helpful but at the same time panicking inside as to what it was I might be about to agree to. I was anxious that whatever it was I wouldn't fail to please him in my endeavours. I had one other concern that needed to be addressed.

"I am usually given my list of duties by Mrs Taylor. Are you saying that is to change now and that I will be responsible to you over the next few weeks?"

He smiled reassuringly. "Not at all, Helen will still be your first port of call as far as Elizabeth and your other household duties are concerned." He drew again on his cigarette. "I am hoping, as I said that you might be able to help me personally in one particular area, and that we might keep that to ourselves."

I felt a bead of perspiration run down my back as I shifted nervously in my seat, wondering what it was he was about to propose, aware I had already agreed to undertake this additional duty no matter what the cost to me personally. I swallowed hard, sensing my throat becoming dry even though I had just finished my tea.

"Of course, I understand and am happy to assist in any way you see fit, especially if it is going to benefit Mrs Taylor in some way." I watched as he put out his cigarette, his hand shaking slightly again. He looked at me for a moment, then placing his hands on his knees he leant forward again.

"I need you to promise me, Ruth, that this will go no further than the two of us, I want to be very clear about that." I felt another trickle of perspiration run down my back as a sudden sense of foreboding overtook me.

"I'm not sure what it is you want me to say sir. I have already agreed to help you and Mrs Taylor in any way I can. I am happy to retain a confidence between the two of us regarding whatever it is you would like me to do if you feel that to be appropriate. Although I should add that I have always been encouraged by Mrs Taylor to be open and honest in our relationship and so keeping a secret of any sort from her is not something I would agree to lightly."

Mr Taylor sat back in his chair, his voice changing and becoming more authoritative.

"I understand your loyalty, Ruth, and I respect you for that. Traditionally I would never ask you to betray that trust. However,

I would also remind you that it is me who pays your salary each month and so on this occasion I am requesting that you do maintain this confidence and keep it between just the two of us, that's not unreasonable is it?"

I felt trapped and increasingly nervous. He was my employer after all and did indeed pay my wages, but what on earth could it be that demanded such a degree of secrecy between us? I knew that ultimately I had no choice but to agree his terms, but was still surprised by the sudden change in his tone.

"I didn't mean to be disrespectful, sir, please forgive me if I appeared to give that impression." I hesitated for a moment as we looked at each other. "I will do whatever you ask." I forced a smile. "What is it you have in mind?"

He rose from his chair and moved to sit opposite me again on the edge of his desk. I watched as he sat staring at the floor for a moment as if considering how best to continue. It felt as though he was deciding whether he really could trust me to keep the promise of confidence between us I had just agreed to, especially in light of my remarks about the depth of relationship and trust held between Mrs Taylor and myself. After what seemed like an age he looked up, wiping his hands nervously down his trouser leg as he did so.

"You are a very attractive young woman, Ruth, are you aware of that?"

I was shocked and more than a little confused. I didn't know what to say but mumbled something about being grateful for the compliment, even though it wasn't a comment I was used to receiving from my employer. I was feeling increasingly uncomfortable as a very real sense of panic began to overtake me.

"Perhaps I should come back at another time, maybe when Mrs Taylor is here and we can continue our conversation then?" I began to get to my feet when his demeanour changed once more, becoming even more assertive. He stood up and took a step towards me.

"That is exactly what we are not going to do, Ruth." He nodded towards my chair. "Please sit down."

I dropped back into my seat as much from shock as from the order itself. I noticed both his hands were shaking now as he brought them together in front of himself. I felt a shudder run through me as I sat waiting, with increasing anxiety, for whatever it was he was planning to say next.

"I thought we'd already agreed this discussion and its outcome would be between ourselves and that my wife would hear no part of it?" I could feel tears beginning to fill my eyes.

"I'm sorry Mr. Taylor, I hadn't forgotten but I was embarrassed by your remark about my looks and you made me feel nervous."

He looked directly at me before sitting in the chair opposite once more. He smiled as if to reassure me and placed the palms of his hands of the arms of the chair.

"I apologise if I was short," his voice and tone softening. "Listen, my dear, my wife, as we both know, is not entirely herself at the moment and there are certain duties that she is unable to perform that I might traditionally and reasonably expect from her, do you understand?" Although unsure of exactly what it was he was alluding to the very fact he was sharing such personal information only served to unnerve me further. I was beginning to feel uncomfortable in the extreme.

"Mr Taylor I am not sure I really understand what it is you are asking of me but I do know I am not comfortable in you talking with me in this way." I rose to my feet and felt a tear run down my cheek. "I think we should end this conversation now, and you should allow me to go back to my work." He also stood up and, taking a step towards me, grabbed my arm as I turned to leave.

"I think you do understand what I am suggesting my dear, I think you understand only too well," his mood becoming darker as his grip tightened on my arm. "And I would suggest that you consider my request very carefully before demanding to leave, unless of course you are asking to leave my employ as well?"

I gasped in almost total disbelief, a real sense of indignation and anger growing inside of me as the full implication of what he was proposing took hold, also as to his threat to my continued employment if I didn't agree to his request. I wrenched my arm from his grasp.

"Are you seriously suggesting I should take the place of Mrs Taylor in your marital bed?" I felt my body tremble as I blurted out the words with both fear and rage burning inside me.

He took a step back, his voice moderating in tone as he attempted to assuage my obvious revulsion at his suggestion.

"That is exactly what I am proposing, Ruth. After all we have already agreed between us how tired Helen is of late and so is therefore unable to carry out a number of the usual duties that might be expected of her as my wife. Of course, as her husband I would be quite within my rights to demand these physical services but, in an effort to ease the burden on her, I am choosing not to."

I could see he was grinning at me although his full facial expression appeared slightly out of focus with the tears in my eyes blurring my vision.

"All I am suggesting, for now at least, is that you help Helen in this particular area by removing one less responsibility from her shoulders. Remember, you have already professed a desire to assist in whatever way you can, and so in a way I am not asking anything of you that you have not already shown an appetite for."

I stuttered in disbelief. "I am prepared to do whatever I can to help you as a family of course, but I never thought for one moment you might suggest something like this."

I took a deep breath, determining to reject his suggestion even if it cost me my job.

"As for considering my future here if I don't agree to what you are proposing then I am afraid my mind is already made up on that front. I shall prepare my month's notice in writing and hand it to you within the hour."

He looked at me for a moment as if considering his next line of attack.

"I should think very carefully about what you've just said if I were you, Ruth. Positions such as the one you enjoy here are not easy to come by, especially without a reference."

I understood immediately what he was threatening but my anger and disgust at his proposal took precedent over any consideration for reflection or common sense on my part.

"I'm sorry it has come to this, Mr Taylor, but I can assure you I have been threatened by much worse than losing my job over the past few years, and I think once I explain my reasons for leaving directly to Mrs Taylor I am sure she will more than understand." Almost before I had finished speaking his mood darkened further. He strode towards me, leaning forward and placing his face directly in front of my own.

"I am afraid that is something that will *not* happen." He hissed at me like a snake about to move in for the kill. "You will not speak to my wife about this conversation under any circumstances, is that clear?"

He remained threateningly close to me as he continued to spit out his venom. "Let me explain exactly why you won't be talking to Helen. Firstly, can you envisage for one moment the impact such a revelation would have on her personally?" He paused as if to allow me time to appreciate the full implications of my threatening to make such a claim. "And of course, there is the potential effect such an accusation might have on our, as yet, unborn child, let alone the damage it would do to dear Elizabeth. Are you honestly prepared to be responsible for such an outcome?"

I could feel my anger turning to something much darker as I began to despise this man standing in front of me, a man who until a few minutes ago I had both admired and respected.

"Naturally I would deny everything of course, which would then leave my wife wondering why you would seek to make such a spiteful allegation in the first place." He was clearly now enjoying his part in our confrontation. I bit back almost without thinking.

"I think Mrs Taylor values my confidence well enough to know I wouldn't lie to her under any circumstances, and certainly not about something as serious as this."

I was attempting to gain the moral high ground at least as we traded verbal blows. He smiled again as if anticipating such a response, already having his answer to my protestations prepared in advance.

"She does indeed trust you Ruth, so imagine her feelings of sorrow and despair when I relate to her my sad discovery of a few days ago in your having stolen certain items from our house to sell on for personal gain. Also, once I explain to her that after informing you of this discovery and that I would have to let you go, you then made up this terrible lie to get your own back at me as some form of spiteful revenge."

I could hardly countenance what I was hearing. "Mrs Taylor would never believe that."

He smiled again as if to confirm his status as the dominant partner in our discussion.

"I readily admit she would find such a sad and unpleasant revelation hard to accept. However, when I show the pieces of china taken from the lounge and her favourite pair of diamond earrings removed from her jewellery box I think she will be left with little choice but to believe me rather than you."

I could feel the tears of frustration and incredulity running down my cheeks.

"But why would I do such a thing?"

"Who knows, my dear, who knows? But of course once I introduce the substantial amount of money recovered from your bedroom as well, perhaps she will begin to ask the same questions herself. Also, as to our ability to continue any longer in demonstrating the same faith and belief we have shown in you to date, not only with the care of our daughter, but more especially as a trusted member of our household staff."

I stood in shock, silent and rooted to the spot. Then as a degree of clarity and reason descended on me once more I spoke up. "It would still be your word against mine."

"Indeed it, would Ruth, but then again why would I go to such lengths to make up a tale like that in the first place? What possible reason could there be in my seeking to protect my own unblemished reputation and happy marriage from a young girl to whom we had shown nothing but kindness and charity towards since the day she first entered our home? That is unless of course, it was in reasonable defence against such preposterous suggestions and vile accusations?" He paused again. Then as if to drive home his point and with telling determination in his voice he continued.

"No doubt that would be a question the police would also choose to ask following my having to report the whole sorry affair to them. Then I would have to reveal the rest of the story about my trying to protect Helen from the sorry truth of your having become infatuated with me over recent weeks and proposing we share the same bed. I would of course tell them I had rejected your advances but that sadly, and as an act of malice, you had taken it upon yourself to, not only steal items from our house but to sell them as a way of raising money to run away with following my decision to tell Helen the truth and have you dismissed."

I stood looking at him for a moment, struggling to come to terms with what I had heard. Could it be true that my employer, a respected bank manager was now threatening to tell a tissue of lies not only to his wife, but also to the police in an effort to maintain his innocence about a fabricated story of theft that he himself had invented along with a proposed sexual liaison between the two of us?

"Why are you doing this to me?" My voice cracked with emotion as I spoke.

He took a step back, his voice softening again. "Listen, my dear, all these threats and counter threats are not doing anything to help the situation for either of us. Indeed, they could all go away by your simply agreeing to assist me in carrying out some of the normal duties that Helen would undertake herself but, for obvious reasons, cannot fulfil at the moment. Is that really so unreasonable?"

I felt the anger rise within me again but tried to contain myself. "If what you are proposing is so natural then why don't you ask me again with your wife present in the room?"

He moved towards me. "Because, Ruth, reasonable though my request may be, I am also certain that she would not view it as such. Something I am sure you are aware of or you would not have asked. The one thing I do know, and that you and I both agree on, is that neither of us wants to upset Helen in her present delicate state."

We stood in silence for a moment staring at each other like a Matador and his bull deciding on their next move of attack. He leant forward, his mood darkening once more.

"You have a simple choice to make, Ruth, you can either agree to my request or you will have to leave this house and our employment. I should add that if you choose the latter it will be without any form of reference or recommendation to any future prospective employer. Further, I will be forced to inform Helen of the reasons for your leaving as being those I have already alluded to. Consequently, not only will you find yourself without work but also facing potential criminal charges by the police." He paused before adding quite deliberately and with a telling sneer.

"Goodness only knows what effect all of that would have on my dear wife? I fear to think about it, Ruth, I truly do."

I fought back my tears and made one last effort to defend myself and my honour.

"Mrs Taylor and I have a very good relationship, she trusts me and knows I wouldn't do anything to harm our friendship let alone agree to the type of sordid proposal you are suggesting."

"I don't doubt that for a moment, my dear, but as I say that would only make the whole sorry affair even more traumatic for her. Consider for a moment the outcome of such a scenario. You would be asking her to choose between the word of her loving and devoted husband of nearly nine years and that of a young woman she has known for only a few months but who, even in that short period of time, she had chosen not only to place her absolute trust and faith in, but more especially the care and welfare of our dear daughter Elizabeth." He stared at me in silence for a moment as if to let the reality of what he had said sink in. "Then sadly I would be forced, against my better nature, to produce the evidence of what I had discovered in your room. She would then be able to see for herself the damming proof of what you had stolen from us and sold on for profit." He paused again briefly. "I think we both know how deeply such a vivid betrayal of trust would both shock and sadden her. Ultimately she would be left with little choice but to accept my version of events and agree we were left with no alternative but to hand the entire distasteful affair over to the appropriate authorities for them to deal with."

I struggled to absorb all I had heard, my brain feeling as if it might explode.

"There is of course another way of dealing with this." He smiled noticing the flicker of hope reflected across my face that there still yet might be a genuine alternative to the two appalling scenarios he had presented to me so far.

"That is, presuming you continue to be unreasonable in your attitude towards what I am suggesting takes place between the two of us." My heart sank.

"I would, as already intimated, have to say that you had become infatuated with me and approached me offering inappropriate favours, which naturally I had rejected out of hand. And of course once that story was in the public domain I would then be free to produce the more damaging physical evidence against you with regard to the theft of our property, thus demonstrating once and for all what a thoroughly devious and dishonest young girl you really are."

He stepped back and I felt my whole body shake as I held my breath waiting for whatever new damming allegation he was about to utter.

"I would attempt to be as delicate and considerate as I could be in speaking to the police about what had transpired, and would intimate that initially I had felt, as had my wife, that you had not appeared, certainly in our early dealings with you, to be the sort of girl to make such sordid propositions and allegations. Also, that we had never experienced any suspicious behaviour on your part in the time that you had been with us, certainly as far as the potential for theft was concerned." He paused, putting a fresh cigarette to his lips and lighting it. "Because of this and the fact you had shown such dedication to us as a family in the time you had been with us one could only surmise that you had now become emotionally and mentally unstable in some way, possibly through the effects of your time spent in the German prison camp?" He drew on his cigarette before continuing. "Of course, Helen and I would want to help you in every way we could, possibly by arranging for you to see a doctor or psychiatrist; the payment for which we would insist on meeting, especially in light of all the good work you had performed to date."

I watched as he inhaled the smoke from his cigarette sensing he hadn't finished and fearing whatever it was he was about to say next.

"I know Helen would want to support you by agreeing to this course of action but it would, at the very least, render you immediately unsuitable to continue in our employ. Also for you to look after our precious daughter Elizabeth, and would most certainly preclude you from any involvement in the care of our new baby when it arrived."

As I stood listening to this liturgy of falsehood I thought back to the times I had been forced to listen to the Nazi guards spouting their equally vile diatribe; cursing me and the whole Jewish community imprisoned in Birkenau. I remembered that I had determined no matter how badly life treated me after my experiences in that awful camp I would never allow another human being to humiliate or control me in such a degrading way ever again. And yet, even with that memory burning deep within me I could feel once again that self same sense of foreboding and panic rise inside of me as my heart pounded and the air in my lungs struggled to surface. It was as though I was suffocating under the tirade of venom being hurled at me. I knew in that moment, determined though I was not to give in, I was defeated and once again the bully had won. I hated myself almost more than my aggressor because of it. Mr Taylor took another draw on his cigarette and smiled as if sensing his victory.

"Clearly, if all of that were to be made public you would never find work as a nanny again, either locally or anywhere else for that matter. And whilst others may also feel a degree of sympathy towards you when hearing of your fragile mental state and its cause, it would still fall to me to inform all of my friends, and indeed any other prospective employer, as to what a lying, spiteful and clearly unstable young girl you had turned out to be. This would sadly portray you as being someone who could neither be trusted nor considered suitable for employment by any self respecting household, no matter how sad the circumstances of your condition. Indeed, it might be considered best for all if you were admitted to some form of institution in an effort to help you overcome your mental stress along with your worrying delusional behaviour."

He stood upright forcing his shoulders back and looking straight at me.

"The choice is yours, my dear, a simple agreement to participate in a natural act between a man and a woman, or the accusation of theft along with the potential for a lengthy custodial sentence, or worse perhaps, the possibility of being held for an indefinite period in an asylum for the mentally deranged?"

I knew without doubt he was serious and would carry out his threats if I refused his demands, also that he was right about how others would perceive me if he spoke out in such a way, but how could I agree to take him to my bed and then ever be able to face Mrs Taylor or Elizabeth again? As these and other desperate thoughts raced frantically around my head and I searched for a way to respond the phone rang. Mr. Taylor answered it and then following a brief conversation informed me he had to speak to somebody at the bank and that I should leave.

"I'll expect your answer to my proposal tomorrow. Helen has arranged to meet with a friend for afternoon tea and I will be home from the bank around three o'clock as I have some papers to attend to. I suggest you come back here at three fifteen to finalise our arrangement, presuming you wish to remain in our employ that is?"

I could hardly believe what I was being asked to accept and agree to. Not only was he suggesting that we betray his wife and family but also, in the same breath, setting out the terms and conditions of his proposition as some form of business transaction.

He moved to open the door. "I understand your reluctance to agree to my request, Ruth, but would suggest you consider more seriously the consequences of such a decision should you continue to refuse my proposal, or as I have already outlined you decide to speak to Helen about our conversation."

I turned to leave, my mind and body numb from all that transpired between us. Mr Taylor smiled as I passed in front of him. "Enjoy your time with Elizabeth now. I'll speak to you tomorrow afternoon."

My gaze fell to the floor in defeat as I left the room and walked away sure in the knowledge my life was about to change for the worse once more. Yet again I was to be forced to exist under the sadistic rule of a callous oppressor and pitiless bully.

FIFTEEN

Jenny was born on October 5th. I remember thinking at the time I would never forget this date as it had been the same day my former best friend from school, Pauline, had been born. I laughed to myself as I took on board the absurdity of that statement. Was I really more likely to remember the birth date of my own daughter, an event that would be forever set firm in my mind, because she happened to share it with an old school friend with whom I had lost all contact some years previously?

My waters broke around four in the morning with harder and more regular contractions following almost straight away. Mum could see it was the real thing even though she had never experienced physical childbirth herself.

"It won't be long now; this little one is definitely on its way."

I think it must be a form of female intuition, a sixth sense if you like that informs a woman when her time is due, and I was in no doubt that Mum was right in her assumption as I recognised for myself that something very different was happening to my body.

Dad kept knocking on the door asking what he could do to help.

"Is everything alright in there? Shall I make a cup of tea or something?"

"Just get yourself dressed and bring the car round to the front of the house, you useless bugger," Mum replied, her patience waning as her concern for me reached fever pitch. "We don't need a cup of tea or anything else for that matter, we just need to get Mary to the hospital, and as quick as possible."

Although I had a growing feeling of apprehension as we drove towards the hospital I also felt secure in Mum's arms as she held me close.

"You'll be fine, Mary, you'll both be fine."

The only sense of panic Mum and I truly felt was in continually having to tell Dad to keep his eyes on the road.

"Jim, for goodness sake, will you stop turning around and look where you're going. The two of us are fine, you just worry about getting us there in one piece, or we'll all be arriving in an ambulance and not for the reason intended."

As soon as we got to the hospital the staff on the maternity unit took over, immediately calm and supportive. They told me all I needed to do was relax, listen to what my body was saying and allow them to use their expertise to help bring my baby safely into the world.

"Don't worry, Mary, everything is fine, you'll soon be holding your baby in your arms." That sounded so good coupled with the knowledge they had been through this experience goodness knows how many times. It all served to calm my growing anxiety as the realisation took hold of me that another human being was about to come out of my body.

"Thank you," I replied feebly as another contraction swept through me. I'm not sure any of this professional encouragement did much to reassure Dad who was by now in a state of panic concerned that not enough was being done, or quickly enough, to ensure the safe arrival of his grandchild.

"Are you sure there isn't something more you should be doing?" he asked, wiping the perspiration from his hands onto his handkerchief. "She's been like this for some time now, are you sure the baby's alright?"

The nurses looked at Mum, sensing her female intuition was about to take control of the situation, at least as far as Dad was concerned.

"Why don't you go and get a cup of tea, Jim? Mary's in good hands now and there's nothing more that we, and certainly you, can do, alright?"

Dad nodded and smiled at me again before wandering off in the direction of the vending machine whilst still throwing the occasional glance over his shoulder in an effort to reassure himself that all was well.

"Sorry about my husband, it's our first grandchild and he's a bit nervous." Mum looked at me, an expression of palpable love and affection etched on her face. "We both are if I'm honest."

"Don't apologise, Mrs Rowland, he clearly cares about you all and that's lovely," said one of the nurses as she began to push the wheelchair I was sitting in towards the delivery area. Mum smiled again and squeezed my shoulder as we headed down the corridor. When we reached the delivery room one of the nurses moved ahead and opened the door. "Now then, Mary, let's get you ready to meet your baby."

Mum helped me undress and prepare for Jenny's birth as the nurses made sure all was in place for her safe arrival.

"Can I get you anything, sweetheart?"

"No thanks, Mum, I'll be fine, we'll be fine. Honest you're as bad as Dad." I struggled to smile in an attempt to reassure her as another wave of pain overtook me. "Thanks for being here with me though, it means so much."

Mum squeezed my hand again. "It means even more to me that you want me with you, more than you'll ever know." I looked up at her as mutual tears of affection filled our eyes.

As I lay on the bed holding her hand and waiting for the next contraction to sweep over me I thought how blessed I was to have Mum and Dad as my adoptive parents. I was determined this baby that I was about to deliver into the world would come to know them both, not only as its grandparents but also in their own right as the deeply loving and thoughtful human beings they had proved themselves to be for me over the past eighteen years. Nobody could have felt more cared for and cherished than I did at that moment and I knew without a doubt this same love would be showered down on my baby and all throughout its life. Secure in that knowledge I lay back and tried to relax, albeit with some difficulty as I followed my instructions to breath, blow and push until Jenny decided to make her grand entrance.

During the next hour or so I thanked Mum time and again for agreeing to be with me at Jenny's birth, not only in her role as my mother but also as my birthing partner in the whole experience. It was certainly never going to be Gerry. Mum played her part to perfection, constantly reassuring me I was doing well and that everything would be okay, especially during those final moments of the delivery itself.

I'm not sure whether it was female instinct or an inbuilt sense of maternal love that gave her the strength to support me in those final hours we spent together; whatever it was I was grateful for her being there. It can't have been easy for her as we waited for Jenny to arrive, thinking back to the loss of her own baby, Holly, who had been born prematurely and died so tragically just a short while later.

Although we never spoke about it directly I think we both recognised the connection in our hearts, and I loved her all the more for showing such devotion towards me without any mention of her own feelings of sadness or of envying me the moment.

Holding Jenny in my arms for that first time gave me an incredible feeling of achievement, not only in having survived the whole process, but more especially in my being responsible for bringing another human life into the world. I became immediately protective towards her and knew in that moment I would happily give my own life in exchange for hers without a second thought or reckoning of the consequences. This was another unspoken bond of love that Mum and I shared as we looked down at this tiny bundle of life, bloodied but so beautiful lying beside us.

Mum stroked Jenny's cheek, tears of love rolling down her face. "She looks just like you did on the day we first saw you, Mary. You may not have come from my body, but I knew immediately that you'd captured my heart, just as this little one has yours, and mine all over again."

We took turns in holding Jenny and fussing over her, recognising that all of our lives had changed forever and that this new and oh so precious life had created the final thread in the tapestry of our family unit.

After a while Mum went to fetch Dad so that he could meet the latest addition to the Rowland family and officially become the granddad he had so proudly been boasting of becoming to his friends for the past few weeks and months. In those few minutes I spent alone with Jenny I wondered how my own mother, at the physical moment of giving birth, couldn't have felt the same about me as I did about my baby girl. If she had then how could she have let me go just a few weeks later?

Such thoughts and uncertainties bothered me greatly over the next few days as I spent time in hospital growing ever closer to and more in love with my beautiful daughter.

Dad entered the delivery room and for a moment I wondered if he had been drinking alcohol rather than tea as he took his granddaughter into his arms for the first time and mumbled almost incoherently about how proud he was of me and how beautiful Jenny was.

"Oh Mary she's so, and you, I… I don't know what to say." I watched as tears of pride and joy fill his eyes. Mum raised her eyebrows and chided him gently.

"You soppy brush. Just say she's beautiful, which is obvious for all to see." Dad grinned at all three of us like the cat that had got the cream.

"Of course she's beautiful, just look at her mother. She's got the same good looks and little nose that our Mary had when she was a baby." I was grateful to Dad for saying that, not because he had compared Jenny to me but more especially because he hadn't made any reference to her father even though her hair was dark as Gerry's had been.

"Have you decided on a name yet? I know we've been talking about it over the past few weeks, but it clearly isn't going to be Peter now we know she's a girl."

Mum looked straight at Dad. "You know there are times, Jim, admittedly few, that I am grateful that Mary is our adopted daughter, because at least she hasn't inherited your brain, or lack of it."

"I was just saying, that's all."

"Actually I have decided," I said, interrupting. They both looked at me intently as I took a breath. "I'd like to call her Jennifer after your mother," I said looking straight at Mum. "Although I'd like to shorten it to Jenny if that's alright?"

Mum's eyes filled with tears again. "Oh, Mary, are you sure?"

I nodded sensing the moment and unable to speak myself.

"Thank you, and yes, of course Jenny's alright. Dad called Mum Jenny wren all the time as a term of affection between the two of them."

Up until that moment I hadn't been really aware of this family nickname as Nan had died when I was only a few months old but it made my choosing Jenny seem even more appropriate.

Dad took her into his arms and held her aloft. "So young Jenny, you're already having to bear the weight of responsibility in carrying forward the family name on your little shoulders. I just hope they'll prove broad enough to carry such a heavy load."

Mum looked at him for a moment and then down at me. "I'm so sorry, Mary, clearly Jenny's arrival has had some sort of detrimental effect on his already deluded mind. Thank goodness you had a baby girl or goodness knows what names he might have come up with had she been a boy, accepting that he'd already discounted Peter?" The room filled with our shared laughter and I was grateful that these were the first sounds to greet Jenny as she began her life's journey. I was resolute in my determination to do all I could to ensure the rest of her life would also be filled with the same sense of joy and love as it had begun.

After spending a few days recovering I was allowed to take Jenny home. At first I found myself treating her as if she were a porcelain doll that might break if I dropped her, and it was with that fear at the front of my mind that I let Mum carry Jenny to the car as we left the hospital. I think Dad felt the same way as I did, driving home at about five miles an hour so as not to shake her about too much. Not that Jenny would have cared if he'd have driven at a hundred miles an hour as she slept during the whole journey. Mum teased Dad and I about our concerns for Jenny and was a lot more confident in her approach towards her.

"She won't break you know. She's a baby not a crystal chandelier."

"You've obviously forgotten the early days we had with Mary," Dad replied. "We practically wrapped her in cotton wool for those first few weeks."

"That's right, and then we discovered like everyone else that baby's are pretty resilient and tend to survive when handled normally. Admittedly we had a couple of accidents between us in the early days but she's still here to tell the story isn't she?"

"You had accidents with me? I can't believe I'm allowing my daughter to become part of a family where her grandparents couldn't even care for their own daughter properly. We'll probably both be scarred for life."

Dad glanced at me in his driving mirror and laughed. "Look on the bright side, now we've got a second chance to get things right. Anyway, I don't know why you're making such a fuss I only dropped you on your head a couple of times." Mum turned to me and shook her head as the two of us held onto Jenny in a silent but heartfelt bond of love.

I was fortunate to be able to feed Jenny myself as it was something I had wanted to do from the earliest acceptance of my pregnancy. Again, I felt sorry for Mum at these times as this was another experience she would never own for herself. Even so she was wonderfully supportive of me and felt privileged to be included as part of the process whenever I held Jenny to my breast.

"I envy you that closeness, Mary, that extra bond. I'm only sorry I couldn't do the same for you."

"I know, Mum, but even though I can do this for Jenny as a physical act, the heart relationship you and I share between us couldn't be deeper and I know you love me every bit as much as I love her."

"Thank you for that, sweetheart. And yes I couldn't love you more, the both of you."

We used to sit together and watch in amazement at how much this little person appeared to be able to consume. She never seemed to have had enough and often cried after feeding. I thought at first it was just wind, but the health visitor said she thought that I might not be producing enough milk for Jenny and suggested we top up her feeds with the occasional bottle. This certainly appeared to work and Jenny soon settled down, becoming more relaxed in both her efforts at feeding and in the resulting patterns of her sleep afterwards. It also allowed both Mum and Dad the opportunity to feed Jenny as well. Dad especially enjoyed his turn with the bottle and would walk around the room singing Jennifer Juniper, the old Donovan song to Jenny as she lay across his shoulder whilst he and patted her gently on the back in an attempt to bring up her wind.

"Dad, I don't want my daughter growing up thinking that's her name, please can you think of something else to sing."

"It could be worse; I could sing "Daddy wouldn't buy me a bow wow" like I did to you when you were a baby."

"Why on earth would you do that to her? Come to think of it, why did you sing it to me?"

Dad smiled. "Don't you remember? When you were very

young we had that lovely old mongrel called Bess. She died soon after your first birthday but you used to make a bee line for her whenever the two of you were in the same room. She was always so gentle with you, but because she was getting on and you liked to grab and pull at anything that came within your reach we kept the two of you apart as much as possible, especially when you used to crawl over to her and yank on her ears. She would look at your mum and I as if pleading for us to intervene on her behalf. You would point at Bess and I would say "doggy" trying to get you to speak. Your mum would laugh and say you'd be better learning to say mummy and daddy." He paused for a moment as Jenny burped in response to his winding efforts. "Well done, that's a big girl." He took her from his shoulder and kissed her lightly on her cheek. "Anyway, that's why I used to sing it to you. My mum had sung it to me as a youngster so it had stayed with me over the years. I used to make a pretty good job of it I seem to remember, although your mother here didn't necessarily agree." He smiled as the memory overtook him and he handed Jenny back to me. "You were such a beautiful baby, just like this little one." I took his hand and squeezed it.

"Thanks Dad."

"What for?"

"Just for being you, and for not calling me Bess or suggesting it as a name for Jenny."

I used to enjoy those times with Mum and Dad during Jenny's feeds as they talked about the past and their experiences with me as a baby. It was as though the arrival of Jenny into our lives had released them to share these earlier memories and events; ones they had, in the main, kept to themselves over the years. Perhaps it was because they had been unsure whether to speak so openly in the past about those times because I had been adopted? Whatever the reason, I think we all felt the benefit of this new sense of freedom that Jenny had introduced into our lives.

We were also grateful for the extra periods of quiet and rest between feeds once Jenny had settled into the routine of breast and bottle. She certainly let us know when she was awake and ready for her next meal as there was nothing wrong with her lungs or the volume of her screams when she wanted to make us aware of her presence. Dad would smile and say he thought she might like to consider becoming a female town crier when she grew up.

"I can just see her in those bright red robes and a three cornered black hat, ringing her hand bell to make sure she has everyone's attention. Not that she'll need a bell with a pair of lungs like that."

Those initial few weeks seemed to fly by, and after the first couple of months I couldn't remember, nor imagine, what life had been like before Jenny arrived. All of this made me question yet again how my own mother had apparently been so prepared to let me go at such an early age and miss out on the daily changes and achievements in her baby's life. It made me angry and upset as I vacillated, in equal measure, between wanting to confront her about what she'd done and resolving never to having any contact with her at all. When I felt like that I was determined not to let her within a hundred miles of my beautiful Jenny, her granddaughter, a granddaughter I would make sure would never be a part of her life.

With that in mind it was interesting when, later on I should begin to make those self same enquiries that I had so vigorously rejected in the past about contacting her, not through my own volition, at least not initially, but through the wishes of Jenny, the very person I had resolved so vehemently to keep her away from.

In those early days though and with Jenny still a baby my thoughts drifted away from Ruth as most of my time was spent focused on caring for this precious gift of life I had been given, a life that had changed my own completely and all for the better, apart from the odd sleepless night! Although even here I felt blessed with Mum and Dad taking on more than their fair share of responsibility for Jenny's care whenever I was tired or simply needed some help, which I so often did.

"You can't do it all, Mary, and apart from that your Dad and I love spending time with Jenny, so you're actually doing us a favour by letting us have her."

I knew Mum meant what she was saying but was still concerned I was asking too much of them both at times, but they never turned me away or denied any request I made on Jenny's behalf. I often wondered what I would have done without them, especially as I didn't have Jenny's father around to do his bit, not that I would have let Gerry come near her once he made his decision not to be a part of her life. That was one of the things I had remained resolute about. Gerry had said he didn't want to be involved with Jenny and even encouraged me to have an abortion in the early days of my pregnancy, and so as far as I was concerned he had made that decision for life. I would make sure he wasn't allowed access to her, either now as a baby or as she grew in the years ahead. I suppose it was this unforgiving line of thinking that also determined how I felt about Ruth at times. After all she was the one who had chosen to let me go so soon after giving birth to me, and so as far as I was concerned in making that decision she had also forfeited the right to see or hear from me ever again.

But if that was true, then why was it, even considering Jenny's eventual desire to know more about her paternal grandmother that I would now agree to make those first tentative enquiries as to her whereabouts? And by following this course of action I was allowing for the potential of her entering my life again, and more especially I would be letting her know about Jenny's existence, something I had determined she would never hear about or have any part in.

I had made the decision long before Jenny was born that I would have nothing to do with her and so consequently, in my mind at least, she had forfeited any rights she might have had in gaining access into the life of her granddaughter. So why, if all that were true, was I now considering turning full circle and going back on all I had been so unwavering about in the past?

SIXTEEN

I closed the study door behind me and headed straight for my room passing Nelly on the stairs. "So what did he want to talk to you about?" she asked excitedly.

In that moment I had to decide whether to tell her the truth or say nothing of what had just taken place between the two of us. I chose the latter, knowing in my heart that Mr Taylor had been right in what he had said about nobody believing me if I chose to accuse him of making an indecent proposal, or worse.

"Nothing," I blurted out, trying not to look directly at her for fear she would detect my misery and frustration.

"He just wanted to clarify arrangements for when the baby arrives, and that I was happy in what had been agreed with Mrs Taylor about my duties." I could feel my cheeks flushed with indignation about what had actually happened and prayed Nelly wouldn't push me further on the matter.

"Are you alright? Your face looks a bit red. Have you been crying?"

"No really I'm fine." I bit my lip to stop myself giving way and bursting into tears or letting the truth flood out. "Just a bit nervous that's all. You know what it's like being on your own with Mr Taylor, he has an air about him that affects your confidence, or at least it does mine."

"You're right. I don't like spending time on my own with him either, not that it happens much anyway. If I didn't know any better I'd say he can be a bit creepy at times, but that's probably just me being silly."

I felt myself wanting to cry out and tell her she was right and for the very reasons I had discovered myself just a few minutes ago. Instead, and with my emotions fit to explode, I forced a smile and carried on up the stairs to my room. "I'll see you later."

By the time I got to the attic I felt as if my lungs were about to burst, partly from my having taken the stairs two at a time in an effort to get to my room as quickly as possible, but also because I could feel my heart beating overtime with both the pain and indignation of what had just taken place in Mr Taylor's study. I leant against the door as it closed behind me and burst into tears. I wept openly, a very real sense of wretchedness coursing through my body as my head raced with irrational thoughts and utter despair. I tried in vain to make sense and reason of the conversation I had just had with my employer but failed on every level. How could a man who, up until half an hour ago, I had both respected and admired so suddenly become the devil incarnate?

I stood with my back against the door for what seemed like an age as if to prevent anyone from entering this new and horrific world I now found myself inhabiting. After a while I moved to lie on my bed, and as I did so my gaze fell upon the picture of my parents and Joseph. I began to cry again as my mind absorbed the terrible truth that the same brutal and bullying hand of injustice we had experienced as a family in Birkenau was about to encompass my life once again. Although I was no longer being forced to exist in that rat infested death camp where torture and murder were a part of the every day fight for survival I still felt no less threatened, with my future safety and well-being now entirely dependent on whether I chose to accept the nightmare terms of my newly appointed tormentor and captor.

How could I allow this to happen, but, equally, how could I not? I certainly didn't want to lose my job, not just for the money and position of trust I held, important though they were, but more because I had genuine feelings for Mrs Taylor and young Elizabeth. They had both become dear to my heart, and I was truly excited by the thought of continuing in my care for Elizabeth and in supporting Mrs Taylor when it came time for the birth of her new baby, and in the months ahead that followed. Up until today it hadn't been simply a sense of duty that had made me feel this way, but more that I was actually becoming part of a real family again. A family that was happy to embrace me in its midst and demonstrate genuine affection towards, perhaps even love. But the events of the past half an hour had shattered all of those hopes and feelings leaving them crushed and broken all around me.

As I lay there on my bed with the sense of hurt and revulsion at what Mr Taylor had suggested burning deeply within my chest I felt my disgust at his proposal turn to anger. I remembered the conscious decision I had made after leaving Birkenau, that never again would I allow anybody to control me or threaten my life, at least not without my fighting back. Now here I was facing the first real test of that resolve. I reasoned that, powerful though he was, Mr Taylor was not an SS guard with a rifle pointed at my head; he was simply a man who had abused his position and authority by threatening me with unfair consequences if I didn't agree to his demeaning and shameful demands. I looked at the picture of my parents and took strength in the knowledge they would agree with my determination to do and say the right thing. I would simply tell him I wouldn't go to bed with him, but that I would agree not to say anything to Mrs Taylor either as long as he never mentioned our previous conversation again. I would also inform him that in future I would only agree to talk with him as long as there was at least one other person in the room, preferably Mrs Taylor herself. Having made this decision I felt immediately better both in and about myself. I looked at the small clock on my bedside table noting that Elizabeth and her mother would be home soon and so hurried to wash my face and make myself presentable for their arrival.

Elizabeth burst through the front door as I reached the bottom of the stairs. She ran straight to me, arms open wide in her usual excited greeting and desperate to tell me about the adventures of her day. Mrs Taylor followed closely behind and, taking off her coat, laughed at the two of us. "Someone is certainly pleased to see you, Ruth; she's been talking about you all the way home." As I held her close Mr Taylor entered the hallway from his study. "Hello you two, have you had a nice time?"

"Very nice thank you, dear, how has your day been?"

He looked at his wife and daughter and smiled. "Oh you know just the usual. And what about you young lady, have you been a good girl for your mummy?"

"Yes I have, haven't I, Mummy?" Mrs Taylor laughed again. "Well, for most of the time yes." Elizabeth grinned at her father but chose to stay in my embrace; an act of mutual affection that offered me a fleeting sense of power over him and one I hoped would let him know he wasn't going win the struggle for power being played out between us easily.

"I'll see you both at tea time," he said, smiling broadly at his daughter and as if dismissing my efforts to hold sway in our battle of wills. My heart sank a little as he turned and walked self-assuredly into the sitting room closing the door behind him. Elizabeth, oblivious to anything but her own existence asked if we could go upstairs and play with her dolls house until it was time for tea.

"Go on then off you go, but don't tire poor Ruth out."

With that Elizabeth took hold of my hand and pulled me across the hallway. "I think we should make a new bedroom in my doll's house," she declared, bounding up the stairs as she spoke. "I was thinking that as Mummy is going to have a new baby then perhaps my dolly might have a new baby as well and she will need a bedroom for it. What do you think, Ruth?"

"That's a very good idea." Even with my heavy heart I couldn't help but smile at this bundle of life and energy running ahead of me.

I envied Elizabeth her innocence as we climbed the stairs together, remembering briefly my own years as a small child when life had also appeared so simple and exciting; the realities of adulthood along with how dark the world would become for me still far away. I squeezed her little hand as we reached the playroom, determined to protect her as best I could, at least for now, from the sometimes brutal truth of what she would come to discover for herself in the years ahead, perhaps even from her own father. Elizabeth smiled up at me as she sat on the floor surrounded by her toys.

"I do love you, Ruth, and I love playing with you as well. You are my very best friend in all the world."

I felt tears of affection sting my eyes. "I love you too sweetheart." I knelt down beside her and allowed the little girl's fantasy world to encompass my thoughts over the next half an hour, moving away from the challenges and exigent conversation that would face me tomorrow.

SEVENTEEN

Those first few years spent with Jenny hold a special place in my memory, with Mum and I becoming ever closer as we discovered together the joy of bringing up a child that truly belonged to each of us from day one. She and Dad had always considered me their daughter and now with the arrival of a granddaughter our family circle was complete.

Mum and I would go shopping together and playfully argue as to whose turn it was to push Jenny in her pram.

"I'm her grandmother."

"Maybe, but I'm her mother and so I get to push her first."

"Yes but if we hadn't brought you up as our daughter then she wouldn't be here."

We often teased each other in this way and on most occasions would happily accede to the other's playful demands. I know all parents like to think their child is the cutest or has the best looks, but in truth Jenny was a beautiful baby. And it was only on the odd occasion when someone remarked how pretty she was or looked like her mother that Carol would become quiet and take a back seat in the conversation. She knew that Jenny had both my eyes and slightly rounded face, but was also aware that she was never going to grow to look like her or Dad with no immediate blood line between them. Even so Jenny still completed us as a family in so many other ways. Dad took endless photos of her in those first couple of years and I became afraid she might develop a phobia about cameras or in having her picture taken. He even bought a Polaroid camera so he could take new photos of her into work and show his colleagues how "his granddaughter" was growing and changing with every passing day, although I'm not sure they were as keen in thumbing through the ever expanding album of Jenny's development as he was!

"Just one more, she won't stay like this forever you know. She'll soon grow and then we'll forget how little she was."

"I don't mind you taking pictures of her, Dad, but do we really need so many? Honestly we'll need a photo album a week at this rate."

"You'll thank me in the years to come. I just wish I'd taken more of you when you were little. You can't get those years or memories back you know."

Mum would tease him as well. "I bet David Bailey doesn't take as many pictures as you do."

"That's because he doesn't have the same three beautiful girls to model for him like I do."

Mum and I would smile and raise our eyes in mock derision at his attempt of flattery whilst acknowledging, at the same time, nothing we could say or do would detract him from his photographic pursuits. Although I wouldn't admit it publicly I did feel a huge sense of pride that my little girl meant so much to him, to both of them.

She grew so quickly in that first year, achieving many small but equally significant landmarks. I remember the first steps she took. We three adults were watching television with Jenny sitting on the floor happily following the movement on the screen in front of her when a dog appeared and she reached out to touch it. Not being close enough she shuffled her bottom a little closer and, placing her hand on the edge of the coffee table, pulled herself to her feet and took three determined steps towards the television before placing her face on the screen in an effort to kiss the dog. We watched transfixed as she waddled forward and then turned to look at each other as if to say did she really just get up and walk? Mum jumped to her feet and gently pulled Jenny way from the television, fearing she might knock it over and hurt herself in her attempts to get closer to the dog. Jenny didn't think much of that and cried out in protest.

"Mum, turn her round to face me, but keep her standing." Jenny was already reaching out towards me for comfort and so I held out my hands in response urging her to walk the few steps across the floor towards me.

"Come on, Jen, walk to Mummy, you can do it." My heart was thumping in my chest as we held our breath and Mum let her go. Jenny wobbled for a moment before breaking into a smile, then after taking one shaky step forward she found her feet and strode confidently towards me as if she had been walking for weeks. That said, just as she got near to me and I leant forward to pick her up and congratulate her on doing so well she stopped. It was as though she had suddenly become aware of what she had done herself. She wobbled again and, reaching out for my hands, lost control of her legs and fell back on her bottom. Almost immediately she began howling, probably as much from hurt pride as any pain she had experienced in meeting with the carpet so abruptly.

"I wish I'd had my camera then. We'll never get those first steps again."

"For goodness sake, Jim, give it a rest will you," Mum retorted. "There'll be plenty of other opportunities to take pictures of her walking."

"Yes, but not those very first steps."

Mum raised her eyes to the ceiling. "Well when you do take one of her walking just write on the back they were her first steps. We won't tell anyone it's not true and I'm sure she won't mind, or care either."

Jenny was by now howling with pained indignation. Mum and I joined her with tears of our own, but ours were tears of pride in what we had just witnessed our little girl achieve. Dad put his arms around Mum and I. "Jenny will experience far greater falls from grace than that in life, but we'll always be there to help and encourage her, just as we have now. We'll pick her up, dust her down and set her on her way again,"

Almost every day in those first couple of years of Jenny's life we seemed to witness some new achievement as she grew, both in size and confidence. I remember the first time she said, Mummy, and the feeling of pride it instilled in me. It was about the only time I consciously thought of Gerry, and although I didn't regret for a moment he wasn't involved with her upbringing, I was still sad for Jenny that there wasn't a man in her life to call daddy.

Dad was determined of course, as the only male in a family of girls, that Jenny should learn to say granddad as soon as possible. So the first time she mumbled something directly at him through her ever present smile he was convinced his genius of a granddaughter had just uttered the magic word, the one he had been attempting to teach her for the past couple of weeks.

"Did you hear that?" he exclaimed. "She said it, she said granddad." Mum and I were not so sure, reasoning that whatever it was Jenny may have attempted to voice had been totally unintelligible, partly because of a mouthful of cereal, and more likely associated with her breaking wind at the same time. This was demonstrated by her bright red face and bulging eyes.

"I think she's more interested in filling her nappy than in talking to you," Mum laughed. "Although you may well have proved the inspiration she needed with your endless attempts to get her to say granddad."

"That's nice, isn't it, Jenny? Your nasty granny and mummy are saying horrid things about us, but we don't care, do we, precious?" Jenny stared at Dad, her face now almost puce. Mum and I looked at each other and laughed.

"There's your answer, Dad, I think she's making it very clear as to what she thinks of you and your attempts to get her to speak, especially as she has more pressing matters on her mind."

The three of us enjoyed so many happy times watching Jenny's development as the months passed by. I look back on them all with fondness, not only for her but for each of us as a family.

I think that's part of the reason I struggled at times in deciding whether to meet Ruth or not and to allow her back into my life, and more especially into Jenny's. I have often wondered what things might have been like had she not chosen to give me away, and how we might have got on as mother and daughter? If she had brought me up how would she have reacted to my becoming pregnant? Would she have been as understanding and gracious as Mum and Dad? Who would have provided the father figure in my life, and would he have cared for me as much as James? All of these differing scenarios played out in my head, only serving to confuse me further. Although I had asked myself these questions a hundred times in the past I had never really given them any proper credence, accepting as I did they were only flights of fancy in my thinking. I assumed I could never truly gain any answers to them, nor did I really want to, at least at that time. I also found it easier and more productive to accept the support and love that Dad and Mum had shown towards me from my earliest memory as the bench mark for family life. Theirs was a gift of love above question and offered unconditionally. They had chosen me alone to be a part of their lives; allowing me to grow safely in their embrace as any traditional set of parents would have done. But now with the very real possibility of Ruth entering my life again I considered once more how different things might have been had I remained *her* daughter.

My mind raced backwards and forwards as I battled with these questions and uncertainties. It was becoming increasingly hard for me to ignore them, especially as I now knew she physically existed and wanted to see me. Chris also encouraged me to make further contact with her.

"Now you know she's out there, you'll never forgive yourself if you decide not to see her or at least hear what she has to say. She may not have been the best mother in the world but she's the only one you've got, if you know what I mean? Just maybe she deserves the chance to tell her side of the story if you can bear to hear it? Either way you'll know the truth and then be in a position to move forward or to close the door on the relationship forever."

Deep down I knew he was right and I did have so many questions I wanted answers to, questions that ultimately only she could answer.

What would our holidays together have been like? Would she have made the angel's costume that I wore in the school nativity when I was younger as Carol had done? Would she have watched with glowing pride as I pranced about on stage knocking over the flimsy wooden stable door and tearing off one of my wings in the process? Would she have comforted me and told me nobody had noticed and it didn't matter that the boy playing Joseph had stamped on my wing in disgust at my ruining his entrance? I knew it was silly even to entertain such thoughts, but those instances were still a part of my growing up, and how Mum and Dad had responded to them and every other seemingly important event in my younger life had all played a role in shaping the person I had become. How could I not think about how different things might have been if those early years of my growth and development had been spent with Ruth?

I was sure they couldn't have been better than all I had experienced with James and Carol but, was that because she had let me go and caused me to resent what had never been, or was it because I had no physical knowledge of how things might have unfolded between the two of us? As these and other random thoughts crowded into my brain the one truth I couldn't escape, no matter how I dressed it up was that it had been me who, after all these years, had made this first attempt at contact between us again. The reasons for doing so hardly mattered anymore, the fact still remained I had opened this Pandora's box and there was no going back to close the lid on it again, no matter how much I may have wanted to.

EIGHTEEN

I managed to avoid any contact with Mr Taylor the following morning before he left for the bank. I busied myself with getting Elizabeth ready for school and in helping Mrs Taylor choose a suitable outfit for her visit later that afternoon to her friends as Mr Taylor had intimated the day before.

I envied Mrs Taylor her extensive wardrobe and the choices she was able to make, having a different set of clothes available to her for each day of the week and more besides. She also had a number of dresses and jackets made especially for her pregnancy and we spent some time comparing them before making a final decision. She was such a generous woman encouraging me to be involved in many of the day to day decisions about Elizabeth or, as was now the case, in helping her choose a suitable outfit for the day. There were times during our discussions, albeit briefly, that I felt more like a friend than an employee, although of course I never verbalised these feelings directly to her.

On this particular day I found it hard to concentrate and struggled to demonstrate my usual enthusiasm in helping her to decide what to wear. I was still thinking about what Mr Taylor had said the day before and, although I knew I didn't want to upset her directly by telling her what had gone on between the two of us, I still found it difficult to conceal my fears and concerns from her.

"Are you alright Ruth dear, you seem a little preoccupied this morning? Is there something bothering you"?

I fought desperately to maintain my composure. "I'm sorry. Thank you but I'm fine. I didn't sleep very well last night and am a bit tired." Here at least I was telling the truth, because I hadn't slept at all well, having found it hard to think about anything else as I'd lain in my bed constantly replaying the conversation that had taken place earlier in the afternoon between myself and her husband. I knew, for now at least, I couldn't say anything to her about that exchange no matter how much I might have liked to have done. I needed both the time and the occasion to be right before I dared speak out about what had happened.

"Well we'll put Elizabeth to bed together this evening so that you can get an early night. You do so much for us, Ruth, and I apologise if we have abused your efforts or goodwill on our behalf of late."

"Thank you, but please don't apologise. I'm fine, truly I am. Just a bad night that's all. I'm sure I'll be better tomorrow." I felt as though I had betrayed her in someway by not telling her the real cause for my restless night. It was as though a wall of lies was beginning to build between us, a wall that would eventually separate me entirely from the one person who really trusted me and whom I also knew would be the most horrified to learn of the truth. Our relationship would be damaged beyond repair should I speak out. I felt trapped but managed a weak smile as I helped her to finish dressing.

The rest of the morning passed fairly uneventfully as I tidied Elizabeth's bedroom and tended to my other duties in the house. Nelly and I had lunch together and she also noticed I didn't appear to be myself.

"Has Mr T been upsetting you?"

"What makes you say that?" I replied, in an attempt to sound surprised and so avert her line of questioning.

"Well you just don't seem to be yourself and I was wondering if he had given you a hard time over something yesterday that you didn't tell me about?" She laughed. "Mind, he doesn't normally order a pot of tea when he's about to lay down the law." I hurriedly made the same excuse as I had done with Mrs Taylor earlier about having not slept well in the hope she wouldn't press me further about my conversation with our employer.

"So go on then," Nelly continued, clearly having no intention of letting me off the hook so easily. "What *did* he want? I know you said it was just the usual stuff but you seemed to be in there for ages?"

"Nothing, honest. Like I said yesterday he just wanted to talk about what happens when the new baby arrives and to know if I was still getting on alright with Elizabeth and Mrs Taylor, which I am." I looked at Nelly and could see she was about to ask another question. "I'm sure he did the same with you when you'd first been here for a while," I said, jumping in and hoping to deflect her thoughts from pressing me further. Nelly smiled as she set her glass of water on the table.

"Like I told you on the day you arrived, Mr T hasn't really said two words to me apart from *do this* or *do that* since I've been here. He's a bit of a cold fish Mrs D says, same as her old man I reckon. They both think they're something special, although I'd never say that to Mrs D 'cause she's smashing she is, deserves better than him. I mean I'm sorry his business failed and all that, but he should think himself lucky that he got taken on here and that he's still working. And he should be thanking Mrs D for putting his name forward when she did instead of moaning at her sometimes that he deserves better. We all deserve better, but you still need to say thank you for what you got, 'cause there's plenty outside who'd bite our hands off for these jobs and to work with people as lovely as Mrs D and Mrs T."

I sat listening in astonishment at Nelly's outburst. I'd never heard her speak out in that way before and told her as much, laughing as I did so. I was also grateful that the conversation appeared to have moved away from my own dilemma.

"Flippin' heck, Nelly, I've never heard you say so much in one go before. " We smiled at each other both recognising the bond of friendship that was growing between us. Here was another person I knew I could trust and who would sympathise with me if I dared speak out about my conversation with Mr Taylor. But I also knew she would feel bound to say something on my behalf if I did as a way of fighting my corner, and that was something I simply could not risk happening for so many reasons, certainly for now.

"I've got plenty to say when the mood takes me," Nelly continued. "Its just that it don't take me that often, and like I say I'm happier to count my blessings and see the good in people rather than tell them what I really think, well at least to their face anyway."

She squeezed my arm and smiled. "I'm glad you're here, Ruth, it's like I've got a real friend now, and I haven't had one of them for a while, not a *real* friend anyway, if you know what I mean?"

I smiled back at her although struggling at the same time to agree with her statement about seeing the good in others, especially our employer. Indeed, at that moment I found it almost impossible to find any good in him at all, let alone seek to bless him.

I really liked Nelly and, as with Mrs Taylor, felt saddened that I couldn't share my secret with her, but I also didn't want her worrying about something that, for now at least, didn't physically concern her. I also didn't want to give myself, or Nelly, the added complication that if I did say something and she then spoke out on my behalf it would cause even greater consternation for all concerned, perhaps even placing her own future and employment under threat as well as my own. I knew I couldn't risk that for either of us. Much as I was desperate to share my story with someone, I decided, for now at least, it had to remain my secret. Who knows, if I did perhaps allow myself a generous thought towards Mr Taylor then just maybe he might also reconsider his own position and in so doing not only regret what he had said to me yesterday and apologise, but also agree never to bring up that hateful conversation between us again. Somehow, much as I prayed that one or both of these outcomes might be realised, I couldn't escape the feeling deep inside that the eventual conclusion to our next meeting would be very different and far less agreeable.

Mr Taylor arrived home just as his wife was about to leave for her afternoon appointment with her friends. "Have a nice time dear." I smiled at him politely and handed Mrs Taylor her umbrella as she made her way towards the front door. He kissed her lightly on the cheek, allowing his hand to run down the full length of her back as she walked away. She turned, offering him a look of love and familiarity that I recognised immediately for what it was, a shared moment of marital intimacy. I had witnessed similar acts of devotion between my own parents, growing up in a home where open displays of affection were common place. However, on this occasion it was being extended as an act of absolute yet unwarranted faith towards a man who was intending to break that bond of trust completely by committing the ultimate betrayal, adultery. She clearly adored him. If only she knew.

He appeared so calm and caring I could hardly believe this was the same man who had spoken to me in such a demeaning and unforgiving way only twenty four hours before. As the front door closed he turned and looked straight at me, his expression changing to one of steely determination and authority.

"I think we can dispense with the pot of tea today, Ruth. Follow me into my study, please." I felt my body shudder, partly from fear but also from my growing resolve to stand up for myself and for what I knew to be right.

He entered the room before me. "Close the door behind you." He moved to his desk and opening the lid of a silver cigarette box picked one up and rolled it between his fingers before raising it to his lips and lighting it. He took a deep draw and then turning his head to one side exhaled a large cloud of smoke.

"I trust you have thought long and hard about my proposal, Ruth?"

I stood rooted to the spot, attempting to exude an air of confidence I knew didn't exist as I felt my legs shaking almost uncontrollably beneath my skirt. I coughed lightly to clear my throat and took a deep breath. "I have thought of little else. I have also decided not to speak to Mrs Taylor about our conversation."

He took another draw on his cigarette and smiled, wrongly assuming the fight had gone from within me and that he had won the first round in our battle of wills.

"Good girl, I knew you'd see sense."

I felt my back stiffen and shudder as I continued, clenching my fists so hard I could feel the nails pushing into my skin.

"I will also not be party to the proposal you made yesterday under any circumstances. Nor will I amend my duties to include anything other than those already stated in my contract and previously agreed between Mrs Taylor and myself."

I kept my eyes fixed on him in the vain hope he might detect some form of resolute determination and associated authority in my shaky demeanour.

"What you are asking me to do is both unreasonable and illegal." I could feel my stomach churning as I took another deep breath. "As nothing has actually happened yet between us and for the sake of Elizabeth and Mrs Taylor I think it best if we both agree to forget our earlier conversation. I also suggest that apart from those occasions when we are physically required to be in each others company we should avoid all other forms of contact between us." I could hardly believe I had been able to say all that I had intended so clearly and concisely feeling as nervous as I did and with my whole body now beginning to quake. I felt a bead of sweat breakout on my forehead as I waited for his reply. He stood quite still and took two or three deliberate draws on his cigarette before putting it out in the ashtray. He slowly raised his head and looked at me, his face showing no sign of emotion.

"That was quite a speech, Ruth, and though I applaud its succinct delivery I am sorry you've come to that decision. I was rather hoping you might see things differently." He paused and took a step towards me.

"Perhaps I should remind you once again of the alternative scenario I spelt out to you so clearly at our last meeting should you continue to reject my proposal."

I stood in front of him unwavering in my determination not to buckle as I waited for whatever it was he would say next. Part of me wanted to turn around and leave the room there and then having said what I had wanted, secure in the knowledge that anything he was about to add in reply was extremely unlikely to improve the situation between us or heal our relationship. I knew that morally I had every right to walk away but the fact still remained that Mr Taylor was my employer and as such I was required to demonstrate a degree of respect towards him as head of the house, something I was finding it increasingly hard to do. My mind struggled to make sense of this apparent piece of perverse logic, with my having no real idea as to why I should trust and obey these feelings of obdurate loyalty to a man who had proven himself to be both shameful and dishonourable in his attitude towards me. Taking another step towards me and glancing at his watch he continued.

"To be honest with you, Ruth, I had half anticipated your reply and continued protestations to my suggestion. So, with that in mind allow me to add some additional detail to the outline of the alternative proposal we discussed yesterday. Can I further suggest you consider what I am about to say very seriously before making your final, and potentially very costly decision?" He stood quite still about three paces in front of me. I could feel the sweat of fear and anger running down my back as I struggled to decide whether to listen to what he was about to say or just slap him across the face and walk away. I hastily chose the former, reasoning just as quickly that whilst the alternative would satisfy my inner rage momentarily, the hurt inflicted on myself and others would, in the longer term, be far greater than the fleeting sting of pain in my hand caused by the slap to his face.

There was a brief yet deafening silence between us as we both stood our ground, each staring hard at the other. It felt as if we were two gladiators awaiting the next move of our opponent and deciding how best to respond and strike back at their foe. In truth I felt nothing like a gladiator, more like the innocent Christian standing before a lion poised to inflict the fatal blow. In an effort not to portray this inner fear I looked deep into his eyes refusing to alter my gaze. I told myself whatever he was about to say could never be as bad as what I, and so many others, had endured under the fanatical rule of the guards in the death camp at Birkenau. Even with this thought rooted firmly in the forefront of my mind I still felt a rising sense of fear move within me as I prepared myself for whatever it was he was about to say. I couldn't believe that less than twenty-four hours earlier I had considered myself to be one of the luckiest young women alive, holding down a job that I loved and working for a family I was becoming more and more drawn towards in my affections. I had even allowed myself the luxury of thinking they might feel the same way about me. And yet, here I was less than a day later not only being verbally abused by one of the very people I had come to care for, and more importantly trust, but now facing the very real threat of him seeking to carry out acts of both physical and sexual violence against me.

Mr Taylor took a deep breath and exhaled slowly as if considering his next response. I sensed a small degree of nervousness in his bearing and body language. Had I scared him off, or was he about to suggest something so awful that the prospect of it becoming a reality was proving a little unnerving even to him?

"As we discussed yesterday, and as you are fully aware, my wife has an attractive and, also rather expensive collection of jewellery. She has told me that on occasion she has allowed you to try on one or two of the pieces for yourself when you have been helping her to dress for a particular event or function that we were to attend, isn't that so?"

After a short silence and with my mind racing to make sense of the point he was making I replied nervously. "Yes that's true. Your wife is a very beautiful lady and fortunate to have so many lovely things." There was another awkward pause. I bit hard into my lip determined not to speak again until I was sure as to where this conversation was headed, but already fearing the worst.

"Do you have any jewellery yourself, Ruth?"

"No sir. Sadly, any that our family had was removed from our belongings on our arrival in Birkenau along with my mother's wedding ring which was taken at the same time." The empathy and compassion he and Mrs Taylor had demonstrated towards me when I first recounted my story about life in Birkenau shortly after my arrival in their home was now missing entirely from both his tone and demeanour as he continued.

"My wife is very careful in looking after her jewellery as you know. Indeed, some of the more expensive pieces are held here in this room in a small safe I have, only being brought out for special occasions." He paused for a moment, putting his hand into his jacket and taking out a cigarette case from the inside breast pocket.

Carefully taking a cigarette from it with one hand he closed the case with the other and slid it back into his jacket pocket.

"Helen mentioned to me that you had commented on how much you liked the particular pair of diamond earrings she had worn recently to the Lord Mayor's Ball. We spoke about that yesterday, if you remember?" I still wasn't sure as to the intended outcome of his story but did recall those particular earrings as they were similar in style to a pair my mother had owned when I was younger. They had been nowhere near as valuable of course with the stones in my mother's earrings not being real diamonds as they were in Mrs Taylor's.

"Yes, they are very beautiful and looked lovely on her." I remembered how my mother had let me try hers on once, but they had slipped from my ear when the clasp loosened and had fallen to the floor. She picked them up and placed them back in her jewellery box until my father was able to get them repaired. I told Mr Taylor I had mentioned this to his wife on the day she prepared to leave for the Ball and that she had been generous in allowing me to hold hers to my ear for a moment. He smiled and, lighting his cigarette, took another step towards me. He leant forward, his face now so close to my own I could smell the tobacco on his breath as he exhaled deliberately into my face which caused me to blink as the smoke stung my eyes. Making no apology for his action he stood up straight again and watched as I wiped an involuntary tear from my eye.

"That's right. Helen also mentioned that story to me on our way to the Ball." He grinned, clearly relishing his part in our discussion. "She told me how she felt sorry for you and wished there was more we could do for you, such was her concern and liking for you." He took another deliberate draw on his cigarette and continued. "The thing is, Ruth; my wife is very fond of those earrings. As I said earlier they hold special memories for both of us: I bought them for her on our second wedding anniversary." He paused as if recalling the event. "Also, to celebrate my becoming manager of the first international trading branch of the bank here in London. It was quite a promotion as you can no doubt imagine." He paused again as if allowing the full impact of what he had said and was about to propose to sink in.

"As I intimated to you yesterday, should those earrings go missing both my wife and I would be devastated. And of course there is also the monetary value to be considered as well." He took another draw on his cigarette. "Can you imagine how she, indeed we, would feel should we discover they had been stolen?" My heart sank as I dared to fear what he was about to say.

"Who on earth would want steal them?" A sudden rush of anxiety gripped me as I began to comprehend the full potential of what he was alluding to.

"Well that's the thing, Ruth, you see it could only be someone who has access to both my wife's room and to her personal belongings, because at all other times they would be locked here in the safe along with anything else of value. So clearly it would have to be someone we both trusted. How else would they know the earrings were in her room and not locked away here in the safe?" He walked to his desk and put out his cigarette in the ash tray. Then, turning back towards me and clearly relishing the moment, he continued.

"Now if I were a policeman I would want to interview all the household staff, including poor Nelly of course. Sadly, she would now come under suspicion herself because she also has the same regular access to her employer's dressing room as you do."

He stood for a moment as if to collect his thoughts, then continuing to play the role of would be detective he took a step towards me. "However, and as we would have to point out to the investigating officer, Nelly has never been afforded any of the privileges that my wife has seen fit to bestow on you, especially with regards to allowing her the same direct access to her jewellery and other treasured possessions, and certainly not with the same freedom of access that you have enjoyed. And it's difficult also to forget the added significance as far as you're concerned when further considering your own mother's earrings and how much they meant to you."

I moved to interrupt now fully cognisant as to where this conversation was headed.

"Mr Taylor if you think for one minute I could…" He put his hand up to silence me.

"We would of course speak up for you as best we could, Ruth. But, bearing in mind your past and the awful things you have experienced it wouldn't be unreasonable to suppose that for a moment perhaps, no matter how brief, you had taken leave of your senses and…"

It was my turn to interrupt. "If you honestly think for one minute I could, or would, ever take advantage of the warmth and affection Mrs Taylor has shown towards me then, with all due respect sir it must be you who has taken leave of their senses." He stood motionless in front of me, as if stunned by the directness of my reply. Then, and quite deliberately he smiled at me again.

"But what about the evidence, Ruth my dear? What about the evidence?"

My mind was racing, trying to assimilate exactly what it was we were now discussing. What evidence was he alluding to? Come to that, what crime was he alluding to?

Was I really to be accused of stealing Mrs Taylor's earrings when we both knew those self same earrings were locked away in his safe?

"I'm afraid I don't understand when you ask about the evidence. What evidence are you talking about?" Before he could answer I spoke again. "Actually, Mr Taylor, I'm not even sure of the crime you are talking about? We both know that your wife's earrings are securely locked away here in your study, you told me that just a few minutes ago?"

He took another step forward. "Indeed they are, Ruth, at least for now, but who knows where they might appear next?" He stared at me for a moment, a look of frustration descending over his face. "Look, I'm getting a little tired of this game we appear to be playing, you know full well what I am suggesting. But, just in case I haven't made myself entirely clear let me spell it out for you one more time."

A genuine sense of fear and panic gripped me.

"We both know that my wife is heavily pregnant at the moment and unfortunately unable to fulfil some of the more intimate duties that I might reasonably and traditionally expect from her, that much I have already made clear, yes?" I stood motionless not knowing how to respond. "I'll presume from your silence that we understand each other thus far. Now, bearing in mind both our apparent desires to make life easier for Helen at this difficult time what I am proposing is that, for now at least, you take on those particular duties. Further, and as I intimated yesterday should you refuse to accede to this request then I am not sure your services here would continue to be viewed either as necessary or as vital as both you and Helen might perceive them to be. This of course would prove especially true should my wife's earrings go missing and then you be found responsible for their disappearance. Sadly, this would result in us having little or no choice but to dispense with your services and allow the full weight of the law and associated authorities to deal with you."

I stood motionless in utter disbelief as the detail of what he had just outlined sunk in. I was beyond anger, and spoke without thinking. "But as you said yourself what about the evidence? He moved towards me. I looked into his piercing dark brown eyes but could find no trace of reason or compassion within his gaze.

"The evidence, my dear young Ruth," his words and delivery both rigid and deliberate, "and you can trust me on this, would be found amongst your personal belongings along with the monies you had already received from selling other valuable items missing from our home."

I could hardly take in what I was hearing as tears of hate and despair began to run down my cheeks. Mr Taylor watched me cry for a moment assuming from my reaction he had made his point, then moving away slightly he took another cigarette from the box on his table. He turned to face me again, his voice and body language changing once more, almost chameleon like, becoming much softer and gentler in tone.

"Listen, my dear, I don't particularly want to unleash such malice or unpleasantness on this house or its occupants. The resultant publicity for us as a family would be somewhat embarrassing I have to admit, but for you of course it would prove utterly devastating." He paused to light his cigarette. "Even if Helen and I agreed not to press charges because of our deeply held sympathies for all you have experienced in the past and not wanting to see you go through further pain or, worse perhaps, serve a prison sentence, the truth would still remain that you would have to leave our employ. Sadly, neither of us would feel able to trust you any longer either with our belongings or, more especially, with the care of our beautiful daughter. Indeed, think for a moment of the effect such an outcome would have on young Elizabeth herself. It could possibly destroy her ability to trust anybody outside of her immediate family ever again, even at the most basic of levels. And I cannot even begin to imagine the heartbreak she would experience in seeing someone she had thought of so highly fail her in such a way."

He drew on his cigarette allowing the nightmare scenario he had painted to take root in my mind. "Would you really want to carry the responsibility for such sadness on your shoulders, my dear, knowing you had scarred our daughter so badly?" He paused again. "Of course, no matter how painful a prospect that might appear to be, the truth is it can all still be avoided by you reconsidering your earlier outburst and offering one simple word of agreement in its place, yes."

I stood there totally dumbstruck, unable to move and not knowing what to say or how to respond. Within those few short sentences he had threatened, not only, the future happiness of his own family, but had also failed me on every level as well. In an instant he had destroyed all the goodwill and trust established between us in the time I had been in working there. My mind raced as he moved towards his desk. I watched as he sat down and crossed his legs, leaning back in his chair and waiting to see how I would respond.

My thoughts went back to Birkenau and how we had been forced to face very real life and death decisions every day. Even though my life wasn't being threatened in the same way now the scenario and outcome, whichever choice I made, was no less devastating. After a few moments he broke the silence.

"Your appetite for confrontation appears to have dissipated a little, Ruth. Am I to assume you are willing to put Elizabeth and my wife's happiness and well being above your own?" His words, whilst wholly offensive in their delivery and intent, made me realise that I had little, if any choice. My earlier objective of denying him his victory lay in ruins on the study floor. If I said no I would lose my job and potentially the ability to find any similar work for some period of time, if ever. I could even face criminal proceedings, with the chances of success in any legal appeal I might try to initiate against a man of such standing in the community as Mr Taylor being limited in the extreme. But above all of that my real concern was in knowing the greatest misery experienced in this whole sorry affair would not be that intended to harm me but more the pain levied upon the two people I cared most about, and had even come to love in a way. I asked myself again, how could a man so readily threaten the future happiness of an entire family for the sake of his own selfish desires?

The ultimate question for me became not so much about the physical act of agreeing to Mr Taylor's demands but more about my ability to live with the self loathing that I knew would accompany such a decision. I stood in silent prayer for a moment asking for some form of divine guidance, but my mind was so confused I could barely remember my own name let alone absorb any spiritual wisdom that might have been extended to me. I suddenly remembered what Sarah had said to during some of the darkest days we spent together in Birkenau. "Do what you need to do to survive." Whilst I recognised the circumstances she had been alluding to where very different from those facing me now, the awful consequences of my agreeing to such degradation appeared no less threatening as I stood watching my tormentor smile knowingly at me from behind his desk. Suddenly his voice interrupted my thoughts and I was jolted back to the present.

"Well my dear?"

I tried to muster as much dignity and defiance into my limp reply as I could. "It appears you leave me little choice."

"There is always a choice, Ruth, it's just a matter of making the right one." He put out his cigarette and leant forward placing his hands on the desk in front of him. "Can I assume therefore that you have made that right choice, for all concerned?"

My eyes filled again as I nodded meekly towards him, the fight suddenly draining from me.

"Well done, I'm sure in the longer term you won't regret it." He rose from his chair and approached me, his voice and manner more relaxed. "You can think of the small rise in your pay that we spoke of yesterday as part payment for additional services rendered if you like. Although, for the reasons I have already outlined that particular detail must remain between the two of us."

I felt a tear run down my cheek as he spoke.

"Now you run along and wipe those tears from your pretty face. After all we don't want anyone to think there is any animosity between us do we, especially as we are about to become even closer, so to speak." He lifted a finger to my face as if to halt my tears. I felt my body shudder and recoil in disgust at his touch and glanced up as he smiled at me again. It was a smile of self satisfied control and dominance and one I had seen many times before in Birkenau after a German guard had inflicted some unwarranted pain or punishment on one of the prisoners. Mr Taylor appeared completely unmoved or fazed by what had just taken place between us. It was as though he had just completed another successful trade agreement at the bank and I had become simply one more business acquisition.

"I'll talk to you later about when we might get together, Ruth, but for now you can go back to your other duties." I felt my head drop in defeat as I berated myself internally over what I had just agreed to. But what choice did I have, especially if I wanted to retain a roof over my head, have food in my stomach and continue to care for the little girl I was employed to watch over and protect. Elizabeth and her safe-keeping had always been my priority, but from now on my desire to protect her would be driven by a fresh zeal and single-minded determination burning within me; from now on I would be protecting her from her own father. My feet, like my entire body, felt leaden as I trudged slowly out of the room. I closed the study door and as I did so I became aware of a new one opening before me, but where would it lead? All I knew for certain was that whatever the destination it would not prove to be a happy one.

NINETEEN

I spent some time alone today thinking about the questions Ruth might ask me questions about Jenny and myself growing up with James and Carol. How much was I prepared to tell her; how much was I willing to reveal about the life I had come to know and love without her?

I got some old photo albums out to remind me of certain times and events in Jenny's life; ones that had proved to be those landmark occasions that stay with you over the years as you watch your children grow. I laughed as I remembered how many times I had told Dad off in the past for taking so many pictures of Jenny when she was younger, but was now suddenly grateful for. I think if I'm honest, my real reason for looking through those albums was to be able to taunt Ruth.

"See what you missed out on, these are the special times in your granddaughter's life that you weren't a part of. And that's your fault, you have no-one to blame but yourself because you didn't want me or love me enough to keep me." I know that sounds spiteful, but sometimes that's the way I feel about how she treated me, although I would never verbalise any of those thoughts to Jenny of course. Like most parents I do the exact opposite and encourage her to be nice to the people who have hurt her, to turn the other cheek so to speak. It's different of course when it affects you personally, but I am trying to be more positive in how I think about Ruth. That said I still don't find it easy to be generous in my attitude towards her. I suppose a psychologist would tell me I'm only hurting myself by holding onto the anger and resentment built up over the years about how I feel she treated me. They would no doubt say she had moved on with her life and rarely, if ever, thought about me or what had happened, although I can't really believe that. If it were true though, then far from letting my pain and resentment go, I would hold it all the more tightly, asking what sort of woman could have a baby and then not only give it away but choose to forget about it altogether. At other times I accept these are just my own irrational thoughts, and perhaps like me she has spent these past twenty eight years wondering how different life might have been for both of us had she kept me and brought me up as her own daughter?

As I looked through the pictures in the album I came across some from the first holiday the three of us took Jenny on as a family. She was nearly two and we went to a fishing village in Cornwall called Gorran Haven. It had a small sandy beach where we rented a house overlooking the harbour. We spent a lovely week there and Dad especially enjoyed looking in the rock pools with Jenny for crabs, shrimps and the like. I well remember the first discovery they made together. Jenny came running across the sand back to Mum and I utterly beside herself with excitement.

"Cab cab," she yelled as Dad dutifully followed behind carrying Jenny's little yellow bucket containing their precious find.

"I don't remember ordering a taxi," Mum said as Dad arrived panting and out of breath, trying not to spill the contents of the bucket on the ground, as he chased Jenny across the beach.

"She's telling you we've found a crab, you silly woman," he spluttered.

"Really," Mum replied, the two of us laughing. "We would never have guessed." By this time Jenny was jumping up and down in elated animation, her arms and legs flailing about in similar fashion to the poor crab as it made a vain attempt to escape its yellow prison. Jenny squealed with delight as she pointed excitedly at their find. "Mummy cab." As Dad placed the bucket on the blanket Jenny decided to prove to us the crab was still alive by kicking the bright yellow container with her little foot in an effort to make the terrified creature move away from the piece of seaweed it was currently seeking shelter beneath. As she did so the entire contents spilled out, causing Mum and I to jump up and scream as the crab raced sideways across the blanket towards us. Poor Jenny became immediately distraught at the apparent loss of her beloved "cab" with her squeals of delight turning in an instant to tears and distress.

"Mummy cab, get cab," she cried as the small animal dashed from side to side on the blanket in its efforts to find somewhere to hide.

"Mummy loves you very much, Jenny, but not quite enough to pick that up." I pointed at the now seemingly demented crab as it ran towards my sun hat. Mum, keeping a watchful eye on the tiny crustacean reached out to comfort Jenny with one hand and gripped Dad's arm with the other.

"Granny feels the same way as Mummy I'm afraid, darling. This is a job for Granddad." Dad, wondering what all the fuss was about, reached down and picked up the crab and placed it back in the now empty bucket.

"Come on, Jenny, let's go and put some more water in here for the crab to play in while silly Mummy and Granny tidy up the mess they've made."

"The mess we've made?"

"Oh so now as well as upsetting my granddaughter with your hysterics the two of you are going to blame her for this little accident as well are you?" He folded his arms in mock disgust at our protest and looked down at Jenny.

"I think when we get back we will both need an ice cream by way of an apology as well if that's all right with you, Granny?" Dad winked at Mum and taking the bucket in one hand and Jenny in the other turned away and headed back towards the sea.

Mum and I laughed as we watched the two of them walk away blissfully happy in each other's company and with their precious find safely ensconced once more in its brightly coloured temporary home.

It was a wonderful holiday and one that only served to cement the love and devotion already established between us.

As I sorted through the photographs of the four of us I realised how much I had come to depend on Mum and Dad over the years. This was born out, not only, through the love and care they had shown me personally but also in the support and concern they had displayed towards Jenny as her grandparents. Now, as a mother myself I could truly appreciate the cost of parenthood and not only in financial terms. To be accountable for the nurture and upbringing of another human being is a truly life-changing responsibility for any parent and for James and Carol it must have placed even greater demands on them at times. They had already experienced the trauma of being told they couldn't have children of their own and, having battled through that terrible period of sadness together, then decided bravely to adopt me as their daughter. When two people choose to create a new life they have traditionally thought about it long and hard before they actually come together as a couple, and once that baby makes its entrance into the world there is an instant bond of love that manifests itself between the parent and child. I know that to be true because from the moment Jenny left my body we became as one all over again. A chord of affection formed between us a thousand times stronger than the physical one that had connected the two of us in the previous nine months she had spent growing inside of me. When I thought about the actual process Mum and Dad had gone through in choosing me to be their daughter, especially after losing a little girl of their own, I realised how deep their feelings towards me must have been and how much I had come to mean to them across the years we had been together. Theirs had truly proved to be a sacrificial love in every sense of the word. They had fought against every possible human emotion when laying aside their absolute and unspeakable grief in not being able to bring a child of their own into the world and then going on to choose someone else's baby to pour out their hearts and love into accepting as they must, that no matter how close they might become to this child, it would never, and could never, be of their own flesh.

As I pondered this gift of unconditional love and security that had been poured out so freely on me by these two wonderful people I wondered again if I was doing the right thing in agreeing, at least in principle, to meet with Ruth? She may have given birth to me but for all intents and purposes had, in letting me go, lost me forever just as Mum and Dad had their own baby girl. The difference being of course that Carol and James had lost their child because of an unfair act of nature and through no fault of their own, whilst Ruth had, in all likelihood, made the conscious decision to remove me from her life.

What had happened all those years ago that had caused her to let me go, presumably in the knowledge that we might never see each other again? No matter how often I wrestled with my thoughts I knew ultimately I did need to talk to her if only to lay to rest once and for all these seemingly endless scenarios that forever tormented my mind. At least I was secure now in the knowledge that Dad and Mum were happy for me to meet with her. The only question now remaining was could I actually go through with it? Did I really want to know this truth, a truth that might throw my life into turmoil all over again or, just perhaps, quiet my heart and its doubts forever?

Dad put it best one day when I was struggling with these reservations yet again. "You'll never know if you don't talk to her, Mary, and ask her what happened. And if you don't then I think, in the years ahead, that the not knowing will prove to be the greater regret to you." I knew he was right.

TWENTY

It was almost a week before Mr Taylor approached me again, but I was immediately in no doubt as to what he wanted. Over the previous few days I had begun to hope he might have realised the folly of his proposal and changed his mind with him making no physical attempt at any form of contact during that time apart from a simple "Good morning" or "Good evening" should our paths happen to cross at either the beginning or end of the day. That said there was still the larger part of me which feared my hopes would be dashed, and so it proved on that fateful Thursday afternoon.

I was in the hallway preparing for Elizabeth's arrival home from school when Mr Taylor walked through the front door. He spoke abruptly and without any form of greeting or personal acknowledgement. "Please come to my study, Ruth."

A sudden dread ran through me as I stuttered my reply attempting to avoid his command. "I'm just waiting for Elizabeth; she'll be home any minute."

Mr Taylor stopped and turned, his voice demonstrating an authority that offered no room for discussion. "And a minute's all I need." He walked towards the study, leaving the door open behind him. "Now, if you please, Ruth."

I followed, also deciding not to close the door in the vain hope that by doing so he might choose another subject to talk about and so avoid the potential of our being overheard if my worst fears were indeed about to be realised.

"Close the door please." As I moved to obey his instruction my heart sank.

"Helen is going away next weekend to her sister Julia's. She is also proposing to take Elizabeth with her. I suggest that might provide the appropriate opportunity for you and I to spend some time together." His words thudded into my head, scrambling my thoughts as I fought to think of something to say that might delay the now seemingly inevitable.

"Mrs Taylor hasn't said anything to me about going away," I stammered, trying desperately to discourage him from continuing this present line of conversation.

"I wasn't aware that my wife and I were required to consult you about the decision-making process of our daily routine? Indeed, I thought we only needed to involve you and the other staff once we have determined whatever it is we have chosen to do? We then inform each of you accordingly as to how best you might serve in fulfilling our needs; isn't that the way it works?" He stared at me purposely, demonstrating no trace of emotion. "Perhaps I was wrong in making such an assumption and you have alternative ideas as to how the employer employee relationship should work within our home?" He paused momentarily, maintaining his unforgiving stare. "Not that it is any of your business but, Helen only confirmed her decision to visit with Julia on the telephone last night. No doubt she intends to speak to you about it later today. Will that suit you, or do you feel I should ask her in future to consult with you directly as to her intentions when planning or making all personal arrangements?"

I presumed his sarcastic and withering response to my remark had been prompted by his frustration at my daring to question his authority. Also, his face was flushed and I sensed a degree of nervousness on his part. This was never going to be an easy conversation for either of us.

"I'm sorry if I appeared rude, sir, I didn't mean anything by it. It is just Mrs Taylor usually gives me due notice when she is making arrangements of this sort, especially if they involve Elizabeth. I hadn't realised she had only spoken to her sister last evening. As you say, she probably intends to tell me about her plans later. I apologise." I spoke slowly and deliberately in an effort to ease the palpable tension between us. Although quite why I was trying to placate the very individual who was threatening to abuse so much more than our already shattered relationship I wasn't entirely sure.

I watched as he took a cigarette from the box on his desk and move to light it, his mood softening as he took a first comforting draw on it.

"Helen met me for lunch earlier today as you are aware and we discussed the detail of her visit then." He took another draw on his cigarette and lifting his head exhaled the smoke into the air. "As you know we haven't been sharing a bed of late due to Helen not sleeping well because of the baby's desire to move around at night leaving her both uncomfortable and tired, hence we were not able to talk fully about her sister's invitation earlier. Julia has invited both Helen and Elizabeth to stay for a few days, and she wanted to talk to me to see if I had any objections which, naturally I didn't. Colin is away on business at the moment and Julia thought it might be good for the two of them to spend some time together. Elizabeth and her daughter, who, as you know, is only a year older, both get on well and so Helen and Julia thought it would be good for them to spend some time in each others company as well."

He took another long draw on his cigarette and smiled at me. "Naturally I gave my approval as it works out well for all of us. I don't suppose Helen will have a chance to see her sister again before the new baby arrives and so I am sure a few days being pampered by her own family will also do her good." There was an awkward silence between us which eventually I broke.

"I'm not sure what it is you want me to say?"

"You don't need to say or do anything at this time, other than to help Helen and Elizabeth pack and prepare for their trip. Devlin will drive the two of them to the house and will therefore also be away overnight. I understand from my discussions with Helen that Nelly has arranged to see her mother at the same time. Apparently she has some leave booked, which leaves only the two of us and Mrs Devlin to consider. As she never tends to leave the kitchen, except when occasionally helping to serve meals that should allow the two of us ample opportunity to spend time together." As he finished speaking I heard the front door open and Elizabeth's voice call out to me.

"Ruth, where are you, I'm home."

"I need to go now, Mr Taylor."

"Of course. I will speak with you again soon to arrange the final detail of our next meeting."

I watched as he put out his cigarette and moving away from his desk walked towards me, his eyes staring straight at me dark and foreboding.

"Remember, Ruth, for everyone's sake, especially your own, this arrangement is to remain between ourselves, am I clear?" I had no words to offer in response and so turned away closing the door behind me.

And so it began.

My heart raced as Elizabeth and Mrs Taylor climbed into the car that Friday afternoon. "Now make sure you look after Ruth over the next few days, Robert, and give her plenty of time to herself. She doesn't need to be running around after you with the two of us away." Mr Taylor leant forward, kissing his wife on the cheek as she leant out of the car window.

"Don't worry, dear, we'll be fine, won't we, Ruth? I promise not to give her anything too onerous to do." He turned and smiled at me, clearly enjoying the moment. Elizabeth's head appeared by the side of her mother's, her dark curly hair catching the breeze and blowing across her face. "Don't forget to read my dolls a bedtime story will you, Ruth?"

"I won't." I made a vain attempt to smile at her, trying my best not to let my emotions rise to the fore as I bit my lip in an effort to hold back the tears I could already feel stinging the back of my eyes.

Mr Taylor and I stood and watched as Mr Devlin got into the car and started the engine.

"Drive carefully, Devlin, you have a precious load on board you know."

I shook my head in disbelief at his supposed concern for the well being of his family knowing only too well his true intentions once they had departed.

Elizabeth called out to me one last time as her mother pulled her back inside the car. "Goodbye Ruth." Mrs Taylor gave a final wave to her husband as she sank back into her seat and closed the window, the two of them blowing a parting kiss towards each other as the car pulled away. I could hardly believe the man standing beside me and demonstrating such apparent affection towards his wife and family was about to betray them in such an appalling way. As he stood waving enthusiastically after the car he displayed no evident sign of any moral conscience to trouble or concern him with regards to his proposed actions against me in the hours to come. I moved quickly back towards the house as the car turned the corner at the end of the road and out of sight. As I reached the front door he drew alongside of me.

"I'll come to your room after supper, Ruth, be ready."

I felt a chill run down my spine as the words I had been dreading exploded into my head like a bomb going off sending my thoughts and heart racing out of control. I turned to face my tormentor.

"Please Mr Taylor I…" The words stuck in my throat as I struggled to compose myself.

"We've been through all of this, Ruth, so please let's not waste any more time in discussing it." He turned and with a final glance down the road to make sure the car had gone strode past me through the open door leaving me to close it behind us as if further demonstrating his ultimate authority over me.

I stood for a moment looking heavenward, offering a silent prayer for help as dark rain clouds moved swiftly across the sky and a chill breeze blew around me. As the first spots of rain splashed my face I felt a shudder run through my body. Was this a reaction to the potential storm brewing in the skies overhead or something far more sinister and threatening that was about to encompass me.

That first time was the worst, with Mr Taylor showing no sign of emotion as he pushed me down onto my bed and, forcing my legs apart, put himself inside me. I turned my face to the wall, remembering what Sarah had told me about her actions during the times when the German soldier had raped her repeatedly. She said she forced her mind to detach itself from what was happening to her body no matter how hard the beating or degrading the sexual demands made of her. Although I tried to do the same and take some limited comfort in the knowledge that at least Mr Taylor was not physically beating me it did little to reassure me as to the violation that was being forced on me internally, nor as to the effect it would have on me mentally, both now and in the days ahead. This wasn't an act of love I was experiencing it was an act of violence and, in its way, every bit as brutal as any physical beating I could ever receive. The mental scars and bruising I would be left with would be equally as painful to bear as any I might receive from a clenched fist or a boot.

When he had finished Mr Taylor got up from my bed and dressed himself quickly.

"That wasn't too bad, was it, my dear?" he enquired, sitting on my chair to tie the laces on his shoes. I stared at the ceiling only aware of his movement from the corner of my eye, refusing to look directly at him or acknowledge him in any physical way. If he was hoping I might salve his conscience in some way by offering any form of gratitude or approval as to his actions then he would have to wait a very long time. He may have access to my body but I would never allow him that same access to my mind or thoughts; those were, and always would be my own. And for now they held nothing but contempt and revulsion towards him for what he had done. I heard him turn the handle on the door as he made to leave.

"I am out for much of the day tomorrow, as I believe you are as well. Helen informed me she had given you some additional time off from your usual duties while she and Elizabeth are away so I suggest we meet here again tomorrow evening around the same time."

I didn't reply but focused my whole being on not crying in front of him although I could already feel the tears filling my eyes.

"I understand this may not be what you had envisaged as part of your contract when you first agreed to work here Ruth, but you did readily commit to helping both Helen and I in any way you could, particularly at this difficult time. Why not think of what you have just done in this way, that in making life less demanding for Helen who already has so much on her mind with Elizabeth and the new baby, you really are doing both of us a great service. I suggest you view this new part of our arrangement as a simple continuation of that earlier stated agreement?" I lay motionless still refusing to acknowledge him as I heard the door creak open.

"You never know, you might even begin to enjoy it." He paused and took a step towards me. "You know, Ruth, whatever you may think of me at this moment you should also be aware that you are now as complicit in any perceived betrayal of my wife as you deem me to be. So don't go thinking you hold the moral high ground in that regard because you don't, not after what we have just done together."

I felt tears of frustration and loathing run down the side of my face.

"Goodnight Ruth." As he closed the door behind him I broke completely and, turning over, wept openly into my pillow. I knew I was trapped, and innocent though I may have been as far as any part of the planning or agreement to what had just taken place between us was concerned, the truth still remained that I was, as he had stated, every bit as guilty of adultery as he was. I looked at the picture of my parents and Joseph and wept again for their passing. Also, that I couldn't talk to them and ask their advice as to what I should do. I lay there, my mind racing back and forth as the tears flowed wondering how, in just a few short days, my seemingly blissful existence had turned once again into a living hell of nightmare proportions. I cried myself to sleep that night and almost every other night during the rest of my time at the Taylor's house.

He came to my room again over the next two evenings until the return of Mrs Taylor and Elizabeth. Following that his visits became more infrequent, limiting themselves to the odd afternoon or evening when the rest of the family were out or the house was quiet.

I did my best to avoid him at all other times and would attempt to make excuses about having to be somewhere else when I was aware of him wanting to be with me again. The worst part for me was in maintaining the ongoing betrayal between Mrs Taylor and myself about what was happening. In a perverse way having survived the horrors of Birkenau, where lies and deceit were an every day occurrence, I was quickly able to adopt the art again of hiding the truth from her whenever we spoke, acting as though everything was as it had been before. There were times though when I would watch her and Mr Taylor exchange a kiss or another show of affection and want to scream out the truth as to what a despicable liar and cheat he really was. I think he sensed these moments, almost relishing the opportunity to taunt me in this way knowing if I did choose to speak out not only would I lose my position, a job that I loved, but also the friendship and trust of one of the few people I genuinely cared about. Our relationship would be destroyed forever along with my association with Elizabeth and the new baby which was due to arrive at any time. It was if he were playing a game of dare with me, a game that would always see me lose no matter which way I chose to play it.

Like everybody else in the house I was thrilled the day Mrs

Taylor came home with a baby brother for Elizabeth. She ran excitedly through the front door and into my arms.

"This is my brother and his name is George, but he can't talk yet so Mummy says I have to tell everyone." I held her close cursing the events of the past few weeks, desperately wishing they had never of happened and that we could go back to the innocence of those first few months spent together.

"George is a lovely name and I am sure he will like having a pretty sister like you to play with when he is a bit older."

"Yes but we must make sure he doesn't touch my dolls because he might break them and then I would have to tell him he was naughty, wouldn't I, Ruth?" I laughed as she pulled away and ran after her mother who was carrying her baby brother towards the stairs.

"You come with us, Ruth. Let's introduce Master George to his new bedroom." I moved to join them as Mr Taylor entered carrying his wife's bag from the car.

"I see you girls are ganging up on my son already," he said, laughing as he spoke. I looked at him wondering if this really could be the same person who had raped me just a few days previously but was now portraying himself as the happily married man and proud father. I hated him with a passion but continued to play my part in this increasingly false game of happy families knowing the cost to everyone concerned, especially myself, would be all the greater if I spoke out.

Over the next few weeks' things settled into a new routine, with my looking after Elizabeth and meeting her daily needs while Mr and Mrs Taylor spent as much time as possible with George. Even better was the fact that, with the two of them being so involved with the new addition to their family, Mr Taylor made no more advances towards me. So for a short time at least things appeared to return to how they had been when I first joined them, with genuine good humour and laughter ringing through the house once more. It was three weeks after George arrived that things changed again, this time forever, and with no chance of a return to the normality of family life I had been praying for.

I had been experiencing occasional stomach pains and bouts of sickness for a few days and so Mrs Taylor made an appointment for me to see their doctor, Mr Anderson, who was also a family friend. He couldn't find anything wrong initially and so after questioning me about my general health and taking a urine sample suggested I come back a few days later for the results. It was then he broke the devastating news that would alter my life and those I cared about irrevocably.

"The results have come back as positive, Miss Cahn, you are pregnant." I sat opposite him bolt upright in my chair, not quite believing what I had heard.

"I can't be. You must have made a mistake."

He leant across his desk and smiled. "I'm afraid there is no mistake, my dear. As I say the test on your urine sample is positive, you *are* pregnant."

I sat for a moment staring ahead in silence, not knowing what to say or how to respond.

"I am assuming from your reaction this was not the news you were hoping for nor expecting?"

I shook my head still unable to speak.

"Mrs Taylor has asked me to keep her informed as to my diagnosis and of any problems she might be able to help with as far as any treatment is concerned." He paused. "Can I presume as you weren't expecting this news then neither will she be?" He leant forward sensing my dilemma. "Would you like me to speak to her or do you want to talk with her yourself first?"

My mind raced: how could I tell the woman who trusted me implicitly on every level that I was pregnant with her husband's baby?

"Please don't say anything, Doctor I'll..." my voice faltered along with my resolve.

He smiled again. "I understand this has come as a shock my

dear, but Robert and Helen *will* need to be informed, preferably sooner than later. This is hardly something that can be kept a secret."

I was now in a complete state of panic and responded as such. "Isn't there something you can do?" I spluttered, not knowing what I was asking, or how to best verbalise the dread and panic running through my head. "Isn't there a way for me not to have the baby?"

Doctor Anderson leant back in his chair, his face taking on a more serious expression.

"I hope you're not asking what I think you are, Miss Cahn, as that is something I would not consider recommending, and most definitely not for you. A healthy young woman with good support, I couldn't consider it. Besides what about the father, presumably you will want to speak to him before deciding on any course of action?"

My heart sank. What could I say in answer to such a question? "I'm sorry of course; it has just come as such a shock. Please don't say anything to Mrs Taylor, or at least not until I have had a chance to speak to her myself."

He sat back in his chair and smiled again. "Of course, I understand, but as I have said already this is not a matter that should be left. No doubt Helen will ask me herself over the next few days what is wrong should you fail to speak with her first." He paused. "She has a great affection for you, my dear, as you are no doubt aware. Helen is a very special lady and I am sure you wouldn't want to present her with any undue distress, especially so soon after young George's arrival into the family. Take my advice and tell her as soon as you are able, it will be for the best I assure you. I am sure she and Robert will stand by you and the load you feel you are carrying at this moment will become all the lighter once you have told them the truth about your situation. They are good people and will appreciate your honesty no matter how difficult the story of what has taken place might be for you to speak of. I make no judgement here, Miss Cahn, I am simply offering you my professional advice."

I could feel tears begin to fill my eyes as he spoke. He was right of course and I was heartened to hear of him speak so openly about Mrs Taylor's feelings towards me, but in a way that only made telling her the truth even harder. How could I begin to explain what I had allowed to happen or why without losing her trust and breaking her heart? And the consequences of informing Mr Taylor of my condition left me almost paralysed with fear.

"I know, Doctor and I…" My emotions overtook me and I began to sob.

Doctor Anderson rose from his chair and walked around his desk, placing a comforting hand on my shoulder.

"Try not to upset yourself, my dear. I can see this has come as a surprise and perhaps not an entirely welcome one but, knowing your employers as I do, I am sure they will seek to support you as best they can once you and the father have decided how you want to proceed."

I wanted to tell him the truth there and then, about what had happened and as to whom the father really was, but how could I and what would he say in reply if I did? I looked up and smiled at him through my tears.

"Thank you, Doctor, I'm sorry."

He sat on the corner of his desk and shook his head. "There's no need to apologise, my dear, I do understand. This can't be easy for you. Can I suggest you make another appointment with my receptionist for a week's time when we can discuss any medical issues pertaining to your pregnancy and to make sure all is well? That will also give you a chance to speak to Robert and Helen, and the father of course." He leant forward and smiled reassuringly. "In the meantime if Helen does ask I will simply say that it is early days and we are still confirming our thoughts, which is not entirely untrue, is it?"

I stood up and shook his hand. "Thank you, Doctor, I'll see you next week."

I stood in front of the receptionist to make my appointment for the following week and could tell from the disapproving look on her face she had already decided that I was yet another young girl who had got herself into trouble. Of course, I knew she wouldn't say anything to the Taylor's, her job depended on her ability to keep a confidence. If she did break this rule of trust she could just as easily lose her position as I was about to lose mine once the truth regarding my condition was revealed.

"We'll see you next week, *Miss* Cahn," she said with a knowing smirk on her face. I thanked her without making eye contact and hurried to leave.

As I stepped outside and took a deep breath the sun came out from behind a cloud and swept over me. I stood for a moment as the sun's bright rays embraced me warming my body but not my heart which ran icy cold with the fear of what was to come, and of the heart breaking conversation ahead of me with Mrs Taylor.

As I arrived home Elizabeth was standing at the front door and rushed down the steps to greet me. "Hello, Ruth, I've been waiting for you so we can play. Let's go up to my bedroom." Mrs Taylor approached the two of us from the sitting room and laughed.

"Honestly, Elizabeth, at least let poor Ruth take her coat off before you drag her away." I smiled at them both.

"That's alright," I said, taking Elizabeth's hand as we began to climb the stairs. Mrs Taylor called after us. "I want to hear how you got on with your appointment, dear; maybe after supper when Elizabeth has gone to bed, if you're not too exhausted by her ladyship in the meantime?" I turned and smiled at her as I continued up the stairs with my excited young charge who had clearly heard what her mother had said.

"What appointment does Mummy want to talk to you about when I'm in bed, is it a secret?"

I smiled down at her, squeezing her hand in an attempt to dispel her concern. "Nothing for you to worry about, darling, just grown up things."

The two of us played happily for the next hour or so until tea time. I made sure I sat beside Elizabeth at the table so as not to be cornered by Nelly or Mrs Taylor asking for the detail of what had been taken place at the doctors. It was later during Elizabeth and baby George's bath time as she rinsed the shampoo from her daughter's hair in an effort to cover her voice that Mrs Taylor spoke to me again about my earlier appointment with Doctor Anderson.

"Please come to the sitting room once the children are in bed, Ruth, I want to hear what he said and if there is anything Robert and I can do to help." A feeling of panic swept over me as I realised there was no escape for me now and that I would have to explain about my being pregnant. The decision I was still struggling with, yet knew had to be resolved, was whether I should tell her the full truth and as to whom the father of my child was? What would she say, and would she believe me? Mr Taylor was sure to deny any involvement if I did speak out about what had happened between us and, no doubt, would carry out his threat to further expose me as a thief if my story was not to his liking?

The next half an hour was spent in getting the children ready for bed and making small talk with Elizabeth and her mother while I battled with my conscious as to what I would actually say when we were finally alone.

Mrs Taylor smiled as she put her head round Elizabeth's bedroom door. "George is asleep already. Hopefully he'll stay that way for a while. He's not really been himself today; I hope he's not coming down with something."

I smiled back as I tucked Elizabeth's blanket around her. "I'm sure he'll be fine."

As I leant over to give Elizabeth a goodnight kiss she put her little arms around me and drew me into her giving me a warm and affectionate hug. Her mother joined us and also gave her daughter a kiss.

"Goodnight, Ruth, goodnight, Mummy."

"Straight to sleep now, darling, we'll see you in the morning."

The two of us closed the bedroom door and smiled at each other in a mutual show of affection. She laughed as we walked across the landing together.

"She loves you very much, Ruth. It's just as well I'm not a jealous Mother." I smiled back at her. "I'm very fond of Elizabeth as well; she's a lovely little girl. You and Mr Taylor must be very proud of her."

"We are, Ruth, and much of that, certainly more recently, is down to you, dear. You have a wonderful calming influence on her." She laughed again. "Indeed I think you've proved to be a calming influence on us all, even Robert speaks well of you. The most I can usually get from him when talking about domestic and staffing issues is a grunt, but he really appears to have taken a shine to you, although he would never admit to it publicly of course. It's not in his nature to make a fuss but I can tell he is impressed with your work." She placed her hand on my shoulder as we descended the stairs together. "And you know how I feel about you don't you, Ruth? You have become a very important addition to our family, and I'm sure young Master George will come to know and care for you with the same degree of affection in the years ahead as his sister has done." She moved her hand onto my arm and squeezed it. "As we all have done."

"Thank you Mrs Taylor, you're very kind."

"Not at all, it is I who should be thanking you. You have made a real difference to this house, Ruth, and I am especially grateful to you for that."

I was touched by her words of affirmation but my heart quickly sank as she spoke again.

"Now then let's go to the sitting room and you can tell me what Doctor Anderson said, I'm sure it won't be anything serious." My mind raced as I tried to think of any possible excuse to delay the inevitable.

"I'll make us a pot of tea as well. Mrs Devlin is out this evening and I don't want to trouble Nelly, she's had a busy day too." Mrs

Taylor laughed again. "I think we both deserve some refreshment after that exhausting hour with the children, don't you?"

"I'll make the tea," I said, feeling uncomfortable enough already about our impending conversation without the thought of her waiting on me as well.

"No I insist. You've done so much already today and, coupled with your visit to the doctor, I think you deserve to be spoilt a little. I've asked Robert to join us as he is concerned for you as well." I gasped audibly. "Are you alright, Ruth, is there something wrong?"

"No, I'm fine thank you," I said, trying desperately to hide the look of trepidation from her that had overtaken me. "I just had a twinge of pain."

"Another good reason for you to be sitting down and allowing me to care for you for a change. You go along and I'll join you both in a few minutes." I walked the few paces to the sitting room struggling to put one foot in front of the other as though they were encased in cement. I heard Mr Taylor's voice call out from the other side of the door as I knocked, nervously praying that he wouldn't be there.

"Come in."

I felt clammy, almost sick as I entered the room, hardly daring to look at him.

"Helen tells me you are not well and that you've have been to see Charles Anderson. I trust he was helpful?"

"Yes thank you, he was very nice."

"He's a good man, we go back a long way." He indicated a chair opposite his own. "Please, sit down. Is Helen with you?"

"She's bringing some tea; she'll be along in a minute." I could hardly believe how considerate he was appearing to be in light of all that had happened between us in recent weeks. As I sat he moved towards me making me feel immediately uncomfortable.

"I hope you are not thinking of saying anything to my wife about our arrangement, Ruth? Nothing has changed you know and whatever you might think of me personally don't forget that you are now equally culpable in the act of adultery. There is also the small matter of the theft with regards to Helen's jewellery to be considered should you decide to be silly and say something untoward. I can promise you if you do you *will* most certainly regret it. We are quite clear about that aren't we?"

The earlier apprehension I had been feeling turned to anger and indignation within me as I realised any initial consideration demonstrated on his part, certainly as far as my health and general well-being were concerned, were driven solely by a narcissistic desire for self-preservation but also to protect both his reputation at the bank and his role as head of the house. Clearly he had no respect for me as a person, and in that one short sentence had demonstrated equally little regard for both his wife and family. Suddenly it became manifestly clear to me as to what I needed to do. Nervous though I was about how my actions might affect me personally I was equally resolute this contemptible excuse for a man would no longer have control over my life, or knowingly deceive those I cared about and that he purported to love himself. Yes I was guilty for my part in what had happened between us, but I was determined to end it now once and for all. I felt disappointed that I'd allowed myself to be bullied in such a way by this cruel and ultimately pathetic man when I had faced far more sinister threats to my existence during my time in Birkenau. If I could survive the terrors of that awful death camp then I certainly had no reason to fear the lies and vilification being threatened towards me by this self serving individual. He took a cigarette from a box on the small table by the side of his chair and smiled at me with a look of self satisfaction. I felt a shudder of apprehension run through my body as I considered exactly what it was I would say when Mrs Taylor returned to join us. I also sent up a silent prayer for strength and guidance at the same time.

For the next few minutes we sat in stony silence avoiding any direct eye contact as we awaited his wife's arrival. I rose to my feet as I heard the door open behind me.

"I'm sorry to have kept you both waiting." I smiled and closed the door as Mrs Taylor moved to the table and placed the tea tray on it.

"Please, let me pour the tea." I was feeling increasingly awkward that my employer, especially in the present circumstances, should be seen as continuing to wait on me.

"No you sit yourself down, my dear, and let me look after you this evening. You've had a tiring day and, as we've already discussed, an equally exhausting time of bathing the children accompanied by the nightly ritual of getting them both to bed."

Mr Taylor shifted uncomfortably in his chair clearly not enjoying the experience of his wife and I being in such close proximity and with him not in control of the subject matter of conversation or as to where it might lead.

"Maybe I should leave and allow the two of you some privacy to discuss whatever it was that Charles spoke to Ruth about earlier?

Mrs Taylor smiled as she poured the tea. "That's very thoughtful of you, Robert, I should have considered that myself." She turned to me and nodded in the direction of her husband. "I apologise, Ruth, Robert is quite right. I was perhaps being insensitive by asking him to be a part of this conversation. Would you rather the two of us spoke in private?" I looked at them both deciding how best to answer and noticed Mr Taylor move awkwardly in his chair again. I allowed myself a momentary feeling of control over him before answering, albeit a little nervously. "No, thank you, I think you should both hear what Doctor Anderson had to say." They both looked towards me, uncertainty etched briefly on their faces. Mrs Taylor leant over and squeezed my hand. "Oh I hope that doesn't mean it is something serious, Ruth? Please be assured whatever is wrong we will do our best to help, won't we, Robert?" Mr Taylor looked up and glanced towards his wife. "Of course, if we can, but I'm not sure what…" his voice trailed away to silence as he shrugged his shoulders alluding to his uncertainty at knowing how best to complete his sentence. Mrs Taylor placed her cup on the tray. "Well, if you're sure then. Now please don't be embarrassed, dear, just tell us what is wrong and how we can best support you."

I took a deep breath, it was now or never. I looked at Mrs Taylor, my emotions already getting the better of me as I struggled to speak. "I'm so sorry to say this to you, Mrs Taylor, but…" She squeezed my arm before moving her hand to take mine. "Take your time, Ruth, there's no rush; it can't be that bad, whatever it is?" I sat for a moment gathering myself as Mr Taylor lit another cigarette and rolled it nervously between his fingers. I breathed in deeply and sat upright in my chair, turning my head slightly to look directly at Mrs Taylor. "I'm so sorry to let you down like this but, I'm pregnant."

There was a momentary stunned silence between them as they glanced, first at each other, then back to me.

"Pregnant, I'm not sure I understand?" She removed her hand from mine and in that second I felt an immediate gulf grow between us.

"I'm so sorry," I said, hoping desperately she would comfort me again as she had done just a few moments previously.

"When, how did this happen? I didn't even know you had been seeing a young man?"

I looked at her wishing I hadn't said anything and could claim back those last few sentences, but equally aware that sooner or later I would have to tell the truth. I could tell from the expression on her face that I had disappointed her terribly. I glanced across to Mr Taylor who was staring at me in almost disbelief and clearly fearing what I might say next.

I turned my head back towards Mrs Taylor. "I'm not exactly sure as to the timing but Doctor Anderson said it is only a few weeks." Mrs Taylor moved her chair back a little as if to distance herself from me. "I won't pretend I'm not disappointed, Ruth, because I am. In fact I'm lost for words, if I'm honest." I could feel the tears run down my cheeks as I looked across at this special woman who up until a few minutes ago I had considered so much more than simply my employer. I had, in more recent times, dared to begin to think of her as a friend, someone I could share my innermost thoughts and confidences with, but whose faith and trust I was about to shatter forever.

Mr Taylor stood up moving to take authority of the conversation; a conversation that for him at least was beginning to spiral out of control.

"Sadly this will mean your having to leave our employ, Ruth and, regrettably the sooner the better. I can't possibly be having a scandal such as this associated with my name, nor indeed with this household." He turned to address his wife. "We also need to consider the effect such a disgrace would have on the children as well, Helen."

She looked at him. "You may well be right, Robert, but shouldn't we hear what Ruth has to say first? Disappointed though I am in what she has done I still feel we owe her that much at least."

He moved away, nervously flicking his cigarette ash in the fire grate as he leant on the mantle piece surrounding it. Mrs Taylor and I sat staring at each other in silence for a few moments as I prayed again, not for strength this time but for the floor to open and swallow me up. Mrs Taylor spoke first glancing at her husband for support but he looked away standing upright and rigid by the fire place drawing hard and deliberately on his cigarette.

"Well, Ruth, are we to hear what happened?"

I lifted my head, the tears rolling openly down my cheeks as I searched for any sign of compassion in her face, but all I could find was look of shock and sadness reflected in her eyes. I knew what I was about to say next would irrevocably change our relationship forever if it hadn't been already by what she had heard in the past few minutes.

"I don't have a boyfriend, well not a regular one at least; I don't have much time for socialising away from my duties here." I noticed her expression change once again.

"I'm sorry if you feel we have been so demanding of your time, Ruth. I thought you were happy here, but clearly we have misjudged you on a number of levels, including a wrongly perceived relationship between us."

I felt my heart break as she spoke, distancing herself from me even further. I knew her words were prompted by a growing sense of personal disappointment in what I had done physically and not me as a person, at least not yet; that particular area of rejection was about to root itself as I spoke again.

"I am happy here, in fact the past few months have been amongst the happiest I can remember for many years. You and Elizabeth have become almost like a family to me, if that isn't too forward. And Nelly and I have also become close, real friends I like to think." I felt myself falter, fearing to speak out the words I knew would destroy any last vestige of affection between the two of us.

Mr Taylor turned to face me. "Well perhaps you should have thought of that before allowing an apparently more attractive avenue of pleasure to distract you from your duties here, as well as betraying the trust of those you purportedly care about. Clearly all that we have afforded you hasn't proved enough or we wouldn't be having this conversation now."

Mrs Taylor stared at her husband; a look of shock displayed across her face in response to the damming nature and inference of what he had just said. Yet within that look I also noted a degree of acceptance in her expression with regards to the general tone of what he had implied.

I looked at him and much though I regretted the hurt I was about to cause to his wife, children and my friends within the house I also knew that if I didn't speak out now this man's lies, deceit and general disregard for his family and others would only continue to fester and grow. Like a malignant growth it would spread, eventually blotting out altogether the light and warmth that had shone so brightly in this beautiful family home up until just a few weeks ago.

Whilst his attitude and actions were not on the same level as the cancer of evil I had endured in Birkenau, a cancer it still remained and as in every other case once the disease is discovered it requires immediate surgery to remove it along with its potential to do further harm to both its victim and to others affected by its vile presence. I felt an inward assurance that I was about to do the right thing, although equally recognised that in so doing I would also be sacrificing my future happiness on the alter of truth in the short battle ahead. I tried to comfort myself in the knowledge that he would become the ultimate loser in the greater war that would surely ensue once I had fallen on my sword and left. I watched for a moment as he turned away, stubbing out his cigarette and throwing it on the fire. He hardly dared face me for fear of what he might read in the growing look of determination in my eyes. Like all bullies when cornered he was beginning to demonstrate the more cowardly character traits of weakness and spite by accusing me of having sinned and failed rather than looking to himself and his part in this wholly unsavoury affair, an affair I was determined would ultimately cost him more than just an admission of guilt. I felt my body shake as I prepared to speak, but this time it wasn't a fear about my own future coursing through my veins but more a nervous determination say the right thing for everyone else and to finally bring an end this liturgy of lies and deception. I also noticed my tears had stopped flowing as I embraced this new and welcome sense of resolve surging through me. I clasped my hands together and took a deep breath.

"Mrs Taylor I need to start by saying that what I am about to tell you is the absolute truth. I would never make up something like this, or ever seek to hurt you, Elizabeth or young George in any way. I hope you can believe that. Nor would I wish to damage the special relationship I like to think we have established between ourselves in the time I have worked for you."

Mr Taylor, now fully cognisant of what I was about to say, stepped forward taking up a position between his wife and I.

"I don't know about you, Helen, but I am not sure I want to hear the grubby details of how this pregnancy occurred. I think we should just accept Ruth has made a terrible mistake and, sorry though we are it has happened, move on to decide the most appropriate way for us to part company; one that will least affect the children and us as a family." He glanced at me, feigning concern for my predicament before addressing his wife again. "I am sure we would both want to be generous in our terms of severance, although of course we would be unable to provide much of a reference taking into account what has happened."

She turned to look at him. "I don't necessarily disagree with you, Robert, but I would still like to hear what Ruth has to say if you don't mind. As I said earlier, we may not approve of the mistake she has made, but we do at least owe her the right to explain herself before we decide any final course of action." She turned to me again. "Please continue, Ruth. Although I should add before you start that Robert is quite right when he says the eventual outcome to your story is still likely to be, for you at least, an unhappy one." She smiled, and although it was not the look of affection I had grown accustomed to during our time together, it was a smile all the same and I took heart from that as I spoke again.

"As I said, what I am about to tell you is the truth. I have never and would never lie to you." She nodded as if in acceptance to that fact at least. Mr Taylor moved towards the door, a look of panic spreading across his face as his worst fears were about to be realised.

"Well I've heard enough, Helen, even if you haven't. The stupid girl has got herself into trouble and is no doubt about to give you some cock and bull story as to how it came about. A story told in the vain hope that it might engender some form of misguided compassion within you towards both her and her cause. Well more fool you is all I can say."

Much as I had wanted to see his face when I explained what had really happened, I was now quite grateful that he was choosing to leave as it might give me the opportunity to speak more openly with Mrs Taylor, although I was equally sure I wouldn't be receiving the compassion he alluded to, misguided or otherwise.

"You leave if you must, Robert, although I think you are being unfair to Ruth who, as I have stated already, and putting aside our personal feelings with regards to her folly in this matter, still deserves the right to be heard."

The two of them stared at each other for a moment before Mr Taylor turned and left the room, closing the door firmly behind him.

"I'm sorry about that, Ruth, though I can understand Robert's displeasure in what we have heard so far. Sadly, I also have to agree with him when he says it will be extremely difficult for us to find a way for you to stay on as nanny to Elizabeth and George following the birth of your own child, especially with you not being married and, up until this point at least, not apparently being prepared to name the father." She took a handkerchief from her pocket and brought it to her face. Her voice faltered and broke as she continued. "Oh Ruth, how could you be so silly. I had such high hopes for you, for us all."

I felt my eyes fill with tears again, but these were not the tears of anger and frustration I had demonstrated so readily towards her husband in recent weeks, these were tears of genuine regret and sorrow for the awful pain I was about to administer to someone I truly cared about. She had become my confidant, someone I knew I could trust with my fears and concerns and yet whose heart I was still about to break.

"I'm not sure where to start and, which ever way I tell you this it won't make it any easier for either of us." I knew I was trying to delay the awful moment of truth as I struggled to find the right words to explain what I had so foolishly agreed to. She looked at me quizzically. "I'm not sure what it is you are trying to say, Ruth, but I promise you no matter how hard it is I will try to understand and also to stand by you as best I am able."

I looked at her wishing what she had just said might hold true but knowing deep inside it could never be once I had finished telling her my story.

"I don't have a boyfriend, that isn't how I got pregnant."

A look of confusion spread across her face. "I don't understand?"

I swallowed hard. "The truth is that I am expecting Mr Taylor's baby." There was a stunned silence as she looked at me trying to compute in her mind what she had just heard.

"He approached me a few weeks ago before George was born and proposed that as you were unable to perform certain duties because of your condition I should take your place in the bedroom to ease the pressure on you."

I continued without looking at her, the tears running openly down my cheeks and my body shaking uncontrollably.

"He would come to my room when you were away and also during your time in hospital. I begged him not to make me do this terrible thing as I knew it would destroy everything I held dear, most especially my relationship with you and the children, but he threatened me with awful consequences if I didn't do as he said." I paused to catch my breath and glanced up at Mrs Taylor, her face demonstrating almost no emotion bar an expression of shock and disbelief which was etched unmistakably across it.

"I'm so sorry I was weak but I was scared of what he would do if I didn't agree. Now in talking to you I wish I had been stronger no matter what the consequences, nothing could be worse than this."

She sat for a moment looking straight ahead, then rising from her chair took a step towards me and slapped me hard and deliberately across the face.

"How dare you say such a thing? Her voice had become brittle and unforgiving. "Isn't it bad enough you've got yourself into trouble without trying to involve my husband in this sordid affair? Robert was right, you are a stupid little girl and we should never have employed you, let alone trusted you with the care of our children." She paused attempting to regain her composure. "I thought we were friends, Ruth? You said you would tell me the truth, but the real truth is that friends don't tell lies to each other, or hurt one another as you have so clearly sought to hurt me in this shameful way. What could I possibly have done to you to cause you to say such unforgiveable things about my husband, knowing how much it would upset me? Why would you lie like that? "

My face stung from the pain of her hand striking it, but the agony of losing her faith and trust in me burned deeper than any physical blow could ever do.

"I'm not lying to you, Mrs Taylor, I promise. Why would I seek to hurt and disappoint the people I most care about if I wasn't telling the truth?"

She moved away from me. "I have no idea, but I do know that I've heard all I want to hear from you this evening, Ruth. I'm going to bed and to talk with Robert. You may sleep here tonight because it is late. We will speak again briefly tomorrow morning about what the two of us decide. I suspect we will simply ask you to leave our employ and house forever rather than getting involved in any additional unpleasantness or further lurid conversations about the circumstances of your pregnancy, along with the appalling and defamatory accusations you have made about my dear husband. I know Elizabeth will be upset but I will think of something to tell her as to why you have had to leave our home so suddenly. Although, and as I have just made clear, I am opposed to lying under any circumstances, I certainly won't be telling *her* the truth, and especially not the grimy and sordid fantasy version of what you purport to be the truth."

I rose from my chair. "Mrs Taylor please, I realise you're shocked at what I've said but I promise you I *am* telling the truth. I ask again, why would I make up such a story?"

"And as I have already stated, I have no idea why you would say such an awful thing." In the brief silence that followed I felt the icy wind of shared misery and sadness blow between us, albeit for differing reasons.

"To say I am shocked and surprised is a gross understatement as to how I am actually feeling at this moment, Ruth. Indeed, I wonder now if perhaps you've ever been totally honest with any of us in the time you've been here, who knows? It may be that your mind has been so affected by your past experiences in the prison camp that you no longer recognise the difference between lying and telling the truth, I don't know. What I am clear about however is, that at this precise moment, I don't even want to be in the same room as you let alone listen to anymore of the slanderous bile you are spouting about my Robert."

She opened the door glancing only briefly towards me as she left the room. "Good night, Ruth." I stood for a moment before my legs gave way and I collapsed back into my chair. I wasn't sure how I had expected her to react, but I certainly hadn't envisaged any of what had just taken place.

I didn't sleep at all that night and rising early waited in my room after washing and dressing fearful of what might happen or be said to me if I ventured outside or went downstairs. Eventually there was a knock at my door: it was Mr and Mrs Taylor. He opened the door and followed his wife into the room. She looked down towards the floor avoiding any form of eye contact with me.

"Good morning Ruth. Helen and I spoke late into the night about your story and I have to say I am equally as disappointed and appalled as she is after hearing what you had to say in your defence and as to how you became pregnant. Indeed, if it weren't for Dr Anderson's confirmation of your pregnancy I'm not sure we would choose to believe even that to be true in light of everything else that has transpired in recent days. Neither of us is sure as to what triggered such a venomous attack, although I have my suspicions and will come to those shortly, but clearly what was said has affected all of our relationships irrevocably." He took a step towards me. "I am afraid following your outburst last night along with the tissue of lies you chose to tell about what you say went on between the two of us I was left with no choice but to inform Helen of our earlier discussion of a few days ago."

Mrs Taylor glanced up. I could see she had been crying as she stood submissively beside her husband.

"I'm afraid I can't bring myself to speak to you personally about this matter, Ruth, but please be assured that I am in full agreement with Robert and in what he is about to say. I am so disappointed in you and can hardly believe some of the things he told me you have said and done during the last few days. I understand you have experienced many tragedies in your life but to strike out in this way against those who…" Her voice cracked as her emotions got the better of her once more.

Mr Taylor took her hand. "It's alright, Helen, we agreed I would speak, please try not to upset yourself again." He looked towards me. "You can see how distraught my wife is with regards to this awful affair, Ruth, as I should add, am I. I had hoped the two of us had found a way to deal with your failures, but clearly you have since felt the need to add malice and spite to your already deluded fabrication of events by going through with your earlier threat of making up this terrible accusation about the two of us with the sole, and entirely selfish, intention of damaging my relationship with Helen." I watched as he stroked his wife's arm in a false pretence at comforting her. As he did so I hated him all the more for his duplicity but also recognised this was not the time to speak out. "That is why I walked out of the room last night," he continued. "I was hoping and praying that you might finally see sense and not go through with your intended web of deceit to seemingly defend the indefensible as far as your own recent actions were concerned."

I felt unable to stay silent any longer.

"I'm not sure I understand what it is you are saying, sir? I told Mrs Taylor the truth last night. My only regret is that she didn't give me the opportunity to fully explain what had happened."

Mrs Taylor brought her handkerchief to her eyes. "Please Ruth, don't say anything else I simply can't bear it. You have let me down so badly. Please just let Robert finish."

I felt her pain every bit as much as my own and wanted to reach out to her but knew at this moment it would be both inappropriate as well as futile. Mr Taylor stepped forward again as if to shield her from me, his voice remaining calm though determined as he spoke.

"I am afraid, Ruth, that following your conversation with Helen last night, and much as I had hoped to avoid doing so, I have been forced to tell her the full detail of all that has transpired between us recently, and not just your malicious version of events, but rather the entire story and the *real* truth."

I stood rooted to the spot, my stomach churning with emotion as he continued.

"I have now shown Helen the items that were discovered in your room after I had noticed them as being missing from around the house along with her diamond earrings; the same diamond earrings you coveted so recently when helping her to dress for a particular function."

"I didn't covet them I simply admired them, Mrs Taylor knows that."

"Please don't argue semantics, Ruth. The truth is you took the earrings along with the other items I discovered here in your room to sell on for personal gain. There is also the sum of money found under your mattress which you also gained illegally from the sale of other objects you had stolen previously. I can only assume that in an effort to deflect attention from your own misgivings or in some crude attempt to get even following my informing you that we would need to contact the police, you decided to invent this unforgiveable story about my being the father to your unborn child."

I felt my chest tighten as I struggled to breathe and looked towards Mrs Taylor who had begun to cry again. I moved to speak but he put up his hand to silence me. "Please, Ruth, have the courtesy to let me finish." He looked at me as a prize fighter might when about to deliver the final and potentially fatal blow to his opponent.

"Ultimately my real sadness in all of this, and particularly for Helen who has invested so much faith and mistaken trust in you, is that not only have you chosen to abuse our previously heartfelt generosity towards you, but more especially that you have surpassed even this betrayal with your latest decision to lie so outrageously about the two of us supposedly having shared a bed together. Clearly, and, as I have stated already, this was presumably done in an effort to create some form of marital wedge between Helen and myself and to throw our deep and loving relationship into disarray."

I felt fit to burst and unable to keep quiet a moment longer.

"Please, Mrs Taylor, you must believe me, I would never do anything like that, to hurt you or any of your family I..." Mr Taylor interrupted me, his delivery becoming firmer and more authoritative.

"I'm afraid it is far too late to appeal to my wife's better nature, Ruth. You should have considered where this might lead before embarking on such a contemptible journey of deceit and subterfuge."

He stepped back, taking his wife's hand as he did so. "Now please listen carefully to what I am about to say as there will be no further discussion after this." He paused for a moment as if allowing the seriousness of what he was about to say to fully register.

"Helen has asked me, against my better judgement I might add, not to involve the police at this stage as we have retrieved most of the items that were taken, along with the monies you gained from the sale of the other goods. Personally speaking, I still feel you should face the full consequences of your actions following a thorough investigation by the authorities. However, because Helen has asked me to be lenient and because none of us would welcome the inevitable publicity associated with such an embarrassing state of affairs I have decided, on this occasion, to acquiesce to her wishes."

I felt my body shake in disbelief and mounting anger towards my accuser, but at the same time felt powerless to respond in any way short of screaming my innocence aloud. I also recognised that such an outburst would have little effect other than to demonstrate my apparent inability to argue my case in any coherent way. Indeed it would simply add fuel to the perception that I was not only foolish and irresponsible but had also lost control of my mind and any sense of responsibility for my actions. I watched as he let go of Mrs Taylor's hand and pulled the cuff of his shirt slightly forward of his jacket sleeve as if to straighten it. Then placing his hands behind his back he continued.

"And so, with all of this in mind, it is with a degree of sadness on both our parts that we have come to the sorry conclusion that you will leave both our home and employment with immediate effect. Further, you will receive no form of reference from us as to your suitability to undertake any similar style of work or service either now or at any time in the future. That is presuming you are ever foolish enough to apply for such a position again, certainly here in the London area at least."

The momentum of his speech and assured delivery increased slightly and I watched as he spat out the odious conditions of his revenge for my having dared to speak out against the orders for secrecy he had demanded regarding our joint deception. I took a small crumb of comfort that soon all of this would be over and I wouldn't have to spend time in his company ever again and certainly not in my bed

"And finally, should we be contacted at some point by another potential employer seeking a recommendation or commendation as to your work and moral ethic we would of course feel obligated to explain the true reasons for our dispensing with your services.

This would be done in an effort to save them from facing the same very real and deep seated personal disappointment in your efforts that sadly we have experienced in recent days."

I looked at Mrs Taylor, sensing she was not entirely comfortable with what she was hearing. Also that she had been left with little room to argue my case by her husband who by now was in full flow and obviously enjoying this opportunity of not only putting me in my place, but also in ridding himself of me once and for all along with any other potential menace I might present to his smug and self-satisfied existence.

"Am I allowed to say anything in my defence?"

He paused momentarily, his voice returning to a more calm and measured tone.

"I'm afraid there is no defence for what you have said or done in recent days, Ruth. Nor as to the upset you have brought to this family, especially my wife, and for that I am afraid I can never forgive you. Helen would argue differently and maintains that there must be some vestige of goodness in you despite all that has transpired. It is because of this and my desire to honour her wishes that I have agreed to pay you in full until the end of the month. This money will serve not only as remuneration for your duties carried out to date but also as severance pay. Although I might add, I would be well within my rights to withhold any further monies from you in view of your recent actions and there wouldn't be a court in this land that would argue differently."

Mrs Taylor stepped forward. "Please, Robert, can we stop this bickering now and leave? You have said all that we intended and simply going over everything again will do none of us any good." She put her hand to her forehead. "I'm afraid all of this tension has made me feel quite unwell. I think I would like to lie down for a while."

I could feel the tears filling my eyes once more as I witnessed the deep sadness displayed across her face and tried one last time to argue my innocence.

"Please, Mrs Taylor, I beg of you to listen to me, none of this is true. I would never do anything to hurt you or the children you must know that?"

She took a step towards me, her face and expression readily portraying her obvious pain and distress.

"I'm really not sure I know very much about anything anymore, Ruth. But what I am clear about is that for whatever reason, *you* are the one at the centre of this whole sorry affair and I won't have my children or my marriage put at risk or threatened by this awful episode any longer. I have trusted you not only with the care of my family but also as my confidant at times, sharing some of my deepest thoughts and hopes with you. And for some perverse reason because of that I find myself still standing here trying to defend your words and actions when I should actually be agreeing with Robert when he says, quite rightly, that all that has happened in the past few weeks is utterly indefensible." She raised her handkerchief again to wipe away her own freely flowing tears. "Whilst not everything may have happened in the way it has been described the truth still remains that certain valuable objects have gone missing from our home only to be discovered in your room, along with money that has apparently come from the sale of other personal items that were taken. Also, we know now that you are pregnant following your visit to Doctor Anderson. The only thing therefore that is in doubt is as to who the father is? It is here I am afraid that both my sympathy and patience for your circumstances evaporate entirely and run dry." She looked directly at me with no hint of the affection we had so often shared between us now evident in her eyes. "How you could ever expect me to accept that Robert might be responsible in any way for the condition you now find yourself in is beyond belief. I have no idea why you would choose to say anything so hurtful, other than to agree with his explanation that you were seeking some form of heartless revenge against him following the discovery of the missing items and money found in your room, and of his threatening to take legal action against you because of this. I can only surmise you had sought to blackmail him in some way and in so doing pressurise him into not saying anything to me. Sadly you have underestimated our feelings for each other as husband and wife. Fond though I may have become of you since you joined our household I am afraid those feelings pale into insignificance when compared to the love and respect I have for my husband, the father of our children and my dearest friend." She paused as if preparing herself for what was to come next. "The truth is, Ruth, you have chosen to betray my trust, and for whatever reason you feel you might have had for doing that I can say without any shadow of a doubt that is something Robert would never do."

I stood motionless, my heart breaking as the tears rolled down my cheeks once more. Mr Taylor took his wife's arm as she continued to struggle in holding back her own emotions.

"I think we've all said enough, and I am sure, despite all the pain you have caused us, Ruth, even you would not want to see my wife upset more than she already is? I suggest for all our sakes we end our discussion here and that the two of us leave you to finish packing while I take Helen to our bedroom to lie down and begin to recover from what has been a traumatic few days for her, indeed for both of us. I will meet you at the front door in fifteen minutes to see you off the premises."

Mrs Taylor turned to leave and spoke without looking at me. "Goodbye Ruth."

As they left the room Mr Taylor allowed himself one more glance in my direction, his smug expression saying more than any amount of words could ever do. I felt my body shudder in an automated response to the door closing and also in the reluctant acceptance of my fate. My thoughts went back to the day I left Birkenau, and horrific though my life and existence had been in that awful place I could still recall the soaring feeling of hope that had flooded my being as I stepped out of that terrible prison camp and on towards whatever challenges the future held for me.

Little did I know those feelings of joy and excitement would turn again so quickly to ones of such deep sorrow and despair?

As the front door closed behind me on the house I had begun to think of as home I felt a distinct chill in the air as rain clouds gathered overhead. I turned my collar up and stepped out to face a new set of challenges seemingly even more uncertain than the ones I had anticipated when leaving the death camp. As I walked along the pavement my stomach lurched and a wave of nausea came over me. Was it simply tension and nerves that had knotted within me or was it a reminder that whatever the future held it was not only myself I had to think about now, but also the new life growing within me?

TWENTY-ONE

I thought a lot over the next few days about what Dad had said and knew that he and Mum were right in suggesting I would be the poorer if I didn't arrange to meet with Ruth and hear her side of the story, a story that for all my misgivings had shaped each our lives and made us the people we were today.

Maybe if I hadn't listened to Jenny when she first asked about my parents, or had taken the easier route and simply said they were dead or that I didn't know anything about them, then perhaps none of the mental anguish we had all experienced in recent months would ever had happened. But it was too late now, the door to my past had been opened and the only way forward was to walk through it and meet whatever lay before me head on. We couldn't change the events of the past but hopefully in discovering the truth about what had really happened we could each move forward to a more settled future.

Jenny was excited when I first told her I had decided to meet with Ruth and asked if she could come as well. I did think about it for a while, wondering if having her with me might soften the blow for each of us and keep the conversation polite and respectful, with neither Ruth nor I wanting to upset Jenny. However, I soon realised this would also mean the two of us, having taken this momentous decision to meet, might then feel constrained in our ability to discuss the deeper detail of our experiences, along with the things we both really wanted discover about ourselves and each other from our past. So after due consideration I eventually said no. I also didn't want Jenny to see her mum upset, and I was pretty sure that I might shed a few tears or show my frustration if the conversation between us didn't go the way the both of us hoped it might. Jenny was fine about it, especially after Mum and Dad supported my thinking. We agreed at some point Jenny could meet her grandmother, providing it was at the appropriate time, and that it was the right thing to do for all concerned.

Even with the correspondence we had already exchanged it still felt strange writing to Ruth and finally agreeing to meet with her. On the one hand here was my mother who hadn't seen me since I was seven weeks old saying how much she was looking forward to seeing me again and talking with me, and here I was asking why had it taken twenty eight years for her to come to this conclusion. I was also interested to know what had changed over the years to make her feel this way. No matter how hard I tried I simply couldn't understand why, if having given your own baby away at just a few weeks old, presumably forever, would you now be so keen to see that same child twenty eight years on as an adult? When I first wrote to her I was fully expecting my request for contact to be rebuffed but the reply I received was the exact opposite. This had confused me and only added to the list of questions I needed answers to. Would she be willing to address those same questions, ones that only she knew the answers to, but for me were still a mystery to be solved? Would she speak to me about what had really happened and be willing to relive her own experiences of that time all over again? I comforted myself with the fact that nervous though I was about meeting her I still had the love and support of Jenny along with Mum and Dad to fall back on should all my hopes and dreams be dashed when the two of us finally spent time in each others company.

When we first started to consider where the best place might be for us to meet I proposed somewhere public, perhaps a café or restaurant, as this would give us both the option to leave if the conversation became too difficult or either of us felt threatened in some way, not physically but more through the enormity of our actually being together in the same room again after such a long time. Dad and Mum suggested meeting in a public place might appear to be a good idea on the face of it but that it would also require us to be aware of everyone else in the room. This would mean, as would be the case if we allowed Jenny to be present, we might then feel reticent about speaking openly and honestly about certain areas or events in our lives, and certainly for me of the perceived failings of Ruth in her love for me as my mother. This indecision about where to meet continued for some time until Ruth herself suggested I might like to visit her at home. My immediate reaction was to say no, but after talking things through with Mum and Dad her proposal began to sound like a good idea.

"If you go to her house you will be free to talk openly," Dad suggested. "And if you find yourself feeling uncomfortable in her company or you're not getting the answers you are looking for you can simply excuse yourself and leave."

Mum nodded in agreement. "Of course you are welcome to ask her here, but if things didn't work out it might prove even more embarrassing if you then had to ask *her* to leave. She might also feel awkward about coming to the house that her daughter had been adopted into and grown up in. Dad and I would go out of course and leave the two of you alone but even so it would place an added degree of pressure on her, perhaps on the both of you? Meeting at her house would also give you a chance to get the feel of what sort of a woman she is. You know, in being able to see inside her home and take note of the pictures and other personal items she has around. I always think you can tell a lot about people from their nick knacks and ornaments."

Dad smiled at her. "Well if that's true I'm not sure what it says about your mother and her huge collection of thimbles. She had shelves of them she'd collected over the years, although she never did any knitting with any of them. Mind If she had she could have used a different one every week for a year and still had a few left over." He laughed. "So what did that say about her, except that she was a stitch short of a knitting pattern to start with?"

"You don't use thimbles to knit with," countered Mum.

"And it wouldn't have made any difference if you did. She still didn't use them; they just collected dust like half the other stuff she kept lying around."

I felt the need to come to Mum's defence. "I used to enjoy playing with Granny's thimbles when I was small. I gave them all a name and she would tell me where each one had come from."

Dad laughed again. "I rest my case. A woman who collects thimbles for no good reason and a granddaughter who gives them names! Honestly what chance does a man have for a sensible conversation around here? Perhaps I should have a word with Chris before he gets any further involved with the women in this house?"

"You leave Chris out of this; he doesn't need your help in forming an opinion about me."

"Well I must admit he doesn't strike me as a *thimple* man."

Mum and I looked at each other. "And he certainly doesn't need to hear any of your awful jokes either, we like Chris remember."

Dad smiled. "I know and I like him too. Chris gets a *thumbs* up from me as well."

Mum and I winced.

"Oh sorry, did I say something?" He was clearly enjoying his own jokes more than the two of us but recognised he had gone far enough. "Okay, I'll stop. Anyway, talking about Chris, what does he have to say about this meeting? We haven't seen him recently, is everything alright between the two of you?"

I took a moment to think and realised Dad was right, I hadn't seen much of Chris lately. I'd been too preoccupied with my own affairs and in arranging this meeting with Ruth.

"We're fine, I think. You're right though, we haven't spoken much over the past few days. I guess I've been too busy sorting all of this."

Mum smiled. "Chris is a good man, Mary, be careful you don't lose him. He may be a big part of your future and you don't want to threaten that because of your past. Jenny likes him as well remember, as do your dad and I, you know that."

She was right of course and I called Chris later that day to talk things through. We agreed to meet together for a drink in our local pub.

I sat staring into my glass of white wine the following evening in the Red Lion feeling a little nervous as I waited for Chris to arrive. We had arranged to meet there after he finished work. Because we had talked about Ruth on a number of occasions in the past I knew he wouldn't oppose my decision to finally meet with her although I was still a little anxious in case he'd had any second thoughts as to how it might affect our own relationship. As I sat there alone with my thoughts I suddenly felt a hand on my shoulder.

"Hello nice lady, long time no see." I looked up and smiled. "Hello you, I'm sorry I haven't been in touch lately but…" He interrupted me. "I know you've been busy with all the other men in your life." We smiled at each other. "Can I get you another drink?"

"No I'm fine thanks, let me get you one."

"No you're alright; I'll be back in a minute." I watched him walk to the bar and thought how lucky I was to have finally found a man I felt I could trust, not only for myself but also with Jenny.

"So what have you been up to these past couple of weeks," he said pulling out a chair from the table and spilling some of his beer as he did so. "I've hardly heard from you, is it Ruth, has she been in touch again?" He licked the spilt beer from his fingers as he sat down?

"Yes and yes. And I'm sorry if I've been a bit distant of late, it's just I haven't really known what to say, but I should have called." I took his hand and squeezed it. "Forgive me?"

"Nothing to forgive," he replied taking a sip from his glass and leaving a frothy moustache on his top lip which made me laugh.

"That's it add insult to injury and laugh at me as well," he said wiping the froth from his mouth onto his sleeve. "You really know how to hurt a man."

We smiled at each other before leaning forward to kiss.

"It's good to see you, Mary, I've missed you."

"Me too, and like I say, I'm sorry." Chris leant forward and kissed me again. "And like I said there's nothing to forgive. So how's Jenny?" I loved the fact that Jenny was important to him and realised yet again by his asking that one simple question why he had become so special to the both of us.

"She's fine and says thanks again for helping out with that math's project she had to do. She got highly commended for her work."

He smiled, lifting his glass to his lips. "Nice to know I'm popular with both the ladies in my life."

I laughed and took a drink. "I am really sorry for not being in contact though, and you're right it was because of Ruth." I placed my glass on the table and took a deep breath. "I've finally made the decision to meet up with her; in fact we're already in the process of agreeing a date." I sat waiting nervously for his reply, but I needn't have worried.

"That's great; I'm really pleased for you, the both of you. Well, all three of you if you count Jenny as well. I presume she's happy about your decision?"

"Yes, although I think she's hoping there will be some dark secret as to why she let me go at such an early age, you know like I was brought into the country by child smugglers or something like that. I told her she's been watching too many police dramas and there's probably a really simple explanation, although I can't begin to think what that might be if I'm honest."

Chris smiled and rubbed my arm. "Well you'll never know the truth if you don't ask and now you've got the chance to do just that." He took a drink and looked at me lovingly. "And whatever she says it won't change the way I feel about you, or Jenny. You're a very special, lady Mary, and don't let Ruth or anyone else tell you differently"

"Thank you, you don't know how much that means to me or how much I needed to hear you say that. I don't want anything to affect our relationship, Chris, although sometimes I worry that…" My voice trailed away and I felt tears sting the back of my eyes.

"You daft brush, I've just told you there's nothing she can say that will change the way I feel about you? What were you, a couple of months old when she let you go, you can hardly be blamed for that now can you?" He sat back in his chair and looked at me quizzically. "Mind you there could be one thing she might be ashamed to tell you that could affect our relationship."

I panicked as a thousand irrational thoughts raced through my head. "What do you mean?"

"Well if you find out that your father was an Arsenal supporter that would of course mean that we would have to stop seeing each other. I couldn't be seen going out with the daughter of a Gunner."

"You idiot, I thought you were serious for a minute."

"I am." I watched as he raised the glass to his lips again, laughing as he took a sip of his beer. "I could never face my mates again."

I knew he was joking but still felt the need for his support. "Seriously Chris, you don't mind me meeting her do you, whatever the outcome?"

"I'd be disappointed if you didn't. I'm glad you've got this opportunity to find out for yourself what really happened. I know Jenny started the ball rolling but I'm sure at some point you would have wanted to know about your real mum and how you came to be in this world. And if you'd left it for another few years, who knows, it might have been too late. So yes, go for it girl, fix a date to see her and ask your questions. And remember, I'll stand beside you whatever happens."

It was my turn to lean forward and make the move to kiss him. "Thank you." Although we sat enjoying each others company in silence for the next few minutes I had never felt as close to Chris as I did just then; the unspoken dialogue emanating between us saying more than a thousand words could ever have done.

Eventually he broke the silence. "Well I don't know about you but I think this calls for a celebration." He nodded towards my glass. "Same again?"

"Please, that would be nice."

"And if we're going to celebrate let's really push the boat out and make it a large glass." He laughed as he spoke. "In fact let's go the whole hog and share a packet of crisps as well." I smiled as he walked back to the bar saying a silent thank you to myself for how well our conversation had gone. As he said I needn't have worried but his reassurance still meant a lot to me.

The two of us spent the rest of the evening talking about everything but Ruth and I'm sure we both felt the better for it, I know I did. I resolved yet again not to let Chris slip from my life nor from Jenny's as the two of us continued to grow closer and more dependent on him both physically and emotionally. Mum had been right when she said Chris was mine and Jenny's future, and I knew I couldn't wreck the prospect of that happiness by letting the past dominate me any longer no matter how nervous I was about what was to come in the weeks ahead. I needed to move forward for everyone's sake and meeting with Ruth would allow me to begin that process whatever the eventual outcome might be.

TWENTY-TWO

I used the money Mr Taylor had given me to buy food and to pay for a small room locally, but I knew it wouldn't last for long and that I would have to find a job quickly to support myself. However, with no references and the threat of action against me by the Taylor's should I seek to gain work as a nanny I knew my options were limited. After a couple of days and with my money running out fast I managed to find work in a back street pub clearing tables and washing the dirty glasses along with pretty much everything else in those dingy surroundings. The landlord wasn't the most pleasant of people either, but at least he didn't ask about my past or as to the reasons for my wanting the job. I think he was just happy to have a young girl in the pub for all of his male regulars to eye up as I hardly ever saw another woman in the bar, and certainly not the sort who were there to enjoy a simple night out with their boyfriend or husband. Most of the women who did occasionally come into the bar appeared to be looking for business of a different sort rather than for a drink. That said, there was often a glass or two shared between her and her would be suitor before they left for another form of entertainment. I got my bottom slapped a few times but I knew it was pointless saying anything to the landlord as I could readily imagine the reply I would have received, especially as he always made great play out of forcing himself against me whenever we had to pass each other behind the bar. I quickly came to hate working there but knew without the money it provided I simply could not survive. I also had this new life growing inside me which only compounded my concerns about what the future might hold for the both of us.

I managed to hide my growing tummy for a few weeks under my apron and by wearing skirts or dresses that were too big for me, but one day the landlord called me into his office. His speech as with his demeanour was basic and to the point. "Are you up the duff, girl?" I looked at him for a moment not quite knowing how to reply. "Cause if you are you can't stay here right, it ain't good for business. Men want to look at a girl with a bit of a shape to them, not some bleedin' beached whale." I felt a mix of emotions threatening to overtake me as I stood before him. Here was another man telling me what I could and couldn't do just as Mr Taylor and the German's had done before him.

"And don't start all that blubbing either, that won't wash with me. If you've got yourself pregnant then that's your own stupid fault not mine." He stared directly at me. "Is it one of the lads from the gas works down the road? I've seen you chatting to them."

"Only to tell them to keep their hands off me," I retorted, feeling anger as well as fear building up inside me.

"A little slap on the bum don't do no harm; you're too precious you are that's your trouble." He shook his head and coughed. It was a deep catarrhal cough from years of heavy smoking and his chest wheezed as he exhaled. "So what, you think you're above some bloke giving your arse a bit of a squeeze but then you're happy to let him get into your drawers is that it?"

Anger was by now far outweighing any fear I had about losing my job; sadly, it was also affecting my rationale and the need for an income along with any thoughts of self preservation I might have harboured.

"I wouldn't let any of your customers come near me for any reason, and certainly not willingly. They're just a bunch of dirty old men with wandering hands and filthy minds. I only work here because I need the money, so don't make the mistake of thinking I enjoy it because I don't."

He coughed again, his face turning red as much from his rising temper as from the need to clear his throat of mucus. "Then you won't mind me telling you to piss off then, will you, if you hate it that much? I only took you on to help you out and 'cause I felt sorry for you. I wish I hadn't bothered now." He shook his head again. "You're like the rest of the tarts that come in here, more trouble than you're worth."

"Suits me, I'll be happy to go and as for…" I bit my lip but it was too late, I had called his bluff and agreed to leave. Fear overtook me again, but the moment for reason had passed and there was no hope now of my making amends or appealing to his better nature following our angry exchange.

"Well go on then bugger off to your boyfriend or whoever it is that's had the unfortunate pleasure of shagging you. I'm sure they'll be only too happy to look after you and your brat when it arrives." He put his hand in his pocket and withdrawing a handful of money threw two pounds across the table towards me.

"That should cover the work you've done over the past few days." He grinned intentionally as he spoke. "If not you can sue me for the rest."

I was tempted to throw the money back into his face but knew that would achieve only a fleeting sensation of self gratification and one that would immediately be replaced by the knowledge I had, through this momentary act of obstinate pride, done something both stupid and very costly. I leant forward and picked up the crumpled and grubby notes. It seemed appropriate that even the money in his pocket should be as dirty and grimy as everything else in this run down back street pub.

"Thank you." I put the money in my skirt pocket and without looking at him turned and left closing the door gently behind me. I didn't want to give him the satisfaction of being able to shout at me again should I have chosen to slam it out of warranted frustration with both him and his attitude towards me.

I spent the next two days in my room exploring my rapidly decreasing options as to what I should do next. The pub landlord may have crawled out from under a rock somewhere but he had been right in saying that my impending motherhood was now obvious to all. The more I thought about this the more I realised I needed professional help and guidance as to how and where my baby would be born. I also needed advice about how to care for it once it arrived?

I decided to go to the hospital and ask to speak to a midwife. The lady at the reception was very polite but it was obvious what she was thinking as she entered my details on the form in front of her.

"So is that Miss or Mrs Cahn?"

My heart sank. "Miss," I replied, my voice hardly getting above a whisper.

"I'm sorry I didn't hear you dear, is it *Miss* or *Mrs* Cahn?"

"Miss." I felt my cheeks burn with embarrassment as I glanced behind me at the other women waiting their turn to be questioned or seen by one of the nursing staff, all of whom appeared endlessly busy as they hurried in and out of the waiting area with their clip boards, checking lists or asking one of the ladies to follow them. I sensed their eyes focus on me and could hear the gentle murmur of derision as they passed their hastily made decisions about me to one another.

I saw one woman lean towards her friend whilst pointing her finger at me. "There's another one. Honestly some of these young girls have no shame or conscience."

I felt like turning and shouting the truth at her but realised it would do no good, or that my innocence would be believed.

The receptionist, also aware of the change of mood in the room, spoke again, this time more sympathetically.

"It's alright dear, just a few more questions and we'll get someone to talk to you."

I smiled praying her change in tone was one of genuine concern and not simply to move me along in the lengthy queue that was now forming behind me.

"Address?"

I told her where I was living, adding this was not my permanent home as I might be moving on soon. I didn't want to say I had no money as I knew this wouldn't help my cause.

"Father's name?"

My heart sank once more as I struggled to reply.

"What is the father's name, dear?" she repeated, smiling at me as she scratched the side of her head with the end of the pen she was holding?

Panicking I said the first thing that came into my head. "I don't know."

Her jaw dropped visibly and I heard another rumble of disapproval verbalise itself from the other women in the room.

"I'm sorry, dear, did you say you don't know? Surely you must know who the father is?"

"Perhaps there's more than one or she's not fussy," came from one of the now fully attentive audience sitting behind me.

"I mean, I can't tell you his name." I looked at her in the vain hope she would understand and end this line of questioning to save both of our growing embarrassment.

The receptionist adjusted her glasses and staring over the top of them looked directly at me. Any sense of empathy displayed earlier had disappeared completely with her voice no longer soft and compassionate but now decidedly imposing and authoritative.

"So let me be clear, *Miss* Cahn. You are not married, you have no permanent address, and you cannot give me the name of the man who is to be the father of your child, is that all correct?"

I nodded sheepishly.

"There is one other question I need you to answer, and I apologise because I should have asked you this earlier, but how old are you?"

I stared at the floor not daring to look directly at her and wishing the ground would open up and swallow me whole as I replied. "Nearly eighteen." Another audible wave of disapproval reverberated behind me.

"I see. So you are actually *seventeen,* is that what you're saying?" I nodded meekly still unable to face her. The receptionist picked up a small piece of pink paper from her desk and handed it to me. I raised my head and with my hand shaking took it from her. I felt lost in a sea of complete and utter humiliation, along with an overwhelming desire to be anywhere but standing in her reception area. Clearly aware of both my obvious shame and the critical audience eavesdropping intently on our conversation behind me, all avidly awaiting our next exchange she smiled, her voice softening once more. "Miss Cahn, sadly you are not the first young girl to find herself in this position and I doubt you will be the last. What I am giving you here is the address of a special children's home here in the London area which is run by nuns. They give help and advice to lots of young under age girls like you and will be able to offer appropriate care for both you and your baby until you are in a position to provide for yourself again. It is called the Holy Order of the Sisters of Mercy and there is a phone number for them at the bottom of the page. I suggest you call and make an appointment for yourself as soon as possible."

She smiled again. "I do hope everything works out for you, but I'm afraid there is nothing further we can do for you here. Certainly not without more of the detail you appear unable to provide at this time. I'm sure the nuns will be able to help." I felt she understood both my discomfiture and my pain, and in her smile I recognised she was also asking me to accept that her hands were tied as far as her ability to do anymore for me was concerned.

"Thank you," I mumbled, forcing the piece of paper deep into my coat pocket.

"Take care of yourself dear."

I walked quickly to the door, not daring to look back but fully aware of the many sets of disapproving eyes that were now focused on me. As I opened the door the word "slut" reached my ears, proffered by one self-righteous and unsympathetic individual and no doubt on behalf of a number of others sitting with her. I stood outside for a moment allowing the tears to flow as I stared up at the cloudless sky above me. Even though it was late winter I could still feel the sun's rays envelope me as they had done outside Doctor Anderson's surgery on the day I first discovered I was pregnant, and as before it was only my outer body that benefited from the warmth not my heart. Once again that felt cold and broken and I despaired that I would ever feel whole again.

I rang the number I had been given for the Sisters of Mercy the next morning, feeling my hands shake as I held the phone to my ear. A woman, presumably one of the Nun's, on hearing my story told me to come and see them.

"You're not the first girl to seek help in this way child, but with the Lord's blessing and forgiveness for your sins we will do our best to put you on the right road again."

I wasn't sure I understood exactly what she was alluding to when she talked about the forgiveness of my sins, or that I liked being portrayed as a fallen woman, but I also knew that I was fast running out of both money and options and so decided to bite my tongue and take up the offer of help she was suggesting.

I took the bus to the home that afternoon and walked nervously up the long gravel drive to the front door. The building itself was large and foreboding and had a dark, almost satanical, ambiance about it rather than the warm and welcoming feel I had expected. I knocked using one of the two heavy bronze rings attached to the imposing front doors and stepped back in surprise as the sound reverberated throughout what I was soon to discover was an enormous open hallway with large grey flagstones covering the floor. A small and diminutive nun opened the door and gestured me to enter.

"You must be Ruth Cahn, we've been expecting you."

As I walked through the doorway the air and atmosphere felt even colder than it had outside. I presumed this additional chill came from the solid grey stone flooring beneath my feet. As I entered I noticed a young girl on her knees scrubbing the flagstones. She was wearing a grey ill fitting smock style dress and her lank unkempt hair fell across her face as she glanced up at me offering little or no expression by way of a welcome.

"I'll take you up to meet Sister Claire," said the nun as we walked passed the girl who had by now lost all interest in me and had turned her attention back to her duties with the scrubbing brush and bucket.

"All the girls here are expected to work for their keep," the nun continued as we climbed a flight of wooden stairs that were wide and polished but with no covering or carpet on them. As our shoes connected with each stair the sound echoed throughout the large hallway below us.

When we finally reached the top she paused for a moment to catch her breath. "Work is good for the soul and focuses the mind on higher plains rather than the sins and mistakes of our past." She smiled at me and put her hand to her chest. "I'm sure those stairs grow in number each time I climb them." Then turning away she strode forward again. "Come along, child, this way."

I stared briefly at the back of her habit as we walked towards a large wooden door that stood imposingly at the end of the corridor. I was beginning to feel unsure as to whether I had done the right thing in coming to the home.

"I'm not sure I understand what you meant," I said becoming a little short of breath myself as her pace quickened and I attempted to keep up.

"About what?"

"About work helping with our sinful past?"

"Sister Claire will explain everything to you in good time," she replied as we arrived outside the door. "Now here we are." She knocked and cast me another brief smile as we waited for a reply.

"Come in." The nun opened the door and ushered me into a large room where another nun sat behind a big dark wooden desk. The room was not dissimilar to Mr Taylor's study, the walls being lined with books and a fading red patterned carpet covering the floor, although I recalled that Mr Taylor's carpet had been blue and in much better repair. The room was well lit by two big windows set either side of the same outside wall at the front of the building. I glanced briefly out of them as I walked towards the desk, noticing the extensive grounds below and the long drive that made its way to the entrance of the home and the world beyond. The nun who had greeted me stood almost to attention and spoke in an equally reverential tone.

"This is Miss Cahn, Sister Claire." She looked at me, her eyes raised above a set of half moon glasses. Maintaining her steely gaze towards me she addressed the other nun.

"Thank you, Sister Margaret, I'll ring for you when we've finished." Sister Margaret offered me another brief and polite smile before backing out of the room and closing the door behind her.

"Come and sit down, child." Sister Claire indicated another chair set opposite her own on the other side of the desk. I sat nervously waiting for whatever she was going to say next and wishing I'd never phoned the Sisters of Mercy in the first place. As I sat waiting for her to speak I reminded myself that I did need help and that these were nun's for goodness sake; surely they would offer me the care and support I had been denied to date by just about everyone else and certainly by the landlord of The Red Lion and Mr Taylor. Sister Claire stared at me in silence for a moment as if assessing me and deciding how best to address me. She leant forward in her chair.

"Well now, I'm led to believe you've got yourself into trouble and would like the Sisters of Mercy to stand alongside you in this time of need and uncertainty is that right?"

I felt my mouth turn dry as I struggled to speak. "Well yes, I suppose. I mean I am pregnant but it wasn't my fault and…"

Sister Claire raised her hand to interrupt me.

"Please, child, don't try and apportion blame for your own failings onto the shoulders of others. God is aware of everything we do and looks deep into our hearts at the sinful intentions behind those deeds and actions we try to deny as our own. He is all seeing and all knowing, and to attempt to present a different picture to him other than the truth will only damn your soul the greater." She stared hard at me with an arrogant look of self-importance and pompous authority.

"If you have sinned, child, as you clearly have, then confession and repentance are the first steps towards forgiveness, absolution and ultimately rehabilitation under God's love and care." Maintaining her gaze she spoke almost without pause as if reciting some well rehearsed mantra that was being delivered without any consideration of its content or as to its impact on the listener.

"God may love the sinner but he abhors the sin, never forget that. How much more will he detest that self same sinner if they fail to fall upon their knees and cry out to him admitting their wicked ways and declare their intention never to walk that same evil path again?"

I sat utterly speechless, not knowing how to respond to such a tirade of personal invective. With my mind searching for hope in all that was being thrown at me I reminded myself that if God was indeed all seeing and all knowing then he was more than aware of the truth of my circumstances. He would know all that had been unfairly exacted upon me, not only by Mr Taylor but also during my time in Birkenau, and was seemingly about to be repeated here in the one place, above everywhere else, that should have been offering me the very help and succour I was so clearly in need of.

I decided, as was being suggested, to indeed put my hope and trust into God's hand but not the vindictive grip of this so called woman of faith who sat before me now. I had come across far worse bullies than she was demonstrating herself to be and survived. I resolved that if the cost of my gaining food and shelter during the next few months until my baby arrived was in having to put up with the perverse and twisted opinions of this sad and frustrated woman in a habit then so be it.

Sister Claire leant forward placing her hands flat on her desk. "Maybe we should start again. Now, let us agree on the facts at least shall we?" She smiled, but it wasn't a smile of comfort more of smug superiority.

"You are clearly pregnant of that there is no doubt, and I assume you are seeking refuge here with us until your child is born. Am I right in my thinking so far?" I nodded.

"Well, we here at the Holy Order do indeed offer shelter and sustenance to wayward girls similar to yourself; to those who have allowed their bodies to be used by a man and have reaped God's punishment on themselves in becoming pregnant. As I have intimated we don't judge you personally, hard though that is when the evidence of your sin is so obviously displayed before us each day." She paused as if sensing her obvious delight in vilifying me might appear as being overly personal and so reverted to a more considered yet still overtly moral tone.

"We accept that only God has the right to judge us individually as surely he will do come the day. But what we do offer here is an opportunity for you to beg his forgiveness and atone for your transgressions through hard work and dedication to the rules by which we live here at the Sisters of Mercy. And of course in all of this, there is the child to consider. God is aware of its existence and although it will be born into sin as we all are, it cannot be held responsible for your wrongdoing and so no judgement will be held against it while it remains in your belly."

I sat in silence hardly daring to believe what I was hearing.

"You will be fed three times a day and given a bed in which to sleep. In return you will be given a list of duties that are to be carried out without recourse or question, is all of that clear?"

I nodded again. "May I ask a question, Sister?" I tried to

remain polite even though every fibre of my being wanted to scream out and tell her in no uncertain terms what she could do with her duties and regulations.

"I'm listening."

"What happens when my baby is born?"

She paused momentarily as if considering how best to answer.

"When the child arrives you will nurse it for a short while until a suitable family and proper home can be found for it. Clearly *you* will not be in a position to provide for it having no permanent address of your own nor credible means by which to support either yourself or the baby."

I felt a sense of anger and frustration building inside me. "But it will be *my* baby. Shouldn't I have a say in its future?"

Sister Claire dropped her head and, clearly unhappy at her authority being questioned in such a way, stared over her glasses at me with a steely and unforgiving gaze.

"It will be your child by birth but not by design. If you were married with a loving and supportive husband by your side then of course all options for its future would quite rightly rest with the two of you. Indeed, the law expects honest and responsible parents to care for their offspring. You and others like you however have, by the very act of becoming pregnant outside of the Holy Order of matrimony, given up all rights to make any such decisions about the future of the precious life you have so recklessly decided to bring into the world. As for the baby itself it will belong, as we all do, to God himself and as such he expects those of us of sound mind and strong faith to do the best we can for it. Surely you would agree with that?" Without waiting for a reply she continued.

"That certainly doesn't mean leaving it in the care of a slip of a girl like you, one who has allowed herself to be used in such a way before she is married. All sexual relations entered into outside of marriage are a terrible sin, and even then are only truly intended for the procreation of the human race. It is certainly not to be seen as some form of pleasure seeking distraction between unmarried and reckless individuals as you appear to have viewed it." She moved slightly in her seat but continued to stare at me demonstrating that she hadn't yet finished speaking. "Now, may I ask you a question?"

"Of course," I muttered, fearing the worst.

"Do you know who the father is? And if you do then why is he not standing beside you supporting you as any worthwhile man would surely seek to do?"

How I wanted to tell the truth, if only to shock her and wipe that self satisfied grin off her face but I knew she wouldn't believe me if I did.

"I do know who the father is but I'm afraid I can't tell you. He has threatened that if I do say anything he will make things worse for me."

"You mean he's married? I presume that's what you're intimating?" The look on my face told her all she needed to know. She rose from her chair and walked towards a bell rope hanging from the ceiling to the right of her desk.

"It isn't what you're thinking, Sister."

"I don't think anything, Miss Cahn, as I say I leave all thought and judgement to God. Ultimately you will answer to him, as will the man in question and, if as you suggest he is married, then an even greater burden of sin will way heavy upon your shoulders for coming between a man and his wife."

"But you don't understand."

"Sadly I think I do, and only too well. I've heard stories like yours many times and, on each occasion, like you, the girl in question claimed her innocence." She pulled the bell rope as she spoke. "Sister Margaret will be here again in a moment. She will show you where you are to sleep and appraise you of your duties over the next few days while we work out a longer term plan for your being here. We can arrange for the collection of your other clothing and belongings at a later date, not that you will be in need them here as you will wear the same simple smock as the other girls. Now, if all of that is clear there is only one other question I need to ask of you."

I held my breath fearing what she might say next.

Taking off her glasses and placing them on her desk she looked directly at me again, the same smirk of derision ingrained across her face.

"Following our discussion am I to assume that you do still want to take sanctuary here at our Holy Order, or do you have somewhere else to go? Accommodation provided by the father of the child perhaps?"

I sat rooted to my chair unable to respond, the fight drained from me as I recognised, at least for the moment, that the bully had won the first round in this early battle of wills between us. I felt totally lost and downcast. She clearly wasn't going to miss the opportunity to remind me as to who exactly was in charge of my fate, certainly for the immediate future at least.

She smiled broadly. "I thought not."

There was a knock at the door.

"Come." I heard the door creak open behind me.

"Ah Sister Margaret, Miss Cahn has decided to join us. Perhaps you can sort out the arrangements to fetch whatever few belongings she has elsewhere and assign her to a dormitory?"

I rose from my chair and turned to witness Sister Margaret bowing almost reverentially towards her superior. "Of course, Sister."

"And she'll need to be placed on the rota to help with Mass, morning prayers and Compline each evening, along with her duties in the kitchen, laundry room and so on."

Sister Margaret nodded in compliance as she moved to open the door. I didn't feel the need or desire to say thank you to Sister Claire as we left the room, I was sure we would cross swords again soon and that next time I would be better prepared to defend my corner.

As we made our way back down the corridor Sister Margaret explained the house rules for the Sisters of Mercy to me.

"We place great store in our prayer life here, Ruth, and in the confession of our sins. I suggest you take both very seriously, not only for the good of your soul but also your own well being. Sister Claire doesn't brook any excuses for missing those allotted times when we are to bring ourselves before God and no quarter is given to those who don't appear at the services or are late. The punishments for non attendance or not adhering to the home's regulations are both swift and severe. Sister Claire says that our Father is a jealous God and so won't tolerate either wanton sin nor those who find reason not comply with our bounded duty to praise and serve him at those fixed and sacred times of the day laid aside for worship. This includes not only you girls but also those of us appointed to his full time service and eternal glory."

I smiled inwardly and thought of others in the past who had insisted on total obedience to their equally unreasonable demands and who were now facing God themselves along with their own time of judgement. Sister Claire may not have been wearing a swastika but she bore all the hallmarks of other tyrannical dictators I had suffered under. I decided once I had regained my confidence and appetite for life that in future when we differed she would fare no better in her efforts to beat me into submission than they had.

My head spun over the next few days as I came to terms with my new set of duties and the daily routine at the Sisters of Mercy. I laughed to myself every time I saw or thought of the word mercy as it was certainly not an expression I would have used to describe the treatment any of us young girls received during our time at the home.

I quickly made two friends, Susan and Diane; they were both about my age and we slept close to each other in the dormitory. We would whisper shared secrets and stories about our past life and experiences long into the night before falling asleep exhausted only to be woken by the sound of a loud hand bell being wrung in our ears before dawn each morning by whichever nun had drawn the short straw in getting us up and ready for the first prayers of the day. The only good thing about attending that early service was that you knew as soon as it was over you could eat breakfast. Mind, the meal that is traditionally accepted as setting you up for the day usually consisted of little more than a bowl of watery porridge and a slice of rough cut bread. Sometimes this would be cremated and presented as toast; presumably to hide the fact the bread itself had gone stale. There were occasions when I felt like complaining but quickly reminded myself, whenever I was feeling hard done by and facing this meagre fair, of the times in Birkenau when I would have happily accepted a third as much and thought of it as a banquet compared to that on which we actually had to survive.

All of us girls looked forward to the days that Sister Rosemary had been roistered for breakfast supervision as she would allow us an extra half spoonful of sugar in our tea or an additional piece of burnt toast if there was any left once we had cleared away and washed the dishes. Susan, Diane and I would always volunteer for these duties, not only for the extra food and drink it might afford us but because Sister Rosemary, being in her early twenties, was someone we felt we could confide in and talk to about all sorts of things that appear important to young teenage girls. She was a diminutive figure and we used to joke at times that she appeared lost in her flowing habit as though it were too big for her. She had piercing blue eyes and a ready smile that we all warmed to and quickly learned to trust. Even when she had to tell us off about something we had done to upset the status quo in the Holy Order we knew that her overall sympathies lay with us. She never actually spoke out against some of the harsher rules or punishments exercised in the home but we could tell from her demeanour that she struggled at times with the reasoning behind them. We spoke to her once about her decision to become a nun.

"What made you want to join the order here at the Sisters of Mercy?"

"Did you have a boyfriend before you came here?"

"I knew I wanted to be a nun from the age of about eleven so never really had time to think about boys. I felt God calling me to his service and just knew it was the right thing for me to do."

"I bet you'd have felt differently if it had been Sister Claire calling you, or shouting in your ear," laughed Susan.

"You mustn't say things like that, Susan. Sister Claire is a woman of great faith and has a lot of responsibility on her shoulders."

"Maybe, but you must admit she can be a bit of a tyrant at times?" Sister Rosemary smiled and shook her head in mock disapproval. She understood our reasoning if not entirely agreeing with our motives for making such a comment. She also recognised we weren't the devil incarnate as sometimes intimated by Sister Claire but were simply a group of teenage girls who had fallen prey to the promises or demands of a man who was probably now getting up to the same thing again with some other poor innocent, another young girl who would no doubt, at some point in the future, also find themselves knocking on the door of the Sisters of Mercy seeking help.

"Do you ever think what it might have been like if you had got married and had children, Sister?"

"I am married, only my vows of love and obedience were made to God and not to a man." There was a genuine look of warmth and sincerity in her expression as she spoke.

"Well I hope he's more faithful than my bloke," Diane said. "Filthy bugger he was, has his evil way with me and then as soon as he puts me in the family way he's off with one of my friends. Well, she used to be a friend, she ain't anymore of course."

Sister Rosemary looked at us and stroked Diane's arm. "God is faithful, girls, and you can always trust him to keep his word. He'll never lie to you or treat you in the way you have been by the men you have been with."

It was my turn to speak. "I wish Sister Claire was more like you. When I hear you speak about God I feel like maybe he does listen and understand everything I've been through."

"You may not always feel his presence, Ruth, but I promise you he is always by your side. When you smile he smiles with you and when you cry he weeps for you."

"So even though I'm a Jew and you're a Catholic it's still the same God we talk to then is it, Sister?"

"Except that we Catholics believe it is through intercessional prayer to Mary the mother of Jesus that we connect with God. As a Jew your thoughts about Jesus as the Messiah are different. Ultimately though I do believe God knows each one of us individually and that he will never forsake us if we reach out to him with an open and contrite heart"

"If I'm honest, Sister, I'm not sure what I think about God anymore or that I want anything to do with him, not after everything that has happened to me over the past few years."

Sister Rosemary smiled. "He'll still be there when you're ready to talk to him again, Ruth. As I say, he'll never leave you or stop loving you."

"Well I don't believe in God and no amount of getting up early and going to bed late to pray will make me change my mind, especially with grumpy old Sister Claire in charge. I mean why would anyone want to wind up all bitter and twisted like her?"

"That was quite a mouthful, Susan, but you really shouldn't be so hard on Sister Claire, she doesn't have it easy you know. She is responsible for all that goes on here at the home including the welfare of you young girls and your babies when they arrive." Susan shrugged her shoulders. "It'll take more than that to convince me I should be like her I can tell you. You're alright though, you know, for a nun." Sister Rosemary smiled and glanced at the clock on the kitchen wall. "Now come along or we'll all be in trouble if we don't make a start on our tasks for the day."

I think if it hadn't been for Sister Rosemary some of us girls would have found ourselves in a lot more trouble than we actually did at times. She would often talk us out of rebelling against Sister Claire's unreasonable requests and non negotiable demands.

Although we knew from experience that babies born in the home would eventually be adopted by families traditionally unable to have children of their own we never chose to think about this being the case with our own babies. This was soon to change though with Diane being almost three months ahead of Susan and I in her pregnancy.

It was a few weeks later that Diane had her baby: a little boy she named Kenneth after her father who had been killed during the war. Following his death her mother had a break down and began drinking heavily, leaving Diane on her own and pretty much having to care for herself. Like so many of the girls at the Sisters of Mercy, she had met a boy who had shown her the attention and affection she craved and that was sadly missing at home. He had made her feel special and she thought was someone who would care for her following the trauma of losing her father and the effects of her mother's breakdown. Sadly the truth, as with so many of the boys and men who promised so much early on, was that when Diane declared herself pregnant the so called answer to her prayers proved to be the exact opposite. He ran a mile denying all involvement in her pregnancy or that he had any responsibility, financial or otherwise, towards her and the baby when it arrived.

The three of us talked together just a few days before she was due to give birth.

"Dad was the only man who ever really cared about me, so if it is a boy I'm going to name him Kenneth after him."

Sister Claire had proved her usual caring self when she heard of Diane's decision.

"You can call the child whatever you like for the short period you are nursing it, but be assured that those who adopt it will be free to name it as they wish once the papers are finalised through the courts."

Diane said that had made her so angry she had answered back

without any thought of the consequences. "Well he'll always be Kenneth to me if my baby is a boy. They might be able to change his name, but they can never change the fact that I gave birth to him, and that's something you'll never experience, you spiteful old witch."

She told us Sister Claire's face had changed to a deep shade of red after being spoken to in such a way and had put Diane firmly back in her place.

"You will miss supper tonight for that remark, but still wash everyone else's plates and cutlery after they have eaten. Might I add, that whilst you may be right about my never experiencing the privilege of bringing a new life into this world, I would also never betray myself nor my relationship with God by allowing my body to be used merely for the act of sinful lust that you so clearly have. I suggest whilst you are clearing away the supper things this evening you think about that and ask God to forgive you at the same time, not only for your part in such an immoral act but also for your ungrateful spirit in speaking against one of his chosen servants in such a way. Who else could you wicked young girls turn to for refuge if it wasn't for the Sisters here at the Holy Order opening our doors to you and your bastard children? Perhaps on reflection you will accept it is you that has sinned, yet again, by speaking so spitefully towards me, when I have only spoken the truth."

Life under Sister Claire was never easy and the three of us would try and make every effort to keep out of her way wherever possible, but never quite hard enough. The problem was that we also enjoyed goading her, even though the resultant punishment metered out for our verbal taunts or acts of mischief were often out of all proportion in comparison to our alleged sinful ways and failings.

"You are wicked, wicked girls," she would shout at us. "It's just as well for you that the good Lord loves all his children, even you, providing they confess and repent of all of their misdemeanours and sins. Although in your three cases I think even his patience, like mine, is sorely tested at times. If the truth be told, I'm not sure any of you are genuinely sorry for the things you do even when you declare them at confession. You would do well to remember that our Father God knows the intentions of all of our hearts better than we do ourselves, so you can be sure he can see through the veneer of your pretence at sorrow and your empty promises not to do the same things again."

We would lie in bed at night giggling to ourselves dreaming up new ideas of how we might tease and torment her next. It wasn't necessarily that we didn't believe in God or in his ability to give us that fresh start we all craved so badly, it was just the thought of attaining it through our acquiescing to the demands of Sister Claire's cynicism and vitriol was a step too far, even for us three desperate young girls. We had all experienced far harsher words and beatings in our lives than she could ever hand out, so why should we believe that hers were being administered as part of God's corrective love for us when those we had received similar treatment from in the past were most certainly not?

Once during evening prayers Susan whispered a joke to me which I attempted to pass on to Diane but collapsed in fits of laughter halfway through which in turn made the other two burst into hysterics as well. We knew we were in trouble when even Sister Rosemary looked towards us in obvious disapproval.

Sister Claire took the three of us to the wash room and forced us to rinse out our mouths with soap and water.

"Evensong is a time to use your voices to lift up praises to God not to tell stupid and inane jokes to each other, so you can each clean the filth from your mouths with a good dose of soapy water." She also made us stand under an icy cold shower for a full five minutes.

"Let us see if the cold water can wash away the heat of the devil in you and teach you to take the Lord's name seriously in future when offering worship to him."

The water froze our bodies and took our breath away as we stood there wondering if the effects of such an icy deluge might cause us to miscarry. Eventually Sister Rosemary came to our rescue, arguing that we had probably learned our lesson by now and was sure we wouldn't let ourselves or the good Lord down in such a sorry way again. Sister Claire grunted, presumably not entirely convinced as to our contrition for our actions.

"I'm sure they'll never do anything like it ever again, Sister."

Sister Claire turned her attention to our young saviour. "I think you underestimate the devil in these three girls Sister Rosemary. However, and, thankfully for them I do have business elsewhere to attend to." With her desire for revenge against us satiated she turned to leave satisfied she had inflicted as much discomfort as possible on us in the time we had spent spitting out soapy water and shivering under the freezing waters of the showers. She also took great pleasure in watching the three of us tremble naked on the cold wash room tiles before turning on her heels and striding out of the room. Sister Rosemary handed each of us a towel.

"You three girls will be the death of me. I like to laugh just as much as you do, but evensong is not the place to be telling jokes between you; Sister Claire is certainly right about that. When we come before God we must remember that we are in a holy place and that he deserves respect as well as our words of praise when we offer up petitions to him, surely you can see that?"

"We know, Sister, and we are genuinely sorry." Even I felt on this particular occasion we had perhaps overstepped the boundaries of what was deemed acceptable between the three of us when it came to winding up Sister Claire and the other nuns.

"We will try harder not to misbehave like that again, won't we, girls?" I looked at the other two who were rubbing themselves hard with their towels in an effort to get their blood circulating again. They nodded in agreement but each of us knew this would probably be a pledge, no matter how well intentioned, we would struggle to keep.

Once Kenneth was born Susan and I would often watch Diane feed him, envying her that intimacy with her baby.

"I can't wait to hold my little one like you, Diane, and feed him, or her, just like a real mother," Susan said one day as we were making our beds.

"You will be a real mother when it arrives, stupid, who else do you think will be giving birth to the wee thing if not you?

"I know that. I just meant I want to meet the little one and hold it in my arms same as you and love it. After all it's not the baby's fault I made the mistake of believing its father when he said he cared about me and that he didn't just want to get inside my pants. In the end he turned out to be like all the other dirty bastards though. Once they've had what they want they soon change their tune and bugger off."

I reflected briefly about my own circumstances, and whilst they might not have been exactly the same as Susan and Diane's the scenarios were very similar. Mr Taylor had also turned against me and denied any responsibility for his actions once I fell pregnant following his earlier pretence that I would be doing both his wife and family a great, if undeclared, service by sleeping with him. Perhaps Diane was right about all men being dirty bastards. But somewhere deep inside I still preferred to believe there may be someone out there who might some day want me simply for myself, rather than for what took place between us in the bedroom.

"I'm going to get a job when I leave here and provide for Kenneth, just you wait and see. He won't want for anything." Diane's eyes filled with emotion. "No-one is going to take him away from me I won't let them."

I pulled Diane towards me and gave her a hug. "That's a lovely thought, but we know that's not what happens to our babies unless of course you find a pot of money or the father changes his mind and decides to do the right thing and stand by you, and we both know that's hardly likely."

"I don't care, I'm not letting anyone take him from me; he's my son. Maybe he didn't come into the world under the best of circumstances but he still deserves all the love and affection his Mum can give him, and not from some stranger who wasn't even there when he was born." She looked directly at me. "I mean it, Ruth, Kenneth's mine and he ain't going anywhere without me and that's that."

Susan and I glanced at each other, recognising between us that same desire to keep our as yet unborn babies but also acknowledging the mostly likely scenario would be they would be taken from us at a few weeks old and given to a family who, if we were honest, would be able to provide for them much better than we were ever likely to be able to do. They may not be able to love them in the same way as we might, as their birth mothers, but they would still care for them and meet all of their needs as the years passed by and as they grew together as a family.

A few weeks later the three of us were working together in the laundry room when Sister Margaret approached us. "Diane, Sister Claire wants to speak with you."

"What about?"

"I'm not at liberty to say, she just asked me to come and take you to her."

We looked at each other wondering what could be wrong. The three of us had been fairly well behaved over the past few days and couldn't immediately think of anything we might have done that had initiated this call from on high.

Susan placed the sheets she was folding on to a table. "I'll come with you."

Sister Margaret stood in her way. "On whose authority will you be leaving your duties, young lady? I don't remember saying Sister Claire wanted to speak with you."

Diane laughed as she followed Sister Margaret out of the room. "It's alright; I'll fill you in on all the gory details when I get back. And if she says I'm in trouble for anything I'll put the blame on you two."

"That's why I wanted to come with you," Susan called after her.

"We know what you're like." She turned to me. "Sister Margaret knows more than she's letting on."

"Maybe, but she's probably as scared of Sister Claire as the rest of us, along with her hotline to God's punishment rota."

Susan smiled. "Honestly for a so called loving creator he certainly wants his pound of flesh when in comes to confession or atonement for our dreadful sins. You'd have thought he'd have a better sense of humour than demanding we receive a beating for putting too much starch in the nuns' underwear so it all dries stiff as a board. It made me laugh so I don't understand why God wasn't amused as well." I laughed. "Sister Claire certainly wasn't though."

"I know, the cow gave me six strokes with the paddle for that, the palms of my hands stung for ages." She waved her hands in the air and blew on them as if to demonstrate how sorely they had been beaten.

We finished our work in the laundry room and were about to leave when Sister Rosemary entered with a concerned look on her face. "You girls might want to go upstairs to the dormitory; Diane has had some bad news."

"What's happened," I asked?

"Her baby has been taken."

"What do you mean *taken*?"

"By a young couple. He's been adopted."

Susan pushed in front of me. "But how, why, surely Diane should have been told it was going to happen?"

"Sister Claire felt that it would be better this way. Diane had always spoken about wanting to keep her baby, she even gave him a name, Kenneth, wasn't it, after her father? That was never a good idea, at least not to name the child after a family member; it simply creates a bond that can never be fully realised. All of you girls know your babies will eventually leave here to live with adoptive parents unless there are special circumstances or your families come forward and offer you and the baby the support it needs. Sadly, that didn't happen with Diane or Kenneth she…" Her voice trailed away as she took on board the enormity of what she had said in repeating, once again, the name Diane had given her son. We both knew what she had said about having to let our babies go was the accepted, if unspoken, truth no matter how hard it was to admit to ourselves. Even so, when the moment actually arrived it still came as a huge shock and was a time of desperate sadness for so many of us.

Susan and I ran upstairs, another sinful act as far as the sisters were concerned but one that we were more than ready to face the paddle for or whatever other form of punishment might be metered out to us for so flagrantly abusing the house rules. After all, this was our friend and she was hurting with a pain far in excess of anything that Sister Claire might choose to inflict on us for an act of such brazen rebellion.

Diane was sitting alone on her bed weeping, punching her pillow and screaming obscenities as we entered the room. "Fucking Sister Claire the bitch, I'll kill her, so help me, I'll kill her."

"Sister Rosemary just told us, they've taken Kenneth away, we're so sorry." I didn't really know what to say but still wanted to offer at least some crumb of comfort to our dear friend no matter how small.

Diane looked up, her face bright red with emotion. "The bitch told me this couple had seen him on two previous occasions and said what a beautiful little boy he was and that they would love and care for him. I told her I would have given him all the love he needed and that nobody else could ever do that as well as me, his real mother. The cow just laughed and said as a child of Satan I had the sin of lust running through my body and so could expect nothing less than God's reckoning for my actions. She said I should be grateful this couple had wanted to offer him a home and that God was sparing him the damnation I was surely destined for by giving him the chance of a new life away from me."

Susan began to cry as well. "She's the evil one, the bitch."

I sat on the bed and took Diane in my arms as she shook with rage and emotion.

"What else did she say?"

"She told me to go straight to confession and seek forgiveness for my spite towards her and the couple who had taken Kenneth away. She said I should be saying prayers of thanks that my son would now receive the love and care I could never give him."

Susan kicked out at the leg of the bed in frustration. "She hasn't got a bloody clue has she? What would she know about love and care, the twisted old witch?"

"That's pretty much what I said to her."

"Bet that went down well?"

"She slapped me and told me to come up here to calm down while she decided what form of punishment would suit my outburst and ingratitude towards the Holy Order."

"What did you say?"

"I told her to fuck off."

Susan raised her hand to her mouth in feigned shock and grinned. "Good for you. About time someone put her in her place. Bet she went potty though?"

Diane looked up again turning her face to one side where we could see the swollen imprint of a hand across her cheek. "She slapped me again."

Susan leant across and gently stroked her face. "I can see. We can't let her get away with this, let's go and have it out with her."

With our passions so highly charged I realised that any further protest just now would only inflame the situation and make matters worse for us. I stood up and attempted to provide the voice of reason.

"Look, we all know what an insensitive bitch she is but when it comes down to it we're all pretty much in the same boat. As long as we're stuck in here someone else is always going to get our baby eventually. We can scream and shout as much as we like but there's nothing we can actually do about it, they have the law on their side." I looked at Diane. "You'll never get over losing Kenneth, and it will be the same for me and Susan when our time comes. It's shit but it's the way the system works."

Diane broke down again. "But I could have tried to look after him; they could have at least given me a chance."

For the next fifteen minutes we just sat on the bed hugging each other and crying. My heart went out to Diane and I knew I would feel exactly the same way when it came time for letting my baby go, even though it had been conceived with a man I now despised.

As I sat there considering my friend's raw sense of loss I recalled the similar feelings of almost unbearable pain I had encountered in witnessing the passing of my brother and parents in the nightmare surroundings of Birkenau. Whilst the conditions under which their lives had been taken were clearly more horrific than the parting of Diane and her baby son, the personal grief and heartache she was experiencing was, to her, no less devastating. For the first time in as long as I could remember I found myself praying with an intensity I had all but forgotten. What if God really did exist? What if he did love us and was aware our pain and fear? What if he wanted to help us in our grieving, rather that simply pour down his wrath and punishment in flames of torment and persecution from on high as Sister Claire would have us believe? I wasn't sure, but I knew I needed to believe in something bigger and better than the cruel and heartless dictates of this woman who held sway over so much of our young lives. In that moment of desperation I committed my friends and myself into God's care in the hope that if he did exist, and was listening, he would, at least for now, take my appeal for help seriously and act upon it.

Over the few days Diane became calmer in herself although no less vindictive in her attitude and manner towards Sister Claire. Eventually it came time for her to leave and step back into society away from the confines of the Holy Order, but after spending so much time in the home and living under such a strict regime it was easy to forget what the outside world had to offer, or even what it was like. We had all become virtually institutionalised in our outlook and acceptance of the austere and unforgiving conditions imposed on us in this claustrophobic and penal style edifice.

Sister Rosemary made sure we had a little time together to say our goodbyes on the day Diane left. "You take care of yourself, Diane. I've enjoyed getting to know you but I hope never to see you again, if you understand my meaning?"

Diane put her arms around the young nun and hugged her. This was as much in recognition of her appreciation of the kindness and understanding demonstrated towards her by Sister Rosemary as it was to say goodbye.

"Thank you, Sister, I won't forget you I promise." She stepped back and looked around the cold and austere surroundings of the entrance hallway, her voice echoing slightly as she spoke. "Although there are those here I will make every effort to erase from my memory altogether."

"Now that's not very nice, Diane. All the sisters, even Sister Claire, want only the best for you and the little ones we help bring into this world. And we offer up daily prayers of thanksgiving for each of you and ask that the good Lord will always keep you safe and guide you in his way."

Diane smiled and chose to leave on a high rather than react negatively again.

"Oh I know that, Sister, I was meaning these two." She gently poked Susan and I in the ribs in what we took to be a display of affection.

"And we'll be pleased to see the back of you as well," Susan retorted, laughing as she spoke.

A wave of emotion overcame me as I took a hold of Diane's hand. "Write to me eh, I'll miss you."

I felt her squeeze my hand tightly in return as we both fought back our tears. "Yeah okay, me too."

She gave the three of us a parting kiss and then without

looking back walked through the large front doors and out into the sunshine. I was briefly reminded of the words of scripture that were so often drummed into us by the nuns, and for once felt them to be truly apt as I watched my friend leave the grim surroundings of the home and move, *out of the darkness and into the light.* We stood for a moment watching her walk away, the gravel on the driveway crackling under her feet as she did so.

Susan and I shouted one last goodbye and smiled at each other as Diane, without looking back, waved her hand in the air in response. My head wanted to believe this was a final act of defiance by my friend demonstrated towards the home but my heart told me it was to hide the tears that she, like us, was allowing to flow. Sister Rosemary put her arms around our shoulders. "Well at least it's only the two of you I have to worry about now."

"Thanks, Sister, we love you too." She rubbed our shoulders and walked away leaving us to watch our friend disappear around the corner at the end of the driveway and out of our lives. The two of us stood for a while hugging each other as the tears continued to run down our cheeks. Eventually I broke the silence. "Come on then or we'll have Sister Claire down here shouting at us to get back to work."

As we moved towards the home and the large front door that was still open waiting to swallow us up again Susan looked at me and smiled. "I'm not sure whether I envy Diane or not. I mean she's out of this place, and that's got to be a good thing I know, but at what cost? She's never gonna see her baby again is she?" I took her hand in silent recognition of that truth and one that would presumably apply to the both of us in the weeks ahead.

Life at the home seemed quiet without Diane. Susan and I didn't have the same appetite for mischief as we had done when it had been the three of us. Equally we were nearing the time for our own babies to be born and so we agreed that genuine fatigue also had a part to play in our general lack of energy and inspiration as to ways of annoying the nuns, especially Sister Claire.

One morning during breakfast Susan suddenly grabbed at her stomach and cried out in pain. One of the sisters came across to our table. "What on earth is the matter, girl?"

"I've got a pain in my stomach, it's really bad like cramp but it's deep inside." Susan's face had gone grey and she looked clammy with beads of perspiration breaking out across her forehead.

"It's probably just your time." There was no concern or sympathy displayed in her words. "Stand yourself up and stop making such a fuss. We'll get you long to the delivery room."

As Susan got to her feet I noticed her dress was wet.

"I think your waters have broken, it won't be long now," I said, trying to encourage her but sensing that all was not well.

As she and the nun moved from the table I saw that the lower part of Susan's dress was turning red.

"Sister she's bleeding."

The nun looked for herself at the red stain that was spreading rapidly and spoke again, her speech and demeanour more consolatory. "Now come along, Susan, hold on to me, we need to get you to the delivery room as quickly as we can, dear." As they left I saw blood was now dripping onto the floor from Susan's dress such was the flow from her body. All of the other girls and I looked at each other; we had seen many others taken to the delivery room, some even as a measure of urgency, but none of us had previously witnessed such a dramatic and bloodied exit.

Sister Margaret entered the room and clapped her hands. "Now come along all of you finish your breakfast and then you can make a start on your duties. It is just Susan's time as it will be yours soon enough so let's not have any fuss about a spot or two of blood, it's quite natural in childbirth to bleed a little." She called to one of the other girls. "Mary Jane, you look as though you've finished so off with you to the wash room and fetch a mop and bucket to clear this up," she said pointing to the blood already staining the wooden floor.

Another of the girls leaned across the table to me. "That don't look like a spot or two of blood to me, do you think she'll be alright?"

"I hope so; she was fine a few minutes ago."

The girl tried to reassure me. "The nuns might be horrid at times but at least they know what they're doing in that delivery room, they've all done their training; well the ones that do the business anyway."

Whilst I remained concerned for Susan I did have to agree that she was in the best hands for her baby and its journey into the world. I decided to knock on God's door again as I cleared away my breakfast things with another prayer for my friend and her baby's safe arrival.

I found it hard to concentrate over the next hour or so in the laundry room as I took my turn in addressing the mountain of ironing that lay all around. It was hot and I couldn't stop thinking about Susan but my own baby clearly decided it wasn't getting enough attention and so kept kicking me as I tackled the seemingly endless mound of sheets and pillow cases that appeared to increase in size each time I turned to take another from the pile behind me.

It was just over two hours later that Sister Margaret approached me. I could tell by the look on her face that my growing fears for Susan, having heard nothing for such a long time, were well founded.

"Ruth, I have some sad news for you." My heart raced as I feared the worst. "It's Susan isn't it, is she alright?"

"I'm sorry, but Susan has lost her baby. If you come with me I'll take you to her, she has been asking for you."

I walked into a small room next to the delivery area biting my lip so as not to let my tears flow as I looked at my friend, her hair lank and stuck to the side of her face which carried an expression of complete loss and bewilderment. She had a tube connected to her arm presumably to replace the blood and fluids she had lost.

As I approached the bed Susan looked up at me, tears streaming down her face. "She's gone, Ruth, my little girl is gone." I took her hand and squeezed it; both words and emotions failing me as I too began to weep.

"I'm so sorry." It was all I could manage as we collapsed into each other's arms. We stayed like that for some time, holding onto each other for comfort, our shoulders and clothing damp with our tears. Eventually our sobbing ceased and I pulled back a little, wiping my face with my sleeve as I did so. "What happened?"

"I started haemorrhaging for some reason which meant they had to get the baby out quickly but the umbilical chord got wrapped around her neck and so she began to panic. The more she fought to be free of me the tighter the chord became and she strangled herself." She paused, catching her breath between sobs of emotion. "They called in a doctor to help with the haemorrhaging. He says I should be alright once they've replaced the blood I lost." She broke down again. "How can I ever be alright again knowing I killed my own baby?"

I took her face in my hands. "You mustn't say that, it wasn't your fault, none of it."

One of the sisters took my arm. "That's enough for now, Susan needs to rest; you can talk with her again soon."

I bent down and kissed my friend on the cheek and whispered, "I love you." It was the first time I had said that and truly meant it for as long as I could remember. We had been through such a lot together over the past few months and I think we both felt our relationship had become much more than one of simple friendship in all that we had experienced in the time we had known each other.

Susan smiled up at me. "I love you too."

I visited her every day over the next week as she slowly recovered her physical strength; mentally though I sensed her mood becoming darker as she continued to struggle with losing her baby under such tragic circumstances. How different her reaction was too so many of the other girls at the home, some of whom almost envied Susan's dramatic loss.

One girl said to me, "Of course I wouldn't want the bleed she had but if the little bugger wants to strangle itself on the way out then good riddance. It's what I would like to have done to the bastard who put it inside me and then buggered off back to his wife that he conveniently forgot to tell me about all the time he was shagging me."

I couldn't understand, no matter what the circumstances, why any girl or woman would wish ill on another human life that they were carrying inside of them, although I must admit some of the stories I heard caused me to question even my own thoughts and feelings at times. Another young girl who was from Ireland, Pauline, was a case in point. "My uncle and his friend raped me on my fifteenth birthday. I'd gone to his house to pick something up for my mammy. I'd never really liked him from the day he married my mammy's sister, he was always a bit slimy towards me, so he was. You know, brushing his hand against my backside when I walked past him or standing in my way and pushing his body up against my breasts that sort of thing. Anyway, so he invites me in and says my aunty has gone to work but has left a special birthday present for me and that he has something to give me as well. I walked into the front room and his friend is there and he sort of smiles at me and says what a lovely looking young girl I am. I said thank you but I felt sick in myself that he should say something like that to me when he didn't even know me as such. I began to feel uncomfortable and said I had better get off home, but my uncle says didn't I want my present first and he grabs my arm and pulls me towards him. He smelt of beer and cigarettes and I tried to push him away, but he tells his friend to come and take my arms and he puts his hand across my mouth and tells me not to scream.

"We just want a little fun that's all and you're a big enough girl now to join in," he says and pushes me back onto the dining table. His friend held my arms above my head and my uncle pulls down my pants and forces himself between my legs." She stopped talking for a moment as the violence of the memory overtook her.

I stroked her arm in a vain attempt to comfort her. "I'm so sorry. You don't need to say anymore."

"No, you're alright; it helps in a way to remind myself that it wasn't my fault." She took a deep breath. "So after he's finished he tells his friend to come and have a go and they swap over with my uncle holding me down. Through my tears I'm begging them to stop but my uncle bends down over me, his face so close to mine that I can smell the drink on his breath and he practically spits out the words at me telling me I can cry all I want but this is going to happen, so why don't I lie back and enjoy it." She stopped talking again, wiping a tear from her cheek with her hand. I could see the pain of what she had been through etched on her face as she recalled the horrific events of that day. "Eventually it stopped. They let go of my arms and I got up, struggling to stand as my legs began to buckle under me. My uncle lit a cigarette and told me I could go home now and enjoy the rest of my birthday.

""If you ever want some more, Pauline, you know where to find me.""

The two of them laughed as I pulled up my pants with their muck still running down my legs."Oh and by the way I wouldn't say anything to your mam as she probably won't believe you, and even if she does she'll not do anything about it." He laughed again and flicked the ash from his cigarette on the floor.

""Do you remember when your dad got killed during the war and I looked out for you all? Well your mam was very grateful if you get my meaning and we became close, very close."" Pauline took another deep breath. "I didn't want to hear what he was saying but he wouldn't let me go until he had finished."

""In fact, your mammy has been coming here regularly over the past few years so we could spend some time together when your Aunty Colleen has been at work, only she doesn't know about that; about how your mammy likes me to fuck her like I have you. So you see if you do say anything to her she'll be in as much trouble as you when your aunt finds out. So why don't you think about that, Pauline, before you go opening your gob to your mammy or anyone else?""

"I told him I didn't believe him and that my mam would never have done the things he said, not with him. I said he was vile and that I hated him, but he just grinned at me.

""Well your mam doesn't hate me; in fact she really likes me, although she does feel guilty about betraying her sister that much is true. But, like I say, I wouldn't talk to her about that as you'll only upset her all the more. In fact she might even think you agreed to come and spend time with me and Patrick here as some sort of revenge for finding out about her and me. What do you think about that, Pauline? Who knows, she might even get jealous so she might, what with you being so young and her getting a bit past her prime if you know what I mean."" Pauline looked at me. "What could I do, especially if he was telling the truth? And if he was then I couldn't even trust my own mam to be there for me. I just went home and never told anybody, but I did begin to take notice of when my mam would go out, especially during the day. I even followed her once and saw her get into my uncle's car, so maybe he was telling the truth about the two of them? Anyway, few weeks later I found out I was pregnant and because I didn't feel I could talk to my mam or anyone about what had happened I ran away and came to England. I left a letter on the table telling her everything that had happened and what my uncle had said about the two of them. Then a couple of weeks after I got here I wrote to her again giving her the address I was staying at in case she was worried about me but she never wrote back. After a while and with my belly growing I had to move out of the place I was staying and had nowhere to go; then someone told me about this place, and here I am."

Even accepting the experiences of my own past I still struggled to understand how one person could treat another so cruelly, with no thought beyond their own selfish and perverse desires.

I struggled to find words of comfort as I listened to her story.

"So if you wonder why I can't wait to get rid of this little bastard growing inside of me, well now you know. They can take it away from me the second it's born. I don't want anything to do with it. I don't want to see it or hold it."

My heart broke for her, and for the child she was carrying, but I comforted myself with the thought that at least her baby might have the chance of a better life once it was adopted into a proper family home; one where it would be given the love and opportunities that Pauline and so many of the girls who found their way to the grim surroundings of the Sisters of Mercy had so obviously been denied.

I went to meet Susan the day she was released from the maternity wing having been deemed fit enough to play an active role in the daily routine of the home again. She looked brighter in herself physically but mentally I could see she was still struggling. "Please, Susie, you shouldn't keep beating yourself up, it really wasn't your fault." She looked at me as we stood in the long corridor between the nun's quarters and Sister Claire's study.

"I know you mean well, Ruth, but you're never going to free me from this feeling of guilt. I just keep seeing the look on the doctor's face as he pulled her lifeless body from me, the blood covering her like some form of awful sacrifice in payment for my sin."

I put my hand on her shoulder. "Don't say that. You mustn't allow yourself to think like that, not even for a moment."

Just then Sister Claire came out of her room. "What's going on here, more idle gossip between the two of you I've no doubt?"

I felt a surge of protective anger rise up in me. "Actually, Sister, poor Susan is struggling to come to terms with the loss of her baby. It's only been just over a week and she's still very upset."

"If she hadn't got herself pregnant in the first place she wouldn't be feeling this way would she? Honestly, some of you girls make me smile with your self pitying. You can't keep your legs closed but then expect others to feel sorry for you when you find yourself in trouble. You should both be grateful for refuges such as ours where you have the opportunity to be cared for and to declare your wrongdoing and fornication before God." She took a deliberate step towards us. "And on that confession, along with a suitable period of penitence and chastisement, you can embrace the blessed assurance of eternal forgiveness for your sinful ways and pray that you will never again be tempted to walk such a depraved path."

Susan and I looked at each other in almost disbelief at what we were hearing.

"Of course I am sad that a life has been lost," she continued, "but clearly God wanted to teach you a very serious lesson in all of this, Susan. Listen to me, girl, although you may be feeling physical pain just now – pain brought on by your own depraved actions I might add – you can take comfort in the fact that God knew your child from the moment it was conceived and, no matter the circumstances of that conception, now has the little one forever in his safe keeping. Surely you should be saying a prayer of thanks to him for that and not standing here whimpering and feeling sorry for yourself?"

"It's *she* that's in his safe keeping, Sister," I said firmly.

"I'm sorry?"

"Susan's baby was a little girl, so it is *she* that will be in God's safe keeping."

Sister Claire scowled at me. "You've always had too much to say for yourself, Ruth Cahn, but then again I have always found those of the Jewish faith to be self opinionated, certainly girls similar to yourself when entering the Holy Order. I would have hoped that time spent with us in a good Catholic environment would have helped improve your understanding as well as tempering your attitude and tendency towards insolence."

I knew that any further conversation would be wasted no matter how reasonably I might present my argument. I looked away so as not to get embroiled in a dispute I was unlikely to win. I was also aware that Susan's physical needs were far greater than my own desire to take on Sister Claire in a battle of words and so, taking my friend by the arm, walked away. Although I continued to feel anger towards Sister Claire in the way she had spoken to Susan and in her attitude to so many other girls in the home, I also felt a growing sense of sadness towards her as a person. How could anybody profess to be the servant of a loving god and yet spew out such vitriol towards the young girls he had placed in her protection and who were so clearly in need of the very care and support she alluded to as being available from this same omnipresent creator? I decided that was a question only he could answer and something that perhaps, in time, I might come to understand. For now I contented myself with the fact that God wouldn't presumably punish me further for putting my arm around my hurting friend and consoling her in her misery and grief as best I could.

Susan was very quiet at supper and struggled to hold herself together during compline and evening prayers. Sister Rosemary allowed me to take her to bed a little earlier as she could see how despondent she had become, although the other Sisters didn't agree with the demand for so much fuss and attention. We both got undressed and into our cot beds with Susan puling the thin blanket tight around her face to hide her tears.

"Feel better tomorrow, Susie." I knew what a pathetic statement that was to make but I was struggling as to what else to say having exhausted all other avenues of comfort throughout the day. I lay there for some time listening to my friend crying as she tossed and turned in her bed. I prayed her tears would act as some form of healing balm and that in the morning she would wake feeling better about herself and what had happened. Eventually her crying ceased and I allowed the aching tiredness in my own body to overtake my mind, my eye lids weighing heavy as I drifted into fitful sleep.

I awoke with a start the next morning unsure of the time but aware that we hadn't yet been greeted by the hand bell so enthusiastically rung by certain sisters in their efforts to rouse us.

This was done no doubt as an act of personal vengeance, carried out against us girls, to display their own displeasure in having had to get up even earlier themselves.

I rubbed the sleep from my eyes and looked across to Susan's cot. My heart leapt at seeing it empty. I jumped from my own bed and ran from the room calling out her name as I made my way down the narrow corridor that separated the various dormitories.

Sister Joan emerged form one of the side rooms. "Whatever is all this noise? Do you know what time it is, girl?"

"I'm really sorry, Sister, but Susan is not in her bed."

"Might she be in the toilet? Did you think of that before waking the whole household?"

I felt immediately admonished. "No, I'm sorry, Sister, I didn't. But she's been so unhappy since she lost her baby that I was worried about her."

She moved to the bathroom door. "You'll have a lot more to worry about if Sister Claire hears about this little outburst. Now go back to your bed and I'll look to see if she's in here."

As I moved away I heard a muffled cry and turning saw Sister Joan step back out of the bathroom, her face ashen and wearing a look of shocked disbelief. "Go and fetch Sister Claire," she said.

"What's the matter, what's happened?"

"Just do as I say, Ruth." She looked straight at me and shouted. "Now, girl, do you hear me, now."

I immediately sensed it was my friend and that something bad had happened. I ran to the bathroom pushing Sister Joan aside as I threw open the door. As I entered so my heart stopped and I caught my breath in both shock and stunned surprise. It was Susan: she had hung herself from one of the overhead water pipes with a strip of towelling.

As I stood in the doorway trying to absorb the full horror before me I could hear Sister Joan's voice behind me talking to some of the other girls who had been woken by our shouting. "Jennifer Riley, go and fetch Sister Claire and Sister Margaret as quick as you can. Get along with you now."

I heard another girl scream having glanced over my shoulder through the still open door and seen my poor friend hanging there, her face red and bloated, her eyes bulging in their sockets. I slammed the door shut behind me and screamed. "Go away, all of you, go away." I slid to the floor, tears cascading down my face.

I could hear Sister Joan telling the other girls to go back to their dormitories and get dressed and to stay there until one of the other Sister's came and told them what to do. I felt the door push against me as she forced it open and entered beside me.

"You should go back to your room, Ruth, there's nothing to be done here, not by you anyway." She spoke gently and crouched down beside me putting her arm around my shoulder.

"But she's my friend."

"I know, child, but there really is nothing you can do, and sitting here looking at her will only upset you all the more." She stood up and smiled down at me. "Now come along, let's get you a cup of tea, you've had a terrible shock. We've both had a shock."

As I struggled to my feet I heard Sister Claire's voice loud and unsympathetic as she shouted at the other girls who were still standing outside the bathroom; the shocking truth of what had happened now passing between them like wild fire.

"I want you girls back in your rooms *now*, there's nothing to be seen here, at least not by you."

I could hear the rumblings of discontent and gossip being shared amongst the other girls as they slowly moved away.

"Did you hear what I said? Get along with you, now!"

Sister Claire entered, still in her nightclothes along with Sister Rosemary who put her hand to her mouth in shock as she saw Susan's body hanging limply from the water pipe. Sister Claire glanced briefly at Susan and then towards me.

"I might have known you'd be here."

Sister Joan stepped in front of me. "Sister, it was me who found her. Ruth came in after me. She's very upset, Susan was her friend."

For once I felt Sister Claire's demeanour soften a little. "Thank you, Sister, I'm well aware of their relationship." A hand touched my arm.

"Ruth, why don't you take yourself off to my study, it will be quiet there and you can be alone with your thoughts." I looked up to see Sister Claire smiling at me; it was a smile of affection, something I'd never witnessed before. I didn't know what to say or how to respond.

"I'll come and talk to you in a little while, there's nothing for you to do here. Sister Rosemary, perhaps you'd like to accompany Ruth downstairs?"

"Of course, Sister." Tears filled my eyes again as I felt Sister Rosemary gently take my arm and guide me towards the door. As we left the room I glanced back allowing myself one last look at Susan.

"Come along, Ruth, there's nothing more you can do for her now."

"I know, Sister, I just wish that…"

"I know, dear, I know."

I berated myself for not having done more to sense the full pain that Susan had obviously experienced in losing her baby; also as to what else I might have done to stop her taking her life. Sister Rosemary and I didn't speak again as we made our way despondently towards the study; there were no words to describe the feeling of utter misery and desolation churning inside of me, nor I suspect were there any real words of comfort the young nun could have offered that would have made me feel any less wretched about myself or what had happened. As we walked together I think we both sensed that silence was the only language which, at that moment, expressed exactly what we both wanted to say as our hearts cried out to God appealing for him to care for dear Susan and to help make sense of what we had just witnessed.

I sat for some time in Sister Claire's study staring at the cup of sweet tea Sister Rosemary had made for me.

"You drink that while it's hot, Ruth, it will do you good. I'll leave you with your thoughts but if you want me just ring the bell and I'll come straight back. Sister Claire will be here shortly."

Time seemed to stand still as sadness and confusion vied for precedence in my thoughts. I picked up the cup but made no move to drink from it, instead gazing blankly at its contents as a myriad of images and memories raced through my mind. How often had I witnessed death in Birkenau, and how many times had I convinced myself not to let it overwhelm me? What could be worse than knowing your own father and brother had been gassed and that you had witnessed your mother being shot, dumped on a hand cart and taken away to the ovens for cremation? I had observed the journey from life to death played out at its worst so why was Susan's passing bothering me so much now? Perhaps I had committed the cardinal sin in such cases of dropping my guard and allowing another human being to touch me again, and made the further mistake of calling her friend as I had done with Sarah in the camp? But if I had made that seemingly fatal error of trusting my heart to someone else once more was that really so terrible? Maybe I had actually learned the greater lesson life has to teach us, that unless we truly love another we will never know nor fully understand the absolute joy and elation that our hearts find in such a relationship. Conversely, and as I was now discovering, to my cost yet again, we are also condemned to experience the numbing pain and grief also associated with those same emotions when we lose that loved one or are betrayed. But without experiencing that very real anguish surging through our being we will also never truly understand what it means to have given our hearts in the first place. Surely that would be the greatest sadness and betrayal of them all?

As I sat there pondering whether I had truly discovered some great truth about life and death or was simply entertaining a series of whimsical ramblings as I had done on so many occasions in the past I heard the door open behind me. I moved to drink my now cold tea thinking it to be Sister Rosemary come back to check I was alright. I didn't want to appear ungrateful for the kindness she had shown towards me.

"Lovely tea, thank you, Sister," I said without turning.

"Good, I'm pleased it helped." I recognised the voice immediately as Sister Claire's. I moved to stand.

"Stay where you are, Ruth." I felt her hand push me gently down into my seat again as she walked past me and around the desk to sit opposite in her large leather chair. Now dressed in her traditional nun's habit and looking more like the tough and uncompromising woman I was used to dealing with I sat waiting for her to unleash a tirade of verbal invective towards me with regards to my earlier display in waking the rest of the house when discovering Susan's body. However on this occasion I was proved wrong and I sensed, for the moment at least, a gentler tone in her attitude towards me. We exchanged a brief and polite smile before her face took on a more serious expression.

"The police are on their way and I will need to speak to them when they arrive."

I moved to stand again. "Of course, I'll leave you alone, Sister."

She waved her hand at me and smiled again. "You'll wear that seat out if you're not careful with all your standing and sitting. I've told you: stay where you are, child. I kept Father Ignatius waiting for a full half hour once so I am certainly not worried about leaving a few police officers outside for a short while. Anyway, they are not here yet so we've a little time to talk."

I felt as though I should smile back in recognition of her remark about Father Ignatius and in demonstrating this lighter side to her character. In any other circumstances I might have done, especially as I had never seen or heard her be anything other than short or derisory in her approach towards me during my time at the home to date.

She placed her hands together under her chin. "You and I haven't always seen eye to eye have we, Ruth?"

I looked down towards my cup suddenly feeling ashamed. “No, Sister.”

“I’m not going to pretend I like you particularly, because I’m not sure I do, but I am aware that you cared greatly for Susan and I respect that. Although I should add that sometimes, in fact most of the times when I had reason to encounter the two of you I…” her voice trailed away for a moment as if to regain her composure.

“Well, let us just say I was not overly impressed by either of you, nor that other girl you took up with during her time here, Diane I believe it was?” She moved forward in her chair placing her elbows on her desk but keeping her hands under her chin as if supporting it. “You girls come here to the Holy Order because you have committed a great sin and in so doing found yourselves pregnant.” My eyes moved to meet her own but I knew this wasn’t the time to protest or defend myself along with the many others who lived under the accusatory finger of persecution that was so eagerly pointed in our direction each day by Sister Claire and her supporters. “Oh I know all about the excuses, that it wasn’t your fault or that a man forced you, but God gave you a tongue didn’t he, you can say no can’t you?

Despite my best efforts to remain silent I heard myself speak out. “It’s not that easy, Sister.”

She sat upright in her chair, any earlier softness and understanding in her voice now replaced by a firmer tone. “Avoiding sin never is, my dear. But we become stronger when we stand against Satan and deny him the room for victory in our lives. And we do that by abstaining from the temptations of the flesh that he so often lays before us.”

I wanted to stand and scream at her, but knew this was a battle I could never win, not with her mind so closed to hearing the truth about how real life was lived out beyond the sanitised walls of the home. I was also reeling from the death of my friend and didn’t feel that an argument with Sister Claire at this point would be honouring to Susan’s memory, although I knew deep down that she would have been the first to enter the fray and protest our innocence if she had been there with me.

I forced a weak smile. "I really don't want to talk about this at the moment if that's alright with you, Sister. I'm too upset about Susan to discuss anything at all if you don't mind?"

Her voice softened again as if in some form of recognition at my emotional struggle, or rather perhaps because she felt she had won this particular verbal joust and that I had simply conceded the battle to her. I knew the truth and that my time would come again. This wouldn't be the last such encounter I would have with Sister Claire but for now was happy to allow her this falsely assumed sense of victory.

"Of course, I understand, although I think the police may want to speak to you briefly when they arrive as you were one of the first to discover Susan's body."

We sat in silence for a moment our conversation clearly at an end and I certainly had no intention of attempting to make small talk with someone I struggled even to respect let alone like.

"May I go now, Sister." Taking her hands from under chin she nodded in mute response to my question. I rose to my feet and walked to the door turning only briefly to acknowledge her. "Thank you, Sister."

"Think on what I have said, Ruth. In the meantime we will all pray for Susan's soul, both throughout the day and during our services."

I closed the door behind me and with tears running freely down my cheeks walked slowly along the long corridor, my feet producing an echo each time they met with the highly polished wooden floor. The sound reminded me of the day I first arrived at the Sisters of Mercy and had made that initial journey of hope to Sister Claire's office. How different the reality of my optimism had turned out to be. How crushed I felt now, so unlike the young girl, who just a few months ago had entered this austere building for the first time, trusting and daring to believe for something better. The world appeared as bleak and depressing to me at that moment as the dark stained oak panelling which lined the walls of this gloomy passageway. I hadn't felt this miserable or despairing about life since my time in the death camp.

As I made my way slowly along that dimly lit and imposing hallway my baby moved inside me. It felt as though God was reminding me that although one life had ended that day a new one was about to begin. I placed my hand on my stomach and stroked it in an attempt to comfort and reassure the life within me that all would be well. If only I could have believed that for myself.

TWENTY-THREE

I was encouraging Jenny to finish her breakfast when Carol entered the kitchen waving an official looking brown envelope in front of her. "I think it's here." I recognised the crest on the envelope as being from the agency who had been mediating between Ruth and I about our proposed meeting and as to where it might take place. I pointed towards the work surface by the toaster.

"Just leave it there; I'll look at it later."

"Mary! It's the letter you've been waiting for, at least open it and see what it says."

"Yes go on, I want to know when you are going to meet your other mummy as well," Jenny interjected through a mouthful of cereal. She had been aware of the various communications between Ruth and myself over the past few months as we edged towards agreeing an actual date to get together. Mum and Dad had long got over any feelings of jealousy or concerns that they might be side lined in some way by my meeting with Ruth. In fact, I think, following the discovery she actually existed and then the three of us operating together to bring about this planned reunion with her had actually worked to cement the relationship between us as a family even further. Although it is fair to say we had each experienced the odd wobble of uncertainty in the early stages of the process. Jenny and I knew without doubt how much the two of them loved and cared for us and that, no matter how my renewed contact with Ruth developed, nothing would ever alter the fact that James and Carol were, and always would be, my real mum and dad and Jenny's grandparents. There might be rules and regulations and various legal documents held by the courts to contest this but the heart makes its own bonds and ours couldn't be more established and committed whatever the law might choose to say about it.

I turned to Jenny who was now pushing the last of her cereal around the bowl instead of eating it. "I'll look at it later thank you. Now come on, young lady, hurry up and finish that cereal or you'll be late for school."

Mum smiled as she leant the envelope against the toaster. "Coward."

I knew she was right and that I was avoiding the inevitable. I was feeling the same sense of panic grip me as had done when the first letter arrived from the agency so many months before informing me they had managed to find Ruth. Again it was a letter I had looked forward to receiving and feared in equal measure. Now here I was with the next, and potentially, life changing part of my future sitting just a few tantalising inches away and yet once again I felt unable to reach across that short divide and seize it.

"I will look at it, Mum, I promise, just not now okay? I don't want to rush it and right now I need to get Jenny to school. Anyway, we've waited all this time so another half an hour isn't going to make any difference is it?"

She sensed my nerves and as always said the right thing in response. "I'll put the kettle on for when you get back and we'll read it together if you like?"

I gave her a hug. "Thanks."

"What about me? I want to know what it says as well," Jenny protested.

"And you will do, just not now alright? Now off with you and clean your teeth or you really will be late. And don't forget to put your shoes on while you're up there as well." Jenny stomped out of the room in protest, complaining as she went that she was a part of this family as well and had a right to know what was going on.

I looked at Carol. "Can't think where she gets that from."

She laughed. "Well at least I can honestly say it's not from my side of the family. Nor your dad's for that matter, we are only the adoptive parents remember?"

"Maybe to me, but clearly I've allowed you both far too much influence in Jenny's upbringing." I felt reassured we could talk so easily about my being adopted and yet still remain secure in our relationship at a far deeper level.

"I'll see you when I get back."

We looked at each for a moment, exchanging that unspoken connection we both instantly recognised and embraced. I kissed her firmly on the cheek as I moved towards the kitchen door. "Love you, Mum."

"Love you too sweetheart, see you soon."

Jenny chuntered away, mainly to herself, all the way to school about how unfair adults were and how they had forgotten what it was like to be young. As we pulled up behind a row of others cars with parents dropping off their children Jenny leant behind her and, grabbing her bag from the back seat, opened the door. "Bye."

I felt she was punishing me for not being more open with her but also recognised that as the central character in this whole affair I was the one who needed to be settled in my own mind before sharing details I wasn't yet entirely comfortable with or sure of myself. "I love you, Jen."

"Love you too, I suppose." With that passing shot she clambered out of the car and closed the door a little more firmly than necessary.

I watched my beautiful daughter walk to the school gates and felt a great wave of pride and love for her wash over me. I tooted the horn as I made to drive away. She turned and waved, smiling now as she chatted excitedly to her friends and, having apparently forgotten the shared awkward difference between us during the fifteen minutes we had just spent together in the car. I waved back thankful that normal service in our relationship had been resumed.

True to her word Mum was getting the mugs out from the kitchen cupboard as I arrived home. “Perfect timing, the kettle’s on; tea or coffee?”

“Coffee please, and make it a strong one,” I said, laughing, as I picked up the envelope.

She reached for the coffee jar. “Jenny alright after her little outburst earlier?”

“She was by the time I dropped her off.” I sat staring at the envelope allowing my mind to ruminate on the various possible scenarios of its content.

“Be a lot easier if you just opened it. Biscuit?”

“No thanks.” I picked up the envelope from the table and began to tear it open. “Here goes.”

Mum placed the steaming mugs of coffee on the table and sat opposite me watching for any reaction as I read the letter.

“Well come on,” she said, having sat as patiently as she could for a few minutes. “It can’t be that bad. I thought this was just meant to be the simple where and when? We’ve already spent all that time on the shall we shan’t we discussions, surely there can’t be anything else?

I folded the letter in my hand and placed it on the table. “Monday week at her house, eleven o’clock.”

We looked at each other with tears welling up in our eyes for similar but also very different reasons. Eventually Mum broke the silence.

“Well that’s good, isn’t it? It’s what you’ve been hoping for. You said you wanted the chance to see where she lived and what her life was like but also have the freedom to walk away if it got too much, so that’s perfect, yeah?”

“I suppose so but, well, suddenly it’s all real you know.” I took a deep breath and felt a tear run down my cheek. “I am actually going to meet the woman who gave birth to me nearly twenty nine years ago. I'm finally getting the chance to ask her why she gave me away and I'm terrified." I took a sip from my mug. "She just better have a bloody good reason for doing so." I attempted to laugh but could feel the tears flowing freely down my face as my body shivered in response to a sudden wave of nerves and shock.

"I'll drink to that." Mum raised her own mug to her lips, also fighting to control her emotions. "I'm grateful she did let you go though, otherwise your dad and I would never have known you and Jenny, or have had you both become the most precious and important part of our lives."

We both sat for a moment wiping our tears and grinning inanely at each other as we acknowledged the very real love between us but also the enormity of the moment.

"This won't make any difference to our relationship, you know that, don't you?"

"Mary, you don't have to keep saying that, we have talked about this so many times. We love you and Jenny and you love us, and nothing will ever change that okay, end of story."

"I know, I just wanted to make sure you knew we felt the same way." Mum picked up the tea towel and playfully flicked it towards me.

"You daft thing, of course we do. So where is it exactly she lives? Near Kent somewhere wasn't it, around two hours away you said?"

"Bromley."

"That's right, but now they've sent the full address, yes?"

"Yes. 35 Primrose Gardens. Primrose Gardens, that sounds nice."

She laughed again. "Don't be fooled by that. You'll probably find it's at the top of a block of flats. That's why they give those sorts of places flowery names so that it eases the blow when you actually get there and find you've got ten flights of stairs to walk up."

"That's not very kind. I bet some of those flats are really lovely. Anyway, why would you call a block of flats Primrose Gardens, that doesn't make sense?"

Mum took another drink from her cup. "I know, bad joke. I'm sure it's a really nice road with lots of pretty houses in."

"Do you think Dad will help me look it up later and work out a route?"

"Of course, and I'll take Jenny to school that day so you can make an early start. You don't want the panic of getting away late and then running into heavy traffic and the like."

"Thanks Mum, I appreciate that." I smiled. "Although no doubt Jen will ask again why she can't come as well and meet her new granny?"

"We've been through that one with her already and agreed it wouldn't be a good idea, at least not for this first meeting anyway."

"I know, but you know what she's like."

We sat drinking our coffee and chatting together for the next half an hour and I found myself wondering if my time with Ruth would be as intimate and relaxed.

"Have you thought about what you're going to talk to her about yet? I know you've written a few ideas down and you want to ask why she allowed you to be adopted but, you can't really start a conversation like that can you?"

I smiled. "To be honest, Mum, I haven't really got past thinking about what I'm going to wear. I mean I want to look and feel confident when I say hello yeah, but I don't want to look as though I'm there for a job interview do I? And I certainly don't want to look too casual as though I haven't made the effort. Oh I don't know, Mum, what would you wear?"

She looked at me and laughed. "I'm glad you've got your priorities right. Here you are about to meet the woman who brought you into this world and ask her some difficult and potentially life changing questions and all you can think about is what to wear."

"Come on, Mum, you know what I mean."

She squeezed my arm. "I'm only joking, love, of course I understand, it's important. You want to set the right tone and feel good about yourself. The good news is we've got the best part of two weeks to get you sorted. Why don't we go shopping together on Saturday and see what we can find, my treat?

"Sounds great, especially the bit about you paying. Mind, it might prove a bit more expensive than you thought if Jenny gets wind of a girly day at the shops." I leant across the table and held her hand. "Thanks Mum."

The next week and a half seemed to fly by as I prepared myself and the final list of questions I wanted to ask ready for the big day. We went shopping and of course Jenny came along too. Mum treated her to a new outfit as well, although that was more to placate her after we said that she definitely wouldn't be coming with me to meet Ruth, at least not on this occasion.

I spent much of the day on the Sunday before what we had all jokingly dubbed "Ruth Day," with Chris. He was very supportive and like Mum assured me that whatever transpired between Ruth and I our own relationship would remain solid and intact.

"You and Jenny mean the world to me, Mary, you know that? I can't think of anything that you might find out tomorrow that would affect our relationship in any way." He kissed me before adding. "Unless of course, you discover you are the love child of that Arsenal supporter. Then, like I said before, I might just have to think again."

"Just shut up will you? Honestly Chris here I am worried stiff about what's going to happen tomorrow and all you can talk about is some stupid football team."

He pursed his lips and shook his head disapprovingly. "Show's what you know about football girl. As the great Liverpool manager Bill Shankly once said, "Some people think football is a matter of life and death, but I assure you it's more serious than that."

"Chris please. I'm being serious as well."

He put his arm around me sensing he may have gone too far. "Sorry love, just trying to relax you a bit." He moved my hair to one side and stroked my face. "Listen, there's nothing you can do about tomorrow or what happens until the two of you actually sit down together, right? So the more wound up you get about it now the more tense you'll be when you actually do meet her, so just try and calm down a bit eh? Don't forget she's probably just as nervous as you are, maybe even more so. After all she's the one who gave her baby away; she's the one who's got all the explaining to do, not you."

I thought for a moment and realised he was right. I was the innocent party in all of this so why should I be nervous? Addressing it logically like that made perfect sense but my head was so scrambled that nothing appeared as it should do, but I resolved to try my best to calm down, as Chris suggested, and wait to see what tomorrow brought. The two of us had lunch together in a local pub and then picked Jenny up on the way back to take her to a local fun fair that had set up nearby. This proved to be a great idea and distraction for the three of us as we took turns in banging into each other in the bumper cars and then trying to win a goldfish on the coconut shy. I wasn't so keen on a second ride on the Wurlitzer though as I felt as I'd already left my stomach on it the first time round.

"Chicken, you stay here then," Chris shouted, leaving me by the entrance. "Jenny and I will go again and show you how it's done, won't we, Jen?"

She happily took his hand as they climbed onto the ride. "You're so rubbish, Mum," she called out as they strapped themselves in.

"I'm happy being rubbish if it means I can keep my lunch in my stomach." I smiled and waved them off watching them spin off into the distance and feeling blessed they were both a part of my life.

We had a lovely afternoon and I was really grateful to Chris for the diversion away from all the thoughts that had been occupying my mind earlier about the day to come. Jenny hugged Chris as we arrived home and got out of the car.

"Thanks, Chris, see you soon I hope," she shouted, making her way up the path. "I'll leave you two love birds to say goodbye. Kissy kissy, yuk."

I watched her go into the house. "She's really fond of you, you know that, don't you?"

"And I'm really fond of her." He pulled me close to him. "But not half as fond as I am of her mum." We kissed, pressing our open lips together as I let him explore my mouth with his tongue. It felt good to be in the embrace of someone I could trust and who cared for me as a woman in my own right and not just as Jenny's mum.

"I'd better go in before she comes back and asks what we're up to?"

"She knows what we're up to, that's why she went in in the first place."

Chris caught my arm as I moved to open the car door.

"Mary, when tomorrow is over, and whatever you decide about Ruth I want you to know I really do care about you."

"I know you do."

"No, what I meant was, maybe we can think about making some plans of our own, you know, about the future?

I sat back in my seat and looked at him. "What are you saying?"

"I'm saying I love you, the two of you, and I want to make a life for us, all three of us."

He put his finger to my lips as I moved to speak.

"I don't want you to say anything now, just think about it. Not that you haven't got enough to think about already at the moment of course." He laughed but I sensed it was to fill the awkwardness of the moment as I struggled to respond, my emotions beginning to get the better of me.

"Chris I…" He put his finger to my lips again.

"Not now, okay? This is hard enough for me to say anyway without you blubbing." He took a deep breath and smiled at me.

"What I'm saying is that when you're ready I'm here for you, both of you, long term, okay? How that works we can talk about, but for now at least I want you to know when you meet this woman tomorrow and whatever you discover about your past you are still loved by me. I want to be your future, Mary, yours and Jen's if you'll let me.

I fought back the tears as I leant forward and kissed him deeply again. "Thank you." I was too emotional to say anymore.

Chris held me close for a moment and then, pulling back a little, cupped my face in his hands.

"Okay that's enough about us for now. Off you go and get a good nights rest before your big day tomorrow." He kissed me lightly on the forehead. "Let me know how it goes yeah, I'll be thinking of you."

I climbed out of the car, squeezing his hand as I did so before closing the door behind me and walking towards the house. After a few steps I turned to face him again. "Love you."

Chris smiled as he started the engine. "You too, see ya."

I watched as he drove away, the worry about what might happen tomorrow fading as I embraced the promise of security Chris had offered me, and Jenny. We had a real future to look forward to and nothing was going to change that. I wiped the tears from my cheeks and smiled to myself as I walked to the house feeling more positive than I had in a long time.

Dad and Mum were equally excited about what Chris had said although, as ever, Dad put his sensible hat on before Mum and I got too carried away.

"Let's get you through tomorrow first and then we can think about whatever Chris has planned for you and Jenny. One day at a time, Mary, and tomorrow is the next big one you need to get through." I smiled at him perceiving a hint of jealousy in his expression as he sensed the affections of another man in my life taking priority over his own.

"Oh don't be such a kill-joy, Mary's just excited, that's all."

"I know that, Carol, and I'm pleased for her as well. All I'm saying is let's see what this woman Ruth has to say for herself first and we can take it from there, that's not unreasonable is it?"

Mum and I looked at each other knowingly. "Ever the optimist, not! Just as well for you Mary that I got the cup that's half full or we'd all be in trouble."

I laughed and gave them both a kiss.

"I'll go and check on Jenny and then have a soak in the bath if that's okay with you? I'll leave the two of you to have your lover's tiff on your own."

"We're not having a tiff. I'm just trying to be practical that's all, for everyone's sake. There's no need to start clambering up the next mountain until we've conquered the one in front of us first."

Mum shook her head, poking him in the ribs as she did so. "Thank you, Sir Edmund Hilary, for that mountaineering lesson."

I laughed again and made my way towards the hall. "Like I said, I'll leave you to it."

As I climbed the stairs I could hear the two of them still playfully squabbling between themselves. I wondered if that's how Chris and I might end up and took heart from the fact that even if we never argued we would still struggle to be any happier than Mum and Dad appeared to be. Mum told me once they had always been close, pulling together as a couple and always seeking the best for each other and for those they loved. I knew this to be true from experience having never had any reason to doubt either their love or commitment to both Jenny and I in years we had lived with them.

I lay in the bath for ages thinking about what Chris had said, his words making me feel as warm on the inside as the water did against my skin. Eventually Dad's more immediate concerns for the day ahead took over and I began to think about all of the questions I planned to ask Ruth. I was pleased I had made a list of them although I was equally sure they would change once the two of us sat down together. As I battled with my rapidly diminishing self-confidence and indecision I suddenly became aware of something I hadn't yet truly considered. How would I respond to any questions she might ask? What if she wanted to know about my growing up with James and Carol or as to how I had brought Jenny up as a mother myself? What could I say without it sounding judgemental of her and would it matter if it did? After all I owed her nothing other than the fact she had brought me into the world. Then again if she hadn't I wouldn't have Jenny in my life nor be the person I was today?

I stared up at the ceiling, my mind frozen in panic, and decided that drowning in the bath was a far better option than addressing the overwhelming feeling of dread that was now permeating through my whole being. I slid back in the bath, my head disappearing under the water. Unfortunately I hadn't factored in that it would immediately fill my open nostrils and cause me to raise my head involuntarily, choking on the warm soapy bubbles as I did so. Perhaps I was being told something? As I sat up struggling to clear my nose and throat I realised a different solution to my problem was required. I clambered out of the bath and dried myself deciding to take Dad's advice and face each challenge and associated hurdle as they presented themselves, one at a time.

I eased myself into my bed that night exhausted both mentally and physically, especially after my earlier exertions on the fun fair rides. I read for a few minutes in an attempt to distract my mind from the meeting with Ruth which had found its way back into my thoughts despite my earlier resolve not to let it. Eventually I put my book to one side and, snuggling down under the blankets turned out the bedside lamp closing my eyes in search of the refreshing sleep my mind and body craved. As I lay there in the dark I was overtaken by a very real sensation of fear. It was as though I were a child again in trouble for doing wrong. It felt as if whatever happened tomorrow I would be the one found to be at fault. It would be me that would be held responsible for the unrest others had experienced and it was me who should be punished for causing such unhappiness. I knew these feelings were irrational and that the exact opposite was true. After all it was me that had been deserted at only seven weeks old and handed over to others to care for. The fact those people were James and Carol and they had showered me with nothing but love was almost beside the point; that outcome couldn't have been predicted at the start of my journey. At that time I was merely a baby, only a few weeks old and given away by her mother. I had always claimed it was Ruth who had rejected me, so how could I be blamed now for what had happened all that time ago?

And yet as I lay in my bed looking at the shadows on my wall thrown there by the sliver of light coming in from under the door those self same shadows all appeared to be pointing towards me and whispering, "It's all your fault. If you hadn't been born none of this would have happened."

Although I felt warm and safe under my blankets my body still shivered, not from any chill in the air but from this unfounded and irrational sense of fear. My mind raced again. What if she hated me for ruining her life as a young girl and wanted to say that to my face? I closed my eyes tight to shut out the shadows of doubt dancing on the walls and pulled the blankets high over me in an attempt to quieten the accusing voices in my head. I lay there like that for some time until the blessed release of sleep eventually overtook me.

TWENTY-FOUR

The final two weeks of my pregnancy seemed to be the longest. Perhaps it was because I didn't have Diane there to make me laugh anymore, or dear Susan to share my deepest thoughts and hopes with. Whatever the reason I often felt alone and abandoned in those last few days, increasingly unsure about my future or that of my baby once it was born.

I was working in the laundry room as usual when my contractions started. It's strange, but although I had never given birth before I still recognised, like so many others before me, that this was my time. My waters broke and I called out for one of the nuns to help me. She took me to the delivery room and I was relieved to see Sister Rosemary walk in as I lay there waiting for the next wave of pain to overtake me.

"I thought I'd come and hold your hand, Ruth. That's if you'd like me to?" She smiled down at me wiping the sweat from my brow with her handkerchief. I nodded my approval and winced at the same time as another contraction took hold. Having her there squeezing my hand and supporting me at every step meant more than I could ever express by way of thanks. I no longer felt abandoned or on my own but rather I was part of something bigger than just myself. The fact that another human being recognised this and was willing to stand by me in my time of need encouraged me in ways that are practically impossible to describe in simple words.

The birth itself went well and took less than three hours in total from the first contraction to holding my baby in my arms. I knew if it was a girl I wanted to name her Rebecca after my mother, and this was confirmed to me as I lay in bed the next day and saw a rose growing in the garden through the window. I remembered how Mama had told me about the first time she had held me and thought of naming me Rose after her favourite flower. Eventually she and Papa had decided on Ruth, but as I lay there holding my own little rose petal in my arms, so delicate and fragile I knew that naming her after Mama was the right thing to do.

Sister Rosemary came again later to check I was okay. She smiled down at the two of us. "She's beautiful."

As I looked across at this little bundle of life sleeping in the cot beside me I felt confused. I knew I wouldn't be able to keep her; that fact had been driven into me along with all the other girls from the day we first arrived at the home. But I also knew for the next few weeks I would be the one responsible for feeding her and preparing her to leave in readiness for someone else to bring up as their own. That was the way it had been presented to us by the nuns as being the best outcome for everyone concerned, especially the baby. Although I had struggled with this reality at times during my pregnancy I had also begun to accept that I wouldn't be able to offer a new baby the home, clothing, sustenance and care it would need, certainly in those first few weeks of its life. But things were different now; her arrival had changed the landscape regarding her future well-being completely, at least it had for me. Now she was real and I had given her a name, my mother's name, even though I'd been told not to as the adoptive parents would be the ones legally charged with doing this as far as all future official documentation was concerned. Also, that it would be a name of *their* choosing and not mine. Suddenly, as had been the case with Diane, I became overwhelmed with a feeling of absolute and unconditional love for this precious new life. She had come from me and no matter what the circumstances of her beginning or arrival she was mine and I wanted to keep her.

The next seven weeks flew by and with each passing day I fell more in love with my beautiful Rebecca as I watched her grow and change. She had a habit of screwing up her little nose while I was feeding her which made me laugh and I swear she smiled at me one day as if to say, "I know you, you're my mummy and I love you." That might sound silly but when you're in love lots of gestures, both spoken and unspoken, that others don't see or understand make absolute sense to you and the other person involved in the relationship, and I had definitely fallen in love with Rebecca. I would spend every moment I could with her, holding her little body close to me and talking about things she couldn't possibly understand, but I didn't care and seemingly from the way she gurgled happily back at me neither did she. Even her smell became familiar to me as I held her up and kissed her face and skin after a bath and when I was drying her. She had totally captivated my heart and I grew closer to her every day, convincing myself that she had the same feelings for me. Any thought of letting her go was, for me, now beyond comprehension and I began to make plans as to how I might persuade the nuns to let me leave with her, and if they wouldn't then how I might smuggle her out and we could make a run for it together. I knew in the back of my mind both scenarios were unlikely to succeed, but at least the possibility of Rebecca and I remaining together gave me hope. There was little of that afforded to any of us girls in that overtly strict and harsh environment, and when Sister Claire was on the war path the same could be said for the rest of the nuns in the home as well.

One day, a few weeks after Rebecca was born, Sister Margaret came to speak to me while I was feeding her.

"Sister Claire is concerned you are becoming too attached to the child, Ruth. You know she will soon be going to a new home, don't you?

"Her name is Rebecca."

"That's another thing, giving her a name is forbidden, you know that only too well sadly from past experience. It will be left to the family she eventually lives with to name her and to bring her up as their own. That was made very clear to you on the day you first arrived at the Holy Order and has been repeated on a number of occasions since, as it has been to all of you girls." She paused as if considering how best to proceed without crushing me entirely.

"Surely, if as you say you are truly fond of the child you would want only the best for it? Try and be sensible about this, Ruth, you couldn't possibly bring her up as your own. What would people think when they saw the two of you together? An unmarried young girl who got herself pregnant by goodness knows who and a baby she can't support; what would any decent law-abiding citizen make of that? If you really want to do what's best for the child then you'll think long and hard about what I've said and see the sense in letting her go to a proper loving family who *can* offer her the opportunities in life that you have so apparently wasted and certainly cannot hope to provide for her yourself.

I looked down at Rebecca who had fallen contentedly asleep in my arms. "Can't you see that she loves me?"

"What I see is a baby asleep who has obviously had enough to eat." She reached towards me. "Give me the child and I'll put her back in the cot while you think about what I've said."

I looked up, my frustration clearly visible as I pulled her little body tight into me. "I'll put her down in a moment, and her *name* is still Rebecca."

Sister Margaret turned to leave. "It will only be yourself you're hurting in the long run by continuing in your obstinacy, Ruth. In a few months time the child will be happy and settled in its new home and you'll be what, pining for a baby that didn't even ask to be brought into the world and all because you couldn't keep your drawers on. Oh yes, a fine mother you would make setting her an example like that."

I watched as she walked away, the metal heels on her black leather shoes clipping the bare wooden flooring with every step. I waited until she reached the door and glanced back towards me as I knew she would. I gave an exaggerated smile and called across the room. "Rebecca says goodbye."

My smile became more relaxed and genuine as I looked down at my beautiful daughter. She jumped a little in my arms as Sister Margaret slammed the door shut behind her. I bent down and kissed her. "That wasn't very nice of the naughty nun, was it?" I whispered.

Over the next few days I did everything I could to make obvious my affection for Rebecca, and at every turn the nuns tried to persuade me otherwise. Even Sister Rosemary appeared to be toeing the party line as we sat together one afternoon.

"Ruth, I don't doubt that you care for your baby, Rebecca as you like to call her, but eventually you will have to say goodbye to her; you simply can't keep her."

I stared down at the floor, unable to look her in the eye. "I thought you would support me at least, you even call her Rebecca."

"I do that for you although I know I shouldn't, and nor should you." She leant forward in her chair. "The truth is, Ruth, that you have no hope of making provision for this little one. Even if you managed to find work to support the two of you ask yourself this. Who would be willing to look after the child of an unmarried young mother while she goes out to work? Even if you did find someone prepared to overlook the stigma surrounding your circumstances, then presumably you would have to pay them for their time as well? So then what? You would have to find other work to pay them on top of meeting your own needs, and so it would go on."

I looked up to meet her gaze. "I told you what happened and how I got pregnant, you said you believed me. So why can't you believe me now and help me to at least try and keep Rebecca."

"I know I said I believed you about the man who got you

pregnant and I do, although if I'm honest I still struggle a little with the actual circumstances, but that is not the point. The truth, and it is one that sadly you are going to have to face, is that you cannot look after this baby no matter how well intentioned your resolve and determination to do so might be. The authorities won't let you either. Even if I and the other nuns here chose to support your appeal they would still say no. Once you leave here you will be on your own, and it would be a dereliction of our sworn duty and commitment to achieving the best outcome for each baby if we ignored that obligation and advised otherwise."

She took my hand in hers. "I'm truly sorry, Ruth, but sooner or later you are going to have to accept that this little one cannot and will not be staying with you, and the quicker you recognise that fact then the better it will be for the both of you."

I looked deep into her eyes searching for any last vestige of hope that she might change her mind and offer to assist in my attempt to keep Rebecca but none was forthcoming.

"I really am sorry, Ruth, truly I am, but you have got to let her go."

Although I knew everything she said made sense and that Rebecca would have a far better start in life if I did allow her to go and flourish within the warmth and safety of real family home, it still did nothing to ease the pain that was tearing at my heart. How could I countenance the thought of losing the one precious thing I had left after everything and everybody I had ever cared for in the past had already been ripped from my life? I fell to my knees and wept in Sister Rosemary's arms. I wept once more for my parents, my brother, for Sarah and all the others I had watched slaughtered so brutally in that awful death camp at Birkenau. I wept for the violence Mr Taylor had shown towards me when raping me, not only physically but also emotionally following the lies he told about the circumstances of what had happened between us and of the actions he had so cruelly inflicted on me. I wept for my friend Susan and all of the other girls at the home who had died either in childbirth or by taking their own lives. I also wept for those who had looked on in horror as their babies were dragged from their arms and handed to another to bring up as their own. And I wept for Sister Rosemary and all of the other nuns who were trapped in this dark and foreboding edifice that purported to offer hope and sanctuary to all who entered its doors, especially us young girls. In reality of course it did little more than to confirm what the so called civilised society outside already thought of us; that we were nothing more than a group of self-seeking and sinful teenagers reaping the rewards of our improper and antisocial behaviour. Further, that we should be eternally grateful for even the small crumb of so called comfort and charity provided by institutions like the Sisters of Mercy. I wept openly and uncontrollably for a long time, unable to stop the flow of tears and rage burning inside of me that regaled against the injustice of it all. I, like so many others was a victim serving a life sentence for a crime I had not willingly committed. My corresponding punishment would be to wear the badge of shame and dishonour awarded my transgression for the rest of my time on earth. Even worse was the fact the real transgressor was able to continue walking the streets boasting inwardly of his wrongdoing yet retaining both respect and standing in the community as a valued and influential member of society.

Sister Rosemary held me gently and patiently in her arms until my sobbing eased. "God loves it when we cry out to him, Ruth, your tears won't have been wasted. I'll continue to pray for you."

I looked up at her, wiping my eyes on my sleeve. "I wouldn't bother if I were you, Sister; I don't think God cares very much about the likes of me."

"You mustn't talk like that, Ruth, God certainly does care about you. He knows every hair on your head and hears every cry of your heart."

I got up to leave, frustrated that even now after our speaking so openly this woman who I had come to think of as a friend, and both liked and respected, still couldn't truly comprehend the reasoning behind my deep torment and distress. How could she know or even begin to understand that the loss of Rebecca would prove to be, for me, the final act in the play that had been my life to date, and one that would break my heart forever.

"Well he must be busy counting the hairs on my head then, Sister, because he certainly hasn't been responding to the cry of my heart of late." I looked down at her and saw genuine sadness reflected in her eyes as to what I'd said.

"You're a good lady, Sister, and I like you, but we're so far apart in our experiences and ideas about religion that I don't think we'll ever find any real common ground. You talk about life and how in God's perfect world it should be lived, but the life I've lived bears no resemblance to those ideals and much of it has nothing to do with God, certainly not the loving God you talk about or that I would like to believe in. If it does then either he hasn't done a very good job at it or I'm missing something."

I placed my hand lightly on her shoulder as she sat in front of me. "I'm sorry if I've disappointed you, Sister, but that's just how I'm feeling at the moment and I don't really want to talk about it anymore if that's alright with you, not to you or to anyone?"

"Of course I understand, but I'll still pray for you." She smiled. "Don't give up on God, Ruth, I know he won't give up on you."

"I don't think it's me God has a problem with, Sister, he already knows what it took to break my heart, it's everyone else's he needs to sort out."

Sister Rosemary looked at me quizzically.

"Since I've been here I've spent a lot of my time working in the laundry room and one of the things I've discovered is that if you put too much starch into the wash things come up shiny and white but stiff and difficult to bend. I think maybe God has placed a bit too much starch in some people and so while they appear all nice and shiny on the outside, inside they're just rigid and not willing to listen or bend."

She looked at me and smiled, tapping the wimple around her face. "I'll try and remember that next time I'm washing this."

I moved to walk away. "Like I said, Sister, it's not the outer garment that's the problem; it's the stiff heart beating inside that wants softening."

I didn't see Sister Rosemary the next day and was worried she might have taken my comments personally and was avoiding me. I still felt what I had said to be true, but I also knew that in Sister Rosemary we girls had at least one friend we could turn to when things got tough. I needn't have worried though as a day later whilst eating breakfast she approached me with her usual smile and cheery demeanour.

"Good morning, Ruth, I hope you are feeling brighter today? I enjoyed talking with you the other day, and have thought long and hard about the things you said."

"I'm sorry if I upset you, Sister, I didn't mean anything personally by it. In fact you're probably the one person who…"

Sister Rosemary raised her hand. "No need to apologise, it is good to air our true feelings at times even if they can be a bit harsh." She smiled. "Or should I say *stiff*?"

I laughed, feeling relieved that I hadn't hurt her feelings, or at least not that she was prepared to make public.

"Sister Claire wants to see you at eleven o'clock in her study, she asked me to come and tell you."

"Am I in trouble again? I'm not sure what I might have done to upset her? I've tried to be on my best behaviour these past few days."

"I'm sure there isn't a problem. I think you worry too much at times about what others think of you, Ruth. She has just asked to speak with you, eleven o'clock sharp. I'll see you later, enjoy your breakfast."

I spent the next couple of hours exorcising my concerns in the laundry room and wondering what I might have done to demand this call from on high. I prayed it had nothing to do with Rebecca and that if it did it would prove to be no more than another reminder for me not to get too close to her. That was a criticism she had levelled at me on numerous occasions in the past already and one that I had both learned to live with and ignore. She could say what she liked I was going to fight to hang onto Rebecca for as long as I had her with me and would do so with every last fibre of my being, even if I did recognise that in the end I might still lose her. While we shared the same roof she was still mine and there was nothing Sister Claire could say that would change that.

I stood outside Sister Claire's study as the big clock at the end of the hallway struck eleven. It emitted a loud gong like sound on each beat which reverberated all the way down the passageway towards me. As the last chord struck I knocked nervously on the door.

Even through the thick wood separating us there was no mistaking Sister Claire's confident tone. "Come."

I entered smiling, hoping to exude a similar confidence to my inquisitor. "You wanted to see me, Sister?"

"Yes, come in, Ruth." She gestured towards the chair opposite her own as a form of invitation for me to sit. As I did so she stood up placing me below her and leaving me feeling immediately vulnerable in her presence. She walked towards one of the large windows overlooking the front of the home. The sun was shining and the light streamed into the room. It bathed the study in a bright and appealing glow; the sun's rays making it feel warm and almost welcoming. I knew better though than to trust the outward appearance of this particular room as it had also born witness to some of our most challenging and damning encounters in the past. I had only ever looked out of the windows myself once in the past but remembered its panoramic view of the grounds and of the long driveway that wound its way from the road outside to the main entrance of the home. I sat still, my hands resting in my lap watching as Sister Claire stared straight ahead as if steeling herself for whatever it was she was to say next. I feared the worst.

"I'm afraid it is time to discuss the future of your baby, Ruth." She maintained her gaze out of the window; I presumed to avoid the potential for confrontation between us by addressing her remarks directly to my face. "I say afraid not with any sense of trepidation or apprehension on my part but, because I know how close you have allowed yourself to come to the child. You will equally know this is something I have repeatedly stated as unwise from the very moment she was born if you remember?"

I moved uneasily in my chair, determined to be firm in my response but knowing also that any attempt to argue outright with Sister Claire would prove, as it had so often in the past, to be a lost cause.

"I do remember that, Sister. But you will also remember I have stated from the very beginning I would like the opportunity, with your permission, to at least attempt to make a life for Rebecca and myself outside of the Holy Order."

Sister Claire turned on her heel and looked directly at me, no longer concerned with either avoiding my gaze or of upsetting me.

"We could trade these verbal exchanges for the rest of the day, Ruth, and still not achieve a desired result for either of us, so please allow me one final effort in making myself absolutely clear and understood in this matter." She moved her hands from behind her back to the front of her habit, placing them firmly together. "You will also remember that I have told you on more than one occasion that you would *never* receive our blessing or permission to attempt such a foolish and irresponsible ambition. Even if we were to consider such a request, which we most certainly would not, then the law itself would step in and take measures to disallow any such arrangement. I understand Sister Rosemary has also taken the opportunity of reminding you of this fact on occasion as well?"

I was stung momentarily by a feeling of betrayal. How could someone I had trusted with my confidences go behind my back and discuss our private conversations with this bully dressed as a nun? I was sure this couldn't be true and so chose rather to believe that she had probably told Sister Claire that particular story in an effort to persuade her not to vilify me yet again, allowing me rather the space and time to come to terms with what I ultimately knew deep down was always likely to be the eventual outcome to my protests.

I sat motionless as Sister Claire took a step towards me, the sun throwing its rays against her back creating the ironic image of a form of halo that enveloped her whole body. I couldn't see her face as the sun behind her caused it to be held in shadow, but there was no mistaking her tone or intonation.

"I have also advised you, along with the other sisters, not to give the child a name. Again this is something you have chosen to ignore. In calling it Rebecca you have not only made the process of giving up the child harder for yourself, but you have also disobeyed my very clear and explicit directives. I don't know why I continue to let that bother me as you have never been a girl to accept either advice or instruction since the time you joined us here at the Holy Order." She turned away and moved back to the window, placing her hands behind her back again.

"I have to be honest about this with you, Ruth, the truth is I won't be sorry to see you leave our care once your baby has gone and you have had the requisite few days to adjust and prepare yourself for the transfer back into society. Although in your case I struggle to imagine what you and the world at large will make of each other. My only hope is that it won't include your returning here again at some point in the future carrying the result of yet another selfish and sinful act inside your belly."

I was seething inside with both rage and humiliation. How dare she speak to me like this? Wasn't she meant to be the ordained custodian of God's charity and grace towards the poor and unfortunates of this world? And yet here she was acting the very opposite, almost as the very mouthpiece for Beelzebub himself.

"Don't worry, Sister, I won't ever come back here, not if I were to become pregnant every year from now on." I stood up clenching my hands tight into a fist. "You set down your list of rules for us to follow: hard work, repentance from sin, a sin almost none of us committed willingly, penance for the wrongdoings of others and attendance of goodness knows how many praise and worship services a day to a God who in your view would rather punish us than care for us. And you in particular are more than happy to administer that punishment, either through the denial of food and basic sustenance or in the handing out of undeserved beatings and any other form of physical abuse and degradation you can dream up in an effort to inflict even greater pain and misery on us girls than we have already endured outside of the home. And you dare to proclaim that you carry out all of this in the name of a supposedly loving creator God." I felt my passions rise as I took a step forward; any thought of compromise now a distant blur. "That's another thing, if he really is a God of love then how come that word is never mentioned in any of your conversations with us or in the actions you display towards us when addressing or meeting our needs?" I knew I had crossed the line of any and all acceptable standards of behaviour but reasoned that if I was going to be expelled by this despot in nuns clothing I might as well go out in a final blaze of glory.

"You're just a frustrated, evil woman who doesn't even know what the word love means. I might be angry at the moment, Sister, but I'll get over that and when I do I will only feel sorrow for you, whereas you will carry the bitterness you feel towards me and others like me who have dared to stand up to you for the rest of your sad and miserable life. I'd rather face God as the sinner I am when my time comes than as the self sanctified empty shell of a human being that you are any day of the week." I wasn't sure where the words were coming from but knew I wouldn't get another chance to speak my mind in this way and was determined to finish.

"Like I say I feel sorry for you, I really do, only at the moment I'm too pissed off with you to show it."

There was a long and awkward silence between us as I stood fixed to the spot not really believing I had actually said all of those things. I suddenly experienced a pang of guilt in my having been so outspoken and wished I had been able to keep my temper under better control. Had I, in being so rude and discourteous, allowed myself to become the very same bitter and twisted individual I had accused her of being? It was too late to apologise now and I wasn't sure in all honesty that I wanted to. Perhaps I could have spoken with less invective in my tone but the basis of what I had said, for me at least, held true.

I watched as she continued to stare out of the window, seemingly unmoved by my verbal assault. A few moments later she turned slowly towards me, a self satisfied grin spreading across her face as she spoke, her voice calm and resolute in its delivery.

"I hope you feel better for your little outburst, Ruth? I'm afraid it will be the last opportunity you have to speak to me in that way during your time here, or indeed ever again." She paused as if to savour the moment. "I will leave it to Sister Margaret to oversee your departure over the next few days now that your child has been handed over to its new family." I watched as she turned towards the window again and waved. My mind raced. New family, what new family? I didn't understand. I ran to her side and looked down at the gravel entrance below as a scene of absolute horror played out before me. I could only watch as a baby in a pale yellow shawl that I instantly recognised as Rebecca's was handed to a smartly dressed couple standing by a dark blue car.

My heart sank. I knew without doubt it was my little girl. I turned to Sister Claire. "You bitch."

"Sticks and stones, Ruth dear, sticks and stones." She smiled, embracing her apparent moment of victory.

I turned and ran to the door flinging it wide, giving no thought to closing it behind me. I raced down the corridor towards the long flight of wooden stairs leading to the front door. My shoes crashed loudly against the grey flagstones as I sprinted towards the exit. Not stopping for breath I pulled open the huge front door demonstrating scant regard for its both weight and size in my effort and determination to get to Rebecca.

As I reached the bottom of the steps and my feet hit the gravel of the driveway I looked up to see the car and its occupants pull away, a hand held high out of the driver's window waving in thanks and goodbye to the nun who had carried my baby to them.

I screamed at the top of my voice, "*Rebecca*," but that only appeared to encourage the car to accelerate in its effort to take my baby away from me.

"It's too late, child, she's gone. Sister Claire said you might react like this and so we, she, decided this would be the better way of doing things." She turned and walked away, briefly stroking my arm as she left. "I'm sorry, Ruth, but it's the best thing for the little one in the long run, you'll see."

I leant forward breathless, placing my hands on my knees as my body shook and I sucked air into my lungs. I watched as the car turned out of the driveway and onto the road taking my baby away for ever. Dropping to my knees I wept openly as I had done just a few days previously with Sister Rosemary; the difference now being the frightening prospect I had earlier envisaged of Rebecca being taken from me had, in an instant, become the horrific reality I had so feared. After what seemed like an age I pulled myself to my feet and trudged forlornly back towards the home, my heart broken and with any last vestige of optimism for a life with Rebecca seemingly gone forever in the back of that dark blue car. I glanced briefly at the building before me which on my arrival just a few months earlier had purported to offer both sanctuary and support for my baby and I. In reality it had provided little more than the existence I had experienced in the death camp, the only discernible difference being in Birkenau we battled each day against physical persecution and torture whilst at the Sisters of Mercy the fight was against mental anguish, torment and suffering. It appeared to me that both systems had been designed to crush all expectancy of our deserving any more from life than we were considered to be worth by those who wielded power over us. This was also true for many others who lived outside this fractured community and viewed us girls as little more than social rejects to be taken from the streets and dealt with as was felt appropriate by the authorities of the day. It mattered not whether we were Jews in the concentration camp or young unmarried mothers at the Holy Order, both institutions appeared to offer little or nothing by way of hope or comfort to its inmates, rather they were designed to salve and satisfy the brutal consciences of those who brought them into being and ran them.

I glanced up towards Sister Claire's study and saw her looking down at me, that self-satisfied grin still spread broad across her face. I knew in that moment my time at the home had come to an end and worse, the same was true for any future relationship I might have hoped for with my beautiful Rebecca.

TWENTY-FIVE

I sat pushing a half eaten piece of toast around my plate as Carol came into the kitchen and nodded towards the table.

"You should eat that; you'll need all the energy you can muster for today. And get that down you as well," she said, pointing towards my almost cold cup of coffee.

"Don't start on at me, Mum, I'm just working a few things out okay?"

"It's a bit late to be changing your mind."

"I'm not changing my mind; I just need to get everything straight in my head about what I want to say that's all." "Come on love, we've already agreed that until you actually meet her and start talking, neither of you know how things will turn out. There's not much point in planning a speech that you'll probably never deliver anyway. Now eat your toast and drink your coffee or I'll set your daughter on you."

Just then Jenny entered the kitchen. "What have I done?"

"You haven't done anything, sweetheart, I was just telling your mum to finish her breakfast like she's always telling you to do."

Enjoying the moment she teased me with a "told you so" look on her face. "Gran's right, Mum, finish your toast or you won't be able to play later."

"Don't you start; you're as bad as each other." I laughed and forced another piece of cold toast into my mouth wishing I had chosen Corn Flakes instead as I chewed on the now almost rubbery and tasteless substance. At least cereal would have had the milk to help wash it down whereas the toast just went round and round becoming ever harder to swallow. I took a swill from my cup and shuddered as the cold coffee combined with the toast to deliver an even worse combination of tastes.

"Say good luck to your Mum, Jen, it's her big day remember?"

"Yeah, good luck, Mum, and remember, whatever this woman's like she won't be a patch on you and Granny okay, you're the best. Well, Granny is anyway."

I gave her a hug as she sidled into me planting a quick kiss on my forehead.

"Thanks, Jen, that means a lot, I think."

She smiled broadly at me. "So can I have some more pocket money then this week and get the new Bay City Rollers single?"

"No you can't, you mercenary little horror. Anyway what's wrong with Donny Osmond, I thought you liked him?

"Yeah I did, but that was years ago when I was little. Anyway he's not as good looking as Woody, he's the one for me." She swooned exaggeratedly as she spoke.

"When you were *little*! Just remind me again how old are you now exactly?"

"Oh, Mum, you know what I mean. Anyway, what about you and David Essex? Yuk or what." She put her fingers in her mouth as if to demonstrate being sick.

"Thank you very much, there's nothing wrong with young David that a few evenings out with me wouldn't cure. Now off you go or you'll be late for school." I stood up and looked at my watch. "I need to get away as well. Thanks again for taking Jen, Mum."

"You're welcome and good luck. Call me as soon you can when leave her house. I'm not sure I can wait until you get home to hear how it all went." She turned to Jenny. "Now come on young lady or we really will be late."

I watched them leave and reminded myself again how lucky I was and that whatever happened today I still had a beautiful daughter and a family who loved me to come home to.

I heard the front door open. “Bye Mum.” I smiled to myself as I put the dishes in the sink and heard the door slam shut behind them. As I stood watching the hot water mix with the washing up liquid to create a mountain of bubbles the phone rang.

“Oh hello, Chris, I was just about to leave.” The line wasn’t very good but it was still nice to hear his voice.

“I won’t keep you, just wanted you to know I’m thinking about you and will be all day. Let me know how it goes yeah?”

I laughed. “Of course. Mind, you’ll have to go to the bottom of the list behind Mum for that. I think she’ll throttle me if I don’t phone her first, she’s already had a go at me.”

“No problem, just call when you can. I know you’ll be tired this evening, especially after you’ve talked things through with Jenny and your parents so maybe the two of us can get together tomorrow for a drink and you can fill me in properly then? That’s presuming your dad and mum won’t mind looking after Jenny of course?”

“I should think they’ll be delighted after having had me bend their ears about everything for the previous twenty four hours.” I looked at my watch again. “Chris, I really need to get moving. I’ll call you later on, and yes to tomorrow night, okay?”

“Love you.”

“You too, bye.”

As I finished drying the dishes I reminded myself that not only did I have a wonderful family and daughter who loved me, but also a man in my life who cared for me deeply as well. I felt bolstered by these truths and in knowing that no matter what Ruth said to me today nothing could change the way I felt about those four special people or in how they felt about me.

I made regular stops as I drove towards Bromley, checking the address and my route each time, determined not to take a wrong turning or worse arrive late through getting lost. I was never a good map reader at the best of times, but now with the added pressure of meeting Ruth occupying my thoughts my confidence in following even the simplest of directions hit an all time low. I decided when I was about half an hour away to stop somewhere and have a drink to settle any remaining nerves. I pulled up at a small tea room just outside of a town called Lewisham and noticing their display of delicious looking cakes decided that a sugar rush alongside a quick cup of tea might help boost my energy levels. I also made sure I used their loo as I couldn't think of anything worse than my opening words to Ruth being a request to use her toilet.

The rest of the journey was event free and I turned into Primrose Gardens ten minutes early. I parked at the end of the road and looked down the tree-lined street wondering which of the red brick semi-detached houses might be hers. Being a few minutes early also allowed me time to settle myself and focus my thoughts. I wiped my hands anxiously down my trousers, the perspiration on them making me feel even more nervous than I already was.

I had decided to wear my blue trouser suit because it meant I wouldn't have to worry about showing too much of my legs if I crossed them while we were talking. I had also put on the bright red blouse Mum had treated me to but was now worried that in might stain and go darker under my arms if I continued to perspire.

"I'll just have to keep my jacket on," I muttered to myself, glancing in the rear view mirror. "Now you're talking to yourself, you silly cow!" I shook my head and felt any earlier confidence drain from me. I knew if I sat there prevaricating much longer I would end up turning the car around and heading home before I had even had the chance to meet with her. I opened the window and took a deep breath. "Pull yourself together, you've waited twenty-eight years for this moment, don't blow it now." I started the engine and looked in the mirror again. "Here we go, girl."

I drove slowly along the road counting the numbers on the doors as I headed towards my destination. Suddenly there it was in front of me, a smart-looking house with a white painted gate and matching fence running along the front of what appeared to be a small rose garden. There were a number of well tended bushes filling the space offering an abundance of colour with their red and yellow blooms dancing happily in the breeze. "Well there's something we can talk about," I thought. "She's a keen gardener, the same as Carol, so that's another thing they have in common as well as being mum to me."

I shook my head. Maybe that wasn't such a good idea. I brought the car to a halt and looked at myself in the rear mirror once more. "Come on then, Mary, this is it." My mind froze and appeared to go into melt down as the question formed in my head, "Do you really want to do this? I took another deep breath and eased myself tentatively out of the car. "Too late for second thoughts now," I reasoned. "And remember, whatever happens here today you still have Jenny, Chris, Mum and Dad waiting for you at home."

I locked the car door and turned to face the house. As I did so I became aware of someone standing on the other side of the front room window, it was her. Our eyes met and I felt my body shudder in both shock and surprise. I hadn't known what to expect but now here she was, my mother, looking straight at me. My first impression was that she looked taller and thinner than I had imagined although I had no reason to think that other than it was just a picture I had painted in my mind over the years whenever I had thought about her. She had a head full of dark and slightly greying hair which was swept up in a bun exposing her face and she appeared to be wearing very little make up which made her natural features all the more striking. Her eyes displayed a look of surprised amazement at seeing me and she put her hand to her mouth, presumably in recognition of the same feelings of disbelief and inner panic that I was experiencing. Could it really be true that after more than twenty-eight years apart we were actually about to meet again, and what impact would that have on our lives? I noticed she was also wearing red, her choice appearing slightly more adventurous than mine, it being a full and flowing Kaftan style dress with a bright blue collar. As she took her hand from her mouth we smiled at each other. It felt as though we were exchanging some form of facial peace offering in the shared hope that this might be, for both of us perhaps, a time of healing.

I moved away from the car and opened the gate, the short pathway to her front door suddenly appearing to be as long as any road I had ever travelled. As I pondered the wisdom of my taking the next few steps the door opened.

"Rebecca?" Her voice faltered. "I'm sorry, it's Mary isn't it? It's just that I've waited so long to…"

I looked up as she smiled, her face wrought with emotion and tears already filling her eyes.

In that moment all my doubts and fears fell away.

I walked forward and into her arms. "Hello Mum."

ABOUT THE AUTHOR

Mark Seaman spent thirty years as a successful radio and television broadcaster and actor before becoming a full-time playwright and author. He also managed radio stations for both the BBC and in the Commercial Radio sector including Premier Radio in London, where he acted as Programme Director and Presenter for the first year of the station's life.

More recently he has established himself as an award-winning playwright and director, whilst continuing with occasional broadcasting and acting work. Mark has a number of published manuscripts that enjoy regular production and stage performances both at home and abroad. Interestingly, *A Corner of My Heart*, started life as an idea for a stage play but Mark felt the characters' stories could be more fully explored in a book and is grateful to The Book Guild for agreeing with him.

Details about Mark's earlier career are available through his website www.mark-seaman.com and his play manuscripts can be found at www.lazybeescripts.co.uk

Mark is married with three children.